Tangled Roots

Published by bluechrome publishing 2008

2 4 6 8 10 9 7 5 3 1

First published in Great Britain in 2008 by
bluechrome publishing
PO Box 109,
Portishead, Bristol. BS20 7ZJ

www.bluechrome.co.uk

A CIP catalogue record for this book is available from the British Library.

ISBN 978-1-906061-40-1 hardback

Printed by Biddles Ltd, King's Lynn, Norfolk

Tangled Roots

Sue Guiney

If there is symmetry in our universe
then who is to say that the stories of the past
cannot coexist with the present,
that the arrow of time
can move in one direction only...

Acknowledgements

Tangled Roots took five years to find its finished form, and during that time I was lucky to have a large group of supporters holding me up and leading me forward. Firstly, I am grateful to those who helped me in my research efforts: Professor Joao Magueijo of Imperial College, London, who, for the price of a dinner, allowed me to ask him a million questions ranging from the number of courses one might teach in any given semester to the meaning of string theory. Next, to Ron Freeman, who shared with me his wide experience and understanding of modern Russia, not to mention an address book full of contacts. Once in Moscow, my wonderful guide, Natalia Grudkina, not only happily took me to all the untouristy places I needed to see, but also helped me define my characters' back stories by constantly asking, "but who was his father?"

I would also like to show my deep gratitude to those friends who willingly read early versions with great care and sensitivity: Kathy Bagley, Sam Cunningham, Helen Freeman, Verity Langley, Sonja Rein, Jeffrey Weingarten, and Sue Booth-Forbes in whose Writers' Retreat, Anam Cara, I found comfort, courage, inspiration, and a home-away-from-home. I am also infinitely grateful to my agent, Randi Murray, who has stuck by me through the various incarnations of this book, always offering a steady hand and a realistic eye. And to Anthony Delgrado of *bluechrome*, who has championed my work in a way I had thought was no longer possible.

The core of my life will always be my husband, my sons, my parents and sisters, and an unbelievably wide-ranging list of friends who have spent years believing in me even when I didn't believe in myself. Nothing could ever happen without any of them. I wish I could name them all, but I must at least mention

Kathy Lavidge, Cassie Murray, Janet Newkirk, Juliette Pollitzer and Susan Weingarten. But in the end, my greatest thanks must go to my mentor, editor and friend, Gabrielle Glancy who did, literally, teach me everything I know about writing. This book simply could not have been written without her.

Sue Guiney

To Don, Alex and Noah

and, finally,

for Sam

Part I

"There are things known and things unknown
and between are the doors."

- Jim Morrison

Chapter 1

John:
Relativity[1]

There I stood, staring in the mirror, straightening my new silver tie over my best white shirt, and I said to myself, "In the galaxy of forty-year-old physics professors, you still look pretty damn good." A full head of, mostly, dark hair. No 'middle-age spread'. Looking at me, you would never have known what a mess I was. But it was all a trick, an easily explained physical illusion that had very little to do with so-called reality. And that's the other thing I was thinking as I stared at myself in the mirror. The silver of the tie, the white of the shirt, the navy blue of the suit − − not really colors, but merely variable frequencies of light, speeding from the late June setting sun, through the frenetic molecules of the shimmering glass window, and refracting back off the mirror. That, in essence, was me.

I was late. I was always late. And I only noticed the time just then because I was wrangling with a cufflink that happened to be stuck under my watch. Let's face it; time is one of my big issues. On the one hand, you could say it's my life's work. I spend most of my days peering at it, poking it and won-

---

[1] See Glossary

dering about its existence. I even calculate it on wall-length blackboards. But none of that ever matters because, in the end, I can't control it. If anything, time usually controls me.

And so it was again on that night. I could already see the wedding guests pulling up in front of the hotel outside the window. I tried to force myself to focus on what I was doing and stop drifting off into space. I tried an old trick I learned back in graduate school, back when my mind was so rarely on the physical world that I often had to fool myself into coming back to so-called "reality." I sang to myself. Old rock 'n roll songs usually did it, and The Doors was the best. "Break on Through to the Other Side" was especially effective.

So there I was, singing and staring and straightening and drifting when there was a knock on the door. I knew it was Lizzy even before I heard her call, "Are you ready yet?" Of course, my big sister would be checking up on me. She always did, under normal circumstances. Phone calls several times a week. Regular dinners "just to chat." Ever since we were kids she used to like to think that I needed her in that way. But, although I was often content to have her take care of me – any mundane concern that I could offload onto her shoulders was one less thing I had to deal with myself – we both always knew without actually saying it that it was really Lizzy who needed me. It had been that way since we were teenagers.

I remember opening the door and being shocked. I expected Lizzy to look beautiful – she usually did, and certainly had at the afternoon's ceremony – but now the sight of her standing there in my doorway in that astronomically priced designer gown amazed me. I think I said something like, "Shit! You could be the bride yourself." I know Lizzy laughed and then tugged at the sides of my jacket and smoothed out my hair as if I was a little kid.

"Can you believe it!" she said, not really asking. I wasn't sure I could. In a minute, we would join the guests downstairs in the ballroom to celebrate my niece's, Lizzy's

12

daughter's, wedding. There I was, all dressed up in my good blue suit. There was Lizzy standing before me looking elegant, almost regal. Somehow, it all made me think about time again. I did the math. My niece, Amanda, was now just a year or so older than her mother was at the time of her accident and to tell you the truth, that plane crash still seemed like only yesterday. Lizzy had often told me that surviving that crash taught her she could survive anything. But nonetheless, from the moment I saw her lying in her hospital bed, her head wrapped in bandages, knowing that one of her eyes was now lost forever, I made it my own personal assignment to ensure that her life after that horrific moment was as easy as possible. Usually that meant making her laugh, although recently I was having more and more trouble being funny.

Lizzy slipped her arm through mine and the two of us walked down the hall. I remember looking at her, but she was looking straight ahead, serious and determined. The eyepatch didn't help. It had become her trademark ever since the crash and no one ever dared question her about it, except me. But I was the little brother. I had a license others didn't. Now, seeing that simple, black felt patch in profile, I decided Lizzy was looking much too serious. I decided to tease her. "Hey, do you remember the first time I called you Queen of the Pirates? You threw a book at me," I reminisced. "Kierkegaard, I think it was. Good thing you've got such lousy aim." Lizzy couldn't actually bring herself to laugh at that. But I knew she had always secretly liked being called 'Queen of the Pirates'. And so she did smile. Then she gave my arm a squeeze and the pressure made me feel like we were teenagers all over again. I remember looking at the carpet stretching down the long hall. It wasn't like me to notice its checkered pattern, but I did all the same, and at that moment I had this wonderful thought that Lizzy and I were actually walking over the grid of spacetime itself. That grid was leading us down the same hospital corridor we had walked all those years before. But now it was leading us to a different place, a different time, and it made me say out loud – I clearly remember it – "Einstein was right. Time *is* curved."

Lizzy looked at me with a smirk and a cautioning glare. "Yes, John. We know. But for now…" We had reached the ballroom and I felt her arm slip away. For a moment I thought about turning and running back to my room with its pay-for-view movies and minibar of comforting little bottles. The noise of the tumult, the heat of the crowd made me feel like I was spinning off onto my own orbit, alone and rootless, and I didn't like that feeling at all. I looked around for help, grabbed a glass of champagne off a passing tray and finally, just in time, found my brother-in-law, Peter. He was in the thick of it, playing the good host, ushering people to the bar. He looked happy. And why not? He was at the reception. The ceremony, the scary part, was over. The tasks given to him by his commander-wife and adoring daughter had all been successfully completed. The buses he had ordered to take the guests from the synagogue to the hotel all arrived on time. They hadn't forgotten the coolers full of champagne and caviar. No one had been left behind. Now he could relax. His daughter was happy, but that was easy. Amanda was always happy. But more to the point, his wife was happy. I've watched Peter struggle with that particular task for over twenty years.

"How you holding up?" Peter asked me.

"Me? I'm all right. What about you?" I asked him back.

"I'm great, as long as I don't start crying. But you know me. All I have to do is look at her…" I did know him and I knew that his no-crying goal was basically hopeless.

Just then, as if on cue in some Spencer Tracy movie, Amanda walked into the room. She was holding her boyfriend's – her husband's – hand. She really was beautiful, but I had to admit she was something else as well. Amanda carried an 'otherworldly' serenity about her that people always talked about, as if she hovered just slightly above the everyday hysteria, untouched by the turbulence that, to me at least, seemed to engulf the rest of humanity. 'Otherworldly' – they used to say that about my mother, too. At least in her old age. But what the hell does that mean, I always wondered. What 'other world' were they talking about? Mars? Maybe it wouldn't be so bad if that was what they had meant, but I knew it wasn't. When people said 'otherworldly', they were talking a sort of spiritual mumbo jumbo that drove me crazy. I'm a scientist, and as scientists go, I imagine myself to be pretty open to thinking about the inconceivable. My entire career has been devoted to doing just that. So, of course, I've always accepted the fact that, for instance, released energy converts annihilated matter into new matter. Sure it does. I understood that theory long ago, doing the calculations myself in graduate school. I've even sometimes fooled around with the question of what happens to all that new matter given the curved nature of spacetime. But quantum physics and human beings are very different things. To assume the same rules apply to both is, at the very least, inelegant. But actually, at the time, standing there staring at my niece in the middle of that hotel ballroom, I was thinking it was downright dangerous. Other world? There is no other world. There's no place else where dead souls that were full of shit on earth are now magically transformed into wisdom and light someplace out there beyond Alpha Centauri. Jesus.

I was about to lose it. I could feel my jaw locking into place, like it did sometimes when I got really angry. Or upset. Or frustrated. Sometimes it got so bad that I couldn't open my mouth at all and I'd end up in some emergency room with a drip of muscle relaxants and sedatives sticking into my arm. But luckily, on that night, before I found myself too far gone, too hopelessly sucked into that infuriating vortex of cosmology and religion, I felt a steadying hand on my shoulder.

"Uncle John!" My eyes focused on Amanda's face. Thank goodness for her. If I loved anyone in this world other than my sister, it was my one-and-only niece. From the day she was born, I felt an affinity with her, a connection beyond calculation. Maybe if I ever had a kid of my own, it would feel something like that. And as for Amanda, I wasn't just *an* uncle. I was *the* uncle. "Happy for me?" she asked.

Was I happy for her? What could I say? I couldn't lie to her. I thought she was too young to get married and she knew it. Just twenty-one. Just graduated from college. What was the rush? Amanda had explained it to me over and over. Tim was joining the Peace Corps – two years in East Timor (wherever the hell that was). They were in love. They wanted to spend their lives together. To do that and still save the world, they had to be married. And there really wasn't anything to complain about. There was nothing wrong with Tim. I once took him to a baseball game and he spent the whole time spouting obscure statistics at me. He was funny and the Red Sox had even won. "And who was I to complain anyway?" I asked myself. "Just the uncle, that's who," I answered. In the minute I stood there looking at Amanda, I was arguing with myself, back and forth. My thoughts were deafening. "If the parents were happy, who was I to say no ... just the favorite uncle that's all ... just the one who understands her the most." The fact that I myself had never been able to sustain a relationship for longer than a year or two had nothing to do with it. Just because I hadn't settled down didn't mean that I believed no one else could. Look at Lizzy and Peter. I knew it was possible. It's just that...

"Hey, look. Tim's a great guy," was what I forced myself to say. "And you love each other. That's all that matters."

"I love you, too," Amanda told me and ran off into the crowd.

It was nearly one o'clock in the morning when I finally got back to my room. It had been a very long day. I've always thought one o'clock was an especially awkward time, hovering somewhere between past and future. But it seemed especially true that morning. My adorable little niece was now a married woman. No more afternoons in the playground. No more ballet recitals. And if Amanda was grown up, what did that make me? I felt myself getting sloppy and sentimental. Clearly, I'd had too much champagne. Every time I sat down to eat, someone dragged me away to dance or run some errand. Now my feet burned and I could feel the beginning of a hangover settle into my right temple. I replayed the wedding's events in my head. Everything had gone according to plan. Peter made it through his toast without looking ridiculous, but with just enough tears to make everyone else cry. I knew Peter was happy. It was harder, though, to know how my sister felt. Lizzy looked happy, but she was too busy being responsible to exude any real sense of joy. No, I decided Lizzy was 'satisfied'. That was the word for it and really, what's so bad about that? Considering she had just watched her only child wave goodbye and walk away to start a new life of her own, a new family … well, 'satisfied' was a pretty good thing to be.

I got undressed, throwing my trousers onto a chair. It didn't matter. I wasn't going to need that suit any time soon. I got into bed and just lay there. I didn't even bother to turn on the TV. I knew there was nothing on the ninety-seven channels I'd want to watch, nothing but some low-budget porno lurking around the higher numbers. Ordinarily, I might have checked it out on a late night like this, a bit drunk and alone in a hotel room. But actually, to be honest, I wasn't usually alone on such nights. Companionship was something I never had too much trouble finding. For a physicist, I was lucky that way. I guess I was smart enough to do my job, but not so smart that I couldn't carry on a conversation with 'normal' people. I could chat, make jokes and at over forty, I had a decent enough build. Women liked me. At least, at first they did.

Take Suzanne for example. She liked me a lot. A year before, when Amanda's wedding was first being planned, I assumed Suzanne would be there with me, peeling back the tightly tucked layers of blankets on the king-sized bed. Amanda liked Suzanne. So had Lizzy. Everyone had started to think that maybe I would finally settle down with this one. But, no. Nearly six months to the day after Amanda's engagement we split up, ending a two-year relationship for the same indefinable reason all my other relationships had ended. It just wasn't enough, I felt. And she complained I wasn't really there.

I remember I poured myself a glass of water and ate the bit of chocolate housekeeping had left on the nightstand. There was one of those complimentary weather cards sitting next to the telephone. I can picture it now, the sun slightly obscured by a dark cloud. 'Partly cloudy' that meant to me and I assumed it would be even worse when I got home to Boston the next day. I remember shutting off the light and laying in bed with my eyes open, waiting for them to adapt to the darkness. It didn't take long. Then I closed my eyes to test how badly the room would spin. It spun, but not too badly. Nonetheless, no matter how exhausted I felt, falling asleep was not easy. I couldn't help but think of Amanda and how beautiful she looked. Twenty-one years old. That's when women were the most beautiful, I thought. Their legs were at their tightest. Their breasts their firmest. And all of Amanda's twenty-one-year-old friends there that night had that look. Strapless, tight gowns. Hair up, show-ing off long necks and bare shoulders. And each one asked to dance with me as if I was something special. Maybe I should have put the porno channel on after all and gotten it over with. But I couldn't. It didn't seem right, somehow. Don't ask me why. Maybe I just didn't want to think about young women any more. In twenty years of teaching, I had never allowed my-self to fall into that trap. But it was getting harder, the older I got. I knew it was pathetic. Such a cliché. But there was this one new, amazing, brilliant graduate student and lying in that hotel bed that night, I couldn't stop thinking about her.

To tell you the truth, I couldn't remember her name, but I did remember our last conversation. Class had just ended. She waited outside for me to ask something about Kaluza-Klein theories. I remembered she made me feel uncomfortable from the start, as if she was forcing me into some corner. She pushed me to think about things I didn't want to consider, like whether the speed of light could be variable after all, like whether Einstein could have been wrong, like whether I could sleep with her.

I started to argue with myself. No, I would not start up with this woman, I said, almost out loud. It would be too ridiculous. I knew other professors did it all the time. It didn't bother them, but it bothered me. I don't know why. It just all seemed so pathetic – the aging professor trying to prove he was still powerful, young, attractive. Forget it. And anyway, I could just imagine my sister's reaction. She would be horrified. And Amanda? Let's just say that it's a long fall from being adored and revered to being an embarrassment.

I opened my eyes and then closed them again. There was no sign of drunken nausea. I took some deep breaths and tried to focus on the rhythm of my chest moving up and down. Thankfully, the tension in my jaw began to relax. My legs felt heavy on the starched sheets. The room's spin slowed down to a gentle flow. Flow – now there was something I understood. I pictured the diagram about p-branes on page 137 of my latest book. Like ruffled sheets of copper, branes of p-dimensions were flowing in waves through the flatness of spacetime. Watching them, I eventually fell asleep, as they drifted everywhere, nowhere, endlessly and back again.

Chapter 2

John:
Particles at Rest

My old roommate, Marty, was still my best friend. Over nearly twenty years of job offers, promotions, research failures and breakthroughs, we've remained each other's most trusted advisors and most formidable rivals. On the outside, we looked like an old comedy routine. I was Hardy to Marty's Laurel, or is it the other way around? Marty was the short, dumpy one, wild-eyed and totally without social antennae. He always said whatever brilliant or outrageous thought popped into his head and felt whatever unfiltered, unconsidered emotion arose in his heart. In all the years that I have known him, I've never stopped being amazed by him. Unfortunately, I think I stopped amazing Marty years ago. More and more it seemed I just exasperated him. He used to say that if I took all the energy I spent thinking about extraneous things like academic politics and relationships and applied it all to my research, I would have won the Nobel Prize by the time I was thirty. Of course, I often pointed out that he hadn't won the big prize either by that age, but I had to admit that everyone assumed he was on the short list. "Look," he always said. "It's all physics anyway, so why worry about anything else?"

Now it might sound strange, but I have to admit that, for me, this friendship was based on a deeply felt, unspoken belief that despite our superficial differences Marty and I were actually the same person. What I mean is that when I looked at him, I saw myself as I would have been if I had been living in the past. Somehow, although a generation younger, Marty had actually grown up in the world of my mother: a close-knit Jewish community in Brooklyn with bright, underemployed parents who had just enough money to buy books, foo and clothing, in that order. If my own mother hadn't realized that there was an entire universe on the other side of the East River and hadn't forced her way across and out, she wouldn't have met her already assimilated husband-to-be, they never would have moved to London and I would have ended up being Marty. If he had ever allowed himself to think about it, he might have envied the places I've been and the sort of cosmopolitan life I've lived. But he never did and now, the older we became, the more I yearned for the simpler, steadier, more clear-cut world that he seemed to inhabit. Put it this way – it wasn't surprising that Marty spent his life thinking about the physical world of condensed matter, while my own head was forever stuck in the cosmos.

My mother. I might as well talk about her now. Her name was Grace, and she cast a long shadow, even after her death. Lizzy and I buried her next to our father in the family plot outside of New York, just a couple of years before the summer of Amanda's wedding. It was very cold the day of her funeral. There was a line of people, many of them strangers to me, who waited in that cold to get into the funeral home and pay their final respects. I remember standing there, seemingly for hours, trying to smile and getting more and more angry as a river of these people passed by, shaking my hand and telling me what a wonderful person she was, how she had changed their lives. She was always there when they needed her, they all said. She had such empathy, such wisdom. Of course, none of them had any idea that my own experience of my mother, this woman that so many talked about as if she was some guru or something, actually had more to do with feelings like rage, pain, frustration and betrayal. How could they? My mother never seemed to be aware of it herself. But by the time we got out of that funeral home and headed out to the grave site, I was screaming inside with fury.

Only five of us went to the grave; I had insisted on that. There were Lizzy, Amanda, Peter, me and Florence, my mother's old nurse and companion during the last years of her life. I remember standing there next to the coffin in the freezing cold, listening to the Rabbi's prayers and thinking, "Who the hell is this guy?" He seemed to know what he was talking about, but I had never laid eyes on him before. And how did he really know anything about my mother, anyway? I mean, how did he know anything about her that mattered? I was furious, all right, but as I stood there in my fury, I believed that it was a fury that no one would ever understand. I couldn't talk about it. I couldn't try to explain it. Anyone I told would only come up with some lame explanation about how difficult it is to believe that God could take away such a wonderful person — as if that was what I was upset about. They would say how hard it was to accept that such a void would now be created in the world. But I knew myself well enough to know that my fury wasn't about any of that at all. What it was about, though, I didn't know.

And so, by the time I was trying to console Amanda, hugging her on the way back to the limousine, I had buried that fury. I told myself I had just let it go, but I hadn't. I had turned myself as cold and hard inside as that stupid rock my sister forced me to place, as a symbol, on top of the casket. I never cried that day. Not once. And I'll never forget how Florence looked at me and said, with a mistaken comprehension, "That's right, John. There's no reason to be sad. We know she's not really dead, is she?" Jesus Fucking Christ. Now that was the last thing I wanted to hear. Sure, I knew there were people like

Florence who believed a part of us never dies, who believed that life continues on as positive energy, inhabiting the universe until it takes on a new form. Who knows – in her old age, my mother might have come to believe some of that herself. But I wanted to have nothing to do with it. Driving back into Manhattan in that limousine, I sat there silently staring out the window. I was praying, all right, but only that my jaw would unlock by the time we reached 68th Street.

Whether I liked it or not (and I didn't), I had a mother who had somehow become beloved by strangers. She drew people to her like a magnet. Everyone was her best friend. Everybody adored her. But I know now that how she got that way was, for me, a big part of the problem. The truth is, she had tried to kill herself back when I was in High School. Not very good timing, as far as I was concerned. But if that wasn't bad enough, instead of dying, she became this new person, full of love and peace and comfort for everyone she met but, unfortunately, leaving her own children to fend for themselves. Or, so it felt to me. Does it sound cruel? Selfish? Okay. Maybe. But all I ever knew for a very long time was that there was an aching inside me, as if there was a black hole in there of such an immense gravitational force that any light daring to come close was sucked in and destroyed. And believe me, there's no singularity quite as destructive as a black hole.

The Monday morning after Amanda's wedding, I was sitting behind my desk, as usual, staring at my computer. And, as usual, eventually I heard Marty's voice. "Hey. Nu?" Each workday started the same way. I woke early; ran five miles or went to the gym. Then I took a brisk walk to the Physics Building and up the two flights of stairs to my office, generally landing behind my desk about an hour before my first class. It's not that my life was particularly orderly. It's just that I couldn't sit still. Marty, on the other hand, always slept as late as he could, threw on whatever clothes he happened to find first, kissed his wife and children goodbye and drove the half-mile to campus.

Ten years ago, within weeks of his marriage, Marty and I learned that we had both been offered jobs at the same university. Now, that was a good day. For him it made his wedding a double celebration, 'two for one'. He now assumed he would forever be with Beth and forever be with me. From the first day of school of that first year working together, he always began his day with a knock on my door. Although my answer was usually as abbreviated as his "Nu?" both of us had come to rely on the exchange as the best way to start. I guess we needed it like we needed our morning coffee.

Next, after the initial greeting, came the important question. Marty usually asked it. "Walk at three?" or four or whatever time worked for that day's specific schedule. I then looked at my desk calendar, made some hesitant noises and figured out the time that suited us both. Most every day, somehow or other, the two of us would take a walk along the river and argue. It didn't feel like arguing to us, but that's what our students called it – 'argue time'. Over the years, it had become a sort of Physics Department institution. At least once a week some student or other would join us, ask some particularly niggling question and then stand back and watch the two great minds argue it out. The fact that our own research lay in different areas didn't matter. By barging into each other's fields and haranguing each other's students, we each kept our minds sharp and our interests broad. Some of our most important work grew out of these 'discussions'. And if there weren't any students around, we then found something else to argue about, usually about physics, but every once in a while about our personal lives. Those walks gave us both a foothold, a safe, stable place to jump off from and come back to.

That specific morning after Amanda's wedding was no different.

"Hey. Nu? Walk at three?" Marty asked.

"Uh…make it four," I think I answered.

By the time four o'clock rolled around, I had already taught two classes, met with a graduate student and become frustrated by my research. As usual, Marty had to find me in one of the half dozen places I was likely to be. You see, Marty didn't share my problem with time. He didn't calculate it or worry about it. He didn't even think about it. He somehow always had a sense of when he should be where he should be. But on this day, I was easy to find. I was sitting behind my desk in my office, staring at the blackboard. Marty walked in. He probably said something like, "Trying to think, or trying not to?" But I remember I hadn't even been aware that he was in the room. His voice startled me. Without saying much, I stood up, picked up my jacket, looked out the window and remembering it was summer put the jacket back down on the chair. We then both walked out of the building into the late afternoon sunlight and down towards the river. Marty immediately started chattering about our true great passion – baseball. The Red Sox had had a good pre-season. The entire roster was healthy and the pitching was deep. Hope and faith were in the air. But I hardly seemed to notice. I was silent. Eventually, he stopped talking and looked at me.

"Okay. So, what's up?"

I think I just shook my head and shrugged. I know I didn't say anything.

"What are you thinking about? Work?"

Still no answer. Marty kept prodding me as we crossed the street and turned onto the promenade along the river. He then tried a different tack. "How many classes you teaching this summer?"

"Four," I said.

"Four? What, are you crazy? It's summer school. Why so many?"

"It's my turn," I answered. I explained it to him. "Three of them are undergrad courses. Basic stuff. But … you know. I like teaching basic stuff." That much was true. I really did believe what my old teacher used to say – "If you can't explain it, you don't understand it." And anyway, I often found that when I explained concepts I usually took for granted, new and interesting questions always arose. My first important article on holography grew out of just such a class.

"Yea, I know," said Marty. "Just seems like a lot of work for the summer. Any time for fun?"

"Fun?" I asked and rolled my eyes. But as soon as I said it, I remember thinking I wished I hadn't. Marty's head dropped to his chest like a disappointed little kid. I knew now he was going to worry about me. I knew he was going to worry about me because he always worried about me.

"Don't tell me you're in one of your moods," he said. "You haven't had one of those in a long time."

"Yea, so I'm overdue." I thought such an obnoxious answer would have shut him up. But no. Now, instead, came the checklist.

"So, what's the story? Research stuck?" Silence. "Lizzy okay? Amanda? Jesus, I can't believe I forgot. What an idiot. How was the wedding?"

So I told him. The wedding was fine. The weather held out. Everyone looked beautiful. The food was good. No, I wasn't upset about that.

By this time we had made it past the bridge and were turning around for the return trip. It was one of those postcard days. The sun glistened on the water. The leaves hardly stirred with the light breeze. Couples eating picnics sat on the grass. Young women in tank tops and very short shorts rollerbladed by.

"Well, if everything's okay then, there can only be one thing left. How long's it been since you got laid?"

Can you believe it? Forty years old and he's still talking about this shit. "Jesus, Marty," I complained. "We're not eighteen anymore. It doesn't matter so much."

"That long, eh? So, who is she? Who's holding out?" Actually, Marty had never grown up. He was still sixteen and always would be. He wanted details and I knew him well enough to know he would never let this go. It didn't matter that I didn't want to talk about it and it didn't matter that there was nothing to tell. Marty was like a bulldog. Once he sunk his teeth into something, there was no shaking him loose. So I told him about the graduate student. I had to. I told him about how beautiful she was, how brilliant and how I couldn't stop thinking about her. Deep down I knew none of this had anything to do with the way I was feeling, but I had to tell him something. With each word Marty's eyes got wider and wider. Finally, he stopped walking and turned towards me.

"Just tell me. Nothing's happened, right?" he asked.

"Right. Nothing's happened."

"Promise?"

"Yes. I'm not an idiot."

Then he laughed. I couldn't see what was so funny and began to sulk. He caught his breath and tried to explain. "Look. You're acting like a Catholic," he told me. "You're a Jew, for Christ's sake. Lighten up. So you 'lusted in your heart'. So what? You didn't do anything. God, we really do have to get you laid."

And for him, that was all there was to it. He knew only too well that I was capable of worrying about things that didn't need worrying about. "Stop looking for trouble," he used to tell me. I longed to be able to take his advice. I did. But I felt that this time I just couldn't. I couldn't because I knew this time it wasn't about the girl. It wasn't about sex, either. It wasn't about anything I could put my finger on. Something was out of synch, like I was going through some sort of conversion-of-matter inside. Some kind of energy was being destroyed, but I didn't know what it would all be recreated into. To be honest, it scared the shit out of me. But I couldn't tell that to Marty. I couldn't tell that to anyone. I believed that if I just ignored it, it would all go away. It always had before. Even my mother's depression eventually passed and she had been much worse off than I ever was.

Right? So, for the umpteenth time in a week, I gave myself the stern talking to that had become a sort of mantra to me. I was not a mass of particles, unglued and orbitless. My internal structure did have symmetry, just like the rest of the cosmos. I was fine.

So, what did I do? I decided to think about the Red Sox. They were playing the Yankees at home that weekend. I decided to go. That was bound to cheer me up and then everything would be okay. Yes, that's what I'd do. I'd go to the ballgame and then, somehow or other, I'd get myself laid – just not by a student.

Who knows how long I stood there by the river nodding my head, convincing myself that everything would be all right, staring off into space and oblivious to the rest of the world outside my own thoughts? Who knows how much time passed? But I do know that Marty stood there for all of it, for however long it took, for however long it would have taken, quietly, patiently, waiting.

Chapter 3

Grace:
So I Said, I Said . . .

It was the traffic light at the corner of 68ᵗʰ and Broadway that revealed to me the surprising fact that I, Grace Rosen, a woman who had moved from place to place always reinventing herself as she went along, who had survived tragedies and infidelities only to cheat death and rediscover life, was finally getting old. I crossed that street sometimes twice a day, to go food shopping, go to the bank. But that goddamned light was fast and getting faster. At first I could just about make it to the other side before the light would turn. Then, I'd be three-quarters of the way and taxis would start honking. One day, I saw another old woman waddling across as fast as she could. I thought, "You better hurry up." but the next thing I knew she was flying through the air. And that's when I said, "Okay, Grace. Enough."

It's funny how my own old age snuck up on me. I was certainly aware that Jack was aging. That seemed to happen the minute we moved back to New York. It didn't bother me, for instance, the way the floor of our new apartment sloped westward. But it drove Jack crazy. His underwear drawer would creep open and steam would come out of his ears. "This shithole," he'd cry. "Goddamn it, I'm living my final days in a shithole!"

"Take it easy," was all I could say as I urged the drawer back into place. In thirty-odd years of married life, moving back and forth across the ocean, in and out of different cities, different buildings, never did we live in a shithole. He knew that just as well as I did. And we weren't living in one then. I remember I usually gave him a kiss to quiet him down. Sometimes it worked. "This isn't anybody's final days, anyway, " I told him. "So just shush."

I was right about part of it. It wasn't a shithole. It was a lovely and expensive one-bedroom apartment on the Upper West Side of Manhattan in a building with round-the-clock doormen and a lobby where every day, on the marble mantelpiece, freshly cut flowers would miraculously appear. The building was old, so the floor sloped a little, but only in two rooms. If it weren't for the drawers opening by themselves, you wouldn't even notice. No, it was a perfectly nice apartment and I for one was happy there. Anyway, after a while, it doesn't matter so much where you are. New York, Boston, London – it's all the same in the end.

I was right about the apartment. About Jack, I was wrong. One night, he had a stomachache. The next night, he had a heart attack. And that was it. As it turned out, those were his final days. Years and years of marriage – the passion in the beginning, the betrayals in the middle, the reconciliations in the end – all over in a breath. In less than a breath. In one sudden, astonishing jolt.

I guess for him it was better that way. I have to admit, it's not a terrible way to go. No prolonged pain. No humiliating dementia. Believe me, I've seen all that too and it's bad. No, Jack was lucky. All in all he was a good man. Sure, he made mistakes. But he did the best he could with his life, withstanding troubles that nearly killed me and changes he never asked for. He deserved a quick death and that's what he got. The end.

But it wasn't so great for me. It was all over too soon. It's not that I was still looking to him for answers to questions that once haunted me. I didn't need to ask him if he really had ever loved that other woman. Or, for that matter, if he ever really loved me. We had stopped talking about all that years ago. He knew I loved him. I knew we forgave each other the best we could. It's just that I wasn't quite ready for his absence. The suddenness was a shock.

It took me a long time to start living again. There was a lot of sitting alone in that 'shithole', staring out the window in silence. In New York there's plenty to watch. Sweaty, overweight men unloading antique furniture. Blond au pairs with cell phones in one hand, toddlers in the other. Old men in fedoras. Delivery boys with boxes of groceries stopping for a smoke. I spent months staring out the window, watching life walk by. It worried the kids. John and Lizzy didn't know what to do with me. But I knew all that watching was giving me a chance to get over the shock. By then I understood that sometimes you just have to let time pass. Of course, I was right. I hadn't lived all those years for nothing. Eventually, I used the time to look at my own life. I sensed that I was ready to look back. It had been ages. Like rereading a book from your childhood. You see more in it the second or third time around. I began to tell myself the story of myself. Out of order. Out of reality. It was as if the white walls of that apartment were my blank paper.

It started with strange images of distant memories, rising out of nowhere from whatever I was doing. I started to see the sycamore tree outside our house in Brooklyn. Then the yellow flowers on my mother's apron as she stood in front of the kitchen sink. There was the old living room couch and the way I could make the color a darker green by brushing my hand against the nap of the fabric. I began to see it all and I began to remember. And I remembered my memory and the way, even to this day, it still holds onto everything. Sitting in our old apartment without Jack, I rediscovered my stories. And so I clung to that shithole like it was the last stone on the last boulder on the final edge of the final precipice.

We lived in London for nearly ten years. Originally we moved abroad for Jack's job, or so we said. It was a good cover. But we really left Boston to leave Jack's mistress in the past. I told him it's move or it's over. So we moved. Desperate? Yes, but it worked. At least for us it did. What it did for the kids was another, very complicated story. At the time it didn't seem quite so bad for John. With a new school and new friends, he looked like he was adapting pretty quickly. For Lizzy, though, it was disastrous. But to be honest, I wasn't really thinking about the kids just then. All I could think about was saving my marriage and I hoped, I believed, that that would be enough to save the kids as well. And like I said, it seemed to work. As far as I could tell, it didn't take too long for Jack to forget Melanie and for London to become our home. Jack and I loved it. And I believe in London we found a way to love each other again. Even as Lizzy and John grew up, settling back in America and spending less and less time with us, London still held us. Not like glue, but like sticky toffee.

We spent our summers in the States and although we enjoyed being there, we were always happy to board the BA flight back to Heathrow. For a while, it was the perfect life for us. One foot in the Old World, one foot in the new and enough frequent flyer miles to keep us all airborne.

A lot happened during those years. Good and bad. I learned most of what I know about death and life walking the streets of London. It was as if the city had seen it all before. Nothing could shock it. Not even my illness. London seemed to know that if it waited long enough, I would heal. Those ancient streets cradled me in a silent anonymity when that was all I could bear. When I was ready, it guided me back to life. Despite everything that happened there, our years in London were some of our best.

Then, something pulled us back to America. It was an embarrassing cliché, a trap I never thought I'd fall into. Our granddaughter, Amanda, was born. She had ten perfect fingers; she had chunky little knees; she had red lips that puckered and suckled in her sleep and she was living with her parents in suburban Westchester. From the day of her birth onward, America had a whole new meaning for us. By the time she was nine months old, we had given up our latest London flat with its views of distant church steeples and its proximity to the pub and moved into our perfectly nice, expensive, noisy apartment in Manhattan.

There had been so many places I had needed to leave. Brooklyn, Manhattan, Boston, London. With each new home came new hope. By the time of Amanda's birth, moving came naturally to me. We'll jog in Central Park and eat at all the new restaurants, I told Jack. We'll watch the newest buildings go up and lament the older ones coming down. It will be just like London, only with grandchildren.

So, again I convinced him and we did all the things we had imagined. I was such a doting grandmother that I got into the habit of putting us to sleep with stories of Amanda's achievements. At four months, she recognized me and laughed. At nine months she climbed into the refrigerator. Amanda was our first grandchild and as it turned out our only one. So I guess you could say we left America because of love and moved back to America because of love. It was good enough for me, but not for Jack. It wasn't just the floors in the apartment that were sloping downhill. We had stopped living our lives for ourselves and started living for the children, but for Jack that was no life at all. He got tired and fed up and disinterested. He became old. Did moving back to America kill him? Let's put it this way. It didn't do him any good.

After Jack's death, I was alone. The kids took turns checking on me. Lizzy was especially good about it, but being the only daughter I suppose that was to be expected. She'd call me on the phone most days and when she wasn't calling she was dropping by. John called, too, just not as often and every now and again he'd fly down from Boston to visit. It was harder for him. I understood that and I tried not to bother him about it too much. But I did worry that he was angry with me for some reason and I did miss him, sometimes even when he was here. But what could I say? I didn't want to force him to talk about things he didn't want to talk about. Making him angrier wouldn't help. All I could do was wait. So I waited and hoped some day it would be easier between us. But then there were Saturdays, when Lizzy brought Amanda in for a trip to a museum, then a visit to Grandma. Those times were the best of all.

Mostly, though, I sat by myself for hours in silence. By that time in my life, though, I had learned a thing or two about being alone and although I was alone, I was seldom lonely. It didn't take long for me to remember who I had become and what I had discovered. I spent a lot of time listening to the silence. It had a reverberating sound as if in it I could hear some distant laughter, or a conversation in another room if ever I wanted to focus on it. Sometimes, I just sat. But other times, I'd listen; there was always something to listen to. No, I wasn't lonely and as I became more and more comfortable with this new chapter in my life, I started to venture out again. I walked through the streets of New York. I even made new friends. I started talking again and as usual, once I started I didn't stop. That's when the children got really nervous. It was easy to look after me when I was sitting in the apartment like a zombie. But how could they keep tabs on me when I was roaming around the city on my own, striking up conversations with strangers?

"Mom, shouldn't you have some help?" they badgered me. "Haven't you earned it?" Until, finally, I gave in.

I didn't like Florence at first. She looked the part, I'll give you that. Her hands were strong and her shoes were white. She was big-boned, big-chested and big-mouthed. Physically, she towered over me and assumed from the start that she could push me around. But I can be just as bossy as she and two bossy women in a one-bedroom apartment is not such a great idea. I think, at first, she wasn't used to working for someone quite so healthy. The fact that I could choose my own dinner, let alone go to the bathroom myself, annoyed her.

"I don't know what you're paying me for," she complained at first. "You don't let me do nothing but keep those taxis from plowing into you when we cross the street."

But I told her, "Don't you worry. Stick around long enough and you'll be filling oxygen tanks to make your heart sing." She laughed at that and then I knew we'd be all right. And we were, especially when I discovered how much she loved to listen to my stories.

Let's say we were pushing the shopping cart down the frozen food aisle. A bag of chicken nuggets would remind Florence of something – "Did you hear Mrs. Birnbaum fell down the steps at that new McDonalds on 72nd?" – which would remind me of my Aunt Mimi breaking her leg in Jerusalem.

Or, we could be sitting outside Lincoln Center looking at the fountain and sipping iced tea. Florence would tell me about her nephew's acne, which would remind me of Lizzy's first piano recital. Until, one day, she said, "You know, you should tell that story to my sister's daughter, Julie."

"What do you mean?"

"Sure. It's a good story. She'd like it."

So Julie came. Barely thirty years old, she was the mother of three small children and the wife of a charming, unemployed musician. Once a month she tried to decide if she should leave him. Twice a month she'd try to figure out why she kept loving him. Her kids were healthy, she had a steady job and there was enough money. But, boy oh boy, was she tired. So, one day, Florence brought her to visit. She came with us on our walk around the park during her lunch hour. She got her complaints off her chest and then she looked at me. Her eyes were full of questions as if I was supposed to have the answers. But I just started to laugh, then Florence started to laugh and although at first Julie looked angry, she soon started to laugh, too. We were all laughing and then, suddenly, Julie stopped and looked at us. "What are we laughing about?" she asked. I remember I said, " You know, all this reminds me of a story." I can't remember now what that story was, but it doesn't matter. I remember it was autumn because I was wearing Jack's old plaid scarf around my neck. There were squirrels everywhere and one nearly ran up Florence's leg. And I remember the sun was bright, because it seemed to make Julie's eyes water.

A few weeks later, Julie came back and she even brought a tape of her deadbeat husband's music. It was pretty good. Something about her had changed. She looked happy. That made Florence happy, which made me happy. And that's how Florence encouraged me to start talking again, telling my stories to anyone, to everyone. When I told my kids about it they said, "Oh, that's nice, Mom. We know how you like to talk." I think they were relieved. But, for me it was fun. I liked telling my stories, changing them every now and then, maybe exaggerating a bit here or there. Sure, it was nice to think that sometimes talking to people made them feel better, too, but as for me personally, it was more than that. You see, all that talking got me living again. And although my stories were about things that happened in the past, actually it didn't feel like I was living in the past. Rather, the past was showing me there was still, somehow, a future.

One time, Julie brought a friend. And then that friend told a friend and then another and another. I never said no. Why should I? When a person likes to talk, it's always better to have somebody to listen. Now, I'm not a fool. I know I repeat myself. One human being's life can only be made up of so many stories. But since my audience kept changing it didn't matter. Of course, Florence was always there. Year in and year out; I don't even like to count. I often assumed she was ignoring me, rattling teacups in the kitchen, boiling water on the stove. She'd hand out cake plates, sometimes help me switch from one chair to another, always fussing in the background. She never seemed to be listening, but once whoever-from-wherever would leave she'd say something like, "Why did you tell that poor girl you moved to Miami straight out of college? You know you didn't get there 'til years later."

Or exasperated, she'd hover over me shaking her head and say, "What do you mean you never slept with that reporter? You know damned well you did."

Sometimes it seemed she knew my life better than I did. I would just sip my tea and say, "Oh, well. It's still a good story."

So, I made friends. Lots of them. And they were all mine – and Florence's. My kids didn't know them. I didn't think they needed to. They just needed to know that I had them. And so, during those years after Jack's death, while my legs still worked and my eyes still saw and those crazy floors kept sloping westward, my life became full again.

But, you know, you can't fight change and you can't fight time. Everything moves along in one way or another and you just have to move on with it. 'Flow' I guess they call it. Eventually, as you'd expect, those old legs of mine got weaker and those eyes got dimmer. But, actually and more importantly, the breathing got harder. That, I suppose, was the clincher. The kids started to worry again and then Lizzy came to have 'a chat'. She sat there on the couch, looking back and forth between me and Florence and I knew something was up. "Mom," she said, "John and I have been thinking." "Oy. Here it comes," was what I thought to myself, because although she went on to say lots of things about wanting me to move closer so she could see me more often, about how it was getting harder for her to take the time to come into the City, about how getting out of the pollution would help my breathing, I knew what she was really saying. "Let's move her out of that shithole apartment while we still can," was what she really meant. And I knew there was no fighting it.

It was hard for me to think about saying goodbye to that place. I had lived there alone for years and then with Florence for even longer. But to me, it was still Jack's last home. Saying goodbye to that apartment was like saying goodbye to him all over again. And like saying goodbye to a part of myself. Because where would I go? There really was only one place – one of those lovely assisted-living buildings with the nice, white rooms, the nurses down the hall and the 'jungle gym' bars in the bathroom. It would be my last move. Of that I was sure. And it frightened me. Not for the reasons you'd think, though. I wasn't afraid of dying. I had already faced that once before and I guess, like anything else, the second time round is always easier. No, I wasn't afraid of dying and I wasn't afraid of losing all my new friends. Many of them would come to visit and those that couldn't would still be with me, only in a new way, as part of some story or other. But there was something else I was afraid of. Florence. If I went, would she go with me? If I was going to talk my way through the end of time, she would have to be there, too.

Florence was an unlikely friend. Only ten years younger than me, she was an old woman herself. She had lived her whole life in The Bronx. She had loved and married her first boyfriend, a God-fearing, Bible-toting Baptist who died too young and left her penniless. She had raised one child, a son who made it all the way to Harvard, but then died in a car accident. She had worked every day of her life, never stepping foot outside of New York's five boroughs. Florence was uneducated, unworldly, but wiser and kinder than anyone I had ever met. In some ways, she reminded me of my mother – a strong, Jewish soul in a big, black body. Why did she stay with me for so long? There were a lot easier ways to make a living than sharing my life. But I won't put words in her mouth. She herself would probably laugh at the question.

"But, will you come, too?" I remember pleading like a little girl. "Will you come to Westchester?"

"Of course I will," she assured me, fixing the striped, woolen blanket over my lap. "I like trees, too."

So, that's the story of how I came to live my final days in Westchester. It's green, I'll give you that. Florence stayed with me, old friends came to visit and I made some new ones as well. I kept talking and everyone kept listening. In the spring, when the weather was warm, we sometimes went out into the garden. We talked, we shared picnic lunches and we laughed. Not so bad. Then, as time went by and the breathing got too hard, I started to do more listening than talking. And that was good, too, because, you know, everyone has their own stories. Mine are no better than anyone else's. They're just mine. They don't have any particular answers in them. But, actually, they don't need to because here's a secret for you – people always say they're looking for answers. But they're not. They're really only looking for truth.

Chapter 4

Grace:
What Kind of Crazy?

My first lover was Teddy. We were only six years old, but that didn't stop us. We sat beside each other in kindergarten, blowing kisses. Our mothers walked us to the park so we could play in the sandbox together, making castles for each other out of dirt and cat poop. I loved him for a lifetime.

One day he moved away. I was alone and broken-hearted. I thought I'd never fall in love again. But then, when I was nine, Manny moved into the neighborhood. He was exotic – a Puerto Rican Jew. "Only in Brooklyn," my mother said, her eyes wide with disbelief. His skin was dark and his hair was curly. And he was older than I was. One day, after Hebrew School, he took me behind the synagogue, back beyond the dumpster and kissed me on the lips. I remember that I liked it. I remember lying in bed, not even ten years old, pretending to kiss him again and again. But one day he wanted to touch me under my white cotton blouse and then under my undershirt and I laughed and pushed him away. Soon after that he found another girlfriend, one I could never compete with. She was eleven years old and she already had tiny button breasts and she was not Jewish.

Even then I was smart enough to know when I was defeated, but I didn't like it. I swore off men completely.

My next few lovers were imaginary. I'd meet them once a week in a magazine or on a movie screen. How I loved Gregory Peck. For my twelfth birthday my friend, Sarah, bought me the full-size poster of *The Yearling*. I tacked it to the wall right by the head of my bed. "The tacks will ruin the wallpaper," my mother said. But my father intervened. "Let her have her picture. Would you rather the real thing?" Falling asleep, I'd lie on my side facing the wall, stroking the shining paper of his leg. Gregory Peck made me happy for a long time; that is, until I started getting bored with playing pretend.

Something happens to a girl in her early teens. It's strange looking down and seeing a body that couldn't possibly be your own. You don't always like what you see. But eventually you get used to it and then you have to decide – what kind of crazy will I be? You see, we all go crazy. That's unavoidable. But some go boy-crazy, while others go book-crazy or fashion-crazy or even crazy-crazy. It seemed as if all my friends knew pretty early what kind of crazy they were. Jeanie was clearly boy-crazy and that gave the mothers the most anxiety. Natalie was book-crazy, which made her mother happy, but left Natalie herself pretty miserable. Laurie became a danger nut, doing things I would never have dreamed of, like climbing over the guardrail on top of the 59th Street Bridge. Who knows what that was about?

I was a different case. I felt pretty crazy inside, but I couldn't figure out what sort of crazy it was. I tried everything. I bounced around from group to group. One week I was a cheerleader. The next week I was a beatnik. I tested out everyone and everything, but I never felt satisfied. That stage lasted, thinking back now, for something like fifty years.

High school was torture. The less said about that the better. The boys I liked didn't like me and the ones who did I hated. But at least after that, like a reward for merely surviving, came college and a life outside of Brooklyn. I moved to Manhattan. We, ladies of the dorm, were tightly guarded (it was still The Fifties, after all), but I did manage to sneak out often enough. I went to jazz clubs in Harlem. I drank kahlua and vodka with my professors. The truth is, I lied to my parents as much as I had to, about where I went on holidays, about whom I spent my evenings with. It's not that I slept around. I wasn't one of those girls. But I felt like every new experience was up for grabs. I lived as if I was always "on the verge".

Most of that first year of college is a blur. All that I really remember are strange boys hanging around outside the dorm. Many belonged to my roommate, Nancy. But then, one night, she brought home Kendall and left him there, almost like a party favor, for me. He was my first gentile. He was beautiful and troubled and I desperately wanted to fall in love with him. But I didn't, although we became inseparable companions for months. It was Kendall who introduced me to Jack.

They weren't really friends. Jack was two years older. But Kendall was auditing a drawing class he was in and decided Jack was the one for me. One afternoon, he found me in the library reading Kierkegaard. His face was flushed and his eyes were dancing.

"I just met your husband," he said.

"Oh really? How is he?" I asked, laughing.

"Perfect."

"I'd expect nothing less."

He pulled me away from my carrel and told me about Jack.

"He's Jewish, but you'd never know it to look at him," Kendall said. That piqued my interest. I raised an eyebrow. "He's artistic, too, but not so much it'll get in the way of his making a living." That annoyed me. It bothered me to know that Kendall understood this would matter. I thought I would have gladly lived in poverty for love. Kendall knew better. "And get this," he continued. "If his drawings say anything about him, he's funny and unpredictable, even if he does seem quiet at first." As far as Kendall was concerned, Jack was exactly what I needed. Something told me to trust his instincts. So we made a plan.

I was to meet Kendall outside of class. He would be engaging Jack in conversation about his latest drawing. I was to be introduced as somebody willing to model nude. Being an architecture student and therefore as much mathematician as artist, Jack would be shocked. But from that moment on, he would imagine the possibility. For a few weeks, it seemed as if we ran into each other everywhere. At first it was the usual places, like the University post office, or the cafeteria. I always tried to have something clever to say. I always tried to make him laugh. Then we began to bump into each other in more unusual spots, like the subway stairs, or around the corner from my dorm. Then he was the one trying to make me laugh. Eventually, he summoned up the courage to ask me out.

"I have to admit, since Kendall first introduced us, I've been wondering what you would look like naked," he started. Now I was shocked. "But lately, I've been just as curious about what you'd look like with your clothes on, say, over dinner." Then I was charmed.

We had that dinner with our clothes on. The clothes didn't come off until much later. As it turned out, Jack was my first love. And Kendall was right. He was exactly what I needed. Jack saw something in me I didn't even know was there. He hooked onto it and held on tight. It was a long time before I understood why, but Jack made it his mission to make me happy. How could I not love somebody like that?

And there were the little things, like the fact that he tucked his shirt into his jeans, he made his bed in the mornings, he recited entire scripts from Marx Brothers movies and played jazz saxophone. He had lived for six months with his family in Africa and had a collection of tribal drums, all of which he could play. He had an artist's heart and a businessman's head. He wasn't boring, yet he was competent. He made me feel safe.

But it didn't last. After nearly two years together, Jack was off to architecture school and I could not, or would not, go with him. He begged me, but I made excuses. I still had a year left of college and although I claimed to desperately want to leave school and follow Jack, I guess I wasn't desperate enough. While most parents of girls back then saw college as a way to find a husband, my immigrant parents saw it as a way to find a life. "There'll be time enough for marriage," they argued. "Your education comes first." I didn't put up a fight. At the time I didn't understand what stopped me. I do now. I had a subversive streak in me back then and marrying Jack was definitely the safer choice. Safety was actually something I ran away from. After a while, I would begin to wonder what I was missing and I'd bolt. I had sacrificed that relationship on the altar of my restlessness.

I finished college. I moved out West. I moved down South. I tried to speak to my family as little as possible. I tried to discover who it was I wanted to be. During that period of my life, men were like handbags – they went with the outfit of the day, but they weren't essential. They just sort of dangled on the side. It took me five or six years to make my way back to New York with some sort of usable identity. Throughout that time I never once heard from Jack. I heard of Jack. I knew he had finished his degree and was working in an architecture firm in Boston. But I believed he was a chapter long since finished.

I met Stan, the scientist, soon after I moved back to New York. My parents loved him and believed that here, finally, was the man I would marry. That doomed him from the start. To me, he was a sensible way to pass the time. A place to land. The more I dragged him to family events, the less they asked me about my future. It worked for a while, but then came Chris. Another architect, but this time an academic one. He was a Dean at Yale and one of the youngest professors ever to make tenure in his department. He had prestige and youth and watery blue eyes that gave him a spiritual sort of look. We met through work. I was assigned to be the editor of his latest book, a popular guide to the Monumental Precursors of the Bauhaus in Europe. Within two meetings, he had stolen my heart away from Stan. First came the furtive looks over coffee cups in the conference room. Then the drink to unwind after work. Then my unnecessary phone calls to Connecticut, followed by his inessential trips to New York. I remember finding all of this exceedingly exciting, though I have to admit it moved a bit slower than I would have liked. Chris was an academic, after all.

Finally, I had had enough and decided to surprise him and bring the first set of proofs to New Haven myself. We had been seeing each other and phoning each other on and off for months. I could have easily sent the proofs up by messenger like I did for all my other authors. But it was October, I remember, and I used the autumn leaves turning to burnt orange along the New England Turnpike as my excuse. It was nearly evening when I arrived, and I drove straight to Chris' apartment for a 'working dinner'. I placed the proofs on his coffee table. He stood behind me, put his hands on my shoulders and then wrapped his arms around my waist. I felt his warm breath in my hair. "Thank you," he whispered. Then we kissed with the kind of desperation that creates life's great memories. For many years after that, on troubled nights, I knew I could conjure up the vision of that kiss and find comfort.

By the time the book tour began, we were openly a couple, commuting between New York and New Haven on weekends, sharing long, breathy phone calls during midweek nights. My parents were in a state. They didn't know which they worried about more – that my present boyfriend wasn't Jewish, or that I was getting old enough, at nearly thirty, to wonder if I'd ever find another one. But I was happy with Chris. I was happy making love one last time in the morning before his Saturday senior seminar. I loved our long, philosophical discussions about art and technology. But secretly I was getting tired of pizza. And all those college kids on wild weekends were starting to annoy me.

We were in Evanston, Illinois, the last town on a five-college tour. Ten days of economy flights and two star hotels were beginning to take their toll. Each stop had its own university to entertain us and its own dinner parties to put us to sleep. I was getting tired of talking about the irrelevant and I was hungry to get back to New York with its freshly baked bagels and premeditated murders. Spending all that time on college campuses reminded me of a hidden truth about myself. Although I fancied myself an intellectual, school actually drove me crazy. And now Chris was driving me crazy. It took all my energy not to scream, So what? during our discussions. I yawned my way through most of the proceedings.

The wide, open spaces of the Illinois campus presented an opportunity for the tour's last lecture. While Chris gave his slide show in a large, partially filled hall, I set myself up in the lobby behind a long table of books and posters. I hid behind a wall of merchandise and finished my week-old *Sunday Times* crossword puzzle.

Suddenly, a shadow fell across the paper and I heard a familiar voice.

"Done any nude modeling lately?"

It was Jack. He looked fantastic, like a grown man in his architect's uniform of khaki pants, pastel shirt and blue blazer. He looked thrilled to see me and he was not wearing a wedding ring. I threw my arms around him.

"Why are you here in this little hick town?"

"Looking up old girlfriends, I guess."

He sat down next to me and showed me the drawings he had brought for his meetings. His firm had been hired to build the university's new Science Center and Jack was put in charge. It was his first big account and I was happy to let him boast. I then told him about my job, the book tour and my return to New York. We talked until the lecture was overand then we exchanged business cards and bittersweet smiles. By the time I got back home, there was a message waiting for me. Jack wanted to see me. It didn't take long after that for Chris to be out and Jack to be back in.

And that's the end of my list of lovers. I married Jack and I remained faithful to him for a lifetime. But, to tell the truth, I'm not sure why. What makes you choose one person over another? Did I just love Jack more than I loved anyone else? Was it just that the timing was right when we found each other again? Who knows? But I do know that, in some ways, Kendall was more intriguing. That first kiss with Chris was more exciting. And there were others, each with their own special moreness. Yet, Jack was the one I chose. He was the one I spent my life with, despite my wondering,and despite his eventual transgressions.

All in all, it wasn't a bad choice. But it was some kind of crazy.

Chapter 5

John:
The Speed of Sound

The light from my laptop cast a shadowy haze over my bowl of Cheerios. The kitchen table was completely covered with the usual morning's debris – a cup of coffee, a carton of milk, the Sports section of *The Boston Globe*, yesterday's mail, a sugar bowl and two or three dirty spoons. I was getting ready for work, doing a million things at once, dressing while eating while reading while typing. There were something like seventeen new emails that morning, the usual amount for eight o'clock on a Wednesday. Most of them didn't need immediate answering. Four of them were advertisements for Viagra. I deleted those right away, but somehow they reminded me to tell Marty about the weekend's Red Sox game. Luckily, Saturday's game was in the afternoon, which meant his kids could go, too. As far as I was concerned, that made the whole thing bearable. If I had to force myself to go out and socialize, at least I'd be with the people I felt most comfortable with, namely Marty, his eight-year-old son and his six-year-old daughter. Even though I was bound to see him in an hour or so, I wrote him an email anyway –

We're on for Saturday. Batting practice starts at 1. Bring the kids.

I was then just about to shut down the computer when I noticed one more message come up on the screen. I pushed aside the dishes and brought my laptop closer. The message was from Yuri Tsypkin.

> *J –*
>
> *A problem with the South Americans. I've heard something. Call me, now.*
>
> *– Y*

The first thing I did was laugh. I could just imagine my old friend all the way over there in Moscow, walking down the halls of his department, wearing a trench coat and dark glasses, sneaking in and out behind classroom doors. "I'll call him later," I first thought. I really did need to get to work. I was all ready to go and had even started the daily hunt around the apartment for my keys. But then I stopped and looked at Yuri's email again. Something felt wrong. The message said nothing. It was basically information-free. But still.

It is true that Yuri had a tendency to see spies in every shadow, but that had to be excused. He had grown up in Russia during the Soviets, after all. And he was Jewish. What better reason for a person to be paranoid? Yuri lived in Moscow still and although Russia was, indeed, changing in this era of Putin and the oligarchs, there were some things inside Yuri I knew could never change. He was suspicious, calculating, aggressive and gruff. In another time and another place, with another head and another heart, Yuri could have been a mob boss, coat slung over his shoulders, fedora on his head, cigar in his mouth. He was everything you might expect a physicist *not* to be. But Yuri was also inspirationally brilliant and enormously generous. He had been a good friend to me ever since we first met in graduate school nearly twenty years earlier. Actually, he was there the first time my jaw locked into place. I was furious over the rejection of an article. It was the first one I had ever submitted to *Nature* and the reviewer was an asshole. I can get myself into a state thinking about it even now. But, the night after I got the rejection letter I couldn't sleep. Hours passed, my brain kept screaming out more and more arguments with each passing minute. By the time morning came, I literally could not open my mouth. I was petrified. Yuri lived down the hall. I pounded on his door, he took one look at me and ushered me to the hospital, staying with me for hours through all the tests, the x-rays, the sedatives. Sitting there by my bed in a ward full of moaning old men, he tried to get me to laugh, reciting horror stories from the old country, even making up State secrets about Kruschev, vodka and Georgian prostitutes. From that day forward, he became the third, along with Lizzy and Marty, in the holy trilogy of people who refused to let me sink.

Yuri was actually one of the first Russian scientists of his generation allowed to study in the West. I always assumed it was because he was so brilliant and because he was a physicist. Russia has always loved its physicists the most. But Yuri eventually confided to me that it was more likely because his father had been Brezhnev's dentist and had once relieved him of a lingering and agonizing abscess. But, patronage or brilliance – it didn't really matter. Either way, he arrived in my life just when I needed him and has stayed there, firmly settled like some huge immovable object, anticipating my needs and somehow reading my thoughts. And I like to think I've done the same for him. Although we hardly ever saw each other, we still somehow always understood what the other was thinking.

It was this mutual intuition which led to our recent collaboration. For the past six months or so, I had been sitting in my office in Boston, playing around with an idea that was so outlandish I could barely even admit it to myself. During that same time, Yuri had been in Moscow, throwing numbers around in the same ridiculous manner and coming up with the same undeniable conclusions. One day, on an impulse, I called him.

"What are you doing?" I asked.

"You wouldn't believe it," Yuri answered.

"Try me."

We weren't at all surprised, then, to find we had been asking ourselves the same seemingly nonsensical series of questions: What if what we know as our three-dimensional universe is actually just a projection of a distant two-dimensional reality? Could it be that the physical processes observed within the universe could actually be described alone by the physics occurring just on its boundary? In other words, what if our world was actually a giant hologram? It was a crazy, perhaps career-breaking idea, but nonetheless, there it was.

As far as I was concerned, Yuri was the only other physicist in the world crazy enough to entertain such an improbable thought. And, I guess, somewhere in the back of my mind, I had always assumed Yuri would be thinking the same insane thoughts as me at the same unlikely time. So, of course, we joined forces. What could be better? At first, we worked at an amazing speed, each of us building on the other's already half-completed ideas. But over the last few weeks, somewhere around the first of May and Russia's annual Celebration of the Worker, something had gotten stuck. The calculations were getting more and more absurd with each new variable. No matter how much we tried to deny it, it was becoming evident that soon we would have to stop, step back and look at it all again from the beginning. It could take months. The time that had been potentially wasted infuriated me. But now, to make matters worse, Yuri seemed to be saying that there was something going on with the South Americans, too. Sure, the first inkling of the holography idea came from a paper out of Argentina a few years before. But since then, nothing. In my heart I believed that I – that is, Yuri and I – were the only ones in the entire scientific community capable of developing this theory. The South Americans had to be wrong, no matter what it was they had come up with. But believe me, the last thing you'd ever want to be a part of was one of those horrible professional races to the finish. Had it really come to that? I remember just sitting there, staring at my computer. I took a sip of coffee – old, cold sludge.

So what did I do? I did the only reasonable thing to do. I called Moscow. It was vaguely morning in Boston, so I figured it must be vaguely evening there. The phone rang only twice.

"*Da? Zdrastvoyte?*" It was unmistakably Yuri.

"Yuri? It's me – John."

"Of course. I knew it. I was waiting. You read my email?" I love the way Yuri speaks English. Grammatically, it's perfect. Colloquially, astonishing. But it's like each sentence is shot out of a canon. Boom. Boom. Boom. Sometimes, it just makes it hard to be serious.

"You really have a James Bond complex, you know?" I said and not for the first time.

"You would say that, there in America, the land of the free. But this is serious." He took a breath. "I should not even talk about it on the phone. But you-know-who from Argentina is getting close to what we are doing. He, his team, they are not stuck. Do you hear? Not stuck. If we do not move, everything … wasted."

"Yuri, calm down." I tried to reassure him. "He's no smarter than us. If we're stuck, then either he's stuck, too, or he's heading the wrong way. How do you know this, anyway?"

"…an early draft of an article … a friend… "

"And he showed you?" It seemed hard to believe.

"No, not that. But we go back many years. He let me know."

"And who is this 'Deep Throat' of yours?"

"Deep throat?" Yuri laughed. "I can't tell you. But I believe him. So come." And there it was, the first light seeping under a closed door.

"What do you mean, 'come'?" I asked.

"Come to Russia."

"Come to Russia. Just like that."

"Yes. Just like that, John. We need it."

"Don't be ridiculous," I said, still trying hard not to take any of this seriously. "I can't just drop everything and run off to Russia. I'm teaching."

"Okay. So don't come." I thought he gave in too easily, but then I heard what his plan really was. "Instead, go to London. There is a conference in August. Six weeks away. Too long to wait, really, but..."

London - the last place on earth I ever wanted to go and Yuri knew it. Now I was getting angry. "Look, Yuri. I don't know..."

"John. I know about you and London and now I don't care. It's enough already. You are forty years old."

"Forty-one."

"Even worse."

London – my own personal house of horrors. Everything truly frightening in my life had happened there. I'd spent almost twenty-five years trying hard not to think about any of it, but when I did, everything seemed distorted and out of focus. I just couldn't bare the thought of facing that place again. I sat there in my kitchen, staring into space, trying not to think at all.

"We need this, John," I heard Yuri say. "You know I am right." Just like bullets.

"But London?"

"The only way. There, they'll send me. Nowhere else. Think about it."

"I'll think about it," I said, just to stop talking about it. Then, I changed the subject as fast as I could. "So, how's Natalia?" There was a long pause. "Yuri? You there?" I could hear Yuri breathing, but he wasn't saying anything. "What? Is she okay?"

"Wait," Yuri finally said. I heard nothing for a few seconds, then footsteps and the rustling of wires. "Okay, I am back. She's fine. But she had a miscarriage."

"What? She was pregnant? But I thought she couldn't..."

56

"So did we. But there is this new program at the medical school. A friend got us in, but really, she is too old. Thirty-eight."

"Jesus, Yuri. I'm sorry."

"It was quick. Maybe ten weeks. That's all. But it gave her such hope. Maybe too much."

Too much hope. That's what he said. I remember it very clearly and I remember wondering to myself, could there be such a thing? All I knew was that there were too many times in my life when I had felt myself longing to have any hope at all. How can you have too much?

"You know, I tell her don't worry. We're happy, yes?" Yuri continued. "But you know what she says? She says, 'Yes, we are happy. But I'd rather live with hope not fulfilled, than live with no hope at all.' That's a Russian for you."

When I got off the phone, I just sat for a moment staring at the black screen of my sleeping computer. I couldn't stop thinking about Yuri. His work, his wife, everything important in his life was in trouble. I could see how everything for him must now really seem like a race. A race to publish. A race to have a child. Here I had been dragging myself around feeling listless and depressed and for seemingly no good reason at all. But look at Yuri. He had a reason, more than one, but his response was not self-pity. It was energy, defiance, determination. I threw my dishes into the sink, found my lost keys and forced myself out of the apartment. "Why can't I be more like that?" I remember thinking, disgusted.

All that day, I paced around my office, starting paperwork and not finishing it, looking out the window and not seeing anything. I was at my most distracted and that's saying something. I couldn't shake the sound of Yuri's voice from my head. That voice was always filled with passion and energy, no matter what he was talking about and if I envied him anything, it was that. I started to feel this overwhelming need to see him, if only to be in the presence of that passion and the feeling grew stronger throughout the day. I could almost feel it sitting there, like pressure building up in the muscles behind my knees. I began to believe that if the two of us could just be locked in the same room and given time to call each other names, argue with each other's insights, then maybe we would find the answers we were looking for – that elusive variable to make the equation fit, or maybe even the reason behind my deepening, blackening malaise.

Obviously, the answers I needed weren't only about my research. To tell the truth, nothing felt right anymore, not me, not my life, not my work. I stood there staring outside my office window at the quad full of well-spaced trees and well-built students and I knew I needed help, even if I couldn't admit it out loud. But now I began to wonder whether some of the answers to my questions, the solutions to my problems, might actually be found somewhere inside Yuri. Strange, I know. Considering that I was a man who claimed to believe in nothing except what I could prove with numbers, it shook me to realize what I was thinking. But I began to imagine that if I could only transfer a portion of Yuri's energy and passion into myself, then maybe that black hole of mine might actually begin to be filled. I had already felt the effects of that energy, just from hearing the sound of Yuri's voice cast out over thousands of miles of space. Imagine if we were actually in the same space, standing next to each other, waves traveling over inches instead of miles. How much better would that be? But London? No way.

Chapter 6

Grace:
Racing Out of the Grand Canal

All too soon the race was on. Not the rat race where you run just to keep ahead of your competitive neighbors. But the race into adulthood. The race where you spend years stretching and practicing and getting your footing just right at the starting line and then, more suddenly than you expect, you're off.

Within a month of reconnecting with Jack we were planning our wedding. Fate had brought us back together, it seemed and who were we to question fate? Kendall foretold it when we were still teenagers in college, but it took us years of denying, forgetting, searching and rediscovering, to finally realize it for ourselves. Once we did, the *rightness* of our being together became our truth. The truth for me was that Jack made sense. He was just enough the same as me to make me feel safe; just enough different to keep me from being bored. An only child of well-off parents, he grew up in a big house in Connecticut. He went to sleep-away camp during summers and came home to the family beach house on Long Island. His parents sent him to Europe as a graduation present after high school. And yet, he was Jewish. It amazed me. Who knew Jews could be like that? And he adored me. He worshiped me. After all the others, I knew he was the one.

The truth for Jack was that I was the missing ingredient needed to spice up his life. With me by his side, keeping him on his toes, occasionally throwing a curve ball into his neatly ordered row of shoes, he could get on with the business of becoming a responsible, well-respected, civilized adult. Jack believed his truth and I believed mine, but to tell the truth, I was always afraid, somewhere deep inside, that what he thought he wanted was, actually, bad for him. Put it another way – he may have loved spicy food, but something blander might have been better.

You see, I knew there was this flutter inside me, that's the only word I could ever find for it. Something inside was fluttering around like a trapped moth. My mother said I had 'ants in my pants'. My little sister, Gina, a force to be reckoned with from the start, loved that phrase of our mother and taunted me with it whenever she could with that obnoxious singsong voice of hers. But I couldn't help myself. No matter what insect you called it, I always felt uncomfortable, squirming around within myself and the world in a way that drove us all nuts. "Settle down," my father would plead. "Come back to earth." After many years, I came to understand what this flutter really meant. It eventually became a tool for me, a sign that it was time to stop and listen to myself. But for a long time, I tried to get rid of it, or at least ignore it. First, I called myself by my middle name, Michelle, instead of Grace, but that didn't help. Then, I raced out of Brooklyn, only to find Manhattan too confining. Halfway around the country and back I ran until I finally realized geography had nothing to do with it. When I found Jack again I began to believe that only his calm assurance could finally quiet me down. But I eventually learned that it's a mistake to think that another person can still that flutter if you have it. That, you can only do yourself.

Eventually, the parents had to meet. I was terrified. I wasn't worried about my parents' reaction to the Rosens. I knew they would be thrilled. My father was temporarily content, happy that I was finally doing something special with my life, moving up and out of Brooklyn by marrying into a wealthy New England family. For him, it was a glimpse of the American dream. My mother was more nervous. Did Jews really live in Connecticut? She couldn't believe it. Who were these people? Were they like us or not? Despite her fears, though, I knew she would be quiet, well behaved, and would smile lovingly at the appropriate times. But what about my new in-laws? They were bound to be less charmed by our simple ethnic ways than Jack was. The Rosens were one generation ahead of us in the American immigrant march away from the poverty of the past into the promised affluence of the acculturated future. I was afraid that William and Debra Rosen would see their only son's choice of bride as a tug back into a world they themselves had worked hard to get out of. And where would we meet? My parents offered to have them over for Friday night dinner, but I couldn't bear the thought of us sitting around that heavy wooden table in a house that smelled of stewed carrots. I was embarrassed. So we met in a little Italian restaurant in Manhattan where there was food my father had heard of and wine my father-in-law would be willing to drink.

The evening actually went better than I had hoped. From the parents' point of view, ours was a perfect match. Jack would give me the key to a larger world, a world I was supposedly meant for and I would give Jack the heritage and tradition his parents had let slip away in their race towards a better life. From that first meeting on, the four in-laws saw each other as often as was necessary and they were always happy to do so.

The wedding was fine, but I'd rather talk about the honeymoon. Everything up to that point was mostly my decision. Jack helped me choose where we would get married and what month it would be, but then he was happy to let me get on with it while he concentrated on work. The wedding ceremony was in our little synagogue in Brooklyn and actually I was happy to have it there. The reception, though, was in Manhattan, despite the inconvenience – a fancy luncheon in a townhouse with leather chairs and chandeliers.

The honeymoon, on the other hand, was Jack's decision. His parents offered to give us a trip as our wedding present and he knew exactly where he wanted to go – Venice. I had never been to Europe. Paris, London, even Rome might have made more sense to me. But in the end, I didn't care. To finally have the chance to walk up to some uniformed woman behind the International Departures counter of the airport and present my passport – to finally have a reason to have a passport – was enough for me. But to Jack, Venice meant something more. When he was thirteen, he and his parents had lived in Paris for a year while his father worked on some big deal for his bank. That year, the three of them traveled everywhere, throughout the greater and lesser capitals of Europe and even to Africa. But one long weekend, they left Jack at home with a French au pair and went by themselves to Venice. From then on, Venice became Jack's place of great romance, the place where adults went to do adult things. So, when it was time to decide where to go, Jack already had it all planned. He knew where he wanted to stay. He knew what view he wanted to see when he woke up in the morning. Before I had even begun to think about it, Jack had ferreted out the best flights and plotted our itinerary.

We had a suite on the fourth floor of the Hotel Londres, overlooking the Grand Canal. Mornings were spent in our complimentary bathrobes, sipping cappuccino on our balcony and eating sweet pastries. Once or twice, Jack took out his sketchbook and drew pictures of the rays of sunlight bouncing off the squiggles and turns of the sculptured palaces around us. I saved those sketches through every move, every new city, every new house. Jack thought they were silly. But I thought they were true to life, true to him. Days, we walked for miles over every bridge we saw, in and out of narrow streets and real-life neighborhoods. Evenings, we ate and drank too much, but not so much as to interfere with our nights of love-making behind opened curtains and street-lit windows. When I think about it so many years later, I still feel us there in that floating city. I don't look back and wonder could those young people in love really have been us? I know they were. Through all the changes the years brought, I can truly say that the Grace and Jack who went to Venice were still there somewhere inside the Grace and Jack who ended up in New York.

At the end of the week we took a speedboat across the canal to the airport. As we bumped along, it felt like all the fits and starts of early adulthood were finally over. We were on the road, so to speak, our chosen path in life and it was full steam ahead. I was newly wed when we arrived in Venice and all the world's possibilities seemed just within our grasp. I imagined our lives together, starting out in our quirky little condo in the best part of Boston. I'd find a job in publishing or at one of the Universities. Every morning Jack would go to his office and dream up beautiful new buildings. Sometimes we'd travel together on business, maybe even back to Europe. We'd make new friends and throw dinner parties. There'd be weekends in the country. Our life was going to be perfect in the way all newlyweds' lives were perfect.

That ride across the Grand Canal to the airport and home wasn't leading us to the settled bliss of young married life, after all. Within a week of being home I realized my period was late. I assumed it was the excitement of the wedding or the disruption of the travel. I decided to ignore it and started circling want ads in the Sunday paper. But a few weeks later, my breasts were getting tender. I felt a heaviness, a sluggishness I couldn't at first explain, but soon enough I realized what was happening. I went to a clinic and took a blood test. I was pregnant.

Jack and I told each other we were thrilled. We told ourselves the timing wasn't what we had planned, but it would be fine. I put aside my job search and tried to prepare myself for motherhood. I bought magazines for new mothers and researched the latest changing tables. I tried to ignore the fact that our fashionable new apartment was now totally impractical. My mother clucked happily; my father shook his head in a sort of resigned understanding. Gina was shocked and, I think, disappointed. Me? I wasn't ready. Even though I couldn't say it out loud, I knew it was all a charade. But really, all I could do was practice my breathing exercises and try to still the flutter.

By the time Lizzy was born, I had turned myself into 'Marine-Mom'. I memorized the rulebook (Dr. Spock), set up the appropriate schedules, stripped myself of any extraneous interests and did everything but shave my head in anticipation of my new life. I think from the start, Lizzy instinctively understood that resistance was futile. She was an easy baby. She slept well, she ate when I fed her and she hardly ever cried.

I loved her. Of course, I did. I even began to believe that motherhood came naturally to me. There grew to be a comfortable rhythm between us. We woke, we ate, we played, we napped, then we did it all again until it was time for our nightly bath and bedtime ritual. We became two parts of the same well-oiled machine, both working together towards the greater good – family.

And Jack? He seemed happy, but it was hard to tell. To be honest, in those early years we hardly ever saw him. He worked very long hours and often had to travel to find new sites and check on new builds. Jack was doing his dream job and I suspect he assumed I was doing mine. If I wasn't, I certainly wasn't about to admit it to him, or to anyone else. From the moment of Lizzy's birth, that old flutter of mine got buried under a mountain of expectations. To do otherwise would have been too dangerous. And besides, I was just too tired.

Chapter 7

John:
A Residual Strong Force

For days after that email from Yuri, I walked around feeling like some kind of combustion engine ready to ignite. I was irritable, angry, frustrated and generally a pain in the ass. But nevertheless, on that following Saturday, just as I said I would, I brought Marty and his kids to Fenway Park to watch the Yankees torture the Red Sox. I had the tickets, after all. I had been buying four season tickets for years now. People were often surprised by that. Even though the Sox rarely won, the tickets were still expensive. Two would have been understandable, even on a professor's salary. But four? I knew it was an extravagance, but, really, it was my only one. Not that I ever paid much attention. Money was just one of those details of life I tried to ignore. Every month I got paid. My paycheck was deposited directly into my bank account and that was that. Actually, a few years earlier, the manager of my local bank decided to pay attention to it all for me.

One day, out of the blue, I got a phone call. "Doctor Rosen, we have noticed that you are maintaining a balance of nearly $100,000 in your checking account," the man said. "Perhaps you'd like to discuss setting up a savings account or an IRA?"

"That's a good idea," I thought and then forgot to make the appointment. I actually forgot about the whole thing, until it came into my head during dinner one night with my sister.

"What?" I remember Lizzy crying in a sort of hilarious outrage. "Are you completely out of touch with reality?"

Soon after that, I was sitting in the office of my brother-in-law-the-investment-banker creating a financial plan. We discussed long-term investments, short-term investments, treasury bills, retirement plans, certificates of deposit. At first, I found the discussion interesting, but then it became boring and my mind began to wander. Until I had an insight.

"You mean, if I keep living like I am and I don't get married and buy a house and have kids, I'd have enough money to buy season tickets to the Red Sox and rent a house on Martha's Vineyard?"

"John," Peter explained to me, somewhat exasperated, "you can do that now." And that's why I had four tickets to every Red Sox home game. To tell the truth, though, I actually bought the extra two tickets for Marty. You see, a single man living like a monk can survive quite well on a professor's salary. But a married man with two children and a mortgage was another thing. With four tickets, there was always room for Marty and at least one kid. Plus, it made me feel good to do it.

So there I was, on that irritable Saturday, walking up the concrete steps to my seats. I've always loved June. It's my favorite part of the baseball season. Everything is in harmony then. The air is warm but not too hot. The team is healthy, the beer is cold and the field is that miraculous shade of green. The feeling I get looking out onto the diamond is the same at forty as it was at fourteen. At Fenway, and no place else, I always felt like I could step out of my world, put my life on hold and just be. The anticipation of that feeling was what actually got me there at all on that day. At least, for a few hours I hoped, there'd be no scientific dead ends to worry about, no emotional turbulence to torment me.

I moved down to the first of my seats and made room for Aaron, then Marty, then Rachel. That's how we always sat when both kids came along. Divide and conquer was Marty's approach to a family outing.

"So, what's Beth doing today without you and the kids?" I asked, knowing the answer.

"Enjoying herself, that's what. She told me to say she owes you big time for this."

"Don't mention it."

Within minutes of our arrival, a horde of vendors appeared roaming up and down the aisles.

"Hot dogs!" one called out.

"Can we?" asked Rachel.

"Popcorn!" called another.

"Can we?" she asked again.

"Don't you feed that kid?" I laughed. It was always the same.

"Yo, hot dog. Yo, popcorn," Marty yelled and soon a parade of food was passed down the aisle, hand to hand. "My treat."

One of the things I loved the most about Marty was that he wasn't a Yankees fan. Although he had spent every minute of the first eighteen years of his life within the borders of New York's five boroughs, he never got sucked into the Yankee's web. He grew up, instead, a fan of the Mets, the team of the 'common man' and was disgusted by all the flash and bluster of that other team up in The Bronx. To Marty, the Yankees' endless string of World Series Championships only proved my own favorite theory, namely the random fallibility of the cosmos.

I remember looking down the row at Marty's kids. I could never get over how different they were. Rachel was always making me laugh. Despite being only six years old, everything about her was big – her cheeks, her belly, her hair, her personality. Marty called her She Who Must Be Obeyed. As soon as Rachel got her food, there was already ketchup all over her face and slurping sounds coming out of her Coke. Aaron, on the other hand, was quiet, skittish, intense and skinny. He seemed to live on French fries and chocolate milk. I could see how Marty must have been just like that at eight years old and it made me long to have Aaron like me. I wanted to be his grown-up pal. So I sat next to him during the game and together we recorded every hit, every catch and every run in Aaron's special book of scorecards. I had given it to him for his last birthday and I bet Marty made sure to remind him to bring it along.

"Uncle John, I've decided to record the hits like this, " Aaron explained to me. "One line equals a single, two lines is a double…"

"Three is a triple, right?" I asked.

"Yea, but look. A run is a star, okay? And an out is an X. That makes more sense to me."

Aaron was very serious about everything he did, but he was especially serious about baseball and absolutely religious about the Red Sox. I took this as a sign that Marty was, indeed, raising his children correctly. He might have been born a New Yorker, but his kids were Bostonians through and through. As far as I was concerned, allowing Aaron to fully experience the angst of growing up a Red Sox fan proved the depth of Marty's commitment to good parenting. He was teaching his son that pain could not be avoided in life, but that it doesn't have to be endured alone. I looked at Aaron and wished I could teach that lesson to a son of my own someday. I'd probably have to learn it for myself first, though.

"So, Aaron," I asked, hoping to make a point. "You gonna' play Little League this summer?"

"Nah, I don't think so," he said.

"Why not?"

"I'm no good."

That's what I had thought he was going to say. I looked at Marty and he just frowned and shrugged.

"How do you know you're no good?" I asked. "I didn't think I was very good, but my team won the Citywide Championship one year."

Aaron looked at his father to see if he should really believe this.

"It's true," Marty said. "I know this story. To look at him now, you'd never believe it, but John was a decent ball-player a million years ago."

"Gee, thanks," I said. "Yea, I was okay. I was the catcher. But there were plenty on the team who were better. But the point is I was okay enough to be a help. And then we won."

"Did it feel great?" Aaron asked.

"It felt great," I said, nodding maybe a little too much and too long.

And, suddenly, I was recalling how, back in that long ago time, baseball was the only thing that did feel great.

I hadn't thought about that summer in years. It was one of those painful memories I had tried to teach myself not to think about. My championship season was the summer after we found out about my father's affair. Actually, to make it worse, I was the one to discover it first. I was fourteen and it was the Sunday just before Thanksgiving. I remember my mother had been acting weird for weeks. It was like she was constantly looking over my shoulder, questioning everything I did. She was acting paranoid and she was making me feel paranoid. I felt paranoid enough just being alive and being fourteen without having my mother creeping around snooping into everything. It was driving me crazy, making me furious. I think I even went storming out of the house one night, swearing never to return. She didn't follow me, I remember. Of course, at the time I assumed that it was all about me. Everything's always all about you when you're that age, isn't it? But then, once, when I picked up the phone to call some friend, I overheard a conversation which still makes my head throb whenever I'm forced to remember it. *Melanie, you know I love you, but I can't right now.* A simple, declarative sentence which began a series of events that changed everything for all of us. Out of desperation, I confessed what I had heard to Lizzy, up in my bedroom after Thanksgiving dinner. Then, my mother found out and confronted my father. Although he stopped seeing Melanie and became overwhelmed by guilt and remorse, the damage had already been done. It was just like a bad case of quantum entanglement. You do something to change a particle and then, no matter what, its relative particle gets changed, too. You just can't stop it.

For me, it all came to a head that next summer. For the first time in my life, we didn't go down to our rental house on the Cape. Instead, we stayed in the sweltering heat of the city. Lizzy didn't come home after her year in college, choosing to work some volunteer job in California instead. My mother sat around the kitchen, staring into space. So, what did I do? I did the only thing I could do – play baseball. I had always been a fan. That summer, I became a fanatic and it was just as well, because baseball provided the one good thing that did come out of those horrible, sweltering months.

I'll never forget that last championship game. It was the highlight of a rather spotty career of childhood sporting attempts. I made two good plays. No – great plays. First, I caught a wild hit that went straight up into the air over home plate, tearing off my catcher's mask and throwing it to the ground, just in time to close out a crucial inning. And then ... then ... I made the last hit to bring us all home, rounding the bases in a whirlwind of dust and sweat and... You know, I played soccer as a kid. I even played rugby in High School, but that Little League baseball team was something else. There were kids there I had never seen before or since, but they were all just what I needed. They took me out of myself and lifted me onto their shoulders into what felt like some sort of parallel universe – a universe where parents sat together on bleachers cheering for their kids, where you always instinctively knew just when that hurtling ball would cross the plate, where you could swing time and time again and never miss. It was glorious. Maybe even poetic. And it felt like it saved my life.

So even though I understood I was now sitting there next to Aaron, staring out onto the field at Fenway, I also knew it wasn't the Red Sox I was seeing out there. Although I was now over forty years old and sitting next to my best friend's kids, I didn't see Manny and Pedro. Instead, I seemed to see Axel and Luke, my teammates, frozen in some time warp. It felt like I was in two places at once. I was aware of the game happening down on the field. I argued with Marty about fielding errors and bad calls. I even stole French fries from the kids. But part of me was also back in the Boston neighborhood of my youth, fourteen years old and tiptoeing around my shattered family. I gave my arms an involuntary shake as if my muscles were too tight for my bones. They always felt too tight back then and they felt that way again sitting there next to Aaron.

The roar of the crowd and a tug on my arm brought me momentarily back to the present. A long, hard drive past the right-field foul line put the Sox ahead.

"Did ya' see that? Did ya'?" Aaron slammed against my side, unable to control his body for all the excitement.

"Right past Pesky's Pole," I heard myself say. "You won't see that every day." I threw my arm around Aaron's shoulder. "Now, how are you going to score that on your card?"

"A star with a big 'P' for 'Pesky's Pole' right next to it!"

I looked down the row at Aaron, then Marty, then Rachel. They were all laughing and hugging. Aaron was jumping up to give his father a high five. Rachel was standing on her seat, draining the bottom of her Coke. They were happy. I pretended to be happy, too, but I wasn't. Despite the home run, I was still like a storm of spinning, accelerated energy, my mind bounced uncontrollably from one irritating thought to another.

And now those thoughts weren't only about the damn South Americans and an increasingly threatening trip to London. They were about an unwanted, dredged up memory from the past as well. *My father was in love with Melanie – that was her name.* I had heard her name mentioned only once or twice, but I never forgot it. Just the sound of the word conjured up images of short, brown hair and mischievous eyes. She was probably dead by now, just like my father, but that didn't matter. For me, she would always be the same age she was then, stuck in time, eternally. The reality of her existence and the effect it had on my life never changed, no matter how many years passed. She always hovered there somewhere like an ultra-dense particle cloud.

I never met Melanie, but I believed I knew what she looked like. Not a great beauty, but pretty enough. Someone you'd like to be around. I was sure she wasn't anything special. It's not like my dad had woken up one morning and found himself in love with some Hollywood starlet. Melanie was just a somebody – nice, comfortable and not my mother. Maybe if it had been some overwhelming passion… If only my father had been caught against his will in some vortex of undeniable ardor, maybe I could have forgiven him or at least understood. But that wasn't what happened. Okay. Maybe I didn't know what actually had happened, but I was sure it wasn't that. I never spoke to my father about the affair. And my father never apologized to me about it either, even though I waited for an apology for years.

All of this was in my head as I sat there at Fenway in the early summer sun and so I found myself thinking more and more about fathers. I thought about how Marty was with his kids, how present he was, engaged and strong. My own father had been like that once, when I was a kid myself, before Melanie came into our lives. It was almost as if I had had two fathers. There was the first pre-Melanie real one, the one I looked up to and adored. And then there was the shadow one, humiliated, frightened, contrite, weak. There were times when I hated that second father even more than I longed for the first. Then, eventually, sometime in my thirties, I decided not to think about it anymore. And I rarely did, except when I was with Aaron or Rachel. Or Amanda, maybe the closest I'd get to being a father myself.

Jesus, I was in a bad way. I coughed. I stood up as if to stretch. I knew I was in trouble if even a Red Sox-Yankees game couldn't distract me. Maybe it would have been better for me to be at work, I thought, lost in the midst of some comfortingly complicated mathematic equation. Maybe there, at least, I'd be making some sort of progress.

"John. Hey, John." Marty's voice came to me slowly out of the distance. "Rachel's gotta pee. Might as well take Aaron, too. Will you?" I felt Marty poking me on the shoulder. "Huh? You there?"

"Yea, yea. Sure. Let's go," I said.

"Are we going to pee in that thing?" Aaron asked.

"Yea. Let's go pee in that thing," I answered, grateful at least to be thinking about something real.

The Red Sox won that day, one to nothing. By the time the game was over, the kids had eaten two Fenway Franks, two bags of popcorn, a giant Hershey's bar, two Cokes, one chocolate milk and three plates of french fries. Rachel could barely walk. Marty lifted her up and carried her down the stairs. Even now I can see her smiling at me and waving from over her father's shoulder. I kept one hand on Aaron's back to guide him through the crowd. It was a long walk after an exciting day and the kids were tired. I was tired, too. I was ready to go home, maybe watch an old movie on TV, eat something and go to sleep. Then suddenly, from the middle of the throng, I heard, "Hey, Doctor Rosen."

I turned to see a group of my graduate students pushing their way towards me. If only I had ignored them. One was my Research Assistant, the "surprising" Phil Priestly. I always

73

called him that. To look at him, you'd think he was your average run-of-the-mill football player with a skull as thick as his neck. But Priestly always got the theory faster than anyone. The more nonsensical the better. He was brilliant and I was always happy to see him. No, seeing Phil wasn't the problem. It was what, or rather who came next that caused the trouble. Coming around from behind Phil was – that woman. Tall, thin, Waspy, confident, smiling, tan. My heart sank.

"Great game, eh?" Phil said. "Doctor Shapiro, those your kids?" Phil winked at Rachel and she pretended to be shy. "We're going to go have a celebratory drink. Wanna come?" he asked.

"Gotta get the kids home, but thanks anyway," Marty answered. I looked at Phil but not his friends. I didn't want to go with them. I had done my duty as a functioning adult and spent the day outside in the fresh air. Now I wanted to go home alone and sit safely in the comfort of my own living room, obsessing.

"Oh, come on, Doctor Rosen," Phil said. "The Sox don't beat the Yankees every day. And I promise I won't let Chloe badger you about Kaluza-Klein theories."

Chloe. That was her name, I now remembered. She moved closer to me, but I tried to appear like I didn't notice. I didn't have to notice. I knew Marty was noticing enough for both of us, noticing, for example, Chloe's smile as she looked up into my face, her easy stumble against my shoulder as the crowd pushed against us. I gave him a quick, but desperate, glance. If I could have transported myself up, out of there and into some other dimension, I would have. But I couldn't move. I wanted to think of an excuse, to think of anything at all. But instead, I just stood there, my eyes roaming back and forth between Marty and the path of responsible adulthood and Chloe and the path of who-knows-what. If only Marty had lied and said I had to go with him to his house. To dinner. To help with the kids. Anything. But neither of us said a word. For all the decisiveness I exhibited, I might as well have collapsed into the mass of base-ball fans and let them physically carry me away. And, to tell the truth, that's actually what it felt like I had done inside – collapse. But instead, what I really did, was give Rachel a kiss, Aaron a hug and then follow my students into the crowd to who-knows-where.

Chapter 8

Grace:
Kendall the Savior

It took me half a lifetime to figure out a lesson my old friend, Kendall Van Brunt, knew from the start: there's no escaping life's tragedies. They come to everyone sooner or later; it's just that they're seldom the ones you expect.

Kendall Van Brunt was a surprising friend with an even more surprising name. He grew up as far from Brooklyn as the Long Island Expressway will take you, and when I first met him, early in my freshman year at college, I thought I had met Jay Gatsby in the flesh. He was just as beautiful, in that blonde, blue-eyed, goyish kind of way. And he had a smile of alarming sincerity. After plumbing the depths of each other's souls and realizing we were not, in fact, in love, I thought that was it. We finished school, he headed east, I headed west and I believed I'd never hear from nor see Kendall Van Brunt, that rich, handsome, distant figure, again. After some time, I settled into a seemingly normal, middle-class, respectable life. As we know, I married the man Kendall had originally found for me and made a home. I rediscovered my parents, my sister. I stopped fighting with myself and found a small, enclosed place inside me to store my dreams. I learned to be content and I tried to be happy.

I never really thought of Kendall much. I dismissed him as just another soul lost amidst wealth and privilege. As I grew up and settled down, I occasionally heard about him from some old college friend. First, he was in the Peace Corps. Then UNICEF. After that he jumped from one government relief agency to another, from one grief-drenched, poverty-stricken third world country to another, as if they were local beer joints. He would wander in, order up a tragedy (a famine or an earthquake or some civil disturbance), gulp it down and move on to the next. I, on the other hand, was always too busy trying to save myself.

I got pregnant again when Lizzy was three, right on schedule. I had done my research and decided that four years between kids was just right. Jack was ready for another baby. Even Lizzy had begun to talk about wanting to be a big sister.

The baby was born in the spring, just like Lizzy had been, but it was colder than usual. I remember because Lizzy, of all people, mentioned it when she and Jack came to take us home from the hospital. "I thought it was spring, Mommy," she said. "Why do I have to wear my winter coat?" I can hear her little girl voice now, but I don't think I gave her an answer. I was so wrapped up in myself and our new son that I barely even noticed her. I barely noticed anything, except the baby's fretful crying and my exhaustion. Looking back on that time, all I have now is a memory of steely purposefulness.

It's hard to talk about even now. It's not just the lump of grief that lodges itself in your throat, or the overwhelming fatigue of loss that makes even the effort to formulate the words more than you can bear. It's the concept that is too hard to explain. It's the essence of the concept. It's the glimmer of a spark around the edges of the essence of the concept that is just too hard. Your grandmother dies and it is sad. It is an expected sorrow, but a sorrow nonetheless. A shifting of a life into the distant realm of history. When a grandparent dies, their funny stories become the myths that uphold your life. There is, perhaps, the occasional longing for their face, for the soft looseness of their skin. But it is easy to incorporate them into yourself. As they pass from their lives, they slip easily into your work-a-day heart like an egg yolk off a spoon.

Your mother or father dies and it is harder. The earth seems to shake. The ground beneath your feet tremors as you realize that the separation is now complete. The separation you fought for, dreamt of, is now real, but not in the way you had wanted. You hope that their best is inside you, but you can't be sure. Who has the self-assurance to completely believe that without the parent, without the solid ground beneath his feet, he can still tread firmly? What orphan is happy to be one?

But when your child dies – when your three-month-old baby goes to sleep at night and never wakes up; when all your screaming and holding and begging does nothing to restart his breathing, ignite his heartbeat; when first there is life and then, for no earthly reason there is none; when that happens to you one Thursday morning amidst the percolating coffee, the popping toast, the melting butter … you die, too. Your body stubbornly continues to function, to pour the coffee, to butter the toast. Your own heart refuses to stop beating. Your own breathing persists in its wretched regularity. But you do, in fact, die. And that is impossible to talk about. From that moment on, there is no foundation. There is no Earth to shake. There is no realm of history. In fact, there is no God. There wasn't for me.

It was strange, but I found myself thinking a lot about Kendall after the baby died. I found myself asking people if they knew where he was. I actually started looking for him. I eventually discovered he was in Ethiopia. "The children are starving and he is saving them," a mutual friend told me. So, I wrote to him, out of the blue, the first and only time in nearly twenty years.

I gave him the facts; a daughter, a husband, a baby lost. I didn't know if the letter would reach him. I didn't even know why I wanted to contact him at all. But writing to Kendall Van

Brunt was the only thing I positively did want to do during those first few weeks. I lived those weeks in a haze. I existed, but it was as if I was forgotten. It was as if God himself had lost me, left me, like a child trembling under the clothes racks in some darkening shop. I poured our cereal into bowls. I walked my daughter to nursery school. I tried not to stare blindly out the window for too long. I picked up my daughter after school and chatted with the other mothers. I told them I was okay. I made dinner. I smelled my daughter's clean hair after her bath. I kissed my husband goodnight. I lived, but I was dead. What would happen to me, I asked myself. Would I ever be found?

Then, on one unspecified numbing afternoon I picked up the mail which had fallen through the door slot onto the weary carpet and there was Kendall's answer. It arrived after I thought I was all cried out. I heard the daily thump of letters onto the floor, I saw that folded blue aerogramme and I knew it was from him. Something made me want to be alone with it, to grab it away, leave the house and find a place of my own, a sanctuary of solitude in which to read it. I told Jack I was going for a walk and told Lizzy I'd be back in ten minutes. I walked down the hill, across the highway towards the river. I found the old, deserted Metropolitan Parks Commission swimming pool, that testimony to the Fifties' belief in the power and the glory of cement and I sat behind the bathhouse on the cracked concrete. My hand tore open the envelope and found his three-fold message:

Don't stop loving.

Let time pass.

Don't give up on us.

I looked inside for more. I shook it open as if I believed a small jewel had gotten stuck in the corner. Was that all there was? I was furious. I remember crying out loud. I believe I actually yelled, "Fuck you, Kendall Fucking Van Brunt." And I began to sob, again, convulsively, painfully with wrenching in my stomach and burning in my lungs. "Who the fuck do you think you are, to say it's that simple?" I didn't know why I wrote to him in the first place. I hadn't known what I wanted from him. But surely it wasn't this.

I can see myself now from the distance of years, sitting there behind the empty swimming pool on the hard, cold, man-made rock, ants scurrying, weeds thorny, clutching that paper to my breast, rocking and clutching and crying and rocking. Clear rivers of mucous streaming from my nose. Whirlpools of tears rushing like rapids over my eyes. What did Kendall Van Brunt know about personal tragedy anyway? What could he know about real suffering? What was he but a rich baby born into generations of wealth? What was he but a baby brought home in a limousine to a mansion by the beach, a baby who grew into privileged manhood? What was he but a big fat baby? He, who grew up to seek out other's tragedies so he could ignore his own. Isn't that what he did? Isn't that who he was?

And then, my clenched fists relaxed their hold, exhausted, resigned and brought the stiff paper with its sharp, cutting edges and its indelible ink up to my eyes to wipe away the tears. I can see myself rising up from the concrete and turning back towards the hill. I held onto the letter, the letter I despised just moments ago and I began my climb back home.

I heard from Kendall regularly after that. Once, sometimes twice a month, something from Kendall would arrive. He never called, so I never heard his voice. He never visited, so I never touched his face. But for a long time, up until years later when he disappeared into the skies in some small plane en route from one unknown place to another, he never stopped sending his messages. And they never stopped finding me. In time, I came to depend on them. I looked for them in my darkest moments and always, always, they would somehow appear. Gifts from his life. Pictures cut from foreign newspapers. Ethnic dolls made of yarn and silk. Once even a tape of children singing to African drumming. Each one was left without description or explanation to find its way to me no matter where I was. They were as varied as the pleas from a frightened heart, except for their one recurring closing prayer, "Love, Kendall." Perhaps because Kendall came back into my life just at the time the baby left it, or perhaps because somewhere in the deepest places of my heart I believe their two souls are entwined, I think of one of them whenever I think of the other and I imagine them, physically, together.

There is a small box I keep tucked away where I've stored my treasures, my favorite pictures of the baby, his teething ring, his first cuddly toy. And nestled on top of them are all of Kendall's gifts sent over the years, like so many firm cushions placed beneath my unsteady feet. Even in my old age I look through the box from time to time. And I think of them both together somehow, Kendall Van Brunt and my baby whose name was Samuel.

Chapter 9

Grace:
Fertility Rites

I was pregnant again too soon. Everyone I knew said so. My parents told me to wait a year, let my body heal and make sure I really wanted to try again. It was sensible advice. Gina said maybe I shouldn't try at all. "One child isn't enough? Why tempt fate?" Gina didn't want children. What could she possibly know about it? "I'm a professional mother. This is what I do," was what I believe I said to her, although I hope I'm remembering that wrong. It is possible, though. I was that crazy.

The first time back at my doctor's office, his nurse gave me a mournful look and even more advice. "You know, we've had three women in this practice who've lost babies and each one has had troubles – thyroid problems, depression, ectopics. Be careful, sweetheart."

Then, of course, my obstetrician went even further, urging me to wait a year and seek counseling. "Losing a baby is the most traumatic event a woman can go through. Even six months after, you're not completely back to normal, physically or mentally."

It's amazing how much good advice one person can ignore. But even now, I won't say they were right. Back then I was adamant about who I was, namely, a mother of small children. Lizzy was four years old, school age, and it was time for another baby. There was nothing wrong with me. As long as I was doing my job I was fine and my job right then was to be pregnant. Jack didn't argue. All he wanted was to be holding a little one in his arms. Only that would heal him.

So we set out on our Campaign to Conceive in a way we never had before. Every morning we took my body temperature and plotted it on a chart. At four o'clock in the afternoon I checked my mucous. I bought a special wedged pillow to put under my bottom so the sperm could swim more easily. Jack would hold me up by my ankles. He switched from briefs to boxers, trying to keep them not-too-warm and not-too-cool. We brought every scrap of medical know-how to bear on this otherwise natural process and it worked. In three months, I was pregnant. Jack was relieved. I was ecstatic. Lizzy was confused.

"So now we're going to have another baby?" she asked.

"Yes, sweetie, we are."

"But this will be a different baby than the last one, right?"

"Right. This will be a different baby."

I don't know how Lizzy remembers Sam's death. I never really asked her, but I can tell you what I remember. It was just another Thursday morning. Nothing special had happened the night before. I was asleep when I heard Jack say, "Shit! I'm late." We hadn't bothered to set the alarm since the night we brought Sam home. He always woke us up. Just a few days before, Jack had started to think maybe it was time to move him into his own room and out of ours, but we hadn't done it yet. It was so much easier having him right there. But, that morning, Sam didn't wake us up. In fact, he didn't wake up at all. It was Lizzy who woke us, coming into our room, wanting breakfast.

I was still half-asleep when I began to sense something was wrong. Everything was just too quiet. No rustling or sucking noises coming from the crib. I wasn't actually alarmed yet, just drowsily curious. Lizzy was quiet as she stood looking down at Sam. It was as if I was still dreaming and couldn't believe what I already knew to be true. That's when I went over to him, but I was moving slowly. Then, somehow, I did know. What started as a vague fear in the back of my mind became a certainty in a split second. I knew immediately and without even seeing him. Sam was dead. It was hopeless. And there was nothing any of us could do.

Lizzy and I just stood there looking at him for a minute. I can remember having one hand on Lizzy's shoulder and the other on the plastic strip covering the railing. It's funny how little things stay with you. I remember thinking how warm Lizzy felt and how cold the crib was. But I didn't pick Sam up. His face was too white. His lips, which he moved all the time, even in his sleep, were still.

Suddenly, for some reason, I jolted back to life. Once I did, everything became a blur. In the same breath, I got Lizzy out of the room and cried out for Jack. I think he was just about to get into the shower, because I had to call his name over and over. Each time I sounded more and more hysterical, even though in some part of me I was trying to control myself for Lizzy's sake. Standing there, I still couldn't pick Sam up. I don't know why. Something about touching him, feeling him like that ... I couldn't do it. Jack rushed out of the bathroom, holding a towel around his waist and what he saw was me standing back, away from the crib, paralyzed.

Jack picked him up. I can see him standing there. I can see the crib. Then I can see Jack holding the baby against his chest. It's not like it's in slow motion. It's more like time is suspended. There is no time. Jack knew Sam was dead. He must have. But he kept saying his name over and over as if he could will him back to life. He spoke quietly at first, then a little louder, a little more insistently. Until he stopped. Then he just stood there, holding the dead baby. I couldn't even bear to look at him anymore.

Eventually the ambulance came. I don't even know how they got there. I must have called them. Jack must have told me to call, but I can't remember his voice. All I can remember is his silence, the hollow look in his eyes and the way he swayed back and forth. And then I remember feeling this overwhelming sense of failure. For a long time that was the word I thought of when I forced myself to remember him and the look on his face. But not Jack's failure. It was my own and although Jack never admitted it, I've often thought that my feeling of failure was somehow communicated between us without words, with just the despair in our eyes. It then seeped into everything about us without our even knowing it, leading us to that empty place that was to follow years later.

And what about Lizzy? Lizzy saw him dead. Can you imagine? A four-year-old looking at the body of her dead brother. It's too horrible to think of. But that's what she saw that Thursday morning and it used to torture me. Lizzy wasn't supposed to know about death yet. At her age, life should have been one long succession of happy, fun-filled days. But she understood Sam was dead. She knew what she saw.

Somehow, I had the presence of mind to call a friend and have her take Lizzy for the day. Later on, when Jack and I went to pick her up, we knew we had to tell her, but we didn't know how to say it. We brought her into the living room and sat her down. Lizzy was the first one to talk.

"Is Sam gone forever?" she asked. When we told her he was, she said, "Don't worry, Mommy. We'll get another baby."

And we did. But it was all different, for better or worse, just as I'd said it would be. All of us had changed, including Lizzy. She got quiet. She became self-reliant and independent in a way that was unnatural for a little girl her age. I was already worrying how Sam's death would scar her. Would she grow up afraid to become a mother herself? But that's not what happened. Somehow Lizzy became everyone's mother. She must have decided it was her job to protect all of us, her parents and the new baby. Obviously Jack and I weren't up to it. She'd follow me around, trying to guess what I wanted her to do.

"I'm cleaning up my toys, Mommy."

"Should I brush my teeth now?"

People began to comment on how mature she was for her age. Lizzy had become ghost-like, wandering through the house, quietly staying out of the way. She developed this weird smile, the kind you put on for a photograph even if you're furious inside. If she laughed, which she sometimes did, she stopped herself, as if remembering there was really nothing to laugh about.

A whole lifetime seemed to go by before I was able to talk to her about it. I felt that if I did, I would be putting terrible thoughts into her head, reminding her of some horrible pain. I was afraid that if I talked about it too much, we'd never get beyond what happened that morning. Eventually, I realized Lizzy had found a way to deal with the fact that first there had been a Sam and then there wasn't. Whatever that way was, it seemed, on the outside, to work for her. But I believe that when Sam died, so did Lizzy's innocence. Something steely grew in its place, toughening up her heart like a pounded down baseball glove and it became who she was. For Lizzy, life began with death. Maybe it helped her survive the struggles yet to come. I don't know. Maybe, in that way her toughened heart became a gift. For me, though, it became one more loss to grieve. The little-girl-Lizzy I had known was gone forever. I tried to act as if everything was fine, but we all knew it wasn't fine. How could it be?

Jack gave himself a couple of weeks to grieve. He was determined to do it right, so he could get it over with and make the pain go away. Good student that he was, he had learned that there were several stages of grief you have to go through and he was determined to go through each one correctly, but as quickly as possible. In the dark of our bedroom, he let himself cry in my arms. He broke down when he saw his mother walk into the house before the funeral. The Rabbi asked him to say a prayer over the grave, which he did, but with a voice choked with sobs. He was a wreck, just like me, but then somehow he found the strength to go on. I guess I did, too. But I did it by burying my heart along with the baby. I denied the hurt and kept showing everyone how okay I was. Maybe I thought that was what it meant to be strong. I don't know what Jack thought, but pretty soon he announced that he was ready to go back to work. And for him, it seemed, that was the end of it. Sam was gone. There was still work to be done, new babies to be made. That was my job.

The second I realized I was pregnant, I swore to myself that nothing would be the same until I was holding my newborn child in my arms. Every stage of development was planned and prepared for, studied and organized. It was like the Normandy Invasion, only without the wall maps and those tiny red flags. No more would I fall prey to nature's caprices. Although with Sam the pregnancy and delivery were normal, I believed something must have gone wrong during his development. Why else would a seemingly healthy three-month-old die in his sleep? No, I would never again blindly hop-skip-and-jump through those months of pregnancy, assuming everything was fine and dandy. That worked well enough once, five years before, when I was younger and more innocent, when I still believed in the invulnerability of youth. But, as my mother said to me just after Sam's funeral, "So, now you know something about life, sweetheart." Yes, now I knew and I wasn't going to roll over and be battered by the waves like some bottle dropped into the ocean. But the energy this all took exhausts me to think about, even now.

The first thing I did was change my obstetrician. It's not that I blamed him. But my first doctor was a kindly, older man who believed in the natural processes of life. People were born when it was time, lived the best they could and died when they were ready. And whenever he looked at me, his sincere, understanding eyes drove me nuts. That was not the kind of doctor I thought I needed. I needed someone young and forceful, on the cutting edge and up-to-date, a doctor with the latest technology and tests at his disposal. I needed an expert from a teaching hospital who published articles in scientific journals; someone who would make sure that this never happened again. So I found Dr. Berlin and talked my way into his otherwise full practice by also agreeing to join his clinical trials. He had gone to Johns Hopkins and then on to Harvard Medical School. His residency was at Columbia Presbyterian and by the time I went looking for him he was running the High Risk Pregnancy Unit in Boston's Women's Hospital. In his hands I felt safe.

Next, I went to the library. Not the public library at the bottom of the street, but the Harvard Medical School Library, which I talked my way into by pretending I was Dr. Berlin's Research Assistant. If I had found the same zeal for researching my college papers as I did for reading those obstetrical journals, I probably could have been a doctor myself. I read everything I could find on fetal development. I plotted out the week-by-week progression, starting with cell division and ending with lung maturation. I read all about diseases during pregnancy – diabetes, hypertension, placenta praevia, fetal alcohol syndrome, I can't even remember what else. Much of what I read I didn't understand, but it didn't seem to matter. Holding those books in my hands gave me comfort.

Then I began to apply it all to myself and this is when my friends really began to worry about me. I started refusing to take the kids to MacDonald's after our trips to the Children's Museum. I canceled luncheon dates in order to do breathing exercises. I'd show up at my doctor's office unannounced, Lizzy in tow and ask to have my blood pressure checked. The nurse, my new "best friend," was usually very kind, very patient. But after the hundredth time, she did take me aside and said, "You know, you're going to have the healthiest newborn on the planet. But his mother's going to be a crazy."

"So be it," I answered and laughed.

Laughing is something else I did a lot of. You can't argue with that. I believed the baby could hear my laughter in the womb and experience my joy, and that, in any case, the movement of my belly was good exercise. It became a ritual. Every night after Lizzy was asleep, I'd put my feet up, pop a video in and spend the evening laughing. The Marx Brothers were always good, no matter what. Charlie Chaplin was too cerebral, as was later Woody Allen. But Mel Brooks was the best. I must have watched *The Producers* a thousand times. Whenever Gene Wilder was backed into that corner, madly caressing his baby blanket, tears would roll down my cheeks. I started quoting the movie at odd times. Washing the dishes, I'd stop, hands full of soapsuds and cry, "I'm hysterical. I'm hysterical. I'm wet and I'm hysterical." Then I'd start to laugh all over again. I now think that such enforced hilarity did keep me balanced in a manic sort of way. It was when I stopped laughing I knew I was in trouble. But that's another story.

In the end, the pregnancy went well. Once a week, Lizzy would help me measure my belly. I would lift my shirt and she would take a picture of me with our Polaroid. Dr. Berlin was satisfied with my weight gain and my blood sugar levels. Nothing was going wrong.

Two weeks before my due date, I packed my bag – several pairs of underwear, two nightgowns, a photo of Lizzy and Jack, a picture of a restful beach scene to focus on during labor. This labor went very quickly. Three deliveries in less than five years does that to you. It was short, but it was brutal. Each contraction was worse than the one before without any time to rest. The baby was coming so quickly I barely made it to the hospital in time. When I did get there, I was nearly ready to push, or so I remember. The memory of that pain is so distant now it's hard to recall, but I'm not sure such a memory is helpful, anyway.

John was born in six hours start to finish, as if he was racing to get out into the world, to get out of me. I took it as a good sign, a sign of strength and determination, two characteristics I always associate with him. He was beautiful and healthy, a long body with a head full of spiky black hair. He latched onto my breast from the first with a workman-like sense of purpose. I always believed that from the day he was born he was able to find his way towards what he needed.

The morning we were due to go home, I was up early. I packed and dressed even before the nurse brought me the baby to feed. When she came I was already out of bed and sitting by the window, a pillow under my arm for support.

"I have a hungry little boy for you," said the nurse, holding him while I fumbled with the hook on my nursing bra. When I was ready, she handed him to me and I could see his tiny face all red from famished crying. I quickly put him to my breast and took a few deep, relaxation breaths to help the milk flow. I can still hear the sound of his eager slurping and his little satisfied groans. He nursed busily for about two minutes, then he slowed down. When he came off my breast, I looked at his face and smiled. At the time, I didn't understand what happened next. What I saw was my new baby looking deeply, knowingly, into my eyes and I felt a shudder, almost like electricity, pass through me. I started to cry and when the nurse came back to check on us, she found John in my arms, happily feeding and me, crying quietly, but uncontrollably.

"Oh, I know how happy you must be," she said, but I knew those tears weren't tears of happiness. Later that night, when we were both safely home, I decided it must have been hormonal. Every new mother experiences sudden, unexplainable mood swings. I blindly decided to forget about it. I now understand, though, that hormones had little to do with it. In his first truly deep look into his mother's eyes, John, like an old soul, was trying to tell me that it was going to be very, very difficult, but that ultimately it was going to be all right. Those weren't tears of happiness. I was terrified.

Chapter 10

Grace:
A Bedtime Story

"Once upon a dime," Gina joked, "there were two little girls. Not quite twins, but so close in age that people could hardly tell them apart." She pulled her chair up close to the head of John's bed so he could hear her over the groaning of the air pump. Gina had ear infections when she was little, which meant she talked too loudly, constantly asking "What?" and mispronouncing words. It drove me crazy when we were young, but now when she said "Once upon a dime," it made me laugh. It was actually John she was trying to make laugh. But he didn't have much to laugh about. His first three years were plagued by endless bouts of croup and asthma. And now he was in the hospital again. He leaned his head against my shoulder, ignoring the plastic wall of the oxygen tent that separated his touch from mine.

Gina held John's hand loosely, tenderly, throwing me a mischievous glance. "It was Halloween night," she continued, "and the two little girls had been looking forward to it for weeks. But they had been arguing a lot about their costumes. Who would they be? Each time one of them had an idea, the other would cry, 'I want to be that; I said it first!' And then there would be tears and shouts until their mother had to come and separate them."

"Grandma, right?" John asked. I raised a finger to my lips.

"Ssh. Remember?" I think for him the hardest part of those terrible hospital stays was trying not to talk. He knew the routine. He had been in and out of that pediatric ward so often he knew all the nurses by name. But he couldn't stop himself talking. I guess he had a lot to say.

"Grandma?" Gina said. "Did I say this story was about your mother and me? Well, anyway, this arguing went on for days and days until their mother said, 'That's enough. I will make two costumes and that is what you will wear . . . or no trick-or-treating.'"

"What a mean mom," I said dramatically.

"I think she had a lot of headaches," Gina joked.

Being the older sister, it was hard for me to keep my mouth shut. I tried to listen without too many interruptions. Gina had been so helpful those last few weeks when John was in crisis, in and out of the hospital, unable to breathe, terrible rasping sounds coming from his tiny chest.

"Go ahead," I said. I was just as curious as John to see what happened next.

"The two little girls kept their arguments to themselves up until the day of Halloween. At school, everyone was talking about their costumes. Joey was going to be Batman-No-Mask. Nathalie would be Cinderella with a special tiara bought for her at Disneyland. But when their friends asked the two little girls what they were going to be, they each said the same thing – 'It's a secret.'"

I saw John's eyes widen. Something had made him smile. I don't know what.

"Finally, school was over and it was time to see what their mother had made. There she sat on the living room couch with two bags next to her. 'Now girls,' she said. 'You know I

am a very busy mother and I can only do so much. One costume was made by me, the other was bought in a store. You can
choose the one you want.'"

"Was she crazy?" I said. I couldn't help myself. Now, as a
mother I know you don't ask kids something like that. You tell
them. I felt smug then thinking this, because I was a mother of
two little kids and Gina was not. Gina may have been a fancy
lawyer in designer clothes making a fortune every year and I
may have only been a housewife with a sick child, but at least I
could still outsmart a couple of kids. I didn't say this to Gina, of
course. I just let her continue.

"The two girls were twitching with excitement. The
mother opened the bags. One was a pink nylon dress with a
pink scratchy frill at the bottom and a plastic mask with holes at
the eyes and mouth. It was the Princess costume from Wool-
worth's down the street. In the other bag were cut-off jeans with
flannel patches of different colors sewn on, a fleecy lumberjack
shirt – just the right size – with suspenders attached and a stick
with a bandana-bag tied to one end. It was a homemade Hobo
costume. And what do you think happened? Both girls wanted
to be the Princess and there was so much crying and screaming
and pulling and pushing that the mother finally said, 'Enough!
You're the Princess,' and she pointed to the older girl. 'And
you, you're the Hobo. And if you don't like it you can both go
up to bed right now.' So the little girls got into their costumes,
grabbed their Halloween bags from the kitchen table and silently
left the house."

I looked at John to make sure he was still awake. His
breathing, although still shallow, had quieted down. He had a
funny smile on his face as if to say, "How can girls be so stupid?"
Gina, on the other hand, seemed far away, intent on her story,
lost in that world she had conjured up. Her eyes had grown
suddenly dark, as if she herself could feel the frustration and anger of the little Hobo. John nudged her with his foot. Gina
shuddered.

"Sorry. Where was I? Oh yea. So . . . the Princess and the Hobo started down the street, ringing one doorbell after another. It was dark already, but the Hobo refused to hold the Princess' hand. She was so angry she didn't even want to walk next to her. The Princess didn't want to take care of her anyway, especially when they ran into a group of friends from school."

Gina gave John's small hand a squeeze and bent closer to his oxygen tent. She pretended to whisper. "You know how big sisters can be." She straightened back up in her chair and with a wink, continued.

"For a while, they were all trick-or-treating together and their bags were getting heavier and heavier. The Hobo's bag was so heavy that she started to lag behind with a different group of smaller girls. After a while, she didn't even know where the Princess was (not that she cared). But then came the time when trick-or-treating was over and the Hobo was standing right near her house all alone. Where was the Princess? What was she going to do?"

Gina got that faraway look again. I was starting to get fidgety.

"The Hobo couldn't go home to mother without her sister and she couldn't go walking along the streets by herself at night. So she decided to wait. There the Hobo stood for a very long time, leaning against the street lamp, the light shining down on her smudged face."

"Oh, really," I moaned. Now I was getting angry. Didn't I have enough problems without Gina making me out to be some kind of ogre to my own son? As if she was so helpless. There sat Gina with this magical life where everything is perfect – a perfect marriage to an adoring husband, a fabulous job, people asking her opinion on important topics. Lost? Helpless? Not her. I was the helpless one with the husband so exhausted and stressed he could barely see me. I could hardly remember the sound of my own voice. But even worse was my feeling of incompetence. Not only couldn't I keep my children healthy, I couldn't even keep them all alive.

I didn't like this story anymore. I started to move away as a signal that we should be quiet and let John rest.

"No, Mommy. Not yet. The story isn't over." Gina looked at me. I nodded as if to say, "Okay. Go ahead." But I wondered if she knew what I was feeling.

"It seemed to the Hobo that she was standing there a long time. But then, from around the corner, she heard crying. At first it was faint, but then it got louder and louder. Soon she realized it was the crying of the Princess. The Hobo ran down the street and there she was. Her plastic mask was pushed back on top of her head. Her nylon dress was covered with dirt and gloppy yellow stains. The pink scratchy frill had come loose from her hem.

'What happened to you?' the Hobo asked, and she touched the Princess' arm.

'Older boys ... down the street...' she said between sobs. 'Eggs ... they threw them at us ... so I ran and ran and then I was lost.'

The Hobo looked at the Princess and gave her a kiss. No, two kisses," Gina looked at John. "One real and one chocolate. That made the Princess smile and she said, 'Anyway, it's no fun being a Princess. Let's just be ourselves.'

And so they were. Together they walked home, hand in hand, each eating their favorite candy. When they arrived at their house, their mother was waiting for them in the doorway. And she wasn't even angry."

Gina smiled; I nodded.

"The End."

Chapter 11

John:
Playing Dice

The bar across the street from Fenway Park was noisy and crowded, but Phil acted like he owned the place. I followed him through the crowd and watched him wave and shout something funny to the bartender. I looked around. Every table was full. Every space occupied. Maybe I'd get a last minute reprieve from all this, after all. But, no. Somehow Phil found a round table against the back wall, big enough for the five of us.

"This is lucky," I said, trying not to sound like I felt, like a man, old, tired and out of my depth.

"Luck? Is there such a thing?" quipped Phil as he pulled out a chair and sat down.

I remember looking at the group of students, studying them. Two men, two women. There were Phil and Chloe, of course. But there was also a woman I didn't recognize, with beautiful eyes (I had to admit) but fidgety, nervous hands. And there was Michio. I hadn't even noticed him before. Michio – the brilliant, new Japanese graduate student whose scientific English was flawless, but who's social English was still a hopeless hybrid of language lab dialogues and *Simpsons* episodes. The first time I heard him shout "Eat My Shorts" across the physics lab, I had to leave the room to compose myself.

"Two plus two," I calculated. "These guys are on a date!" That little brain wave gave me a sense of relief out of all proportion. Maybe the fidgety girl was going out with Michio and better yet, maybe Chloe was dating Phil. That would make sense. They had similar interests. They were about the same age. What an old idiot I was, I thought and then grabbed a chair like a man having made a narrow though, to be honest, slightly regretted escape. I sat next to Michio's date and reached out my hand.

"I'm sorry. I don't think we've met. Are you in my department?"

The girl looked uneasy and started to answer, but Michio interrupted. "Oh, I am sorry. This is my friend. Her name is Laura. She is in Mathematics."

"Nice to meet you, Laura." I shook her hand. "Some of my best friends are mathematicians. No, really. Do you work with Professor Hoffmann?" I made small talk to the poor silent girl, turning my back to the others. It didn't really matter to me what I was saying, as long as I didn't have to worry about Chloe anymore. But every now and again I could feel her trying to move into the conversation and every time she did that nervous knot in my stomach came back. I tried as hard as I could to avoid any real contact with her. Maybe I was rude. I don't know, but then again, I was petrified. It took a while before I realized I had been babbling, overwhelming Michio's date with any stray thought that popped into my head. In between clauses, I took a breath and looked at those beautiful eyes of hers that I had noticed before. They had glazed over. My mouth went dry. I stood up and said, "Okay. First round's on me. Who's having what?"

I made my way through the crowd to get the drinks. The room was full of laughter and loud cursing. The lighting was harsh and there were thirty years of signed Red Sox photographs on the walls. This was no "yuppie" bar. It was a cheap, old-fashioned dive that happily reminded me of my own student days twenty years before. For a moment, I felt safely cocooned in the crush of people around me, but then I felt a hand – Chloe's hand – on my arm.

"I thought you might need some help with those drinks," she said. I looked to my right and there she was, smiling at me. She pushed her long, black hair off her face. Her eyes were blue. Blue eyes, black hair. An unfortunately irresistible combination.

"Oh. Okay," I stammered. I took a deep breath and tried to convince myself I had nothing to worry about.

Chloe then started to talk about the game and knowledgeably, too. Pedro had had a great outing, I recall and she knew enough to notice. I said something like, "You sound like a fan."

"A fanatic is more like it," she explained. "My dad grew up with these guys. Even though he moved out West, he always stayed a Red Sox fan. I guess I'm the son he never had."

So much for that disproportionate sense of relief. This woman was getting more and more perfect every minute. The barroom noise became a buzz. My ears seemed to ring. My face felt hot and the skin on the back of my neck went clammy. It was like I was fucking sixteen all over again. I was almost afraid my voice would crack. I turned to pick up the beers, just to give myself something to do. Chloe reached for the wine glasses. I decided I better not say anything else and just walk back to the table. But instead, even without realizing it, I blurted out, "So, are you dating Phil? He's a great guy."

Chloe threw a look at me back over her shoulder.

"Phil and me?" she laughed. "You kidding? He's not my type."

I heard that and shook my head. I was doomed.

Sitting back down at the table, I discovered Phil and Michio already embroiled in a heated discussion. When I heard the topic, my heart sank even lower.

"But you see, for me as a Buddhist it is quite simple." Michio spoke calmly. "In my religion, it is all about energy, how it moves within us, how it affects one thing after another."

"So to you, God is energy," Phil said, taking the drinks and offering them around. "That certainly makes it a lot easier. No old man pulling strings…"

"…or rolling dice," Chloe added. "Isn't that what Einstein said?"

"I believe Einstein said God does *not* play dice," explained Michio.

"Yes, but Hawking said he might and I bet if anyone knows, it's him," Phil countered.

I wriggled and fidgeted. "Right, this is what graduate students talk like," I reminded myself. I hated this sort of pseudo-philosophical-scientific talk back when I was a student and I hated it even more now. I took hold of my beer, drank nearly half of it in one gulp and looked around the room, trying to distance myself from the discussion. Maybe I'd see some long lost friend in the crowd. Maybe there'd be an escape.

"But, Professor, you understand me?" Michio's voice was calling. "Professor Rosen? You know about *chi*, yes?"

"*Chi*? Me?" I said, trying to make a joke, stalling for time. "Well, I don't know. Not really…" I let my voice trail off, trying to make it clear that this was a topic I was not at all interested in pursuing. Anyone who knew me at all knew that this was one discussion I never wanted to have. Religion, God, spirituality – it all annoyed me. I didn't know why. It just all seemed so personal. So much so that I didn't want to talk about it even with myself. The whole religion thing always felt like a sham to me, more trouble than it was worth. And, for some reason, it also made me think about my mother and I never wanted to do that. But graduate students are persistent, earnest little creatures and Michio, in his innocent confusion, persevered. He looked at me and waited for as long as he could before speaking.

"But, Professor, you are Buddhist, right?" Now even Phil knew that the situation was getting awkward. He took a swig of his beer and looked at his feet. The quiet, nervous girl remained quiet and nervous. Even Chloe could do nothing to help the situation. Buddhist? I thought to myself. On no. Not again.

Actually, it was my own fault. Back when my mother was dying, I came up with this joke. People were always trying to be nice, to ask how I was, if I was going to take time off to be with her. I didn't know what to say. How could I explain that I wasn't going down to New York because I didn't think she needed me? My mother was surrounded by people, strangers to me, who were practically sitting vigil with her. Florence said they were sharing their good energy, seeing her off to the next world. So, I made a joke. I said she was allowing her soul to escape to Nirvana and she didn't need a skeptic like me getting in the way. It was stupid. It didn't even make sense. But, I guess I said it a few times too often because people started to believe that my old Jewish mother from Brooklyn was actually a Buddhist. Then, when that word filtered down to my students, they assumed I was, too. The whole thing was absurd, but for some ridiculous reason, the joke took on a life of its own, living on even after my mother was dead. Marty said that's what I got for joking about religion. I guess he was right.

"No, Michio," I finally answered. "I am not a Buddhist." I tried to keep my voice calm. "I'm a sort of Jewish-nothing. It was just an old joke. A bad joke. Sorry."

Michio nodded his head in thought and I relaxed a bit believing this unbearable part of the evening was now over. But then, suddenly, surprisingly, quiet Laura spoke up. Her voice was high and shockingly childlike.

"Oh. I know who you are now. You're that guy." Chloe shot an angry look at the girl and tried to change the subject. Phil and Michio squirmed in their chairs. But if Laura saw any of this, she ignored it. Her naiveté actually made me smile. Who knows what the hell she was talking about? But I couldn't hold her lack of social antennae against her. I knew she couldn't help herself. She was a mathematician, after all.

"Yes," I laughed. "I guess I'm that guy."

"Cool," she said, nodding. And then, finally, that was it. The end of the conversation and now, I hoped, the end of the evening.

I drank the last bit of foam from my glass. "Yes. Well, I can see that you all have many important questions to hash out. But I gave up on those issues a long time ago, so I think I will say goodnight. But I must warn you," I continued (and, if I do say so myself, I think this was an especially good parting line), "I don't think God likes physicists very much – especially cosmologists like us. We're always poking our noses into his business. But mathematicians, on the other hand," I finished up, looking straight into Laura's nervous eyes, "are undoubtedly his favorite children. See you next week." Not bad, eh? Phil and Michio called out "See ya' " and "Thanks." I could hear their voices continuing the discussion as I walked back through the crowded room and out the door. I was feeling pretty pleased with myself. A narrow, though remarkably graceful escape. The quiet and warmth of the summer night air was soothing. I would have drunk it deep down inside me if I could have. I think I looked around for a taxi at first, but then decided a good, long walk was what I needed. I started off, but soon, amidst the street noise, I heard Chloe's voice calling after me.

"Professor? John. Wait a minute."

I turned around to see her running up to me, her bag bouncing over her shoulder, her rubber flip-flops in her hand. When she reached me, she was breathing heavily. I gave her a second to catch her breath and caught myself looking down at her bare feet, smiling.

"I don't know if I'd walk barefoot around here," I said. "Who knows what you could catch."

Chloe slipped her flip-flops back on her feet, steadying herself by placing a hand on my arm.

"I just wanted to say I'm sorry about that whole thing back there. I hope you're not angry. People can be so insensitive sometimes."

"No, don't worry," I reassured her. "It's my problem, not theirs. Just because I have this thing about God doesn't mean other people have to. And anyway, I'm a grown-up. I know how grad students can be." Sure, I may have said I was a grown-up, but I certainly didn't feel like one. I had no idea what to do next. Should I be the first to walk away? I didn't want to be rude, but I didn't want to encourage her either. In any case, I knew I had to act fast. "Thank you, Chloe," I said. "But really, it's fine. Go on back to your friends. I'm just going to walk home."

"Oh, but I'd rather not go back. It's so crowded and noisy. Couldn't I just walk a bit with you?"

Shit. Here was trouble. Chloe's boldness, her confidence shocked me, but I must admit those were the qualities which attracted me the most, as well. This was the moment when I could have said "no", a real, unequivocal, definite "no" to her, to the entire dangerous scenario, to everything. But I didn't. I just started to walk and I let her follow me.

It was a long way from Fenway Park through the Back Bay, over the bridge and into Cambridge. But the route took us through some of the most beautiful parts of town. It was getting late, but the moon was bright and the air still warm. The old brick buildings lining the wide avenues took on a turn-of-the-century sort of look. In my already unsettled state, it was easy to forget myself. The conversation with Chloe was light and comfortable, when there was conversation. But sometimes we walked in silence, as if listening to a distant dialogue galaxies away. I felt surprisingly calm, even relaxed. Or maybe I was just finally resigned. Either way, there was a sensation – call it a release – that had been missing from inside me for too long, as if whatever battle had been going on inside me was now finally surrendered. Now that I felt that "release" again, I wasn't going to let it go so easily.

I had no idea what time it was when we finally crossed the river and arrived on campus. The streets were deserted. Most of the buildings were dark, except for the eternal lights streaming out of the scattered laboratories.

"You must live somewhere near here, I suppose," I said, turning towards Chloe. I can still see myself standing there close to her. Closer, surely, than I should have been. I can remember smelling the faint floral scent of her shampoo and my heart began to race.

"Where do *you* live?" she asked.

I waited a minute before answering. But I wasn't thinking, or analyzing, or worrying, or calculating. I was just waiting.

That's when Chloe took my hand. I couldn't stop her. Again, there was that damned boldness of hers. She then lifted her foot an inch off the ground and rubbed it against the inside of my leg. I swear, it's true. And that was it. I was gone. The overanalytical brain, the whirlpool of paranoid anxiety, all of it – out the window. The only thing that mattered to me any more was the gap between her T-shirt and her jeans, that exposed bit of skin at the small of her back and all that it led to. My fingers went searching. Her bare skin radiated heat into the palm of my hand. I left it there and slowly led her home, allowing her to lean closer and closer against me with each step.

I slipped my key into the keyhole and opened the door. As I walked up the stairs, I felt Chloe pressing against me from behind, her head on my back, her hands rising up to my shoulders, her energy flowing into me. Even at that moment, I couldn't help but be aware of all the energy that had been expended getting me and Chloe to that point in time and space. Energy, with its fields of color and strength, was constantly swirl-

106

ing around the universe, leaving one place, entering another. It was just like Michio had said. Maybe the Buddhists were right after all. Everything is energy and although we may be able to calculate it, I already knew too well we can never escape it.

Chapter 12

John:
The Arrow of Time

The Monday morning after that weekend's fateful Red Sox game, I got to work early. Chloe had stayed well past lunch the day before and once she left, I spent the rest of the day wandering around the apartment. I tried to clean, but everything distracted me. A stray back copy of *Theoretical and Mathematical Physics* led me to a bookshelf with a coffee cup on it, which bounced me back towards the kitchen and an open empty box of Rice Krispies. Back and forth, up and down, for hours in a random pattern of movement I spent the day and most of the night. By the time 7:00 Monday morning came, I couldn't wait to get to the office. I was desperate to throw myself into my work and retreat into an endless equation of trustworthy numbers, letters, marks and symbols. And so there I sat, staring at my computer, rubbing my eyes, punching keys and manipulating the tiny universe I saw before me – a universe I myself had created – but which made no more sense to me on that day than the enormous, supposedly real universe I was theoretically a part of.

I remember having a splitting headache. I could almost feel the electrons beaming out of the computer and piercing through the membranes of my eyes. From the time I was a kid, I had imagined there was something like a movie screen inside my head. It shimmered when I closed my eyes, with little specks of silver which somehow amplified the images it displayed. The young me imagined it stood firm somewhere between the back of my eyes and the front of my brain. I once even drew a diagram of it, that's how seriously I used to take these things. It looked something like this:

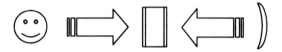

The image would go through my eye on the right, hit the magic screen in the middle and reflect back onto my brain there on the left which would, in turn, interpret it all for me. And that's how it still seemed to work. Beams of light jetted from the computer's brain to mine, creating on their way shades of light and dark like an interference pattern on my internal screen. But that day, that's all those images meant to me, just lines and dots, as I sat there staring and tapping my foot. Maybe if I stared hard and long enough, I thought, something would break through, something would jump out and make sense enough that I could show Yuri. Then Yuri would relax, I wouldn't have to go to London and I could go back to depressively obsessing about my personal life. But the more I stared, the less I saw. It was all meaningless patterns of light.

Eventually, I heard a voice. "Any idea how long I've been standing here watching you do nothing?" I looked up to see Marty standing in the doorway. "What time did you get home Saturday night?"

"Time? What's time, anyway?" I sneered at him.

"Very funny." Marty walked into the office and looked over my shoulder at the computer screen. He was clearly impatient. "That's pretty, but I can't help but wonder ... what happened after we left you Saturday?"

I knew there was no escape. I would have to talk about Saturday night. Marty would somehow get it out of me. When Marty wanted to know something he was like a bull terrier, tugging at your trousers until he got what he wanted. This quality of infuriating persistence made him a great physicist and an annoying, but even greater friend. So once again, I collapsed into my fate, shutting down the computer and standing up to face him. I was doing jack shit there anyway.

We left the building in silence. I wanted to be silent, but Marty was clearly biding his time. For once, though, the world was on my side. Silence was everywhere. The campus was nearly empty. There were fewer students in the buildings than during the school year and the ones who were there were different, more purposeful and less boisterous. The streets were emptier, too. I used the silence like an invisibility cloak. I hid inside it, shielding myself from unwanted questions. A part of me believed that if I didn't talk, I didn't actually exist. It was an old trick I used every now and then, but it was annoying as hell when I did it. I knew I could never get away with the silence trick in front of Lizzy, for example. If I tried, she'd just punch me in the shoulder and yell, "Cut it out." And then I *would* cut it out because I remembered all too clearly where that old trick came from – my mother.

My mother was the master of the silence trick. Back during all those months of her depression, she just sat there in her hospital room, refusing to talk. To me, it looked like she was using her silence to erase herself from the world. It was if she was saying, "Okay. I may not have actually killed myself, but as far as you're concerned, I might as well be dead." She was unreachable. Her eyes would be open, but there was nothing there behind them. I remember I went to visit her in the hospital, once.

They didn't want me to go, but I insisted. I walked into her room, and saw her sitting in a chair, dressed in a sort of tracksuit thing that she never would have worn otherwise. At first I thought maybe it wasn't her sitting there after all. And, in a way, I was right. It wasn't her. It was more like some waxwork out of Madame Tussaud's – it really wasn't anyone. Actually, it was horrifying. At first I wanted to give her a hug, but seeing her like that, sitting there with those dead eyes of hers, I just couldn't. I couldn't bear to touch her. I'm pretty sure I left her after just a few minutes, having said little more than, "Hi, Mom. It's me – John." I know she said nothing at all in return. She didn't even look at me. So I left and I didn't see her again until she finally, months later, came home.

Those months of my mother's silence were the most painful of my life. I felt like a guinea pig in some cruel alien's science experiment. "These earthlings are ruled by something called *emotion*. Let's see what they are," the alien would say and then, one after another, I would feel horrible, painful things. Fear, anger, betrayal, anger again, love, despair, loneliness and of course anger. It all came back to anger and it was that anger, I guess, which never really left me. So, sure, I would pull the silence trick sometimes when I thought I could get away with it. But I never kept it up for long. I'd always back off once it started to upset somebody else. I guess I'm just too nice a guy.

This time the silence was shattered anyway once Marty and I reached the river. Suddenly, the whole world seemed to come alive again. The river itself was a highway of sculls with cox shouting orders. On the paths, teenagers whizzed by on scooters and bicycles, runners dodging between us. Sounds bombarded us from every angle. There was no longer any escape. Marty and I moved to join the crowd, waiting for the right moment to step onto the path, like cars merging onto a highway.

"So, what happened after the game?" I knew this was what Marty had so desperately wanted to ask all day Sunday. It was, of course, the question I most wanted to avoid.

"I had a drink with them and then I walked home."

"And ?"

"And ... did you see the moon Saturday night? It was glowing." A ridiculous, desperate attempt to change the subject.

"No, I didn't see the glowing moon." Marty now sounded aggravated, which was as close to anger as I had ever seen him. I didn't want to talk, but I didn't want to make Marty angry, either. I suppose I gave him a look which said without words, "Go ahead. You can ask," because he started in again.

"So..." Marty spoke, enunciating each word as if he was recording a language lab tape. "Did you walk home alone?"

"No, I didn't walk home alone," I answered, mimicking him. "I walked home with Chloe."

"Oh, Chloe. So now you know her name."

"Yes, now I know her name."

"And?"

"And I guess I know other things, too."

"Jesus, I knew it." Marty had a rare, inscrutable look on his face. I could almost always tell what he was thinking just by looking at him. But this time, for once, I couldn't tell if he was happy or mad or worried or what.

"John, I don't know what to think."

"Me, neither."

"Well, wait a minute." After a few steps I realized Marty had stopped walking and then, with a quick hop, started again. "How bad is this, really? I mean, she isn't in one of your classes now, is she?"

"No, but she was last term and could conceivably be again."

"You're not her advisor, are you?"

"God, no. But look, you can't make this any better than it is."

"But people *do* do it..." Marty said in a feeble little voice.

"Yes, I know," I tried to explain it to both of us. "But not me. Not up 'til now. Hell, she's a graduate student in my department. I'm a full professor. At best, it's unethical. At worst, harassment…"

Marty shook his head. "Well, are you going to see her again?"

I remember not really knowing the answer to that question until the words were actually out of my mouth. I said something like, "I guess I have to. I mean, how can I not? Wouldn't it be worse just to sleep with her once and then ignore her? And anyway, it's not I like wanted this to happen. I just couldn't…"

"Resist?"

"Yes, resist, okay? Look – she's amazing, she's beautiful, she's smart. And to tell you the truth, she's the one who came on to me."

"Okay, okay," Marty said, shaking his head. "You don't have to rub it in. We all know you're irresistible."

By this time, we had walked to our usual turning point, but it was obvious Marty wasn't ready to go back. There was an empty bench just beyond the bridge and he rushed to claim it before someone else did. I was happy just to follow. I could sit for a while and watch the boats stream by, if that's what Marty wanted. I felt wasted and tired, as if all the energy had been sucked out of me.

"Well, what do you think? Do you really like her? I mean, *really* like her?"

"Yes, I suppose I like her." I was reluctant to say it, but I had to. "But it's not what you think."

"What do you mean, it's not what I think? You slept together. You like her; she must like you."

"Yea, but I'm pretty sure she's not going to fall in love with me. I can tell. She seems too … chipper." Marty was about to say something obnoxious about that, I could tell. So before he had the chance, I continued, "And anyway, I'm not going to fall in love with her, either. It's ridiculous. The whole thing's absurd. But, hey. If it makes you feel any better, I still feel like shit, despite Saturday night. So much for that solution to my problems." And that, more than anything else I might have said, was the closest to the truth.

I could see how intently Marty was listening to me. I watched him shake his head again and then, as if on cue, we both looked down at our feet. Actually, we both looked at Marty's sneakers. Those sneakers were ten years old and the rubber at the tip had been glued back together three times at least. I called them Marty's his 'security sneakers'. If only I had had a pair for myself, then maybe I would have known where I stood. We sat like that, quietly, for a while, long enough for me to begin to hope the conversation was over. But then Marty breathed out loud and mumbled, "Now I'm really worried."

To be honest, I was worried, too. It was this worry which had been driving me crazy since Sunday morning. But understanding what I was worrying about was another story. Believe it or not, the situation with Chloe wasn't really bothering me all that much. Everything that happened so far with us had happened thoughtlessly, that is, without any thought on my part. No decisions had been made in advance. Everything just happened. No, I really wasn't worried about Chloe. That was just a cover. Instead, I was beginning to realize I was actually worrying about the fact I was worrying. It's hard to explain. Sometimes, I would just feel bad and for no good reason. And then, the longer it lasted, the more I'd roam around worrying about why I was feeling that way. "What the hell's wrong with me?" I'd ask myself. And when there wasn't a good answer I'd really worry, because I knew what that sort of worry signaled – a looming depression which was, unfortunately, not unfamiliar to me.

I had felt that sort of depression twice before in my life – once during graduate school, once around the time I got tenure. But this was different. Those other times, I could pinpoint my reaction to an event or a circumstance. In graduate school, I fell into a black hole after my first real girlfriend, my first real love broke up with me. It was soon after that I had my second bout of lockjaw, too. That's when they finally decided it wasn't tetanus or some weird dental disease. It was just me being crazy. They gave me some anti-anxiety pills to take, which I still occasionally pop when I need to and recently, to be honest, I've been popping them more than ever. (I hate the way they make me feel, but at least they keep me out of the emergency room). But, anyway, that time back in graduate school, it took me nearly a year to pull myself out of the depression, pills and all. That was somehow understandable, though, if perhaps a bit extreme.

The depression after my tenure appointment was more of an existential crisis; a "what now" sort of a hole where the pain felt less acute, but the blackness just as dark. But, what I was feeling now was even different from that. Now, nothing was really wrong. I tried to think it through. I was a man with a job I loved. Okay, my research was stuck and Yuri was playing spy games halfway around the world. But still I believed all that would come right in the end. And now I was even getting laid, just as Marty had so maturely urged me to do. Granted, this particular woman was a dangerously improper choice, but if nothing else she was making me feel better about being in my forties. And what was so bad about forty, anyway? Nothing really. I did my own checklist. I could still think well enough; I was physically fit and I guess still attractive enough to be able to sleep with a twenty-something. And anyway, it was summer and in a few weeks I'd be walking along the beach on Martha's Vineyard, eating lobster rolls for dinner. Even before the episode with Chloe, I was aware of feeling like shit and of not being able to figure out why. And as much as I hated to admit it, sometimes being smart just isn't enough.

By now, the afternoon sun was at its most intense. I felt it burning the back of my neck. I knew I couldn't sit there any longer and squeezed Marty's shoulder. "Enough. Let's go," I said. We both stood up and walked back along the river to campus. Marty was unusually quiet, which was fine with me. It was all too tiring to talk about.

Months later, when I looked back on this episode of my life, I realized that talking was actually what I had needed to do most. The fact that I was avoiding it so much was really a sign of just how necessary it had become. Even then I had begun to think seriously about seeing a shrink. My doctor had been urging me to do it for years, especially when I started asking for refills of those anti-lockjaw pills again. It wouldn't be hard to find one. The school's health service had a whole team of them. But I just couldn't imagine what I would say. What would I talk about? Where would I even begin? Myself? What would I say about myself? My father? Let dead men lie. I liked to believe I had forgiven him, anyway. Then what? My mother? I couldn't bear it. The older I got, the more she haunted me. But she was the last person I ever wanted to talk about. No, I just couldn't do it. Then, in the midst of all these thoughts, I heard Marty's voice. He had stopped walking and turned to face me.

"Look, buddy," he was saying. I can remember every word. "I'm not good at this sort of thing. You know, I look at you and see the man who has everything. You're smart, you're handsome, you've got money. Everybody likes you. And yet, something important, even more important than sex, is missing from your life. You don't know what it is. I sure as hell don't. But maybe you should talk to somebody who can figure it out."

It was as if Marty had read my mind. "I've been thinking the same thing," I had to admit. "But every time I do think about going to a shrink I get crazy. It just seems like so much bullshit," I said, but actually, I was lying. I knew that talking did help. It was the one thing which eventually helped my mother, after all. After her months of silence, it was actually the talking that got her better. By talking she had been able to recognize her anger and over the years she had become nothing but anger. She explained it to me herself. She was angry at the world, she told me. She was angry at God, at herself and until she had been able to let go of that anger, she couldn't let go of her depression. She also told me about her months of silence, what it felt like and why she had done it. All this came out one morning, or maybe it was afternoon, as I sat there in our kitchen in London, eating a bowl of Weetabix for breakfast. It must have been just a few weeks after she came home from the hospital. She stood there with her back against the sink, smiling and watching me eat and then she told me. Everything. I don't know if I said anything back to her in reply. I can't really remember. But I do know I just continued to sit there, eating, trying not to look at her and feeling like it was all too little, too late. So I heard then, whether I wanted to or not, that the talking did help. And from time to time, as I grew older and faced my own sort of depression, I couldn't help but think that maybe it would be good for me, too. But I was just too scared to try.

I couldn't yet admit it, but in my heart I knew that it wasn't actually the shrink that frightened me. I wasn't afraid of the doctor himself, or of sitting on his couch and revealing all my secrets. Instead, I was much more afraid of the possibility that I would need a shrink in the first place, that I was turning out like my mother. But I was determined not to succumb. I would never let myself fall apart like she did. I would fight this threatening blackness on my own, in my own way. And I wouldn't hurt anyone else in the process.

By the time I had thought about all this, Marty and I had made our way back to campus and were standing in front of the physics building. I looked at him. Everything from his uncombed hair to his untied shoelaces seemed to show me just how much he was thinking about me. At that moment, I think I knew that I loved Marty and Marty loved me as much as we loved anyone in the world. It seemed silly but, you know, it gave me hope. Just the fact that Marty was there, annoying me, challenging me, worrying about me, meant that I wasn't really alone. I found myself thinking about all the people in my life I cared about. Lizzy and Peter, of course. Amanda, out there saving the world. Plus Marty, Beth and the kids. Even old girlfriends, like Suzanne. I still cared for her. The world was full of people

I loved or had once loved. And that thought, more than anything else, helped me believe, at least for a little while, that I would be all right.

"I'll be able to pull myself out of this, Marty," I tried to reassure him. "I will. You'll see. Don't worry so much." As we opened the door, I felt the air-conditioning wash over me and I remember thinking it felt like I was being cleansed, bathed in some restorative ozone solution. I walked towards my office and Marty walked back to his lab. With every step, I felt something inside me harden. I would turn my fear into determination. My anger into strength. I would be fine. I didn't know how I would do it, but I'd find a way. I thought about the beach on Martha's Vineyard. Perhaps a change of scene would do me good. And maybe an old-fashioned heart-to-heart with Lizzy. Yes, that's what I would do, I thought. As soon as I got back to the office I'd call Lizzy and invite them down to the Vineyard for a long weekend. Yes. And the Red Sox were bound to continue their winning streak. That would be good, too. It would all be good. Time would move forward and everything would be fine. I just had to be patient.

By the time I was scheduled to teach my next class, I was completely frazzled again. There were too many thoughts in my head. Trying not to worry about myself just made me worry more about my research. What if Yuri's paranoia was right? I shot off a quick email to him: "Any more news? Nothing here." For a while, I searched the physics sites on the Internet, hoping to find something that would spark a thought. But it was useless. Despite my good intentions and assurances to Marty, everything I did only made me feel worse.

Disgusted with myself, I left the office early and walked down the hall to the classroom. I needed a moment to focus on the present reality, namely, "Topics in Physics." Somehow I had to find a way to teach it. The room was quiet. There was a large window overlooking a quad full of green, but other than that, the room was overwhelmingly white. Soothing, actually. I liked teaching there. Its medium size suited me. I hated those large lecture halls with rows and rows of seats looking down on me as if in some ancient amphitheater. There, my students were too remote. I might as well be talking to myself. But the little symposium room was just as bad – ten chairs in a circle with a small blackboard behind them. That was too close. I couldn't breathe. So I was content to be in the medium-sized room. It reminded me of an old elementary school. It was a room where I could play teacher, write terms on the board, ask questions to raised hands, stroll up and down between the desks. I could lose myself there.

I took a moment to look out the window. I didn't really see anything; I just looked. With a few deep breaths to clear my head, I tried my old rock 'n roll trick. I conjured up that famous Doors' organ solo which always made me think of a single right hand chasing itself over the keys, tripping back and forth over scales full of eighth notes. Then came the lyrics, and soon I was mumbling them out loud:

You know that it would be untrue.
You know that I would be a liar,
If I was to say to you,
Girl, we couldn't get much higher.
Come on, baby, light my fire.....

I think I stood there for a while, staring and singing to myself until I heard voices and footsteps behind me. Nodding hello to my students, I forced myself to smile. This was an undergraduate class, full of smart-enough students, but it was summer and nobody really wanted to work very hard. They all looked tan, relaxed, underdressed and very young. Anyone could see there wasn't a real physicist among them. I liked to call this my 'baby class', the give-them-anything-you-feel-like physics class created to introduce future doctors and architects to the *elegant beauty* of physical science. Basically, I walked into the room twice a week and talked about whatever came to mind. As long as sometime during the term I danced around quantum mechanics, mentioned inflation and paid homage to Einstein, I was all right. I could do that. I could lose myself for now in basic physics. And I wouldn't think about Chloe or Yuri or anything else. Teaching would do that for me.

I scanned the room to see if everyone was there. Two of the girls looked at each other as they rubbed their bare arms and shivered. The air conditioner was on full blast and the room was freezing. It gave me an idea and I opened the window.

"Okay, everyone," I said. "Let's get started. So, why did I believe that opening up the window would warm up the room?" We were off.

"Hot air rises," someone shouted.

I probably scowled. "We're not talking up and down, we're talking side to side. Try again."

"Heat travels from something hot to something cold," someone else said tentatively.

"Like from a light bulb," said another.

"...or a hot place to a cold place..."I heard from the back row.

"Yes," I said, and then slowly making a big circle with my arms, I prompted them "...or like from the..."

"Sun!" several people called out. I actually don't think they minded being treated like High School kids. It was fun for a change, and easy.

"Okay, then." I walked to the blackboard and scrawled *The Second Law of Thermodynamics.* "What's that?"

A brief silence and then a raised hand. "Entropy increases?"

"Yes, it does." I then wrote *entropy* on the board. "And what is entropy?" Now the class started to come alive.

"Chaos."

"Disorder."

"Doesn't it have something to do with dispersion?"

"Yes. Now we're getting somewhere." I sat on the edge of the table. I could feel a part of myself come back to life as I sparred with my students. My imagination began to run, creating an energy inside me that seemed to come from nowhere. I was teaching. "Entropy is a measure of the amount of disorder in a physical system," I said, and I continued with an example I'd used for years. One of my favorites. "You go to the beach. You bring a blanket, a chair, an umbrella, two physics books, a cooler of beer and a boogie board. You create your own little physical system there. Now, if you are a dangerously A-type compulsive sort of person, you'd sit in your chair, your blanket might be rolled at your feet, your books stacked neatly on top of the cooler. Everything frighteningly neat and tidy. Low entropy. But if you're like me, you throw the boogie board down next to the chair, use the books to weigh down the blanket, take out a beer and lie down with your little system as spread out as possible in complete disarray. High entropy. And the 'Second Law of Thermodynamics' says that it is much more likely that my second little beach scenario will take place than the first. In other words, energy disperses and you can measure it."

I looked around at all the pens hurriedly scribbling in notebooks and stood up. I continued talking, walking around the desks, peering over shoulders. "But, so what? How does that affect us?" This was a familiar speech of mine, one I've said a million times over the years. I can basically recite it by heart. But this time, it somehow felt new and full of energy. "Well, it means that the fast moving molecules in the hot air outside would move towards the slower moving molecules in the cold air inside, as long as they weren't hindered, i.e. the window was open. But that's kind of obvious. Everyone knows that. A more interesting question is, how does this affect the universe?" I hesitated for a second, and then impulsively blurted out, "Or even better, how does it affect time?" I walked back to the blackboard and wrote in large letters *The Arrow of Time*. Now, this was a concept I never included in this lesson and had never intended to introduce to these particular students. "The arrow of time" sounded simple, but it was a knotty problem, *the* knotty problem.

It had been sticking its head into my research and consuming my thoughts for years. But there it was, written in black and white on the board. There was no turning back.

I pointed to the words. First, there was silence. I paced around the room. One hand went up.

"Well, do you mean the direction that time moves in? Like the future?"

"Yes, time does seem to us to go in one direction only. And one speed only, right?" I would have to ease them into some sort of understanding. "But let's not forget about Einstein."

"You mean, relativity?" someone eventually said.

"I mean relativity," I answered and then continued as clearly as I could. "We've already seen how your experience of time is necessarily different from mine, depending on where we are, what we're doing and where we're going. But remember. Each of our experiences, our 'nows', is specific to our own point in the grid of spacetime. We discussed this last week." The more I talked, the more concentrated I got. "But this is really important here because – get this – if everything that has ever happened and ever will happen is actually a point on this so-called grid, then is there a future? I mean a real future as we think of it, as distinct from the past? Something that has not yet happened? Or is it all, actually, the same?"

I stopped and looked around the room. At first, there were only blank faces, but then I could see glimmers of energy in a few sets of eyes. Some pencils began to tap. I remember wondering if I should continue or not, but I was having too much fun to stop. "Therefore, is there really an arrow of time, a single direction in which time moves? Think about it. If there is symmetry in the forces of nature, which there generally seems to be, shouldn't there also be symmetry in time? Would time really move in one direction only? And what does all this have to do with the Second Law of Thermodynamics and entropy?"

I positioned myself at the front of the room and looked at the row of faces. Whatever glimmers of understanding had begun in some of those eyes were now well and truly lost. I could almost see the "does not compute" sparks shooting out of their ears. With all of my questions, I had taken a relatively orderly group of brains and thrown them into disarray. It was great. But I did feel bad for them. A *Physics for Poets* class shouldn't be too taxing, especially not in the middle of July. So I decided to laugh it off. "A little much, huh?" I think I said. "Well, that is just to show you the type of question we cosmologists grapple with in our research. And, of course, we do it all with numbers. It's enough to make you stay in medicine, eh?" The class laughed and their faces began to relax. I guess I then babbled some soothing words of explanation and reminders of homework deadlines. Soon enough, it was time to dismiss them. As the class walked out of the room, their energy increased and the noise level grew louder. I stayed behind, laughing to myself. I remember it was the first good laugh I had in a while. On that old screen behind my eyes I could almost see a graph of the movement from order to chaos going on in those undergraduate minds. "Yes, entropy increases, all right," I thought to myself. "And you can measure it."

Chapter 13

John:
The Event Horizon

Lizzy was forever telling me that I thought too much. She was right, of course. Every minute of every day my brain raced, sometimes frantically like a microscopic world of quantum jitters, other times like a little kid running around in circles. It wasn't always a bad thing. Sometimes it allowed me to come up with elegant new approaches to seemingly intractable questions. It also made me a fascinating teacher, if I do say so myself, not to mention pretty good at dinner parties. But it was exhausting – not so much for me (I was used to it, after all), but for those around me. One of my girlfriends, years earlier, claimed to have found the answer in meditation. She convinced me to go to classes with her, to sit in silent stillness for longer and longer periods of time. The sitting was never a problem. Neither was the silent stillness. I actually liked it, which made my girlfriend happy, at first. But when I told her I liked it because the longer I sat, the more different ideas I could think about at one time, she got angry. She said I had missed the point – again – and that was the end of meditation and soon after, the end of her. Don't get me wrong. I can focus. Just not on any one thing for very long. But that doesn't mean my focus isn't intense and clear.

Everyone knows the more intensely you focus a beam of light, for example, the more powerful it becomes; the more powerful it becomes the more you can see. That's what lasers, not to mention holograms, are all about, after all.

At the moment in time I'm thinking about now, though, after weeks of teaching and worrying about my research, after the third or fourth "romantic" Saturday night dinner with Chloe followed by a late session of "physical exploration," I was exercising my laser-like focus on Chloe's left pelvic bone. There it was, jutting out in a harsh angle as she lay asleep on her side. It protruded so distinctly I could nearly see its shadow in the morning light. I remember being surprised to realize, though, that it didn't actually attract me. I felt no desire to touch it, or even worse, be touched by it. I just stared at it and followed with my eyes the line of its contour, up her side, down the roller coaster of her waist and back up again to her equally visible rib cage. I turned on my back, closed my eyes and became lost in thought, secretly yearning for something else, smoother, fleshier, more substantive. I guess a lot of time passed, because at some point I started to fidget. I was probably getting restless.

Soon after that, Chloe woke up. I felt her move next to me and touch my shoulder. I turned on my side to see her puffy eyes and smiling lips.

"Good morning." She spoke with the ease of a woman who had spent every morning for twenty years waking up next to that specific man she now found lying beside her. True, we had slept together a lot over the past few weeks, but I was still amazed at Chloe's nonchalance.

"Good morning," I said, smiling back, but weakly.

Chloe sat up and stretched, lifting her hair off her shoulders. I knew it was an invitation. Instinctively, I reached up and softly traced a wave pattern down the middle of her back. Chloe turned and placed a quick kiss on my lips.

"Gotta' go to the bathroom. I'll be right back."

I lay in bed and watched her walk across the room, moving like an animal, unselfconscious, unaware of her nakedness or her actions. She scratched the top of her leg, shook out her hair and hopped over the doorjamb into the hallway. Seeing her that way, I thought she looked even younger than she was. Her body was thin and tight. Tidy, actually. There was no real sign of the twenty-five years of life she had lived, as if all that living had happened in her head, her body barely along for the ride. Her breasts were good, though. Nice nipples. And I have to admit that's what I was thinking as Chloe came back into the room, knelt on the bed and straddled me.

"You awake?" she teased, weaving her fingers through the small hairs on my stomach, working her way further and further downward.

Yes, I was awake. I watched my hands move as if they had a mind of their own. I saw them reach for Chloe's breasts, circling around them from underneath. They then slid upwards towards her shoulders as Chloe's legs tightened around me. I concentrated on her face as she lowered herself down, bending her elbows until our lips touched, then our chests, our hips and thereafter the rhythmic movement up and slowly down.

By the time I had gotten out of bed, taken a shower, got dressed and had a quick cup of instant coffee, it was nearly two o'clock in the afternoon. I was starving.

I called to Chloe in the bathroom to see how much longer she'd be. I felt irritated. She wasn't taking all that long, but however long it was was too long for me. I needed food, some real coffee and fresh air.

"Almost done," I heard her call and so I began to rummage around the living room while I waited. That's when my attention was drawn to the printed notice I received in the mail a week before. I was lost in thought, reading it over and over again, when Chloe finally appeared, dressed and ready to go. I hadn't even noticed her there, standing close behind me, reading over my shoulder.

"Imperial College London? Are you going?" she asked, startling me.

I folded the paper secretively and put it inside my pocket as if I was trying to hide some evidence. "I'm famished. Let's go to the diner." My need to be out of the apartment became overwhelming. I felt like the walls were closing in on me, so I got Chloe out the door as fast as I could. She didn't seem to notice.

"So, when is it?" she asked as the hot July sun hit us full in the face.

"When's what?" I was stalling for time.

"Imperial College. You know."

"Oh, that. End of August." I pushed forward to the diner and its all-day Sunday breakfast. I was quiet, distracted and barely aware of Chloe's constant talking. As I opened the door to the air-conditioned restaurant I caught the word *London* in the middle of one of her sentences. We may not have been having an actual conversation, words bouncing back and forth between us, affecting our thoughts, changing our positions. But we were definitely thinking about the same thing.

I had tried to ignore that official conference notice when I first received it. Of course, I had known it was coming. Nearly every day I got a new, pushy email from Yuri asking about my plans. "Decided yet?" "Tickets booked?" And each time, I sent back the same reply. "I'll let you know." The inevitability of my going was becoming more undeniable every day, but still I was waiting to say for sure. What I was waiting for, I didn't know. But maybe I was just waiting for a good cup of coffee, because as soon as Chloe and I sat down at a table and were handed our menus, at that distinct moment when I put my filled coffee cup to my lips and took my first sip, I decided in an instant probably calculable to something like 10^{-23}, that I would go.

"Yes, you know," I finally told Chloe and myself, " I think I am going to go."

"To London? Cool. Sounds like fun."

"Well, I wasn't so sure at first. It might just be a lot of the 'String Theory Mafia' guys." I was explaining it all to myself as much as to Chloe.   "But then I heard from Tsypkin." Chloe's eyes frowned. She didn't know who Yuri was. Of course not. "Yuri Tsypkin? Never heard of him?" I tried not to sound too patronizing. "He's a physicist out of Moscow – one of the most important ones. I first met him years ago when he was a student over here. He's a great guy. Real smart, too. So anyway, he's going to be there and he wants me to go." I took another sip of coffee and glanced at Chloe over the top of the cup. She was sitting there, listening, drinking, easy and unbothered by anything. So annoying. I could have left it at that. I didn't need to explain anymore why or if I was going. I just was. I certainly didn't owe Chloe any more of an explanation. And by the looks of her, she wasn't expecting one anyway. But for some reason I kept talking. "You see, we've begun to collaborate on a paper. You know that holography research I've been doing? We're at the point where we probably need to talk about it in person. To tell you the truth, the pressure has been getting pretty rough." Why did I tell her that? What did Chloe, or any graduate student for that matter, know about the politics of science? How could anyone that age really understand the pressure professors like Yuri and I were under? For all they knew, science was just about being smart and doing the work. Ha.

I watched Chloe put another packet of sugar into her coffee. She looked so satisfied, so content. Obviously, she didn't care enough about this "rough pressure" of mine to let it come between her and her breakfast. Maybe, at one point in this inane relationship of ours, I had deluded myself into thinking that Chloe might actually give me an excuse *not* to go to London. But I now knew, for no particular reason, that was not going to happen. If anything, she was probably giving me one more reason to *go*. I think I began to mumble.

"So I guess, sure, I'll go. Yea, I suppose I should. But it is a long way to go for a weekend..." I could feel myself trying to back out again.

"Well, it doesn't have to be a weekend," Chloe suggested. "Make it a week. Go wild. Sounds like fun."

Again, I was amazed at the gulf between us, at how nothing ever seemed to worry or bother Chloe and how everything seemed to worry and bother me. I was tired if it, tired of obsessing about every move I made. It never seemed to make any difference, anyway. If nothing else, being with Chloe had taught me that. No matter how much I had worried about it, there I was: with her, a student, having breakfast in a local diner after a morning of sex. Clearly, all of my worry and bother couldn't stop the fact I was moving inexorably towards something whether I wanted to or not. Something's gravitational pull was drawing me in and it was stronger than any jitters I could thrust in its way.

Looking back on all this, I eventually came to see this moment in time as my 'event horizon', that imaginary line surrounding my life marking the point of no return. *This* moment was when gravity took hold and began to pull me into the unknown. Within a month's time, I was going to be back in London. That was becoming clearer every second. I didn't really have to go. Maybe I could have figured out a way to see Tsypkin in some other place or some other time. But I had said I was going to go and so I would. It hadn't actually been a decision. It was more like a stumble. That was what I was doing all the time those days, it seemed. I was stumbling through my life, bouncing around like some wayward photon, waiting to see where I'd end up next. Now, you would think that even someone with as little self-awareness as I had back then would see that I was embarking on some sort of confrontation with my past. It had to happen. Imperial College was literally around the corner from where I used to live. But, no. I wasn't thinking about the future. I wasn't thinking about the past. All I was thinking about was the waitress standing beside my table, her pencil poised above her pad and the word 'pancakes' coming out of my mouth.

But there was one thing which even I knew I had to do. Chloe's suggestion about lengthening my stay still hung in the air between us. But it had hidden ramifications. I did some calculations in my head, voicing them out loud at the same time.

"Extend my stay? Let me see," I began. "School lets out in a couple of weeks, then I'm off to the Vineyard – some family stuff. It's a long planned thing." I rushed through that part. To be honest, I didn't want to give Chloe the chance to suggest joining me there. The Vineyard was my refuge and the last place I'd ever want to see one of my students, even one I had been sleeping with. "That takes me to mid-August and just about the time of the Conference. I could go for a week or so and be back in time for the start of school." I know I then started to eat with great intensity. I must have looked ridiculous, staring down at my plate and stuffing one mouthful in after another. You see, I knew that I had just told Chloe that this was pretty much the end of us. We wouldn't be seeing each other much over the next six weeks. And then? Well, I wasn't going to think beyond then. How could I imagine anything beyond this trip to London, anyway? But I didn't know if Chloe would be upset. I had no idea how she felt about me or about what we had been doing together. She always seemed so content. It was bizarre. But she certainly didn't make me wait long for an answer.

"Yea, the summer is flying by," she said between bites. "I'm going to be out of here pretty soon myself, I think. Did I tell you I just about finished my project with Doctor Ellis, or at least as much as we can do now?" She began to stir in her chair and look around the diner, not in any agitated way, just kind of restlessly. It may have been my imagination, but it looked like she was ready to jump up and out the door right then and there.

"I'm heading up to the Berkshires to see my folks by the end of next week. I was just going to tell you. Then my schedule's kind of up in the air."

And that was that. So now I knew. Chloe had had her summer fling with a professor. It was fun; now it was done. I couldn't believe it. Actually, I was able to believe Chloe's indifference. After all, I had always known she wasn't in love with me. I told Marty so myself, weeks ago. But what I couldn't believe was my own reaction to her indifference. My ears got red, not with anger, but embarrassment. All that agonizing, all that worrying, I thought. The long walks with Marty, the imagined arguments with Lizzy. All for nothing. For a simple summer fling, the type of superficial thing that young women had so easily these days, but that I had never been able to have. It was humiliating; not because it had happened, but because I was so embarrassed by it. It just didn't make any sense to me. But, then again, nothing was making any sense to me then. I may have been on the verge of some great change in my life, but I couldn't begin to imagine what that change could be. Sure, I may have reached my so-called "event horizon", but did I have even the slightest clue of what could be on the other side? No way.

I finished my cup of coffee and licked the last remnants of syrup off my fingers. I heard that Chloe was already happily onto some new topic of conversation, but I could barely understand what it was. Words had stopped having any meaning. Nothing had much meaning anymore. But nonetheless, I was nothing if not polite, so I nodded my head as if I was following what she was saying and signaled the waitress for the check. Really, what else could I do?

Chapter 14

Grace:
The Blur

There was a time in my life when whole years seemed to disappear. It's not unusual. Many people find the child-rearing years a blur, sleepless nights blending into overwrought days. One child's bout of projectile vomiting hurls itself into another child's recurring ear infection. As with any difficult period, it's easy to forget that those years are only a chapter in your life, and not the whole of it. "Well, here I am," I used to think. "This is me forever." Sometimes I stopped and looked at myself in the mirror during that time and saw not exactly a stranger, but a person I didn't recognize. And I assumed that bizarre morph-of-a-person was the ultimate me, the final product.

   Thirty years later, when the children are grown and on their own, you remember what you once knew for certain. I understood so much about life when I was nineteen, twenty. For instance, way back then I knew that my strength came from solitude, but my joy came from my union with the rest of the world. I didn't mind being alone, because I knew that there was always, somehow, a sustaining connection that would stop me from being lost. By the time I had finished college, I knew there were many paths I could take in my life. I had the sense that one path would lead to another and that there would always be one more taking over from where the old one left off. But I lost all that wisdom somewhere amid the discarded jars of baby food, and it remained forgotten during the rush to ballet lessons and the tears over long division. I had nothing to say to anyone that wasn't confined to the four walls of my house or the lives of my children. It's not surprising that I slowly lost touch with my sister. Gina was a lawyer, traveling all over the world doing deals, full of opinions, important. She had a husband, but no children and so, for a long time, we had nothing in common. Or so we thought. We saw each other on holidays, of course. My mother made sure of that. But we stopped really talking or even trying to remain a part of each other's lives. Over the years, we became so remote that it took a trauma to bring us back together.

The memory of my former wisdom only came back to me after the blur was over, but it took a long time. Longer than for most people, I think. Forgetting what I had known necessitated a painful process of rediscovery. People joke about past lives, but you don't have to actually die in order to be reborn.

During those years of blur, Lizzy and John grew up. They went to school and, usually, did their homework. There were music lessons, haircuts and pierced ears. John outgrew his early breathing problems and had become a sports fanatic. Each new season brought a new sport and an endless series of practices. Throughout it all, Jack and I kept working in our own ways, stopping to enjoy ourselves whenever the occasion allowed, but basically pushing forward so as not to fall back. At first, we instituted the "weekly date." One night a week we went out, just the two of us, to dinner or the movies. It didn't matter where. We'd splurge on a babysitter and give each other a few hours of our undivided attention. It was a good idea and worked well for a time. Once or twice a month those dates even led to sex, something that was becoming more perfunctory and less passionate, to be honest. Again, not an unusual story. We were exhausted. Our work preoccupied us – I built our family while Jack-the-architect built his buildings – and when we did come together,

134

usually late at night in bed, we were comfortable enough just to take a deep breath and fall asleep.

For a long time that life worked fine for Jack. His eyes were always focused clearly ahead of him. But it was dangerous for me. My own eyes naturally focused inward, and during those years I had to train myself to keep an eye on everyone else at my own expense. I forced myself to ignore the fluttering inside me, that restlessness that had always annoyed me and kept me searching for more. But now, there just wasn't time for it. As a child I already understood that there was something beyond the limits of my skinny little legs and bony arms. That fluttering had kept me searching for whatever that something was. But by ignoring it, I ignored an essential part of me.

Years went by. I myself became a blur, somehow not completely there. It was almost as if you could walk right through me, I was so much a phantom of myself. As teenagers, Lizzy and John both acted in ways to try and jolt me without even realizing it. They didn't want a mother who was just a shadow of a person. They wanted and needed a solid presence, a full-bodied, complete human being with her own distinct goals, beliefs and needs. But I couldn't be that for them. For too long I had stopped existing as myself. The responsibility for my children's lives and deaths had overtaken me. It became who I was. I had, indeed, stopped being me so they could be them.

Chapter 15

Grace:
The Spy Who Loved You

There was a time, so long ago, when every conversation between John and me went something like this:

"Everything ok at school?"

"Yea."

"How're your friends?"

"Fine."

"Do you want to talk about anything?"

"Mom, lay off, will ya?"

It's not that he had been acting strangely, exactly. But he had a different look in his eye back then that was hard to decipher and that made me want to push and prod until I could make it go away. I didn't think it was drugs. He didn't look like a pot smoker to me. I never smelled it on him. His eyes were never glassy. But there was something else, something more sinister and I didn't know what. Then, one afternoon, pushing the shopping cart down the frozen food aisle, it hit me. There it was, among the fish fingers. Guilt. Yes, John had started to look guilty and once I thought about it I realized that I knew that look. It had been in his eyes when he peed in the sand box in kindergarten. It was the same look he had when he was caught cheating on his math test in fourth grade. When he was twelve and stole some money hidden away in his sister's jewelry box, it was there, too. The dullness in the eyes, the darting glances, the tightened lips. What was he guilty about?

The more I probed, the angrier he got. The angrier he got, the less he talked. He once even threatened me. "I'll leave this house right now if you don't leave me alone." Every day after school he went straight to his room, slamming the door, without even saying hello. He accused me of snooping through his things, of not trusting him. I lied and said I did trust him. "Anyway, what are you so worried about if you don't have anything to hide?" I snapped.

Maybe I was overreacting. Maybe it was just the perversity of adolescence and nothing more. I had been lucky with Lizzy. Her teenage years went pretty smoothly, I thought. But now I wonder if I had really even noticed them. At the time, I assumed it had to do with my excellent parenting skills, my instinctive understanding of her every need. But no. Now I think Lizzy's adolescence went smoothly because it didn't dare not to. I was forever setting rules, drawing lines. At sixteen, her curfew was eleven o'clock. It didn't matter that there was an important party or a once-in-a-lifetime concert. She had to be home when I said she did because I couldn't bear to stay up worrying about where she was. There was always plenty to worry about, anyway, without looking for something new. Jack and I argued about it – he always tried to *loosen me up* and come to her rescue – but Lizzy and I never did. Maybe it would have been better if we had. But I was tough back then. I've got to admit it. And now it seemed it was John's turn.

One Sunday morning I called Lizzy at college.

"Mom, what's the matter?" she yawned.

"Nothing, sweetheart." I couldn't just blurt it all out. "I was just missing you and wanted to say, Hi." But Lizzy wasn't buying it.

"Couldn't it have waited a few hours? What's wrong?"

I had been sitting on my bed. I stood up, then I sat down again. I couldn't keep still. Now what was Lizzy trying to hide? It wasn't that early, nearly eleven. I imagined her hungover with a wet washcloth on her forehead. I imagined a man, a naked man, lying there next to her. I started babbling.

"Well, nothing special to report here. Your father's in the middle of a big project, a lot of travel and late nights. Your brother, well, he's a teenager. You know how that is." Lizzy grunted. "Have you talked to him lately?"

"To John? I don't know. I guess a week or so ago, not that he ever says very much. Why? What's he done?"

"Nothing. I don't know. Do you think he's done something?"

"No, Mom. I don't think he's done anything. He's fifteen. Leave him alone."

And that was the end of the conversation. I realize now there wasn't anything else. No how-are-your-classes. No how-are-your-friends. Just me, my worries, and my snooping questions about her brother. I was so obsessed with my fears that I couldn't see what was going on in Lizzy's life. I never stopped to look. It's amazing she didn't hate me. Or maybe she did. Maybe they both did.

One day, I found that I couldn't control myself any longer. I became a spy, lurking in dark hallways, hiding behind doors. I purposefully interrupted John while he was doing his homework. Was he really doing his homework, or was he playing video games? Would I catch him reading *Sports Illustrated* instead of his biology textbook? I lingered in the hall outside his bedroom when he was on the phone. There was a perfect spot between the closet and bathroom doors. I stood there folding sheets to put into the linen closet, washing down walls that had never been dirty. I couldn't stop myself. Standing in the shower, I conducted imaginary interrogations. Where are you going? Who are you seeing? Weeks passed and I discovered nothing except my own unhealthy knack for espionage.

Once, while Jack was at work and John was in school, I went into John's room. I picked the wet towels up off the floor. I put the dirty socks into the hamper. There were always stacks of magazines and stray papers to straighten, the bed to make. But then I opened his closet. I saw his jackets hanging neatly next to his trousers. I reached towards the pockets in his shirts at the same time as I said to myself I shouldn't be doing this. I started to walk away, but the door remained open. I had to go back to close it, to cover my tracks, but there I was again and this time I didn't stop myself. One by one I searched his pockets inside and out, upside down and around, looking for I didn't know what. Everything was empty, and that should have been enough. But it wasn't. I went to the bookshelf and tipped forward rows of books, peering into the recesses behind them. I felt beneath his mattress and under his pillows. I opened magazine covers and looked into his pencil box. There was nothing, but it left me with a sick feeling in my stomach. I didn't find the answers I was looking for. I didn't find anything except a disgust for the person I had become and a loathing for the lonely, untrusting place where I was going.

Leaving the room, I spied one last drawer to open. It was full of stuff, old homeworks, scraps of paper with unlabeled telephone numbers, an overdue library book or two and some old photographs. I picked the photos up. There was a picture of Brian, John's best friend, the summer before at the Town Pool, cut-off shorts, no shoes, no shirt, showing off the beginning of a muscular chest. Then, a wallet-sized school photo of a girl I had never seen, all long curls and a smile full of braces. There was a picture of Lizzy, Jack and I that John had taken two years earlier in Disneyworld. Lizzy looked annoyed. Jack looked surprisingly happy, with an arm around each of our shoulders. My mouth was open and my eyebrows arched, staring straight at John. Obviously, I was shouting out some instruction or other to him. There were lines around my lips and a fatigue in my eyes. I couldn't bear to look at it. I hardly recognized the harrowed woman I had already become. I thrust the photo back in the drawer and slammed it shut.

Then came Thanksgiving. Not knowing what else to do, I threw myself into the holiday preparations with an unparalleled zeal. Lizzy and John were both home. Jack could only take the day, but at least he wasn't traveling. We were all going to be together. I tried to act 'normal'. My fears were in my head, I decided, and I was going to ignore them and get on with my life. No more spying on my family. "There's nothing to worry about," I repeated to myself. "Nothing's wrong."

I don't remember much of that weekend. I know we had a big dinner, much too much for just the four of us, with the usual turkey, stuffing, pumpkin pie. I do remember the kids teasing Jack about the amount of wine he drank, more than a bottle just on his own. While I wrapped up the leftovers into neat little packages, I could hear Jack and the kids in front of the television. Occasionally, I strolled over to the doorway to see if I could hear what they were saying. Jack asked Lizzy some cursory questions about her classes. John teased his sister until he made her stomp out of the room.

"Jesus, John. Will you grow up?" she yelled back at him.

"What? What did I say?"

Then there was only the TV noise of marching bands and college football. I walked into the television room, the roll of cling film still in my hand.

"Hey, what's going on?" I asked both Jack and John who were now staring intently at the screen.

"Notre Dame's up by a safety," said John.

"That's not what I meant," I said, so Jack answered. He hurled his words over the back of his shoulder at me while looking straight ahead at the television.

"John was teasing Lizzy about her new boyfriend, is all."

"Lizzy has a new boyfriend?" I asked. "I didn't know that."

"Yea, can't you tell?" John groaned. "That's why she's acting so ... you know."

No, I didn't know. Maybe I didn't know anything at all. I felt tired. I sighed out loud as if I was sighing for the whole world.

"John, please," I said. "Don't pick fights with your sister. Not today. Go upstairs and apologize, will you?" I must have sounded like I was begging. I know I felt like I was going to cry. John looked at me with annoyance. Jack didn't look at me at all.

I went back into the kitchen and tried to busy myself. I started to wash a few pots, but the sound of the running water irritated me. I wondered what was going on upstairs. Had John apologized? Had he come back downstairs again to plop on the sofa with his father who just sat there, unable to think of anything to say? I turned off the faucet and moved towards the opened kitchen door. There was nothing to hear but the hum of the television. I peeked into the room. Jack was in there alone. I tiptoed to the bottom of the stairs. Lizzy and John were talking, I could hear that, but I couldn't make out what they were saying. They weren't arguing exactly, but their voices sounded too strained. Despite my best intentions, I found myself sneaking up the stairs to get to the door.

I leaned against the wall so I couldn't be seen. Finally, I was close enough to hear them more clearly.

"Lizzy, you have no idea what it's been like around here," John was in the middle of saying.

"Oh, please. Don't be so dramatic."

"Really. You're off at college. You don't know. Mom's like a maniac, snooping around all the time. She's tired. She's irritable. And Dad…"

"What about Dad?"

"Nothing."

I heard John moving around in his room. It sounded like Lizzy sat down on the bed.

"Don't say 'nothing'. You brought it up. So what is it?"

"I just don't know if I should. It's bad enough that I know."

"Know what?"

What was John talking about? What did he know? Suddenly, my legs felt weak and I gripped the banister. I quietly stepped up another stair.

John's voice was cracking. "He was on the phone in the kitchen, and I had just come in. I couldn't help but hear." Their voices got very low. Who was on the kitchen phone, I wondered. Jack? Was he talking about Jack? I was now standing behind the door, right outside John's bedroom. They couldn't see me, but I could see them. John's head was hanging low, his straight black hair falling forward onto his hands. Lizzy had her arm around his shoulders trying to comfort him.

"I heard him, Lizzy. 'Melanie, you know I love you, but I can't right now.' That's exactly what Dad said."

"Melanie? We don't know any Melanie, do we? Like a cousin or something?"

The room went quiet. I leaned against the wall to keep from falling over.

"So that's why Mom's been so weird lately," Lizzy finally concluded. "It must be. Poor Mom."

Suddenly, I found myself in the middle of John's bedroom. I didn't know how I got there, and I didn't know what I was going to say. A pounding started in my temples and I massaged the skin over my eyes, but I knew this headache wouldn't go away that easily. For a long time nobody said anything. John and Lizzy were staring at me. I was like a zombie. I looked around the room.

There was the caricature made of John years earlier, a baseball glove on one enormous hand, a Superman cape flying off his back. On the shelf above John's desk was his line-up of soccer trophies and his baseball cap collection. There was even Dinky, his first teddy bear, eyeless and bald, stuffed into the end of a bookcase. Everything was both familiar and strange at the same time. Even my children. I stopped in front of them, sitting there silently, obviously frightened. At first they looked tiny to me, fragile and confused, huddled together. I wanted to kiss their foreheads, smooth their hair. But they weren't really tiny. They were big, very big. Bigger than me it seemed and far away, looking back at me from a bleak distance of years. Their eyes were dark and watery, like stagnant pools in a forgotten wood. Looking into their faces, I suddenly heard myself speak.

"It's cold in here, isn't it?" was what I said.

Chapter 16

Grace:
Sliding into Home

It was the summer of life-changing decisions. I felt as if we all stood on the edge of two rocky paths, but the woods around our family had grown so tangled and dark that none of us could see beyond the first few steps. Lizzy had finished her freshman year of college. She had been miserable, but had decided not to transfer. Jack was still frozen after a very long, very stormy winter. I had begun to recover from my paralysis after discovering Jack's affair. And John emerged, bruised but still fighting, from the jungle of Middle School into the warm, green expanse of summertime baseball.

The ballpark benches were hard, but at least they weren't crowded. Jack sat beside me, but he left a space as if Lizzy was about to come back any minute from the bathroom. Of course, she wasn't coming back from the bathroom and if she was, I doubt that she would have sat next to him. That summer she was working in San Francisco, teaching English to children of migrant workers. The air was warm with a slight breeze. The sun glared down on us, bouncing off the rims of our baseball caps. The game was about to begin.

"You do realize, don't you, how important this game is?" John asked us at breakfast. "We win this and we're in the championships. If we don't, the summer's over."

"The summer isn't over," Jack corrected over the top of his newspaper. "You still have three weeks until school."

"And six weeks until the autumnal equinox," I added, not really trying to be funny. Nobody laughed, anyway.

"You know what I mean," John said sternly, looking into the bottom of his cereal bowl. "Baseball's over. For the summer. That's what matters."

That summer of all summers, baseball was the only thing that mattered to John. It was the only thing that mattered to the rest of us, too, because it was the only thing that made any sense.

The benches were, indeed, hard. The conversation between Jack and me was even harder. At home we could avoid each other by hiding in different rooms, or talking on the telephone, or sleeping in front of the television. In the car we could listen to the radio and pretend to sing. But there, on that bench among the bleachers behind a high school in an unknown, faraway part of town, there was nowhere to hide. So even while nothing was happening, we sat and watched, staring into the blank sky, silent.

Eventually, the game began with our team at bat. Over the past few weeks I had gotten to know some of John's teammates. I even looked forward to hearing them swearing in the kitchen. Their intrusion into our days gave me something to talk about with my son. For instance, I knew that Luke Santini, right field, had a mother who was a journalist and his house was always full of faces you'd see on TV. Eggshell Dolan, the pitcher, had had four dads in fifteen years and knew the entire dialogue of all three *Godfather* movies by heart. My son, John, was the catcher and had the ability to bring out the best in everyone else while hiding himself behind a mask. Over the summer I realized that baseball positions were like dogs – they fit their owners exactly.

Play started off slow and sloppy. Both sides were nervous and although there were more fielding errors than there are brands of corn flakes, our team couldn't capitalize on any of them. The score remained 0-0 as they fumbled their way through the batting order. It wasn't pretty and the fans were getting restless. Jack and I just sat there, quietly and waited. Waiting was something we could still do together well.

After the third out, a heartbreaking fly ball nearly to the back fence, our team took the field and the excitement started to build. John, dressed like an armadillo, covered from head to toe with protective padding, squatted behind home plate.

"I'll never understand how he can squat like that and catch the ball at the same time. My thighs ache just looking at him." I was speaking to Jack, I guess, but I still stared into the field.

"He's strong," Jack answered, also looking straight ahead. "Stronger than me." He slid to the edge of the bench and took the classic male baseball-watching position – knees bent, elbows on knees, hands clasped in front of mouth. I looked at him. He was wearing an old Grateful Dead T-shirt, cut-off jeans and a Red Sox cap. For a minute he looked like the man I married twenty years before. I smiled. I couldn't help myself. And although he didn't turn to see it, I know he felt it. As the first batter walked up to the plate he yelled, "Blow it past him; you can do it!" and clapped his fist into his palm. I suddenly had an overwhelming urge for popcorn.

"Yo! Popcorn!" I yelled and a sweet-faced ten-year-old boy brought over a baggie full of Jiffy Pop and a can of Coke, courtesy of the Team Moms. I held onto the bag and I put the can down in the space between us.

Jack was right. The first batter had nothing and the pitches flew right past him into John's open glove. The first two outs were easy, but then came the biggest fifteen-year-old I had ever seen. He was big and he was fat and he was menacing. John sprang up and down on his knees and pounded the inside of his glove.

"Jesus," Jack said. "Look at that kid."

"Maybe he's slow."

"He better be."

The first pitch came in and the batter swung wildly. I gasped. I thought he would knock John's head right off. I held my breath. The pitcher nodded to John. John nodded again and placed his glove in front of his face. A swing ... and then the thud of contact. The ball flew straight up like an arrow, over home plate, over the head of giant-boy, into the glaring sun. John jumped to his feet, hovered back and forth underneath and squinted into the glare until the ball ran out of steam and fell straight back to earth into his waiting mitt.

"You're out!" screamed the Umpire.

"Yes!" screamed Jack.

"Yes!" I screamed and both of us jumped off the bench and clapped each other's hands in the air. John turned towards the bleachers to look at us as the team walked off the field. Jack and I gave him the thumbs up and then settled back down on the bench, still laughing. I hadn't felt that good in a very long time.

From the moment I decided to spy on my husband and catch him in the act, from that first moment of decision to the split second when that baseball hurtled into my son's ready glove, I was a changed person. I had become someone different, someone undreamed of. And so did my children. It was like waking up one morning and finding you were living in someone else's house, in someone else's life. I could find the silverware drawer, but I didn't recognize the hand reaching for the knife. And that was the worst part of it all. Sure, I wanted my husband back. Sure, I wanted things to be like they were. But most of all, I wanted *me* back. I had worked too long and too hard to find me in the first place to let some asshole, even an asshole I loved, take me away. Everyone told me to leave him. My already divorced friends, of course. Lizzy, at first. She still wasn't talking to him, really. My married friends, too. And my gay friends. Everybody. Except my sister, who hesitated.

"I hate him," she said over a tearful coffee. "I have always loved him and now I hate him. But I want to love him again. It hurts too much not to."

"So do I," I cried. And that's when I decided to find a way to stay.

I was luckier than many. It was clear to me from the start that he didn't love Melanie. Not really. He was devastated when I confronted him. Contrite, pleading. And the more I threatened to leave, the more he felt his children's fury, the more desperate he became. That was fun. A bright moment in an otherwise nauseating chapter. And I was brutal. I never let him know what I was thinking. I never made any plans. I never made jokes. I never made small talk. I just wandered through the days like someone anaesthetized. It was torture to him.

Unfortunately, it was also torture to John, our only child still at home, mired in the debris of adolescence anyway and now living with the walking dead. At first his grades sunk. But that was understandable. I didn't say anything. Then he threw himself into his studies, working all the time just so he wouldn't have to be near us. His grades soared. Again, I didn't say anything. Then school was over. John and Jack started to ask when we were going to go to our rental house on the Cape, like we always did. I don't know, I said. Soon, maybe. I had no intention of going. No intention of leaving Jack alone up there in the city. But, poor John. Hanging around the city with nothing to do but sweat. Actually, it reminded me of my own childhood summers back in Brooklyn. We never went away to some beach house. My parents were always working. They certainly never planned anything for us to do. So we hung out. We ran in the open fire hydrants to cool off. We played ball in the street.

But one day in late June, John had had enough. "I can't take this. I hate you. I hate dad. I hate this house. I hate my life." He was crying.

I stopped what I was doing, probably drinking coffee in the kitchen and staring into space and looked at him. I know my eyes were dead. There was no emotion in my voice.

"Okay then," I said. "Go outside and play ball."

And he did. He found a game. Then he found a team, then a league and then an entire season and as far away from home as public transport would take him. He woke up in the morning, grabbed his bat and his glove and went out to play. At first he wouldn't even come home for dinner. Then, he did come home and his friends started to come home with him. They would watch baseball games at night on TV, still wearing their caps and mitts. They ordered pizza. Sometimes Jack would watch with them after work. Sometimes I would linger as I passed through the living room. The kids would talk and laugh. Jack would exchange statistics and trivia with them. It began to look like a normal house again, to the untrained eye. Baseball not only became John's life that summer. More than that, baseball saved John's life. It saved our family, too.

Now, here we were at the game. The first four innings were typical – long spans of tedium punctuated by unexpected instants of hysteria. John's first time at bat he grounded out to first. The second time he hit a single. There was already one man on base and the score was still 0-0 with two outs. It was a great moment. There are times, as a mother, when you have to sit still and let life happen. You spend so many years trying to protect and control and then you realize you're done. All you can do is watch. It was like that. The pressure was on. John walked up to the plate looking almost like an adult. He did his pre-hitting routine, pounding the bag with the bat, knocking the dirt off his cleats. Then he stood and waited. He knew the ball would come to him and he knew he could hit it. He doesn't always connect. No one does. But when it works, the sound rings through the air with assurance and weight. Again, we were on our feet.

"Way to go. Yes, yes!" Jack screamed.

"Run. Don't stop," I cried.

"Safe!" called the first base umpire and the bleachers exploded with cheers.

"That's my boy," called out Jack, turning to me. There was love in his eyes, unadulterated joy as if, for a moment, he had forgotten he was miserable. He reached towards me in congratulations, but I froze. I tried to respond to him. I did. Yet, all I could manage was a gentle pat on his back.

The next batter came up. It was Jose Sanchez, a New York City kid spending the summer with his aunt. I had heard about him. John and his friends thought he was tough and at first he frightened them away. But as his hitting got better he became a real part of the team. Eventually, the boys were all cursing in Spanish.

"Hit the ball, Jose," I yelled. "You can do it."

"Bring 'em home," cried Jack. "Bring 'em home."

And although it took three fouls, two strikes and two balls, he eventually did. The hit wasn't strong enough to empty the bases, but it brought home the man on second, leaving runners, John included, on first and third. The score was 1-0.

Jack was on his feet. "Bring my boy home," he called out, but it wasn't meant to be. Three quick strikes and the inning was over, leaving John stranded on third and kicking the dirt.

The next four innings went by in a time of their own. Some were over quickly, some dragged on endlessly. There was a lot of time to sit, to think, to try not to think, to avoid conversation. It was exhausting. Being angry had exhausted me. I was ready to give up the battle, if only I could figure out how. I remember looking around me and thinking, where the hell are we? There were maybe one hundred people in the stands, people of all ages, little kids, brothers and sisters, parents, grandparents. But I couldn't even understand what many of them were saying. Yes, some spoke English. But many spoke Spanish or Portuguese or an English that was English but still incomprehensible. And I knew none of them. But I did begin to realize, sitting there, looking all around me, that I did know something about each one, just by the fact that they were all there in the first place and mostly wearing baseball caps.

We were in Boston so, of course, there were lots of Red Sox caps. But not exclusively. There were caps with university logos. Plenty from local businesses. A few imaginative, indecipherable ones. Even some Yankees caps. But all baseball. All American. At that moment, the whole world was American. At that moment, it felt like anywhere there was summer, there was baseball. There was America. We could be American anywhere. We could play baseball anywhere. We could live anywhere and still be home. Couldn't we? It made me think.

Jack could see how lost I was. He knew after all we said and didn't, there was nothing more to say. Instead, he screamed into the air. "Ducks on the pond!" he would yell when the bases were loaded. "Slide!" he bellowed whenever a batter ran towards a base. So the innings ticked by, flowing one into another the way one day flows into the next leaving you with a life spent too soon. And as they did, Jack's clichéd bantering began to make sense. It seemed to be all there was left to say, after all. And strangely, almost imperceptibly, it started to be enough.

Then, in the bottom of the eighth, tragedy struck. It was some kid from Providence with long arms and skinny legs who found the hole and hit the ball just hard enough to make it roll out of reach. A teammate, who had walked to first and then stolen second, ran home. The score was tied. One more inning of regulation play to go, but I knew we could run into extra innings if we had to. It was a tempting thought. There we were, Jack, John and me, in a part of town we had never dared to go before, surrounded by people who until that day led lives that had nothing to do with ours. With each walk from the dugout, our son would check on us. He would check not only that we were watching, but that we were still there, sitting on that hard bench together, his mother and father, next to each other. And we always were still there, together. I now realize that somewhere along the way, we had begun to feel more at home at the ballpark than we did in our own house, than we did in our own lives. If we could find home there, of all places, then maybe we could find it someplace else, too.

I suppose I should tell you how the day ended. Two outs. Luke singled to first, which propelled Eggshell to third. John came up to bat. He swung furiously. He hit the ball like his life depended on it. All three boys circled the bases, and then, one by one, slid into home. And I guess that's really the point of the story, the point of baseball. It's a long, torturous game, but it can change in a second. For us the season wasn't over, after all.

Chapter 17

John:
The Elusive Theory of Everything

Large chunks of lobster meat in a white hot dog roll. The simplicity of it was perfect. I nestled the lobster roll into the brown paper bag, right next to the lemon iced tea and underneath the bag of potato chips.

"Let's go eat on the jetty," I said to Lizzy and Peter and started to walk down the road to the dock. It was crowded in the village – August on the Vineyard is always crowded – but I didn't mind. I was content to dodge the cars and bicycles, the baby strollers and dreaming tourists, while Lizzy and Peter walked behind me, single file, past the antique shops and fish markets and then out to the beach. At six o'clock, the sun was still strong, but everyone was already anticipating another Vineyard sunset. The sunsets on this part of the island were famous. The entire sky filled up with pinks, reds, purples and yellows. It was so beautiful that people actually applauded. I often joked that those sunsets were almost enough to make me believe in God.

Considering the crowds, it was surprisingly quiet. I could hear the ropes clanging against the flagpole. The water made that kind of 'slurshing' sound as it rolled back and forth against the hulls of the fishing boats. Somewhere a child was crying. But other than that, we were surrounded by a quiet which I could almost feel, as if some old, well-worn sweater had been thrown around my shoulders. I felt warm and comfortable inside it. What a difference a hundred miles can make. Maybe getting out of Boston was going to do me some good after all, I remember thinking. I then started to smile. I know I was smiling because I also know I hadn't been smiling all that much since Lizzy had come to visit. She had definitely noticed. I could tell by the way she kept staring at me out of the corner of her good eye. So, when I realized I had actually begun to smile all on my own, I turned to look at her full in the face, to make sure she saw it. From the moment she arrived on the island the previous night, I could tell she was watching me. I have to say it still unnerves me the way her one good eye can transmit all the intensity that most people need two eyes for to convey. Maybe it's the contrast of the green of her seeing eye against the black of the patch over the other empty socket which makes her look so intense. But for the past twenty-four hours that eye had been boring into me like some electromagnetic sensor designed to find hidden answers in otherwise unreachable recesses. It made me uncomfortable, to say the least. So when I caught myself smiling, I made sure she saw.

The jetty was over a hundred years old. Somehow, it floated finger-like out into the sea; nothing but enormous, old boulders of mismatched rocks wedged together. Actually, it was a giant stonewall, just like the walls that dotted the landscape, originally dividing acres of farmland and now dividing acres of expensive views for wealthy holiday home owners. But this wall, this jetty we now approached, did not divide. Or, so it seemed to me. Perhaps it was originally created to separate the dock from the beach, or one sort of tide from another. But now I felt as if the wall of stone was combining – combining the land with the sea, my own heavy footsteps with the tails and fins of the

156

bluefish below and the particles that create me with the particles that create everything else.

"How far do you want to go?" Lizzy's voice eventually reached me. I guess I had forged ahead, hopping from one boulder to the next, while she was stepping more carefully, making sure each footfall was secure, her arms instinctively stretching out for balance. Peter was close behind her, but he knew better than to offer his hand for support. Lizzy never wanted help. "Let me fall," she used to say. "Just pick me up if I do."

"Let's go to the end, past the fishermen," I said. "We're almost there." It never occurred to me that walking over a hundred yards of uneven, jagged boulders could be hard for her. Nothing ever seemed hard for her and so I suppose I had long ago stopped thinking of her as handicapped in any way. But the truth is, that with just one eye she had very little depth perception and an unreliable sense of balance. No one would ever have guessed it, though. After surviving that plane crash and losing her eye, she could have gone through her life timidly, one tiny insecure step at a time. But she didn't. Instead, she plowed forward with the determination of a Sherman tank and she expected everyone else to do so as well. No, Lizzy no longer amazed me. I just accepted her strength as a given, like the pull of gravity, like the strong force between quarks.

When I reached the end of the jetty, I sat down leaving space for the other two and their bags of food. Soon, I felt Lizzy's hand on my shoulder as she lowered herself onto the rocks beside me.

"This is terrific," Peter said, sitting down beside her. "You feel like you're at the end of the world. Nothing but blue sky and blue sea everywhere you look."

"I married him for his poetic soul," Lizzy teased, "but can we eat now? I can't wait another second for this lobster roll." I was the first to take my sandwich out of the bag and hold it up to my mouth. I then looked at Lizzy, who did the same. The two of us turned to Peter to complete the set of three poised

157

lobster rolls, but instead, out of his bag Peter pulled a cheese-burger. What an abomination!

"Cheeseburger?" Lizzy and I both said at once.

"What? 'The Lobster Trap' makes great cheeseburgers, too." Peter took a bite and purposely allowed a yellow-red smear of ketchup mixed with mustard to linger on his chin. "You both are too judgmental. That's your problem," he proclaimed and not for the first time in our lives. I shook my head, looked at Lizzy and laughed. Not even the boorishness of my brother-in-law could keep me from my most favorite meal in the world.

We sat there for a while, happily eating in silence. Behind us, I remember two boys were dangling long fishing lines into the water. In the distance, a trawler sat fixed as stone in the middle of the Sound. An occasional sailboat glided by. I took a long sip of iced tea and closed my eyes. "This must be what peace feels like," I thought to myself.

A short time later, I heard the rustle of a paper bag. Peter had gathered together his trash and was standing up. "Where you going?" I asked.

"Thought I'd go for a walk along the beach. You two stay here. I'll meet you at the lifeguard chair in a little while." I had guessed this moment would come, that Peter (good husband that he was) would find a way to leave Lizzy and me alone. Of course, Lizzy was worried about me. But then again, I hadn't done anything to make her not be worried. To tell you the truth, I secretly liked having her worry about me, especially now that Amanda was halfway around the world. I had somehow convinced myself that by letting her worry, I was actually doing my sister a service, giving her something to do with her time.

"So. Worried?" I said, pretending to laugh.

"About what?" Lizzy tried to act confused, but the attempt didn't last long. Neither one of us could ever hide anything from the other. "Well, okay, now that you mention it, I am. What's going on with you?"

I tried to cover it all up at first – a sort of knee-jerk subterfuge, I suppose. "Nothing really. I don't know. I guess I've just been a bit down lately. But first, tell me more about Amanda."

"I showed you the pictures last night. They're healthy and happy and still married. Try again."

"Look," I said, facing the inevitable. "It's not that I don't want to talk about it, it's just that I don't know what to say."

"John ..." Lizzy was using her exasperated older sister voice.

"Lizzy, with that tone you'll get nothing."

"Okay. I'm sorry to sound impatient. But I've been hearing something in your voice every time we speak on the phone and it's been going on for months. I know you're not a big talker, but I also know you're unhappy." She leaned closer to me. "Have you had another one of those attacks?"

"What? The jaw thing? No, not exactly. But I'm back on those pills, just in case." As a joke, I patted out a rhythm on the pocket of my shorts so she could hear the rattle of the bottle inside. She didn't think it was funny.

"Jesus, John," she said, looking down into the sea and shaking her head. "Please. Talk to me."

So there it was. The big push to talk. But my mind went blank. I thought I was willing to talk. Really. That's why I had set up this visit in the first place. But, suddenly, I couldn't think of anything to say. No, it was even more than that. Actually, I couldn't think at all. Maybe it was the sea air. Maybe it was the lobster meat. But sitting there on the edge of the jetty, staring out into the vast, endless array of energy fields, quantum particles, string-like vibrating waves, my mind did go blank. I have no idea how long I sat there like that. At that moment, there was no time. But Lizzy waited.

It was strange what happened next. Slowly, eventually, individual ideas started to form in my mind. I could almost see them popping up out of nowhere on that mental screen of mine. First came the equation I had been working on before vacation. That was still a disaster. No matter what I did, the solution continued to be infinity or, to put it bluntly, nonsense. Infinity is great as a concept, but as the answer to a mathematical equation there was nothing worse. I guess I started to think about that, but then the idea passed and again there was nothing. I know I was vaguely aware of Lizzy sitting there wanting something sensible to come out of my mouth. I would have obliged her if I could, but I still couldn't think of anything to say that she would want to hear. I remember becoming increasingly aware of the breeze rushing over the hair on my arms. I mentally followed the sensation as it moved up my forearms to my biceps. Automatically, I flexed my muscles and felt the tension contract and then release. I did it several times – contract, release, contract, release – until my arms became tired. Thinking of my tired arms, I looked some more at all the water surrounding the jetty. Tired arms and water, a familiar childhood memory. Now here came a thought I could actually utter.

"Did I tell you I'm going to London?" I blurted out.

"What? When?"

"In a couple of weeks."

"A couple of weeks? You're kidding, right?"

"No, I'm not. And not only am I going to London, I'm going to South Kensington to a conference at Imperial College practically around the corner from the old flat." I stated all this in a rush, with the boastfulness of a man accepting a dare.

"Well, now I know something's up with you," Lizzy said, shaking her head. "After twenty years of avoiding the place, now you're going?"

"I haven't been avoiding it," I claimed. "I just never had a good reason to go."

"Bullshit," Lizzy argued with me. "You don't need a good reason to go to London. Everybody goes to London. Jesus, it's not like it's Siberia. Even I've been back. And my memories of the place aren't so great either, remember?"

Remember? I couldn't forget. It was the Christmas when I was sixteen that all the trouble started, or so I believed. Lizzy was in her last year of college and didn't want to come to London for the holiday. If anything, she had been boycotting the place. I knew even then, that she never understood why we had to move there. Other people's fathers had affairs, she said. They didn't pick up and move to the other side of the world. It made her feel deserted and angry. I understood that and had tried to explain it to my mother. But she didn't listen. She put her foot down and made her fly over. Then the airplane crash landed, Lizzy lost an eye and almost died, my mother felt guilty and tried to kill herself. Twenty years later, that's still how I described what had happened. One, two, three, cause and effect, all as simple as that. But, of course, there was nothing simple about it. Nothing is ever that simple, not when it comes to physics and certainly not when it comes to family. Some might say my refusal to see the complexity of my past was what led me to that moment there in the first place. Lizzy probably would have said just that. But sitting there on that jetty, I still believed there was a logical explanation to everything, an answer to every question just waiting to be discovered. There, more than anywhere else in the world, I felt connected to everything around me – the air, the sea, the ground – and all of it made me believe even more than I usually did in what we cosmologists call "TOE – the Theory of Everything" – that one, single explanation that encompasses all matter and all forces. I believed it exists for quantum physics, and so it must exist for people. I just hadn't figured it out yet.

I looked at my sister and then, instinctively, surprisingly, did something I had never ever done before. I reached up to her face and let my fingers brush over her eye patch. I couldn't believe I had done it and half expected her to swat my hand away. But she didn't. She didn't move at all. Then I heard myself ask the question that used to bother me a lot, but I had long ago given up trying to answer. "Lizzy," I asked. "How come you're not angry?" A lump lodged in my throat and I began to wonder, with great astonishment and embarrassment, if I was actually going to cry. It was ridiculous. "What the hell's going on with me?" I thought. It must be the wind, not that there was so much of it, but it was the only possible explanation. I'm sure I was about to apologize for ... whatever ... but Lizzy started to speak. I could barely hear her over the surf.

"Why aren't I angry? Maybe because you're angry enough for both of us." I said nothing, so she continued. "Look. Go to London. Go to the old house. Eat where we used to eat. Drink where we used to drink. Then let it go. For God's sake. Mom did the best she could. The rest of us forgave her. Why can't you?"

"It's not that easy," was all I could say.

"It *is* that easy. I did it."

"But maybe I'm just not as strong as you, okay? And it seems I'm getting weaker all the time," I muttered under my breath.

Lizzy started to protest. I knew she wanted to argue with me, tell me how silly I was, tell me she loved me. She certainly had said it all before. But every time she did, it turned out the same way. She tried to bolster me up, but it always just made me feel small. And although I had originally meant to allow this little talk to happen, now that it was here, I couldn't stand to go through with it. And besides, I didn't want to ruin the buzz of a good lobster roll.

"Look," I finally said. "I don't want to talk about it. I don't want to talk about *her*. But I will go to London. I have to go anyway, to meet with Yuri, to try to figure out this mess we've created for ourselves. And while I'm there I'll say hi to all the old ghosts for you." Then I started to laugh, remembering one of my favorite old toys. "Remember that old Ghostbusters gun I used to have? The one with the backpack attached and the sparks that came out? Maybe I should bring that along. What do you think?"

I could see Lizzy was trying hard not to laugh, but it was useless. We both remembered too well that old photograph of the little-kid-me decked out from head to toe in every bit of Ghostbusters gear our parents could find. Of course Lizzy had to laugh and so did I. I moved in to give her a quick hug, but she held on tight and for a long time. Even after we had both stopped laughing, I let myself rest there for a while, staring into space. Over her shoulder I saw a family of piping plovers hopping along the beach and in the distance, the lifeguard's chair and my brother-in-law, waving.

Chapter 18

Grace:
Gifts

London. The Old World. Not traditionally the home of casta-
ways and refugees. Not historically the place you run away to,
not the first place you think of for that. Quite the opposite. But
that is what we did and where we went and we weren't the only
ones.

It was simple. In one month, the decision to move was
made. In another, we were there. Six months later it felt like
we'd been in London forever. I realize not everyone finds moving so easy. But not everyone is running away as hard as Jack
and I were.

Jack immediately threw himself into his work. He loved
London's architecture, the old and the new. All of it seemed to
energize him. Back in Boston, work had become an obligation.
Now, he was so excited by it that he seemed to forget why we
had come to London in the first place, or so I hoped.

The move, at first, was hardest for John. He was lonely for
Boston, for his friends, for his baseball team. But soon his
school, which was populated by parents swamped in the guilt of
up-rooting their children, enveloped him in a Disney-like imita-
tion of American life that was even better than the real thing.

Halloween became a two-day festival. Hot dogs and Cokes were served at the soccer games. No head was without its baseball cap, no foot without its Nike. But there were the extra bonuses of pubs, a drinking age of sixteen, and the Tube, which was safer than the T and which his mother let him use, on his own, at night.

Lizzy, unfortunately, closed the door to her college dorm room and tried to make believe it wasn't happening. She would receive phone calls, but not initiate them. She refused to come visit. And she still wouldn't talk to Jack. As for me, I must admit, I was pleased with myself. I had done it – moved us to another part of the world, to another world entirely, created a home where our lives had a reliable rhythm and our surroundings comfort and familiarity. But most importantly, I had kept our marriage together. My self-satisfaction expressed itself, I see now, in an initial euphoria exhausting for those around me. But after what I had been through, I felt I had earned it.

We arrived in London in the midst of an epicurean explosion. Chefs had become the new celebrities. Restaurants were opening and closing like jack-in-the-boxes. I threw myself in with a dizzying delirium I hadn't felt in years. I even began to cook. I haunted the specialty spice shops of Westbourne Grove and the Asian markets along the Edgeware Road. I'd start off in the morning, my *A to Zed* in my pocket, in search of a new neighborhood treasure, that latest restaurant you could only get into for lunch, that open-air market full of unusually shaped South African fruits. A perfect day was to stumble upon an alien-looking vegetable all spiky and brightly colored in some obscure market, race home to experiment with its preparation and read restaurant reviews while strange smells simmered on my stove. I became what was then called a foodie. John tolerated it as long as he could have his weekly Big Mac. Jack loved it. He loved the excitement of not knowing what new taste he'd find at home. I think he loved the energy he was sensing in me and the passion I had unearthed in myself for new discoveries.

It was all very exotic. Charging around the city with the rest of the ex-pats made us feel exotic, too. In time, the two of us, together, began to heal.

After a few months of chicken jalfrezzis and porc cassoulets, squid-ink risottos and slow-cooked lamb tajines, it was my birthday. It wasn't a big, important one. My fiftieth had already come and gone right in the middle of my worst time with Jack. I hadn't felt much like celebrating then. But this birthday was different. We were in the midst of our new beginning and so Jack asked me how I wanted to celebrate, *if* I wanted to celebrate. I really wasn't sure. I didn't want a party. A visit to Boston was out of the question. It was still too soon, the specter of Melanie would have haunted us constantly. I would have loved to have the four of us together, but Lizzy wouldn't come and I didn't want to expect too much from John, either. That left Jack and me to celebrate on our own. Maybe we were ready, but maybe we weren't.

I couldn't help remembering Jack's own fiftieth. It was a disaster. He wanted to pretend it wasn't happening, but at the time I couldn't understand why. Of course I realized later it must have been the very beginning of his relationship with Melanie. The guilt probably hadn't even kicked in yet. He was still held captive by the passion and the heat of this new intimacy. The secret messages, the hurried caresses, the sweat, the racing pulses, the burning skin, all of it. Sometimes at night, later on, after I knew, I lay awake imagining what it must have felt like. Well into middle age, nearly fifty years old, there he was, overwhelmed by that fevered rush we had assumed died out decades earlier with the first pregnancy, the first mortgage. I had to admit it must have been wonderful. Of course he didn't want to be reminded of his age. He was ageless, fifty years old and mooning around like a teenager. When I thought about it later, I realized I was horribly jealous, insanely resentful, but not only about that woman. Not only about his relationship with her. What I resented just as much was that he had that feeling deep in his gut, that fire lodged somewhere above his groin, behind his spine, that spread every time he closed his eyes or smelled his fingers or touched his hair. He'd had that feeling again and I hadn't. This was the torture.

Of course, I didn't understand all that at the time. I didn't know why he wanted to ignore his birthday, why he didn't want any gifts, any acknowledgements. I thought it was just some mid-life crisis I could jolt him out of. So, despite his protestations, I threw him a party. It wasn't exactly a surprise. I told him our friends were taking us to dinner. At least that way I knew he'd leave the office and get to the restaurant. But when he got there he saw our table in a private room, twenty guests standing waist-deep in balloons and candles and flowers. Champagne flutes, caviar hors d'oeuvres and my triumphant face. Instead of delighted surprise, what I saw was glaring anger in his eyes, a distraught shaking of his head, and his back as he marched out of the room. I made a joke of it. I got him to come back in, but the damage was done.

Now it was my turn. What did I want? I knew, but I couldn't say it out loud. It wasn't jewelry or a trip. I didn't need to be surrounded by the cheers of friends and family. Any of that I could have just for the asking. No, the gift that I longed for was much harder to get. What I really wanted, was the feeling of that fire somewhere deep inside, still burning.

So what did I do? I went shopping.

Jack had booked us into the newest restaurant run by London's latest *enfant terrible*. It would be just the two of us among the studied petulance of waiters and silent culinary orgasms at the tables around us. John would be spending the night at a friend's house. Looking through my closet, I realized I needed a new dress. Despite all the cooking and eating, I had done enough walking and running to still look okay. Standing in a cubicle, surrounded by three mirrors, I looked at myself and thought of my mother. At fifty, she wore a girdle. Her hair was frosted. She wore 'hose' to hide her varicose veins. But not me.

The skin on my upper arms was slightly loose, but not flabby. The cellulite on my thighs was noticeable, but not horrifying. And my stomach, somehow, was flat. I found a dress cut slightly low in the front, lower in the back and long enough to make sense. It was silk and cool to the touch. The green was deep and varied and I hoped it would remind Jack of my eyes.

I was happy to meet him at the restaurant. I enjoyed the solitary cab ride through darkening streets. I sat back and looked out the window as we drove past Buckingham Palace. down the Mall and in towards Piccadilly. I imagined that people passing by would look at me and wonder who I was, famous or rich or somehow notable? It was a silly thing, but it made me feel good about myself. It made me feel valuable.

Jack was waiting at the table. That was the first treat. He was so often late I had taken to bringing a book with me wherever I went. He greeted me with a kiss, a glass of champagne and a look that was genuinely, I believed, full of love. There may have been gratitude there, too. I'm sure there was some relief mixed in. But, yes, there was love in that look and I remember briefly closing my eyes to store away the memory for future reference.

I remember everything about that meal, exactly what it looked like, smelled like, what it felt like to be sitting there amidst the linen napkins and crystal champagne flutes. It was magnificent. Every moment held a heightened importance and when I recall it, as I often do, I think about it as a time separate and distinct, unrelated to the past yet a gesture to the future.

I still know exactly what I ate. Pan-fried foie gras with a calvados glaze to start. The bite of the apple brandy was sudden on my tongue, a thrilling surprise and it smoothed the way down my throat for the firm-soft creaminess of the foie gras. Jack and I fed each other and when I offered mine to him, he received it with an opened mouth and steady, serene eyes. Those eyes. They were the first thing I ever noticed about Jack. A person's eyes are not always what you see first – for me there have been forearms stretching out of upturned cuffs, a muscular back working beneath a white T-shirt – but with Jack, it was definitely his eyes. When we first met in college, the day Kendall introduced us standing on the granite steps outside the library, the intensity of the blue of his eyes trapped me, the way they shone out from beneath his thick, dark brown eyebrows. And when I saw him once again after years of separation, striding across the marble foyer outside some other university's lecture hall, it was those deep-set, piercing blue eyes that assured me it was Jack, really, after all. That night, he looked at me in a way he hadn't for a long time. I let myself believe that he wanted what he saw. That was the best birthday gift of all.

My main course was a brochette of lobster and scallops. I remember actually gasping when I saw the plate. The fish sat perched like satisfied angels on a dune of roasted peppers and sun-dried tomatoes. It was like a piece of sculpture had been placed in front of me, but with an unworldly aroma. I just sat there, shaking my head, laughing. Next, Jack's sea bass arrived. We bent our heads over the dish to admire more closely the swirling brushstrokes of lemony green pesto. Jack leaned close to me. "I feel like I'm in the National Gallery of Food," he whispered. The waiter bowed and bid us "Bon appétit," but it took us several minutes before we dared disturb those creations with our forks.

It was perfection. It was absurd. But it was more real to us at that moment than much of what had happened during those difficult months before, when life was like a mire of anguish and confusion, sucking us downward like quicksand. It's not true that time heals wounds. Time is too unreliable. But our belief in each other and our belief that there could be such an absurdly perfect meal for us, Jack and Grace, on such a night, on the other side of the world, in a new life such as this … that did heal us. And so, the food really was more than exquisite. Its tastes were more than divine. And all because finally and without our realizing it, we had begun to be able to see and taste and feel again.

We sipped the wine slowly. It brought a delicious numbness to my brain, but an intensity to my senses. Each taste, each scent, each bite, each sip, each swallow infused me. With every forkful another shred of the pain lifted to reveal that something unexpected had taken its place. I didn't have a name for it then, but every time I thought back on that night, I remembered it the same way, and I know it is true. In place of pain, there was faith. We discovered it together and nurtured it first in that restaurant. And it was there, with us, throughout the cab ride home, into the front door, through the foyer and up the stairs to our bedroom, where a dozen red roses were waiting on the nightstand and the lights were low but still on.

Chapter 19

Grace:
Running in Place

It's nice to have money, especially when you blow up your life in one place and try to make a new life someplace else. You can buy fancy meals, fancy furniture, fancy trips. It keeps it all exciting for longer. But money can be dangerous, too. It can delude you into thinking you can protect yourself from life and the more money you have, the easier it is to delude yourself.

A few months after we settled into our flat in London, I hired a private trainer. To tell the truth, I probably hired her more for her name than anything else. Fiona Gladstone. Now that's British, for you. She was blonde and tall, with perfectly outlined biceps and a bottom like you read about in magazines. I felt healthy just being near her. Twice a week we'd meet in Hyde Park, rain or shine. First, we'd stretch; then, we'd run.

I have to admit I hated it. I never liked exercise. As a teenager I convinced myself it was anti-intellectual. Much better to be weak and misshapen. At least then you could fool yourself into believing you're too busy thinking to bother with that weird thing attached to your head, namely your body. But as you get older, your body starts forcing its existence on you. You realize you have to take care of yourself. If you don't, there's no amount of money that can save you. I learned that the hard way.

So, although I hated all the bending and lunging and squatting and running, I did it anyway. You see, I liked the talking. Fiona was my first friend in London. True, I had to pay her for her time, but if it hadn't been for her, I wouldn't have talked to anybody except Jack and a bunch of cab drivers for God knows how long. Within a month, Fiona and I told each other everything. She told me about her father in Essex. She told me about her boyfriend-the-disc-jockey who her father-in-Essex hated, about her brother in Spain with his two little boys who spoke Spanish better than English and who she hardly ever saw. And she told me about her mother who had died of breast cancer. I told her all about me and Lizzy and John and Sam and Jack and even Jack's affair with Melanie. The whole thing. I think she thought I was crazy because, despite the difference in our ages, I told her so much. And I'd say things just to make her laugh. I loved to tease her.

One day I said to her, "There are a hundred reasons not to exercise. Especially in England where it's always dark. If you grew up in Brooklyn like me, you'd know without being told you never run in the dark."

Fiona was usually a few strides ahead of me when I'd say things like that and then, just for spite, she'd speed up. But I can be stubborn, which she also came to know and her running faster just egged me on. I'd watch her legs pumping in front of me. Up, down, up, down. It was hypnotizing. But it kept my legs going, too. And my mouth. With each mile I listed another reason not to exercise. Heart attacks, physiotherapy bills, the exorbitant cost of sneakers – I had a million excuses.

When you spend that much time with someone, it doesn't take long for you to get attached. And attached I got. I started to feel like Fiona was my little sister. But she was a little sister without the complaints, the judgments, the expectations and the jealousies. My relationship with my own sister had become dif-

174

ficult. I think I felt worse about it than I let myself realize. I know now my attachment to Fiona wasn't only about Fiona. I somehow believed running behind her twice a week would make me feel better about Gina.

"You're running away again," Gina yelled at me when I told her we were moving to London. I tried to explain but I couldn't make her understand. I believed to save my family, we had to leave Boston. We had to get away from its memories and temptations. We had to get away from Melanie. But Gina would have none of it. "If there's a problem with your marriage, it's going to follow you to London. Make it work here." I felt misunderstood and that made me angry. How could my own sister judge me like that after all I had already been through? Of course, I realize now what Gina instinctively knew. My reasons for the move sounded good, but they weren't the only reasons. To be honest, Gina had been too easy on me. I was doing more than just running away. Now I know I used Jack's affair as an excuse. But that old flutter, that old, horrible restlessness had started to torture me again. I had buried it for a long time, but I hadn't tamed it and when it came back, it nearly drove me crazy. I began to feel as if it actually would drive me crazy if I didn't do something about it. But instead of trying to figure out, once and for all, what the flutter was all about, I ran away. I forced us to move. And not just once. First, to London and a huge rental flat in South Kensington. Then, barely a year later, to a house overlooking the canal in Regent's Park. Fiona thought I was nuts.

"Grace, why move house now? You just settled in. And you have such a lovely view."

I tried to explain that the flat was never meant to be permanent; it was just a place to land. A house would feel more like a home. Regent's Park was that much closer to John's school. But it was all nonsense. I couldn't really give her a decent answer, the same way I couldn't really explain to Lizzy why, once again, we were moving.

Lizzy was the other person upset when we left Boston. But that I could understand. Even though she had gone off to college and moved away from home, she still felt abandoned. It was bad enough that her father strayed in the first place, but as long as he had agreed to give up Melanie, she didn't understand why we couldn't go back to the way we were. She had almost lost her father, but now she was losing her home. And that was my fault.

"Mom, you say you want me to feel like London's my home, but how can I when you keep jumping from one part of it to another? Forget it. I'd rather just go to Aunt Gina's in New York."

Gina had surprisingly little to say about this next move. Probably because I didn't even tell her until it was all decided. At that time, we weren't talking very often. She was always in a meeting or on some business trip. I relied on my mother to fill her in on the necessary details of my life. It was easier that way. Just like it was easier to move than to settle, to run than to stop and look at where you were.

You know what they say about hindsight. But the fact remains I couldn't have done anything differently. That's who I was back then. Not long after the move to London I began to fear that I was in more danger than I realized. I felt more unsettled than ever. Even though I had saved my marriage, moved my family and created a new home, something was still wrong inside me. It doesn't matter anymore what name you give it – restlessness, lack of confidence, fear – something was devouring me. I was blind to all the warning signals and still I kept running. I didn't listen to myself, never mind anyone else. I can see it now like some old, silent film. There I was, hurtling forward like a runaway train, straight towards the edge of a cliff. No matter what I did, I couldn't stop myself. How much more would it take before I was actually tumbling over the edge?

About a year after we moved, Gina came to visit. It was the only time she came to London. She was at a conference in Paris and stopped overnight on the way home. Even now, I can remember vividly what she was wearing. Gina always dressed beautifully. She made a lot of money at her job and she spent plenty on her clothes. It used to make me jealous. But now, that image of her in her simple, incredibly expensive, black Armani pants suit makes me proud. She was smart, confident, elegant. She always looked just right. She always knew what to do. But I was aware even then she looked pale and drawn. Maybe she was just jet-lagged, I thought at first. I didn't look so great myself. We were just about to move to the new house. There were boxes all over the flat and I had been running back and forth between Kensington and Regent's Park every day for weeks. I was exhausted. I was also nervous about the visit. Even though a year had passed, I was worried that she was still angry with me. I was afraid of her disapproval and desperately wanted to believe that one hug would make it all better.

The sun was surprisingly strong that afternoon and the air was clear. We went to lunch at an expensive restaurant in Holland Park. I was hoping to impress her. I wanted to drink some wine and eat something fattening. She let me order it all, but I noticed she didn't eat much and hardly had anything to drink. I needled her.

"You're so thin. Eat something. Have a glass of wine. You don't have to work today."

And she tried, just to make me happy. But she distracted me by changing the subject and asking what I was doing with my days. I ranted a bit about not letting John get too wild. It was a dangerous time for him, I told her; he had more independence than ever, but still not a lot of brains. Just like when he was two. Then I found myself telling her about Fiona. I described the loop we did around the park. I mentioned all the landmarks we regularly passed – the Albert Memorial, the Serpentine. I wanted to make my life sound glamorous. It was my way, I suppose, of saying, "Look at me. I live in Europe. I've done something with my life, too." But when I think about why I happened to tell Gina about my personal trainer just then in the way that I did, I believe there was more to it than just showing off. Something outside myself, beyond my own hurts and disappointments, compelled me to talk about Fiona. She was ill and for some reason I wanted Gina to know. I remember exactly how I described finding out about it all.

"We're running," I said, as if it was a story. "She's ahead of me, I'm a few steps behind, blabbering between gasps for air about nothing in particular, when suddenly, nonchalantly, as if she was just asking the time, Fiona says over her shoulder, "They found a lump." I was so shocked I stopped running. It was right near the statue of Peter Pan. Fiona circled back to get me and found me holding onto Tinker Bell." Gina put her fork down, I remember, and stared at her roasted sea bass. At the time, I thought she was commiserating. I kept talking. "She said the doctor told her it was the size of a lychee nut. Can you believe that? A lychee nut, like you get in Chinese restaurants. What is it with these doctors? So, now she's having surgery, chemo, the whole nine yards. And she's only twenty-eight. It breaks my heart." I was talking so fast I took a sip of wine to slow me down. But when I looked at Gina, her face seemed funny. I thought she was about to cry. She pushed her chair back away from the table. What was she trying to get away from, I wondered. Was it me? What had I done now?

"What, Gina? What is it?' I asked.

At first, Gina tried to laugh. She used her napkin to dab at nothing on the side of her mouth, and then cleared her throat. Without even hearing one word from her, my heart sank. Whatever it was, I knew it was going to be bad. She pulled her chair back under the table and rested her chin in the cup of her hand. I could barely hear her behind the wall of her bent fingers. Her sigh sounded more like resignation than anything else.

"I have something to tell you," she said.

Gina's cancer was already advanced when she told me about it. The date for her surgery had been set. The tumor on her brain gave her headaches. Sometimes her eyesight would blur. She explained that she was lucky to have been able to continue working as long as she had, but she knew she would soon have to stop.

I began to cry. We had to leave the restaurant. When I finally was able to control myself, I started to say all the hopeful things I could think of. I can't remember them now. They were meaningless even then. It wasn't long after that visit that I was visiting her in the hospital in New York.

During Gina's operation, I sat with my parents in the waiting room. We drank too much coffee and didn't say much. Every once in a while my mother would say something like, "At least now they've cut it out of her. She's still young. You'll see." Then, my father would just look at the floor and try not to say what he believed was the horrible truth.

After the surgery, Gina had six months of chemotherapy. I called twice a week to check on her. I also called my parents at the same time, but those calls were harder for me to make. The veil over my mother's hysteria was very thin. Thirty-five hundred miles of ocean couldn't even muffle it. My father rarely got on the phone at all. When he did, I could hear centuries of old world fatalism in his voice. "Now you know something about life," seemed to echo in my head.

Sometime during all this, Fiona, too, had her operation and radiation treatment. She recovered well and was soon back with me twice a week in the park. It didn't take her very long to regain her pace. As for me, I was running faster than ever.

Chapter 20

Grace:
Ghost Town

Sometimes strange things happen to me. Maybe strange is the wrong word. Maybe I mean unexplained, unexpected. Or maybe these are the same sorts of things that happen to everyone, only I am more disrupted by them

I remember sitting in the backseat of a yellow cab. I had flown into New York from London a couple of days earlier. I knew it was going to be a terrible time for me. I was worried about having to leave Jack and John on their own. John was still in high school and I felt guilty not being there to help with all the frenzy of homework and late afternoon soccer games. And Jack... I never liked to be away from him. Maybe it's true that once the marital bedrock is shaken, it never really feels solid again. All this is to say that I was in something of an emotional state – uncomfortable with the reality of the city I left behind and troubled by the ghosts in the city I had come to.

For me, New York had become a ghost town. Not like in the Westerns. Not a ghost town where the town is empty, weeds tumbling in dusty wind, doors creaking off their hinges. But a town vibrant, kinetic, alive – yet full of ghosts. There were faces I knew too well, old teachers, neighbors, corner store owners. And then, there was the blurred background of painful memories. The city was overflowing with ghosts who seemed to jostle the living for space on the already overcrowded streets. Now I had come back, too, to add my own physical presence and emotional weight to the concoction, balancing the scales temporarily towards the temporal. But only briefly. I knew I had come, after all, to oversee the birth of another ghost.

The traffic was terrible. Gridlock on every corner. I had booked myself into a very expensive hotel halfway between my sister's apartment in the West Eighties and her hospital in the East Sixties. I had come not only to see my sister, but also to help my brother-in-law. I was shopping for meals; I was cooking meals; I was freezing meals. I was maid and secretary all rolled into one, doing more housework for my sister's family than I ever did for my own. My sister, of course, had her own housekeeper and cook and secretary, but suddenly they were paralyzed. They had become the walking dead, always getting in the way, never getting anything done. So I did it all. And not only was I doing housework, talking with doctors, fielding endless phone calls from well-meaning friends, but there were my daily cross-town trips to the hospital and then, worst of all, the phony brave face and the fake chirpy voice I put on to keep us all going. So, I spent a fortune on a hotel and told myself I deserved it. I needed it. I needed the turndown service. I needed the white, fluffy bathrobe. I was needy, all right. But the truth of the matter was I needed something I knew I could no longer have. I needed my sister, healthy and functioning. I needed her to be the sensible one, the one firmly rooted in reality. Although I was older, Gina always had two feet on the ground. I was afraid I would be lost without her and something as silly as a fluffy bathrobe wasn't going to change that.

So every day, sometimes twice a day, I would sit in a taxi in that traffic. I'd make notes, phone calls. I'd manufacture logistics and formulate strategies. Anything to keep my mind off what was happening. I found myself reverting to my old New

Yorker ways. I barked through the change window, "Don't go through the Park, you'll get stuck at Fifth," Or, "New York Hospital … you know where that is? You don't know where that is? Ok, go like you're going to Bloomingdale's and I'll tell you what to do next."

Then I sat back and checked out the driver's ID posted on the dash. I made note of his medallion number, checked the photo against the face I saw in the rearview mirror and tried to decipher his name. Was it Abdul Mohammed or Mohammed Abdul? I thought all those London cab rides had dispelled my basic mistrust of cab drivers. But New York survival instincts die hard. Within a week, I was just another skeptical, impatient fare, fidgeting in the back seat, trying not to throw up from the pungent sweetness of the deodorizer dangling from the mirror.

I kept myself busy in those cab rides. Maybe I should have used them as a much-needed quiet time, a moment to reflect on the inevitable pain around the corner. But I couldn't. I kept myself busy in the cabs, in the apartment, in the hotel room, even in my sister's hospital room. I talked with the nurses. I secretly read the notes from the night before. I patted my sister's hand and told her stories. I was always creating sound and static in my head to drown out the small, frightened voice inside me trying to make itself heard. Joking on the outside, I was screaming on the inside. I couldn't remember ever really screaming before. I could barely imagine what my voice would sound like if I tried. But the scream of terror, of anger, of frustration was there, deep inside me and it filled my head with a high-pitched squeal that, when I stopped to listen to it, sounded unmistakably like the word NO! As the days turned into weeks I took on the glazed look of a prisoner of war. It was like I was force-fed the minimum I needed to survive, but I was still starving. In my case, it wasn't for food. I had enough room service and hospital ham sandwiches. It was for something else. What, I didn't know.

One evening, I decided to go back to the hotel early. Gina had urged me to go and get some rest. I had already had a full day of preparing meals and commiserating with my brother-in-law. And my sister had a good day, that day. She was sitting up for a while. She ate some soup and Jell-O. She said hi to Jack when I called home. And she smiled when John got on the phone to say, "I love you." We had both accomplished a lot and she seemed stable. There was an available taxi with an English-speaking driver right outside as I pushed my way through the revolving doors and out into the night air. I told him my destination and sat back in the seat. I actually relaxed. I stared out the window and felt my hands unclench. I was able to crack my neck. Slowly pulling away from the hospital I noticed the first shoots of green starting to break their way through the hardened flowerbed. Spring would be coming soon.

I could feel myself smiling. I looked out the window. The traffic seemed unusually bad for that time of day.

"Lots of traffic tonight," I said. "Is something going on?" All of a sudden I felt surprisingly chatty.

"I dunno," the taxi driver answered over his shoulder. "But sometimes when they put up those parade barriers they divert all the traffic."

"Parade?"

"Yea. They've closed off all of Fifth Avenue. Tomorrow's Puerto Rico Day. You from out of town?"

I didn't know how to answer. Was I from out of town? I just grunted and sat back against the cracked vinyl seat.

New Yorkers love parades. I had forgotten. Whenever they can, they love to close down major traffic arteries and throw the whole city into chaos just so they can have an excuse to celebrate. The Puerto Rican Day Parade was always a big one. That and the San Gennaro Festival were good excuses to leave Brooklyn and head into the City when I was a teenager. "Mind your sister and don't forget to hold each other's hands," my mother would shout after us. Thinking back on it, I can't believe she let us go like that. God knows, I never would have let my own kids go to a parade in Manhattan, into that unpredictable crowd. There was one time, I suddenly remembered sitting there in that taxi, when Gina and I tried to get to the front of the crowd, squeezing between legs, ducking around elbows. For some reason, I was determined to make it up to the barrier. I kept tugging Gina along, but when I had broken through the front of the crowd I realized her hand was no longer in mine.

"Gina!" I cried out. Everyone around me looked, too. "Gina!" I screamed again. And I was just about to hurl myself back into the crowd when she came pushing through.

"Are you okay?" I asked, grabbing her hand. "Jesus, you scared the shit out of me."

"Sorry," she said, kind of laughing. "But all of a sudden someone lifted me up. It was like flying." Then after she saw me grimace, she said in a very matter-of-fact way, "Don't worry so much, Grace. I can take care of myself."

I must have sighed out loud then, because the driver glanced over his shoulder and said, "Sorry, lady, but the traffic's terrible. I'm doing the best I can."

"I know. So am I," I heard myself answer, and stared out the window again.

We reached Madison Avenue and were turning uptown. For no reason, the traffic suddenly lightened up. There was Ralph Lauren, Donna Karan, Calvin Klein and I barely had any time to peak in their windows. I started to think that here I was in New York and I hadn't done any shopping. Maybe I could take a couple of hours tomorrow morning and just go. Jack and I had planned a trip to Morocco over Easter and I could use a couple of summer dresses.

That's what I was thinking when we slowed down for a traffic light. Suddenly, we were the only ones on the street. No cars ahead of us. None beside us. I turned to look out the back window – the street was empty for blocks. The driver was silent as if nothing strange was happening, but I knew there was. Where did all the cars go? I couldn't explain it. Suddenly, in the middle of a detour. How unexpected. Where were all the people? The light seemed to stay red for the longest time. I could hear the engine idling, but that was all I could hear. No screeching motorcycles. No honking horns. Just the taxi, idling, in a suddenly empty street.

Then something startled me. It was a woman's face, come close up to the car window. She wasn't old or young. She wasn't ugly or pretty. She just was. And she was smiling. Then I realized she held in her hand a flower, a lily, like the ones I had seen at the hospital, but this one was in full bloom. For a split second, I even thought her hands were stained with dirt, as if she had just dug it out of the ground herself. She wasn't offering it to me. She didn't want me to buy it. She just wanted me to see it, to see her, to acknowledge them both. She stood there looking at me, smiling, the flower in her hand. As the cab pulled away, I turned to watch her until she was too far away to see.

I knew at that moment my sister was dead. And I was right.

Chapter 21

Grace:
Home for the Holidays

The night before her accident, Lizzy and I had a terrible fight. It was her last Christmas holiday in her last year of college and it felt like she was on the verge of leaving us forever.

I had started to miss her terribly. Now that we had moved to London, I hardly ever saw her. She made it very clear that we had moved away without her (which we had) and that she had no intention of making London her new home (which she didn't). Whenever she had a break from school, she had gone off to visit her Aunt Gina in New York. It made sense. It was cheaper, that's for sure, but it made me jealous. We fought about it all the time. "How can you not want to come to London?" I'd ask. "Everybody wants to come to London." But she was stubborn. It's true – I never did consult her about the move. She was already in college. I thought it didn't really concern her. How wrong could I have been? My one consolation, though, was that it was good for my sister. As Gina got older, she wished she'd had children after all. She never actually said so to me, but I knew it was true. Lizzy became the daughter she never had and in the end, she was a great comfort to her aunt.

But now that Gina was gone, Lizzy's feelings of anger, desertion, betrayal and fear were magnified a hundredfold. If only I had understood all that at the time, I might have been more gentle with her. But I didn't and so, instead, I put my foot down, believing it was best for both of us.

"Come home for Christmas, Lizzy," I said. "It will be wonderful, a real old-fashioned London Christmas. Just the four of us. The streets will be quiet. We'll hear the church bells ringing. We can peek into people's windows to see the lights on the trees, just like we did back in Boston when you were little." The more I described it, the more desperately I wanted it to happen. "Don't go off with your friends. Just come home." It started as a suggestion, but somehow changed into an order.

First, she called to tell us about a ski trip. This was the beginning of negotiations that would last through November. I was walking down the stairs and I could hear Jack on the phone in the living room.

"Aspen?" I peered into the room, already shaking my head. He gave me a look.

"Tell her no," I said. "Tell her I got theater tickets."

A week later, she called with another idea. This time it was a chance to meet her boyfriend's parents. It was my turn. "Really, sweetheart," I said. "I'm sure they'll understand. They'd probably be more impressed anyway, to hear that you're spending the holiday with your family instead of staying to see them." She didn't like that at all. Even Jack thought I was grasping at straws when I told him about it. By that time, I was like a machine on automatic pilot. I kept pushing forward unable to turn, blind to everything around me except my own desperate need to control. This time, Lizzy was getting the worst of it. It became torture every time I spoke to her. The argument hung over every phone call like a missile waiting to explode. Eventually, around Thanksgiving, Jack began to waver.

"Come on, let her stay out there if she cares so much about it," he said. "What's the big deal?"

"It is a big deal," I snapped back. "I want her home for Christmas. Period. Is that too much to ask?"

Jack was always trying to win Lizzy over. Ever since his affair, when Lizzy was so furious she didn't talk to him for over a year, he'd been trying to make it up to her. But I wasn't going to stand for it. I held my ground. Finally, I simply sent her the plane ticket. For a week or so she seemed to have given in. You see, I said to myself, it isn't such a tragedy. So she'll come and spend a few weeks with her family in London. How horrible could that be? I even planned a shopping trip to Paris. The night before she was due to fly, she started in again.

"I don't know why you're insisting on this, Mother," she yelled into the phone. "You have some happy little fantasy of what it will be like, but it's your fantasy. Not mine. London might be your home, but it's got nothing to do with me. I'm coming, but I'm not happy about it."

"What a selfish bitch," I said to myself. "What a spoiled brat!" I put my hand over the phone's mouthpiece and whispered furiously to Jack. "We're her family, goddamn it. She could spend some time with us." I was seething. Why was I so angry? Why had I turned this into the final showdown? Knowing the answers to those questions now doesn't change anything. Back then, it was all I could do to stop myself from saying the horrible, hurtful words which were on my lips. What I did say, though, and with undisguised pain in my voice, was "Well, at least *I'll* be happy to see *you*."

The details of the crash are still sketchy. I don't think they ever figured out exactly what happened. Just before touchdown the engines lost power. Instead of the easy drifting down onto lowered wheels, the plane literally fell out of the sky onto unforgiving tarmac, tons of metal flung onto the ground like a cartoon anvil hurled out of a skyscraper. Three people died. There were broken necks and terrible burns. Lizzy fell forward onto something sharp.

When Maggie from British Airways called, I almost got sick right then and there. I remember Jack sat up and looked at me and then gently took the phone from my hand. At first, I felt fear and nausea, but when I heard him say, "Western Ophthalmic Hospital, near Paddington Station," I felt two other sensations in quick succession – relief and then guilt. We threw on some clothes, pulled John out of bed, and ran out the door to hail a cab.

She was alive, they assured us. Some bad bruises and minor burns, but mostly the damage was to her eye. We walked up to her room, but before Jack could open the door, I grabbed his arm. I couldn't go in. I was paralyzed with fear.

"It's my fault," I said. "She'll never forgive me." It was John who eventually found the courage to open the door.

There she lay. Even from the doorway I could see the large, blue-black bruises on her arms and cheeks. She had a massive white bandage swathed around the right side of her head. Fresh stains of wet blood were seeping through it. Her bottom lip quivered. I looked at her. She said nothing, but a steady stream of tears poured out of her one, good eye. Slowly I approached the side of her bed, afraid that she would push me away. I reached out to her and gingerly cradled her hand in mine. When she left it there for me to hold, I began to sob. "Forgive me, Lizzy. Please, forgive me."

Lizzy spent that Christmas in the hospital. New Year's, as well. Jack went over every day after work. He'd bring flowers, tell jokes, smuggle in chocolate ice cream – the expensive American kind. At first I came early in the morning and was the last to leave at night. But then the nurses said my being around so much upset Lizzy and was hindering her recovery. So I stopped going as often. I had to stop. Even though every moment away from that room was a new torture for me, I couldn't hide from the truth. I had to see myself for what I had become, the one great obstacle in my daughter's life.

John was a surprise. Since our move to London I sensed that he and his sister were growing apart. Lizzy resented our move and the more her teenage brother grew to love the freedom and worldliness of his London life, the more Lizzy resented him, as well. But from the moment he saw her lying there in that hospital bed, he took charge, providing an emotional stability that neither Jack nor I could muster. While I was crying at her side and Jack was standing silently in the doorway, John made his way over to Lizzy's left side, pulling her vision towards him. "Thank God you're alive." Every morning, he'd pop out of bed early and rush over to be with her. He brought in a mini-stereo and set it up on the windowsill and the two of them spent their days listening to music. Sometimes, when I did visit, I would stand in the hallway outside her room for a minute and listen to their easy conversation and the soft tones coming from behind the slightly opened door. From that moment on, John became Lizzy's ballast.

After nearly a month, the bruising was gone, the pain had subsided, but her right eye was so damaged it was permanently shut. For the time being, there was nothing left for them to do but send Lizzy home. When the three of us arrived to collect her, she was dressed in her jeans and the new cashmere sweater I had bought her for Christmas. A black patch covered her eye.

"Well, gorgeous, ready to get out of here?" John asked.

"Why aren't you in school, you sluggard?" Lizzy teased. "How long a holiday do you Brits get, anyway?"

It was good to hear their banter and I allowed myself to relax a bit. Although I couldn't wait to get her home, I was also frightened. Once she was there, there'd be no escaping her anger or my guilt. She said she didn't blame me, but I knew that in her heart she really did. And she would continue to blame me, whenever there was a reminder of her new disability. I watched what I said every minute of every day. No mere mentioning of somebody's beautiful eyes. Forget about eye make-up. Even her photography class seemed off limits. And her boyfriend? I didn't dare bring him up at all. I was so busy trying not to cause her any more pain, I could barely talk to her. All I could do was stand by her side, smiling inanely, and touch her shoulder whenever she'd let me.

Lizzy herself was contained. She was a highly-glossed titanium safe, shining and smooth on the outside, but impenetrable. Locked away was all the fear, remorse, fury and horror she was trying to ignore, but I knew it would come out. It had to.

The doctor finally arrived to do his last examination, to officially release her back into the world. He was tall and thin. He dressed like a banker in his pinstriped suit. He looked tired.

"I'd like to see you in one month's time…" He looked at me, about to continue.

Don't say anything else, I thought. Just shake our hands and let us go. I remember feeling almost a sense of panic inside; I was so desperate to get us out of there before someone said something to make it even worse. But I couldn't stop him.

"There is one thing you'll want to consider…"

"A glass eye?" Lizzy asked and she sat up in her chair. Her back went rigid.

"Well, they're not made of glass anymore," the doctor started to explain, but she interrupted.

"No," she said quickly. "I've already thought about it and I don't want it."

"You have time to decide." The doctor was startled.

"I said, No. I won't spend the rest of my life pretending this didn't happen." She rose from her chair. She started to leave.

The doctor looked at Jack, who shrugged.

Lizzy picked up her suitcase and steadying herself on her brother's shoulder, she walked away. The doctor, Jack and I watched her pass slowly through the door and into her new life. As she made her way down the long corridor, I could see that she was talking to John. Her face, as it turned towards him, was serious and firm, but calm. Her voice was quiet, but I could still hear her.

192

"It's my decision," she was saying. "I see it all quite clearly, just the way I am."

I couldn't admit it then, but I know now I was starting to see more clearly, too.

And what I saw petrified me.

Part II

"People like us, who believe in physics, know that the distinction between past, present and future is only a stubbornly persistent illusion."

- Albert Einstein

Chapter 22

John:
The Uncertainty Principle

Back in the 1920's, a physicist named Werner Heisenberg developed a theory he called *The Uncertainty Principle*. Basically it says that you can't know two things at once. If you know the position of a particle, you can't know its speed and the more you know one, the less you know the other. So, it's where you're going vs. how long it's taking you to get there. Take your choice, but you can't have both. Sometimes, if you know anything at all, I guess you just have to count yourself lucky and leave it at that.

The one thing I did know was that I had already been to London and back again. I could clearly remember sitting in a series of conference rooms, listening to panel discussions about *The Theoretical Effects of Inflationary Perturbations* and *Entropy in an Accelerating Universe*. In my briefcase, I still had the crumpled napkins and half-torn handouts on which Yuri and I had scribbled possible solutions to the scores of 'what if' questions we had hurled at each other. Over those few days in London, we had snuck out of the proceedings half a dozen times. Whether it was in the corner of a deserted classroom or over beers at a local pub, being together kick-started us like a power jolt to some beat-up old engine. Sparks of new ideas jumped back and forth between us, generating a renewed sense of urgency and belief in our work – just as we had thought it would. But for me, it all happened in a blur. The speed of that trip, not to mention the speed of the few weeks that followed, was impossible to calculate. It made my head spin as if it was clamped into some high-speed proton accelerator.

I tried to explain it all to Marty the day I returned to Boston. They invited me over for dinner. I sat there with him, Beth and the kids, trying to collect my thoughts in between bites of mashed potatoes. But they were all shooting questions at me, then interrupting my answers with even more questions. Did I meet with Yuri? Did I see where I used to live? Where else did I go? Did I ride on a double-decker bus? It was exhausting. Talking to Lizzy the next day was even harder. She wanted details. Was I near Hyde Park? Could I see into the windows of the old flat? Was that pub, the Ferret and Firkin, still there? Did I go? I could come up with answers to those kinds of questions (yes, yes, yes and yes), but I knew that Lizzy, for one, was not really satisfied. What she really wanted were answers to the big questions that all those little questions were leading up to. How did I feel while I was there and how do I feel now? I would have loved to have been able to tell her that by going back to London I did actually break on through to the other side, in the words of that old Doors song. But I just couldn't say for sure. So much had happened and so quickly, that I couldn't keep it all straight. But I was able to come up with one story that I knew would satisfy her.

On the last day of the conference, I decided to take myself for a walk. After a few minutes I did find myself wandering into Hyde Park, just as Lizzy had imagined. I ended up on the steps of the Albert Memorial. There it was, looking like it did twenty-five years before. Nothing about it had changed. Even my reaction to it was the same. The statue amazed me. It was enormous, both in size and value. So much gold. But it was the symbolism of it that really floored me. Could it be true that

Queen Victoria had loved her husband so much that when he died she built this unbelievable monument to him? Could anyone really love somebody that much? I couldn't believe it when I was a teenager and I couldn't believe it now.

I took my time walking up and down and around until I had seen all 360 degrees of the monument. Then, I sat down to rest on the bottom step and closed my eyes. That's when the strange thing happened. A memory came to me, but not through my brain. It came through my nose. I had somehow closed out all the sounds of the cars and the people around me. I had even stopped being aware of the unusually intense August heat and the near-naked young women who had come to sunbathe in it. Instead, I focused on what I was smelling and I realized it was something I had smelled hundreds of times before, but not for many, many years. I was smelling the unique aroma of a London stroll in the park. Lilac and rose. A distant hint of diesel. Freshly mown grass and horse manure. I used to love that smell. It subdued me, calmed me. That's what it did when I was sixteen and it was doing it again now at forty-one. But it was doing more than that.

Suddenly, in that space behind my eyes, I could see myself in my memory. I was writing a poem for a High School English class, of all things, and the poem was exactly about that smell. I remembered being furious that I had to write the damn thing in the first place. But, as I sat there that day decades earlier, the poem just came to me. Without even realizing it, I had been noticing all those aromas and analyzing each one as if I was performing some science experiment. And then I wrote it all down. Everything was there for me in the park that day, ready and waiting, clearly explained and demonstrated. I only had to take a deep breath, think about it and set it out in short, choppy phrases. It was the first and last poem I've ever written and I hadn't thought about it forever.

That's what I told Lizzy about and the story did satisfy her. I let her read as much into it as she wanted. I certainly didn't make any connection between having such a memory and moving one step closer to some sort of mental health (especially since I still woke up at least one of those mornings in London and reached for my little vial of pills). But Lizzy probably did make such a connection and that was fine with me. If it was true, then great. There was my "breakthrough". And if it wasn't, then ... well, I was no worse off.

So, that was my trip to London. Five days altogether, over and back. I listened, talked, done a few calculations and brainstormed with Yuri. Then I went home. But it soon became clear to me that, just because I was back sitting in Marty's dining room it didn't necessarily mean that the trip was really over. Getting on an airplane, getting out of Boston, spending time with Yuri, imagining what else could be possible in my life, all set up a kind of chain reaction. One step led to another and the next thing I knew, everything was changing. If I had been on automatic pilot before, now I was like an unmanned rocket, zooming ahead at unbelievable speed, attaching myself to a course of action which would eventually carry me away to who-knows-where. Even before I had unpacked, I was standing in my Dean's office, leaning over his desk and convincing him to grant me an emergency three-month sabbatical. I gave my classes for that semester to other already over-worked professors. Marty and Beth agreed to check on my apartment from time to time so I wouldn't have to sublet it. One by one, all details fell into place with remarkable ease. So much so, that some might have said, "it was meant to be".

So, soon, before I had time to realize what I was doing, I was sitting in yet another airplane. I buckled my seat belt, made sure my tray table was up and stared intently out the window at the clouds rushing by. To the casual observer, I might have looked like a man afraid of flying. But it wasn't the flight I was afraid of. I probably knew more about the mechanics of air flight, not to mention the practical applications of Newton's Third Law of Motion, than anyone else on that plane, including the pilot. But as I sat there on that early September morning, it was finally beginning to dawn on me that I actually was afraid. It had been just three short months since Amanda's wedding. For some reason, that event stood out in my life like the starting gate at Churchill Downs. So much had happened since then and all at break-neck speed. I tried to replay it all in my head, but everything I thought of seemed totally unbelievable. First I had started and then ended an affair with a student. Never before and, hopefully, never again. Next, I returned to a past home that had been haunting me my entire adult life – and survived. Also, in the midst of it all, I found myself locked with my old friend Yuri, in the kind of furious, blood-boiling scientific race that I always associated with *Around the World in Eighty Days* or *Those Magnificent Men in their Flying Machines.* And, to top it all off, I was now flying away from Boston just when the Red Sox seemed unbeatable. If all that could happen in three short months, then what would come next? You bet I was afraid.

It seemed like only a minute had passed before I heard the clunk of the landing gear lowering into position. Hardly a second more and I felt the jolt of the plane hitting the tarmac. I took a deep breath and looked outside. The sun was bright and the sky was blue and clear. A long, unexceptional two-story building came into view. Lots of cement. Not much glass. And then, as the plane turned to taxi into its gate, I saw a row of huge white letters attached to the roof. They weren't English letters, but they were all recognizable nonetheless: "MOSKVA." Where was I going? I still didn't know for sure. But at least this was a clue.

Chapter 23

John:
Entangled Particles

"Nice car," I joked. There I was, sitting next to Yuri in the front seat of an old, blue Skoda, watching the Russian landscape speed by.

"It is my sister's," Yuri explained, at first with a content, almost smug look on his face. He obviously hadn't gotten the joke and it was just as well, because I soon looked down at the odometer - 128,314 and counting.

But then he said, "Okay. It is old. But it still works. In Moscow cars are not so easy to get."

"Well, believe me, I'm grateful for the lift. I guess I didn't realize how tired I'd be. Thank your sister for me."

"You can thank her yourself. We eat at her *trater* tonight."

"*Trater?*"

"Restaurant. There. Your first Russian word. But now we go to your new flat."

Yuri had arranged everything – the visiting professorship, the university-owned apartment, even access to that highly secure palace of science, the Lebdev Institute. It was astonishing.

"You know, I still can't believe it," I said staring out the window while I talked. "How long ago were we at the London Zoo, sitting in that horrible bird house?"

"Three weeks. I love that place."

"I hate it."

"Of course you do. You and your nightmare memories."

"I know, I know. But I spent too many hours there as a kid, hiding away from, well, everything. But it should show you how good a friend I am that I even went there with you at all."

"Yes. And now you see how I repay you. A whole new life."

I was beginning to realize, speeding down the highway, how Yuri had probably been waiting all conference long for just the right moment to "pop the question" about this so-called new life. It was almost as if he had gone to London with the express purpose of bringing me back to Moscow. Everything must have been arranged in advance. It was the only answer. How else could all of this come together so quickly? A Russian trap, if ever I'd seen one.

"Well, I do have to admire the way you pulled this off," I said, but it was impossible to hide the skepticism in my voice.

"Oh, well, the University was easy. A Visiting Professor from America? And you come cheap. Convincing you was much harder."

"You took advantage of me in my weakened psychological state."

"You have been in that weakened state too long. You need some good Russian cooking, some vodka…"

"And I suppose I need you?" I laughed, but Yuri wasn't really joking.

"Yes, you need me. We are tied together. *Pravda*? Like, we say, a 'quantum entanglement'. You are pushed in Boston. I fall over in Moscow."

It was an old joke between us, but it seemed to become truer all the time. And now that we had been working together, our brains were even more in synch than ever. It was eerie, actually, but somehow also comforting.

Yuri pulled off the highway and drove across a four-lane bridge. We were well and truly in Moscow now. Everywhere I looked I could see the gilt dome of another church, the arrow-like steeple of another government building. I was squirming around in my seat, trying to see everything as it rushed by. Yuri started to laugh. "You know, I just had a funny thought," he said. "Remember the time I first met your mother? Back in school? Back in the old days?"

"Yea ... so?"

"Her nurse. What was her name?"

"Florence." Just the thought of her made me laugh, too. "She was so big."

"And such dark black."

"And bossy. Jesus."

"Never did she believe I was from Russia. Like it was some joke. Even then, when my English was not so good. She would not believe it."

"I know."

"And now you are here, too. Yourself."

"I know."

"Funny, yes?"

"Yes. Funny."

Over the next few miles, Yuri tried to point out landmarks as they sped by. "This, the hotel where artists lived. Over there, the Cathedral, rebuilt." But soon, barely slowing down, he turned into a side road and parked. "Okay. First stop."

Now, this moment I can never forget. I got out of the car and looked up. I stood there for a few seconds, walked back several yards and looked up some more. I could hear Yuri chuckling behind me, but I couldn't help myself. I had never seen anything like it. "*This* is the University?" I asked.

"The main building. Administration, some classrooms. You can see it even from across the river."

"No shit." The building was gigantic, a huge white stone structure flanked by two enormous towers. Each section narrowed its way up to a point, the wings housing blue and gold clocks, the central tower topped by a silver spear holding a Russian star. "It's absolutely massive," I said, shaking my head over and over. "It makes me feel…"

"Insignificant?"

"Yea, like some atomic particle or something. Like a neutrino."

"Yes. I think that is the point," Yuri said, rather hushed, I recall. "But don't worry. You get used to it." I thought I had known before what it was like to feel small. But living in the shadow of this, I thought I might lose myself completely. "Come," Yuri said. "Your apartment is just here."

I followed him into a tall, cement-block building and watched as he babbled in Russian to an old woman, complete with *babuschka* on her head, sitting behind a desk in the foyer. Slowly, she pulled out a box of index cards and thumbed through, one by one, until eventually she found what she was looking for. Only then did she nod. It seemed to take forever. In the meantime, I noticed a large bulletin board off to the side. It was covered with printed flyers and handwritten notes, all of them in Russian, of course, all of them indecipherable, except one. Pinned underneath a stack of sheets, barely visible, was one small notice in English. It read, English Lessons. Typing. Call Olga. For some reason, that made me feel even more overwhelmed. I remember imagining, while I stood there waiting for Yuri, me walking the dark halls late at night, looking for this Olga – maybe old, dumpy, short hair sticking out of a scarf on her head – just to have someone to talk to. Not a pretty thought and for the millionth time in the few hours since I left Boston, I found myself wondering, "What the hell have I gotten myself into?"

"Okay, I have the key," I heard Yuri behind me. "Come. We move you in. Then we eat." As we walked into the elevator, he showed me a single key on a red ribbon. "Tenth floor. Almost the top. Good views, maybe even across the river. We will see now." The elevator jolted and clanked at each floor. I kept thinking how lucky I was to have traveled so lightly. Moving an entire life's-worth of stuff into this apartment building would have taken forever. Eventually, the door slammed open and we were in the middle of a long hallway with whitewashed halls and flickering fluorescent lights. Yuri's stride was twice as long as mine and by the time I arrived at my new home, the door was open and he was inside. I watched him walk around the flat, motioning at each door, each window. What I saw made my old apartment back in Boston look like a palace. Basically, here was one large room divided into three smaller spaces, punctuated by an occasional piece of institutional wooden furniture – a bed, a desk, a table, some chairs. I don't know what I had been expecting – the worst probably – but what I saw certainly didn't exceed it by much. I wasn't unhappy, I don't think. It was clean and it was quiet. But that was about it. As I tossed my bags into their appropriate areas, I noticed Yuri standing by the window. He was nodding and smiling. "Yes, look. You do have a view of the river. John, you will live like a Tsar," he said. "Three whole rooms, just for you. Even a bathroom."

"*Even* a bathroom?" I remember thinking. Well, welcome to Russia.

By the time we finally pulled up in front of his sister's restaurant, I was exhausted and ravenous. "Vodka right away," Yuri advised. "Then you feel better." He pulled open a thick wooden door and led me downstairs through a second, inner door, which in turn led to the *trater*. I looked at him and saw a ridiculously proud smile plastered all over his face. "Now you meet my women," he said.

Two rooms stretched out in front of us, separated by a small bar. Everything was blonde wood, simple, clean and comfortable. The sound of Russian voices and Russian laughter was everywhere and it helped me relax. A tall, slim woman with black hair and excited eyes approached, talking as if in mid-conversation. Yuri gave her a kiss and even before he could introduce her, she was embracing me and kissing both my cheeks.

"At last. It is John," she said with a deep, guttural accent which was surprisingly appealing.

"John," Yuri said with a dramatic flourish of his hand, "my wife, Natalia. Natalia, *this* is John." Finally, after all those years, a face to fix into the stories and the long-distance concern. She was beautiful, but in a way I had never really seen before. Her smile held a sort of stillness in it, which gave her a natural, easy quiet. She was nearly as tall as Yuri, but barely a quarter of his size. Yet, she was far from fragile and seemed to fill the space she inhabited completely. Is there such a thing as a shadow with substance? If there is, then that was how she seemed to me from the moment I first saw her.

Natalia took my hand and led me through the restaurant to our table. The air was warm and filled with the scents of tomato, oil frying, lamb and cinnamon. Already waiting for us were four small glasses filled with the clear liquid that could only be one thing. I remember watching Yuri reach for a glass even before sitting. He raised it as if to make a toast, but then a shout came out from behind the bar and a woman rushed over, shaking her head and clicking her tongue. It had to be Elena.

"What? You don't wait? What's wrong with you?" she scolded Yuri, kissing him at the same time. Then she pulled me to her and kissed me as well. She started to laugh as she handed out the rest of the glasses. "Now we can start. To John. Welcome to Moscow. Welcome home. *Na zdarovya.*"

"*Na zdarovya,*" echoed Yuri and Natalia.

"*Na zdarovya,*" I said, too, remembering the words from my childhood, from my grandfather's resonant voice at the end of the dining room table. I watched the three Russians finish their vodkas in one gulp. I did the same, but with a small cough at the end.

"Like a real Muscovite," Yuri teased.

It's hard to describe the dinner that followed. Everything felt magnified. Tastes, smells, language, music were all new and yet, somehow, familiar. Everything seemed to echo something from a distant, though suddenly retrievable past. I felt as if I was ten years old again, listening to my grandparents' stories of 'the old country'. Sitting there in that crowded *trater*, I could almost feel the overly heated air of my mother's old Brooklyn house lingering on the back of my neck. Maybe it was the jet lag, or maybe it was the vodka, but I remember everything feeling more intense, more spirited than anything else I had felt for a very long time.

Elena had arranged a traditional feast. One after another a new platter came out of the kitchen, filled with food I could remember from years back. Only this was better. Now, I liked what I was tasting. First borscht, then salad, then a plate full of different fish, some smoked, some fried. Cabbage filled with minced lamb and raisins. Eggplant smothered in tomato and onions. And more and more vodka. I can just imagine how red my cheeks were by the end of it all. I know I rolled my shirt-sleeves up above the elbows, sat back in my chair and patted my stomach.

"Look at me," I said to them. "One meal in Russia and I'm already acting like my grandfather."

"I knew you were Russian," Elena said, lifting her glass once more. "One look in your eyes and I could see it." That was the first of a million such tossed-off declarations of faith Elena filled my head with over the next few months. It got to the point that I could see one coming a mile away. But this time I wasn't prepared.

"You could see it? See what?" I asked, laughing.

"Your Russian soul."

Now Yuri began to howl with laughter and slapped me on the back. "Watch her," he said, pointing to his sister. "She believes. She takes scientists' brains and turns them in and out."

"Oh, yea? We'll see about that," I said, raising my glass. "You don't scare me, Elena. I have a big sister of my own, you know." I downed my last glass of vodka for the night and slammed it on the table. But I think I stood up too soon, because the room started to sway and I had to steady myself against Yuri's shoulder. He took me by the arm and turned me towards the door.

"To bed," he demanded. "Tomorrow, it all begins."

Chapter 24

John:
Dark Matter

That first night in my little bed in my little apartment with its little view of the Moskva River was not easy. I was exhausted beyond anything I could ever remember and that was the good news. That exhaustion was probably all that stopped me from picking up my bags and heading back to the airport. Sure, I'd had a fantastic dinner and a wonderful evening with Yuri and his family. But now that I was alone I felt lost, bewildered, anxious. I didn't head back to the airport, though. Instead, I poured myself a glass of water from the kitchen sink (could I drink the tap water and not get sick, I wondered?), took one of my pills (could I take one despite all the vodka?), and got into bed.

The day replayed itself like a movie in my head. How many hours ago had it even begun? When was it that I locked up my apartment in Boston and drove to the airport? It felt like a lifetime, though, because before I knew it, there were the 'Seven Sisters', those enormous matching skyscrapers, looming beyond the river, piercing the sky over Moscow. And there were church domes, hundreds of them in blues, golds, reds and yellows. Yuri had called them 'the people's testimonials to the survival of God'. And finally, on the way home from my 'Welcome to Moscow' dinner, seated again in the front seat of the old Skoda, I saw that most famous sight of all, St. Basil's and Red Square. Was all of that in just one day? Even taking into account a notion of accelerating spacetime, it seemed inconceivable.

After dinner, Elena had offered to drive me back to my apartment and I was too tired to argue. The vodka had worn off and left me with a dull headache and a sense that I was somehow floating in space. As Elena drove through the city, I noticed a sort of communal silence that the entire city seemed to share with us, until I broke it with my first glimpse of St. Basil's. The sight of it made me inhale so strongly that even Elena had been able to hear my gasp over the rumble of the car engine. "Okay. Come," she told me, pulling off to the side of the road. "A short stroll through Red Square before bed."

It was actually a beautiful evening. Moscow wasn't an eternity of winter, after all. The September night air was just as I would have expected it to be in Boston. Crisp, cool, but with lingering warmth from a still strong sun. Elena led me through the red brick gate and, without a word, gestured to the scene around us. Within a few steps, there they were ... the domes of St. Basil's. The building was lit so that the colors looked electric, the textures swirling. I was speechless. I couldn't even begin to understand, no less articulate, what I was feeling. It was as if that one building stirred up every image, every association I had ever had with Russia. Dr. Zhivago riding on an endless, curving road. Snow and bare trees. Julie Christie in her fur hat and long coat. Horse-drawn wagons with fur blankets. Balalaika music. Even, I had to admit, that wretched Disney song, 'It's a Small World After All'. From somewhere deep in my past, a romantic fantasy of the indomitable Russian spirit pitted against a harsh Russian reality flooded into me.

Then, just like that, for the first time that day, probably for the first time ever, I fully realized what I had done. I didn't mean to say it out loud. I didn't even know what the words really were until they came out of my mouth. "Shit. I'm in Russia," is what I said. Not very profound, nor very eloquent. But Elena looked at me as if I had just divulged my deepest, darkest secret.

Sometime later – who knows how long – I was lying in my new bed, in my new apartment. It was still night and the light from the street lamp cast a halo outside the window. I couldn't sleep. My body was well past exhaustion, but my thoughts were still hurtling along. "Tomorrow I'll unpack, first thing," I thought. I'd find the cables and converters and set up my computer. "The sooner I get to work, the sooner I'll feel at home." Home, whatever that was. It wasn't Boston right then. Not really. Now it was these few rooms which Yuri had so quickly pointed out were luxuriously 'just for me'. I shifted position to try to get more comfortable. I could see the stack of suitcases piled up against the wall and I remembered the photo of Lizzy, Peter and Amanda at the wedding I had packed at the last minute. Just three short months ago. Jesus, it was hard to believe. I could see Amanda standing there in her gown. I could remember being forced to dance the hora with Lizzy. And now Amanda was in some island in the South Pacific. I was in Europe – shit, I was nearly in Asia. We had all been together and now we were spun apart. But Amanda was with Tim. Lizzy had Peter. And me?

I closed my eyes. The light from outside moved like a phantom behind my lids. It created a circle, an image like the sun with thousands of photons shooting out in random patterns into the surrounding dark matter. The longer my eyes stayed closed, the more darkness took over the light. It didn't scare me, the darkness. The whole idea of dark matter was something I always found somehow comforting. The universe was full of it, even though it couldn't be seen; maybe that's why I loved it. I couldn't see the dark matter. Nobody could. But I knew it was there. I could feel it. It had mass, because it had gravity and so I could calculate it, bring it into my own small world and make it mine. Dark matter was inside me now, I knew, behind my eyes, working its way around my brain and down into my arms, my legs, my chest. I had taken it inside me and it filled me up. The darkness wasn't the lack of something. It was a substance of its own. It had matter, reality. I had matter, reality, and that thought finally consoled me, there in that bed which was now just for me, alone.

Chapter 25

John:
When Beams Collide

Bodies are adaptable, even mine, and it didn't take long before my legs could automatically make their way from my apartment to the office I now shared with Yuri. 'Shared' was really overstating the case. In fact, it was Yuri's office with Yuri's books on the shelves and Yuri's scribblings on the blackboard. I had been given a table under the window, just large enough for my laptop and a glass of strong tea. When I first saw the set-up, I must admit, I mumbled something about playing the part of Yuri's 'lovely assistant', but I felt bad about it as soon as the words came out of my mouth. I didn't mean to complain. It was a wonder they had found any space for me at all in that dusty, dark, cramped, old physics building.

It hadn't taken long for Moscow University's Physics Department – Cosmology Sector to start getting their money's worth out of their new visiting scholar. There had been a one-week settling-in period, then came the request for a special graduate lecture on holography. Preparing the talk had been much harder than I had thought it would be. It's not that I didn't know what to say – if anything there was too much to cram into fifty minutes. I knew the topic better, perhaps, than anyone else in the world (that's why I was there in the first place, after all). But nonetheless, I was nervous, not energized or revved up as I normally would have been. I was really nervous – shaky hands, tightened jaw muscles, the whole bit. But I didn't know why. I spent the morning alternately staring at my notes, then at the brown streaks of dirt on the window above my table and then at the small vial of pills I kept hidden in the back of the desk. I hadn't thought of hiding them, but when Yuri saw me unpack them on my first day at work, he threw a fit.

"John, what is this?" he scolded, as if he was my mother finding a bag of pot in my underwear drawer. So I told him.

"I take them sometimes. They help with the tension, the jaw thing."

"And how do they make you feel? Good?" he asked, not even trying to hide his sarcasm.

"No, not good." I had to be honest. "More like tired, not really there, but at least functioning."

"Barely. How can you think with these?" he yelled at me and actually tried to grab them out of my hand. I wouldn't let him. I don't know where I got the strength to push him back. He's so much stronger than I am. But I suppose I was still more desperate than I had realized. No, I wouldn't let him take them away from me, but I did have to promise I'd stop using them, or at least try to stop. It was quite a scene and a good thing one of our students didn't walk into the room just then. It must have looked like we were in the middle of some barroom brawl. Actually, though, Yuri was the only person who ever challenged me about those pills. Not Marty, not my doctor, not even Lizzy. I never talked much about them, but I never hid the fact that I was on medication, either. Their existence just hung there among us like some thickening radiation cloud, something we all knew was bad, but something we all tried to ignore. But not Yuri. "When you were a kid, okay," he yelled at me. "You were fucked-up. I know. But enough. Be a man, John." Easy for him to say, but, truthfully, I did want to stop using them. I hated the way they clouded up my brain and made me feel outside the rest of the universe. It was just choosing the right moment to stop that was the problem. And this moment, before this lecture, my first one before a room of Russia's most inquisitive young scientific minds, couldn't possibly be the right one, could it? So I sat there with the vial in my hand, not opening it, but not letting it go, either.

Eventually, sitting there and staring and thinking about what I was actually going to say to these people in that lecture hall, I began to have an inkling about what the problem might be. It was the students themselves. Sure, they spoke English. But there was English and there was English. It first dawned on me that this might be a problem, when I told Yuri the title of the talk. I had been told that the poster for the departmental notice board needed a shorter title than the original, 'Emerging Applications of Holographic Research to Theoretical Physics'. Something snappy, I thought. Something cute. "How about: What is Reality?" I had asked Yuri. He then looked serious, nodded and rubbed his chin. "Get it?" I urged. "It's kind of a joke?"

"Yes, I understand. What is Reality? An important question of philosophy. But a joke?"

That's when I realized that Russians, Russian physicists at least, don't do cute. Intense, serious, impassioned, visionary, yes. But cute? And that was a problem for me. For years I had believed that 'cute' was my best bet for getting into my students' hearts. And getting into their hearts was the surest route into their heads. When I taught, I teased and mocked and joked and wheedled and did every sort of tension-reducing trick I could think of. Because I knew that if physics students were anything at all, they were tense. And if they continued to be tense they could never open themselves up to entertaining the nonsensical, crazy, counter-intuitive ideas that were the key to theoretical thought. But how could I do that here in Moscow? I could just see myself standing at the front of the lecture hall, looking up at row after row of those earnest, furrow-browed faces and dying a thousand deaths. In nearly twenty years of teaching, I had never been so nervous.

I needed a break. The hall outside my office was deserted even though it was the start of a new school year. Where was everybody? In class? Hiding? One young student, clearly an undergraduate, was sprawled half-asleep on a bench carved into the cement wall. Other than that, though, I was alone. Walking down the hall, I passed one severely closed door after another, each one covered with thick red leather padding as if a series of Doctor Frankensteins were hiding behind, cackling. After a couple of weeks, the place still gave me the creeps. When Yuri brought me there on my first day of work, I couldn't hide my reaction, no matter how I tried. The halls were dark. The floor was dingy. There were hardly any windows. "Institutional, yes?" Yuri had laughed, seeing my face.

"Yes, 'institutional,' as in mental institutional," I think I said. I didn't mean to be insulting, but I couldn't help myself.

"I know," Yuri admitted. "But only because it is old. There is no money to fix the building. But the people are good and the research, important. And the history – you will see. It is everywhere."

Walking alone to the end of the hallway, I now found myself in the midst of all that history. The foyer was full of glass cases housing decades of important papers, photographs, even military medals. The entire story of theoretical physics was displayed around that room. The pre-war era, the Soviet age, and now here, today, and my looming lecture. Separating each case was a wall full of portraits and name plaques, many of them Nobel Prize winners. It was intimidating but, to be honest, it was inspiring, as well. The longer I stood there and the more I looked around, the more proud I became. Slowly, I began to realize that I, too, had now taken my place, if only for a short time, among this astonishing tradition of scientific thought.

Yuri found me staring at a portrait of Einstein. "Okay," he said. "So he wasn't actually Russian. But we adopt him anyway. Like we adopt you."

"So, there you are," I said. "Finally. Walk with me, will you? I need to bounce around some ideas."

Together, we walked down the stairs and past the building's caretaker behind his wall of glass. This nameless old man ruled the building like some mythic gatekeeper. Without his approval, nobody entered and it took some time and Yuri's insistence before he gave that approval to me. Now I knew just to nod without smiling and grunt out "*Dobriyi outra*" in the morning and "*Dosvedanya*" at night. Yuri and I wound our way down the street, through a grassy quad, to the river. The Moskva River, which meanders around the rest of the city, runs straight beside the university campus. Now that morning classes were over, the pavement beside it was full of students, some rushing off to their next lecture, some strolling in the autumn sun.

"It's not the content of the lecture," I tried to explain, barely looking around me. "I'll keep it simple to start. First, define the process – I'm sure they already know how holograms work, but it's good to remind them of the basics. Beams splitting, beams colliding, that sort of thing."

"And the interference pattern slide? Did you get the projector?"

"Yea, I hadn't realized I had to order that in advance. But I got it. Then I thought I'd go on from there to black holes…"

"…and entropy, yes…"

"Then I'll talk about Maldecena's calculations and ease them towards what we're working on."

"Oh, no. Do not do that." Yuri's face clouded over.

"Why not? It's his early stuff. And anyway, we haven't heard a thing from the South Americans in over a month."

"Yes. Exactly. And that is why not. There is an old Russian saying…"

"Oh, no, not another one," I teased. But Yuri wasn't joking. He stopped walking and pulled me off to the side and out of the rush of passing students.

"No joke, John. In English, it is, what?" He paused and looked up into the sky for help. "Yes. Listen. 'You need not be afraid of barking dog. Only silent dog.' *Da*? You understand?"

"Okay. I understand. Don't tempt fate. "

"Yes. Don't do it. Not now. Talk about our work a little, if you must. But not theirs."

When we started to walk again, we were both silent. What Yuri had said was true. All had been quiet on the South American front. It had lulled me and allowed me to settle into Moscow and get on with my work. But Yuri was not to be lulled. "Okay," I eventually spoke up. "We'll leave the South Americans out of it. But the fact is, I have to give this lecture in a couple of hours. And I've got a problem."

"Okay, then. What problem?"

"The problem is how to get these kids to relax. I can't start getting those students to consider m-brane theory if they're rigidly sitting there taking notes and believing everything I say. I mean, how could they begin to imagine that the reality they know might actually be just light beams colliding to make a three-dimensional image reflected off some distant boundary? Now really – how can I get them there without humor, without loosening them up first?"

"And Russian students, they do not have humor?"

"Maybe in Russian they do. But in English?"

By this time, we had come to an intersection full of cars and trolley lines. I stopped and noticed where I was for the first time. In front of us was the entrance to the Metro. Across the street was a sign with Cyrillic letters even I could understand – MacDonald's. Everywhere I looked I saw students. Every one of them was wearing jeans; all the men wore sneakers. There were baseball caps – too many with New York Yankees logos –

and T-shirts with American slogans and pictures of rock 'n roll bands.

"See? Students," Yuri said. "They are the same everywhere. Here. London. Boston. No different."

At that moment, a teenager walked by. He was striding very purposefully, almost marching, to some place or other. But around his head was a pair of earphones and on his T-shirt a picture of Bart Simpson. 'Eat My Shorts'. I read it in English and then said it out loud. "Eat My Shorts. See that T-shirt?" I showed Yuri. "Even my Japanese students back in Boston know that and think it's funny."

"You see? All the same. So, be cool," Yuri said and started to laugh.

At ten to three a bell went off on my computer. Yuri had gotten me to start using the computer as an alarm clock. It was terrific. Why it had never occurred to me before, I couldn't imagine. But now, without having to rush off in a panic, I could gently come out of whatever hyper-focus I was in and calmly switch gears to the next task at hand. "Once again, you've changed my life," I joked to Yuri.

"A pleasure. *Nyet problem.*"

I grabbed my box of slides and opened the desk drawer looking for my note cards. There was the vial of pills. I took a look around the room to make sure I was alone. I opened it and took one out, but I didn't put it in my mouth. Instead, I put it in my jacket pocket next to where I had just put the cards. I knew I wouldn't need to look at those notes, but they were there, just in case. And so was the pill. Whether I would need that or not was yet to be seen. I then headed down the hall to Lecture Room 307. The door was closed, but a sheet of paper was tacked to the board on the wall. The top half was in Russian, but then beneath it read:

Professor John Rosen, Cambridge Massachusetts

This lecture will be conducted in English

Yes, 'in English', it said, as if it was some apology, or the small print at the bottom of a contract. For the first time in my life, I longed to speak another language. I had always hated language classes in school. In High School I took two years of French and then switched to Intro Spanish, just to get out of the requirement as quickly and easily as possible. But now I was beginning to realize there was more to this language business than I had thought. It was not so much that others couldn't understand me when I spoke English. They could. But language was more than just the meaning of a string of words. There were nuances, references, things more subtle than merely a batch of definitions lumped together. And as long as I couldn't express myself in those more complex ways, I could never show myself to be the whole, full person that I was. And I was a whole, full person. True, it had been a long time since I felt like one. For too long, I had felt like a hologram myself, just a barren projection of some other, truer reality. But now things felt different, as if the sketchy outline of myself was beginning to be filled in. But how could I show who I was, if I couldn't really talk to anyone?

The Lecture Hall was empty and dark. I found a row of switches on the wall and flipped them all. One by one, randomly, lights began to flicker and hum along the ceiling. I looked around. Shit. I hated teaching in this sort of room. It was much too big. The floor was pitched at a ridiculously steep angle and there must have been twenty tiers of benches and desks leading down towards the front. I had to be careful not to stumble and drop all the slides. The projector was already set up off to the side and a silvery-white screen hung down from the ceiling. The rest of the wall was one enormous blackboard, which could roll up and down with the crank of a handle. I set aside my materials and looked back towards the top of the room. "This is like a giant step back in time," I thought and just stood there for a moment, staring silently, in wonder. Yuri was right. This place oozed history. It was everywhere, from the dust balls hiding in the corners to the chalk dust embedded in the crevices of the small wooden shelf beneath the blackboard. What words had that dust once written, I wondered? What symbols and calculations had it revealed? And now, there I was, too. Me, with my own energy, my own thought patterns. Soon, particles from my own scribbles would be added to that chalk dust, mingling with the history of scientific thought, thousands of miles away from anywhere I ever thought I would be.

In the midst of this reverie, my hand slipped into my pocket. There were the cards. There was the pill. But already students were beginning to take their seats. Soon the room was nearly full and scores of eyes were looking down towards me in anticipation. Yuri himself was standing against the back wall, arms crossed, head nodding. I looked back at them all and became aware, quite suddenly, that I wasn't nervous anymore. Somehow that feeling had passed completely on its own and now, all I felt was ready. I realized it was time to start and I just started, without any hesitation or thought. I took my hand out of my pocket and reached for a piece of chalk.

"Good afternoon," I said and then continued as if I had said it a million times before, "*Zdrastvoytye.*"

Chapter 26

Grace:
Unforgiven

For the first month after she was home from the hospital, Lizzy haunted the house and my life with an eerie, angry silence. She never talked to me, so I never knew where she was. I would assume she was in her bedroom, then she'd suddenly appear behind me, pale as a ghost, her good eye glaring. She'd stand there as if she was waiting, but whenever I tried to approach her, she'd move on, leaving a chill behind her. She looked terrible, as if she was there and not there at the same time and the fact that she rarely wore the eye patch in the house made it for me even worse. That raw, naked, phantom eye haunted me like some dead animal I couldn't bear to approach. It was everywhere, although Lizzy seemed nowhere and it was all there was between us.

I know John saw everything. It looked to me like he was living his own life normally, but it must have felt like he was trapped in some horror movie. He would often come home from school to find Lizzy shut away in her bedroom and me brooding.

"Mom, I can't stand this anymore." He eventually confronted me. "She's obviously creeping you out and she's pissing me off. I'm going to talk to her."

He marched into Lizzy's room, slamming the door behind him. I followed and listened. I heard nothing at first until suddenly there was laughter. The sound startled me and I fell back away from the door. John soon opened it and saw me lurking there. He sneered.

"Jesus Christ, Mom. You treat her like she's dead. Get over it."

But getting over it was exactly what I couldn't do. Even then, I knew I had to. I knew I must let go of the horror of Lizzy's accident and that my guilt was swamping both of us. I barely even spoke to Jack. It seemed the more Lizzy shut me out of her life, the more I shut myself into some solitary, shadowy, ghost-like place. John was right. Lizzy was 'creeping me out', but I was also creeping myself out and I didn't know how to stop it. We went on like that for a long time until something changed.

Three thirty one afternoon. I'm hovering around the living room, fluffing already fluffed pillows, when Lizzy appears like an advertisement for American youth, wearing jeans, a gray Gap sweatshirt, a blue Red Sox baseball cap, her sneakers and now, her eye patch. She sits down on the couch and stares silently toward the front door. I guess John finally convinced her to go for a walk, because when he burst in, already in mid-sentence, Lizzy was slowly starting to raise.

"I'll be right with you," John said to his sister. "Let me just take a pee."

Lizzy sat back down and so did I. I looked at her and she looked at the floor. We sat there together, wordless, until we heard the bathroom door open and John's voice once again.

"Lets go to HMV, ok? There's a new record I want."

Lizzy began to put her weight on one leg to stand. It suddenly dawned on me how difficult it was for her to find the

226

ground beneath her feet. She was clearly testing to make sure she could tell where the floor was and I realized then she had been doing that all month. My normal impulse, any normal mother's impulse, would have been to reach out to her, to offer help and an arm to lean on. But I couldn't move. I just sat there and watched her stumble until John lent her his hand.

"There you go. No problem."

"Ok, but go slow. And don't leave me alone in any of the aisles." She sounded like the little girl I once lost among the GI Joes in the giant toy store back home. John sounded, amazingly, like himself. Silently, I watched them walk out the door and then shouted, "Have a nice time." But I had found my voice too late; they were already gone. I went to the living room window and watched as they made their way to the corner. John was obviously laughing. His head bounced as he walked, turning from one side to the next other as if he was doing a stand-up routine. Lizzy seemed to be staring straight ahead in deep concentration. Every now and then she'd reach out for John's arm, using him like a crutch. Watching the two of them slowly walk down the street, I felt a painful recognition, a sudden understanding of Lizzy's struggle. It must have been so hard for her, listening to her brother ramble on while also trying to figure out where to put her feet, how to judge the distance between herself and other people, how to shield herself from the glare of the sun. Just watching it was more than I could take. I sat down on the couch in precisely the same spot Lizzy had been sitting. The cushion was still warm from her presence although she was gone. I sat there in silence and I remember thinking I should have been feeling hopeful, but instead I was feeling bewildered and exhausted.

After that first walk, Lizzy became braver and braver. It must have been hard for her. I know what it's like to go out into the real world after you've been shut in for a long time. Later, when it happened to me, I found that things I never used to notice became strange and threatening. Bicycles careening down the sidewalk were like galloping dinosaurs, toddlers like moving obstacles. After weeks of being an invalid, you lose all confidence that you can handle anything yourself. But, if your body and mind are ready, that sureness comes back quickly. After a few days, I could see that Lizzy was regaining her confidence and I found the courage to tell her so.

"Thanks," she said. She actually smiled.

A couple of weeks must have passed. The timing of it all is a blur to me now, but an unmistakable lightening of the atmosphere in the house started to happen once Lizzy walked out into the world. Her face regained some color. At night, I could hear her laughing with her brother. She even once bought herself a silk scarf in Camden Passage. Jack was thrilled, clutching desperately to each little change as a sign of progress. I tried to be happy, but I still couldn't. My downward spiral had already begun. I couldn't escape the memory of her accident, that woman's sincere voice on the telephone, the brightness of the lamps in the recovery room. I couldn't forget the image of my child lying bandaged and crying in that hospital bed. And I could still hear the cold anger in her voice during that last phone call before her flight. All of this kept replaying itself in my head, waking, dreaming – it made no difference. It was my nightmare and although Lizzy was waking from hers, I was still trapped in mine.

I watched what was obviously the beginning of her slow recovery with what must have looked like detached interest. I plastered a smile on my face and added a pseudo-sweetness to my voice. Actually, I was dying inside. Literally dying. My long list of sorrows had finally started to break me down. I now realize I was in a sort of shock, like a victim of war, or a witness to a horrific crime. No wonder Lizzy couldn't talk to me. She refused my infrequent offers of help. It felt as if she was watching me, haunting me and waiting for something which I could never give. I don't blame her. And if she had acted differently, I don't think it would have made any difference. She did eventually make an overture to me, but the fix was a temporary one. Someone must have urged her to do it – whether it was her brother or her boyfriend or somebody else, I never found out – but, one day, she came into the kitchen where I was idly reading a Thai cookbook and said, "I'm going to Regent's Park. Wanna come?" I was shocked. Those few words were more than she had willingly said to me in months. I didn't know what to say, but I jumped up and grabbed my jacket. It was longer than I had ever walked in my life, but I didn't dare say no. I didn't dare say anything. I just followed.

It never rained, but the sky was a February gray, as I remember, and the air felt damp. Lizzy's pace was surprisingly fast. At one point, I wondered if she was trying to wear me out, to leave me behind once and for all. But, somehow, I kept up. We hardly spoke and I tried not to stare too much at this silent, wispy figure leading me onward. It was almost two hours later when we returned home. My legs were throbbing.

"Thanks, Lizzy," I said, collapsing onto the couch.

"It's okay," she answered and went into her bedroom.

Something must have felt all right to her about that first walk, because a few days later, in between rain showers, she asked me out again. We did a loop around Holland Park. Two days after that, it was Notting Hill and Portobello Road. We never stopped to look in store windows. We never stopped for lunch. No talking, just walking. Eventually, I went with her most every day, most everywhere. I felt like I was on a roller coaster. Sometimes I allowed myself to hope, other times I fell into despair. But mostly I was afraid to feel anything. Even as Lizzy was coming back to life, chatting to John in the living room at night or listening to her father's conversation over dinner, she was still vague to me, just as I was vague to myself. The Lizzy I had known was gone and the walks we were taking together felt like walks I was taking alone, but with a painful, persistent memory.

Eventually the time came for Lizzy to leave us in London and return to her normal life. The doctors proclaimed her fit. She knew where to put her feet. She wasn't so wobbly. It was what she had been waiting for and Jack and John were thrilled for her. I wanted to be happy for her, too, but I couldn't. I had already stopped knowing how to feel happy. Lizzy was going back to college, eye patch and all, back to her studies and her boyfriend, but as the day grew closer, I became more and more agitated. I didn't yet realize how exhausted I was and how I was already lost in the dark cave of my self-hatred. I'd sit up in bed and worry out loud to Jack.

"Maybe she shouldn't go back. Why can't she transfer to someplace over here?" And then,

"What about the QEII? She doesn't have to fly... " It was my last morbid attempt to take some control over our lives, but it was futile. Each time, Jack would hear me out, patiently and quietly. But I was being handled. Without knowing it, Jack was trying to stop me from doing what we were both fearing – falling apart.

When the actual day came, Jack and I drove Lizzy to the airport. We stayed until the plane had safely taken off and then we went home. I know Jack hoped another traumatic chapter in our lives had been neatly concluded. I remember being angry at the smile that came to his lips as he drove back into London and thinking to myself, "Does he really think it's all better now?" It disgusted me to think that he assumed we could just get back to normal. I knew we couldn't, because I knew I couldn't. After we got home from the airport, I felt more tired than I had ever felt in my life.

What happened next must be told with calmness, but don't let that fool you. Those memories are painful and can still make me cry. But now, when I think about this chapter in my life, there is also gratitude, a crucial lesson learned later, and that must be remembered as well.

I went to bed. At first I thought I was 'emotionally drained' and needed a day or two to relax. But that day or two turned into weeks when I couldn't bear to do anything. Even the slightest task was too much. I thought I had contracted some weird disease. All I wanted was to stay in bed. The household fell apart. I stopped buying groceries, stopped doing laundry. Days would go by without my changing clothes or even taking a shower. I let go of everything – my husband's life, my son's life, my own life. I stopped making decisions, turning off my brain as if it was an old, staticky television. Jack called the doctor, but when the time came to leave the house for the appointment, I went back to bed and fell asleep. Eventually, our GP made a house call and took some blood. When the results came back negative, he recommended psychotherapy and a course of anti-depressants, but Jack refused to believe it. I suppose it's understandable. Jack had watched me go through so much. When our marriage was in danger, I found a way to keep us together. Even the death of our child hadn't broken me. Over the years we had all trusted in my strength to pull us through, to carry us forward. Now, with Lizzy nearly healed and functioning again, he couldn't believe I was really falling apart. If he was ok, then I surely was. But I knew I wasn't and I feared I wouldn't be for a long time.

I didn't tell any one that I was crying for more and more hours every day and I didn't let on that my headaches from years before had returned with a fury. I didn't mention any of it, I think, because I was too tired to care. I just turned over in my bed and faced the curtained window. But in the midst of it all, I was lucky. I had made a friend in London, a relatively new friend and she pushed her way into our lives and refused to ignore the truth.

Some people have dozens of friends all the time. I was never like that until much later. For most of my life I just had acquaintances, people with whom I happily passed the time, but without any sense of attachment. But there was always, in each chapter of my life, one woman there acting like the midwife, delivering me into the next phase, the next set of stories. During those months in bed, behind closed eyes, I spent many hours thinking about all of them, but especially about my mother and Gina. Every now and again I would get out of bed and sit in the chair by the window, telephone in hand. I wanted to call my mother, but I couldn't. I couldn't bear to burden her with how I felt. She would never understand, I thought, and telling her the truth would only hurt her, just as I was hurting everyone else.

But, eventually, Jack did call my parents. He had to. But first, he called Katherine. She was another mother from John's school. She had twin boys in sixth grade when I first met her and we sat on the same library committee. Tall, thin, with jet-black hair and expressive hands, she was always organized, always busy. She grew up on the Mainline outside Philadelphia, went to a finishing school in Michigan and college in North Carolina. She was as different from me as she could be, but she liked me. During my years in London, Katherine became my companion in the good times and my confidante in the bad.

At the start of my illness, she called every afternoon to check in and every day I would assure her I'd be better tomorrow. Then tomorrow came, and I wasn't better. Katherine started bringing over vats of homemade soup, but it became more and more difficult for me even to say hello to her when she peeked her head into my room. That's when she knew I was in danger, she told me later. Katherine took it upon herself to do the research, call the doctors and then talk to Jack. She was a woman of quiet confidence. I knew and liked that about her from the start. But I hadn't realized how generous and determined she could be as well. It takes a great deal of love *and* guts, to barge into somebody else's life. But that was what was needed and only Katherine had the ability to do it. And so she saved my life.

One evening, she came by the apartment. Jack was already home and I heard them moving around. I think they were having dinner. I was in my room, a cold compress on my head, pretending to be asleep. I remember hearing the phone ring, but I ignored it. Jack must have picked it up because I heard his voice. I could hear him through the haze of my isolation as he paced back and forth outside my door.

It's strange how I remember what happened as if I was really there. But, of course, I wasn't. I wasn't really anywhere. It was as if I had become a ghost, observing from afar, detached, vaguely interested, but mainly alone with my pain. I know the phone rang. I know Jack answered it to find Lizzy on the other end. According to Jack, years later, he tried to have a pleasant, superficial conversation with Lizzy, listening to her updates about school, avoiding any discussion about what was happening at home. He was trying to protect her, just as he was trying to protect us all and when Lizzy asked to speak with me, he told her I was taking a nap. That's when Katherine snapped. After weeks, if not months, of bringing over food, talking to doctors, neglecting her own family in order to keep ours going, she told Jack she couldn't stand to listen to him lie any longer. They started to fight. Somehow I knew what was happening, almost as if I had been expecting it. I dragged myself out of bed and went into the hallway. There they all were, Jack and Katherine, and John off to the side, arguing as if it was a scene out of Tennessee Williams. But with my arrival, they froze and stared at me. I could still hear Lizzy's voice on the phone, so I took the receiver out of Jack's hand and spoke to her. I don't remember what I said; it wasn't anything particularly meaningful. But it ended both that conversation and the argument in the hallway. I went back to bed.

At first, it was so quiet I thought they had all left. But I think they were in shock, because eventually Jack was sitting on the bed beside me, with Katherine peering in through the door. He started to talk, but my look told him to stop. I knew what he was going to say. He was going to tell me to get help. He was going to tell me he loved me and that everything would be all right. When I wouldn't let him speak, he reached over to at least kiss me, but I moved away. I couldn't bear to be touched. The pain that was once only inside, now was on the outside, too, and it was too great.

"Please," I begged. "Please, leave me." But Jack persisted. "Don't you understand?" I pleaded, hoping the humiliation of it all would force him away. But Jack had obviously decided he couldn't turn away any longer.

"Don't I understand what?"

I realized then I would never have any peace. Something must be done. I tried to answer him. It took every last ounce of energy inside me to do it. But I eventually did, not well enough, but it was the best I could. I said, "Don't you see, it's unforgivable. All of it. Everything's that's happened to us. It's all my fault and it's unforgivable."

There was silence for a moment and then they both tried to argue with me. "It's not your fault. There's nothing to forgive." But it was too late. I had come to hate myself too much, hate myself and all the terrible events of our lives, which I somehow took responsibility for. I had spent my life trying to run everyone else's, to protect them from danger and sadness and I felt like I had failed. Miserably. Repeatedly. I had to forgive myself and I couldn't.

I begged Jack and Katherine over and over to leave the room and leave me alone; they finally did. For hours after, I just lay there, listening to the sounds of doors closing, lights being turned off. I assume Katherine eventually went home. Jack got into bed. But these sounds no longer really reached me. They were muffled, as if heard through some tightly woven gauze. I pretended to sleep, but I was waiting for John and Jack to be asleep themselves and for the entire world to be hidden away in its darkness. I got out of bed feeling nothing in particular, but acted without thought or sensation. I walked into Lizzy's bathroom. I found the sleeping pills and painkillers left over from her operation. I took them all.

Chapter 27

Grace:
Brush Cutting

The first hours were black. Life was both real and not real at the same time. I could hear, but I didn't comprehend. I don't remember anything about a white light; there was nothing beckoning to me. There was only darkness and a sense of being alone and disconnected. But there was still, somehow, sense.

Eventually, parts of me must have begun to function well enough to allow the Emergency Team to 'bring me back'. But in the meantime there was nothing. Looking back years later, I think I say there was nothing because that makes some kind of sense to me. But actually, I was in a state between nothing and something. There were thoughts and a sort of consciousness even in the darkness. Even while they worked on me with their rush of machines and shouts and flashing lights, even as I heard muffled yelling and people calling my name waiting hopefully for a reply which I know I never gave, I was always there thinking to myself and recalling, step by step, what I had done.

I had poured pills into my mouth and some felt lodged uncomfortably in my throat. They were small, round, dry and tasteless. The bathroom floor then became cold on my bare feet. I stared at my face in the mirror, that face which I no longer recognized. I felt the cold from the floor rise up into my legs and into my deadening heart. Then came the relief of this semi-aware darkness. Lying on the bathroom floor, being carried on the stretcher, driving in the ambulance, I lived it over and over. The thoughts were there. I could see them like a newsreel behind my closed eyes, but the feelings were missing. I felt sensations, but it was as if they didn't have anything to do with me. I watched it all with a vague, intellectual interest, but the emotions were gone. No fear, no remorse, no hope, no love. Nothing. That was my death and I now know it had started long before the night I swallowed those pills and lasted long after the rest of the conscious world believed I had come back to them.

There were days on end in the hospital when I didn't know if I was asleep or awake, whether the blinds were opened or closed, or if I even cared. I was in a hole where everything was gray and nothing mattered. I never put up a fight. I did what they told me to do. But always in silence. I wasn't in a coma or catatonic. It was more like I was one of the undead, walking the hallways but not really alive. I was both aware of things and not aware of them, living the way I imagine an animal would live. An animal might step on a jagged rock and pull its paw back in pain. But when the pain is over, the thought of the rock is gone, too. It might hear the honk of a car horn as it dashes across a road. But if it lives to cross to the other side, the sound of that horn no longer lingers meaningfully in its ears. Aware, but unaware. So, when the phone rang in the nurse's station I turned my head towards the sound, but I didn't really hear it. If I saw a bright light, I shielded my eyes. I felt pain, like when they jabbed my bottom full of sleeping medicine or clamped my head inside an x-ray machine. Those things made me wince, but none of the sensations made any difference to me. I took it all silently, giving nothing in return.

How can I describe something for which there are no words? I know now, that some people can take that leap of faith, can believe in a reality that can't be named. Eventually, I was able to do this as well. But back then, in the blanketing grayness which was my hospital life, I could neither find the words nor utter them. In that way, I was not really alive.

Every day was the same.

The Nurse comes in. I always know when she's there although I'm sure it doesn't seem like it. It's not that I don't notice her. It's just that I don't notice anything. She talks to me. I know what she says, but it doesn't register. Every morning the same routine. The sheets hurt. Too cold. Starchy, like pinpricks on my skin. Too white. I sit still. The air in the room feels like nothing. There's no smell, no color, no sound. I sit still and look straight ahead wondering, is it morning already? I swallow my pill. The orange juice tastes like nothing.

The Nurse puts her hand on my elbow; helps me out of bed. The floor is cold. Those backless, spongy slippers slip off my feet. She ties the bathrobe around my waist. I just stand there. She walks me down the hall. The fluorescent light flickers. Other nurses say hello, but I look straight ahead and say nothing.

There is a room with people. They know my name but I don't know theirs. The Doctor says hello. The radiator makes clicking sounds.

Then it is night. I eat whatever is put in front of me and eventually wonder, am I sleeping yet?

And so it continued. The sheets, the light, the cold floor. And the Nurse. She was always there, her hand on my back lifting me off the toilet, guiding me through the hallway. She would ask me questions, always questions. I heard her, but I never answered.

Sometimes, walking down the hall, we passed a nurse's cart. It was always gray. The walls were gray. The faces were gray. That room again and those people were gray. And the radiator made clicking sounds.

Often, she put the television on in my room. "Do you want to watch television?" "Do you want to get into bed?" She put me in bed and would leave me staring at the black and white screen, listening to the gray noise.

One day, the Nurse took me to a different room. There was a table. Two chairs. I remember dust on the blinds. The Doctor was there. His hands were folded and his fingernails were short. He asked questions. I knew his voice. I understood his words. I even looked at his face. But I said nothing. He handed me a photograph in a plastic frame. The corner pricked my finger. It was a photograph of Jack, John and Lizzy. The Doctor wouldn't let me see them, not yet. But I could look at their picture. In it, they were smiling. But it didn't reach me.

I walked down the hall by myself and hardly noticed that the Doctor had given me the photo. It dangled loosely from my hand. I walked back to my room, then passed it. I didn't go in. I walked further down the hall and then back again. With each step the slippers slipped off my feet. Some doors were open. One man smiled. A woman sat doing nothing. I walked back to my room.

On that day, I heard my voice in my head, but I couldn't make out what I was saying. Maybe I wasn't saying anything.

Every morning I took my pill. One, in the morning, with orange juice. Eventually, I began to notice if the orange juice was cold. Then another day, after the nurse pulled up the blind, I saw the sun in the sky through the window. I remember looking at it. The gray of my world began to be less opaque. I suppose the pills were finally beginning to work. Shards of light were trying to break through. I didn't fight them or reach out to them, but I did begin to notice.

One night, the Nurse pulled down the blinds and the room got darker. "Do you want to watch television?" she asked. I looked at the photograph of Jack on the table. I shook my head and soon was asleep. If I close my eyes now, I can still see the dream I had. My children are young. There are three of them. They are in my mother's house. We are playing cards. I am young, too. I'm laughing out loud. Jack comes in. He is my father. He is wearing my father's black fedora and rubbing his hands together against the cold as if he's just walked home from work. He comes into the room and puts his arms around us. He laughs. I smell brisket in the oven.

One day after that, I got up and got dressed. I pulled up the blinds by myself. The sun was already there. The Nurse brought me breakfast and my medicine. I had coffee, too.

In the afternoon I walked down to the end of the hall and found a room with many chairs and a bookcase. One book was *The Complete Sonnets of Shakespeare*. It was surrounded by a mess of hardcover books and paperbacks, leaning against each other or lying face down on the shelf. There were old, torn Agatha Christies, a collection of the novels of Barbara Cartland, an assortment of Dickens. But my hand reached out instinctively for the Shakespeare. I had seen many of his plays since moving to London, but it had been years since I had actually read any Shakespeare myself. And I don't think I ever read the sonnets right through. But I sat down then and read them:

Like as the waves make towards the pebbled shore,
So do our minutes hasten to their end...

I still know those words. I can still hear them in my head and when I do, I see the view from outside the picture window in that room. There was a park, a church steeple and always some woman in heavy white shoes pushing a baby carriage. Even now, years later, I associate those ordinary images with Shakespeare's words and together, I link them with my return to the living world. It seems hard to believe it now but it is true. From the moment my fingers touched the spine of that book, it all started to matter somehow. Suddenly I knew I was waiting for something.

> *When to the sessions of sweet silent thought*
> *I summon up remembrance of things past,*
> *I sigh the lack of many a thing I sought,*
> *And with old woes now wail my dear time's waste...*

Time passed and something did change. Thoughts started to come in long sentences with many clauses. I realized they were my thoughts, no longer disembodied. It started with Shakespeare's words, but then came my own. I remember beginning to say them to myself in my head as if I was saying them out loud. My words helped me understand something. I didn't know what yet, but something.

Then there was one particular day – same Nurse, same orange juice – only now there was color. The orange juice was yellow. So was the sun. The bathrobe on the foot of my bed was not white or gray, but pale blue. Suddenly it felt as if there were colors in the world and I was seeing them. I felt my heart beating inside me. It was irregular, like a child playing bongos. I felt it in my chest and inside, my stomach tickled me. There were two feelings, together, and they reminded me of something long past. I remembered there were moments in my life when I had been happy and although the memory surprised me, it made me think that perhaps, one day, I could actually feel again.

Later, as I sat in the Doctor's office, I saw the room differently, more distinctly, as if a bright light had been turned on.

The walls were brown, like wood. They weren't wood, but they reminded me of wood. His carpet was dark blue with little white specks. On his desk was a red box full of pens. I was seeing the colors as I probably had been for a while, but without realizing it. Now, at the same time, I also heard the words for them in my head– brown, blue, white, red. Those words, those names gave the colors definition and that definition gave me a way to define myself. I was no longer a part of an all-consuming grayness. There were now variations in the world around me. If I saw something, I could find its name. And if I could find its name, I could respond. For the first time in months I wanted to speak, if only to bring those words out of my head and back into the world again. Sight, language, speech. From one to the other. It was the movement of life, from outside to in and back out again and I was beginning, finally, to reclaim my place in it.

I noticed I walked alone all the time. The Nurse no longer came with me everywhere. I went to the toilet myself and even to the book room. I walked down the hall past opened doors. One day, I looked into one of those rooms and recognized the face of the woman there sitting alone. She was young, like one of my children. She looked at me but she didn't smile. We looked at each other without smiling, without even nodding. Her head had short, very black hair. It was so black everything else around it looked white. The air around her black, black hair was clear and shining. The sun came in from the window behind where she was sitting. It made the room a yellow-orange. The orange of the light and the black of her hair reminded me of Halloween. I remembered, yes, there used to be Halloween and then there was that sensation inside my stomach again. I realized, for a moment, I was happy. Inside my head I said to the young woman, "Thank you."

By that time, I was reading myself to sleep every night. It was always Shakespeare. His words were like a balm, like something you rub on a sore muscle.

> Let me not to the marriage of true minds
> Admit impediments...

Their sound alone gave me comfort, even without understanding the depth of their meaning. Reaching out to switch off the light, I often saw the picture of my family smiling at me. Then I would fall asleep.

There then was another day, perhaps the most important day, when I woke up tired. I had been dreaming. The dream is still with me even now, when I want it to be, but then it haunted me without letting me know what it was. It lasted like some unrecognizable, growing insistence inside me. I took my medicine and drank the orange juice the Nurse had left. She hadn't woken me or said good morning. I went to the bathroom. On the way up from the toilet I saw my face in the mirror. I touched my face and hair. My dream was in my head but I still didn't know what it was. There had been something about a forest. There were trees and brown twigs all over the ground. I looked down at the bathroom floor. I lifted one of my feet as if to step out from the tangle of branches. When I looked back up into the mirror, I was crying.

Later that day, I was back in that room with those people, but I noticed some were different. Maybe they had been there a long time, but they seemed new. How long had they been there? How much time had passed, anyway? They were speaking. They no longer asked me questions as if it was understood, even by the newcomers, that I would never speak. I sat there on a plastic chair and noticed that the plastic was blue and the chair legs were silver. I looked around. All the chair legs were silver and there were more colors everywhere. Then, I noticed a painting on the wall. It must have been there all along, but it felt as if I was seeing it for the first time. It was a painting of a garden full of wild flowers. A woman with a wide-brimmed straw hat was working in the garden. The flowers had colors. There was sunshine on the woman's back. I stood up and walked to the painting. There was still talking all around me, like a buzz, a swarm of noise around my head. But inside my head it was growing quiet and clear. I was the woman working in the garden and the sun was on my back. It was a yellow sun.

That night I got out of bed. New feelings and thoughts had been stirring inside me all day and they lasted into the night. These feelings, I know now, were the beginning of my understanding of what had happened to me. I recall I couldn't sleep. I tossed and turned for a while before swinging my legs over the metallic edge of the bed. Although the room itself was dark and quiet, a dim light shone beneath a crack in the doorway from outside in the hall. There were a few distant voices. I went to the bathroom and turned on the light. The sudden flickering hurt my eyes. I looked in the mirror and touched my lips.

> *What is your substance, whereof are you made,*
> *That millions of strange shadows on you tend?*

"What is my substance?" Perhaps this was the question I had needed to ask all along, but for which I hadn't known the words. Suddenly, I knew the words and understood their meaning. I wanted to speak. I needed to speak. I opened my mouth, but at first nothing came out. I remember being afraid that, maybe, I would never be able to speak again. It had been so long since I'd tried. I took a breath and pushed the air out of my lungs and up into my throat. It made a *'w'* sound. "What" was all I managed to whisper.

The following morning, I was awake when the Nurse came in. She gave me my food, my medicine, my coffee and orange juice. I went through my breakfast routine, but I didn't look at her. I was thinking of something. I had woken up thinking. In my mind I could see the painting from that room. I could see a garden with cuttings all around the ground. I saw the trees nearby with branches lying under them. I imagined I was actually there, in that garden, picking up the twigs, looking at them, then gently clearing them away. I was imagining all of this, I knew. But it was real. I waited until the Nurse left the room. I got out of bed and walked to the window. The yellow sun was already there. I reached down to pick something up, something from the garden. When I brought my hand back up it was empty, of course, but I still felt something. I can feel that something even now. I looked at the ghost-of-a-something in my hand. I examined it and put it off to the side. I was *brush cutting* – at least those were the words I said to myself then and that's what I still call it. I was putting it all aside, all of it that had been in my head, one by one, with care and precision, but also with tenderness. In my mind, I was looking at the flowers that had died, lying on the ground. I felt myself forgiving them for dying. I looked at the growing pile of cut branches and twigs beside me. I let go of them. There was a beginning of a path clearing in front of me. Just the beginning, but I imagined it there growing wider and longer, the more I cleared, the more I let go. I thought I was going to laugh, or cry. Then I heard a sound behind me. It was the Nurse. Over her white uniform she was wearing a green cardigan and she looked at me with a question.

"I'm ready," I said.

My silence had lasted four months. It had taken that long for me to recover my ability to feel, to rediscover the words associated with those feelings and then, most importantly, to decide I wanted to utter those words. When I began to speak again, I began slowly. My thoughts and feelings didn't rush out in a torrent of words, but rather in a slow, methodical drip.

The very first thing I told the Doctor was my dream. I told him about the garden. I painted the picture for him with my own, hard-earned words. Then I cried. My voice sounded strange to me, but I knew that would change. It would all change.

Over the next few weeks and months, we did my brush cutting together. The Doctor understood and helped me to, as well. I looked at each event in my life, cried over it and put it aside. Sam's death. Jack's affair. Lizzy's accident. All of it. They were the tragedies of my life. Everyone has their own – there is no immunity from that. But I didn't cause those tragedies. Maybe I did have some responsibility for Jack's affair. I accepted it. I even had a role in what happened to Lizzy, certainly for the course our relationship had taken. I accepted that, too. But all of that was not the sum of Grace. There is more to me, to anyone, than their sorrows and their mistakes.

When I left the hospital, I was not a new person. I was the same Grace, just as I am now. But I had begun to let go. And the more I let go, the freer I became. My hands were empty. I could fill them with anything.

Chapter 28

John:
A Magnetic Moment

My hand remained on the receiver for a while even after I had hung up the phone. It just felt as if my body wasn't yet ready to let go of the connection. I sat on the couch in the sitting area off my kitchen, staring into space. Every now and then I heard a car pass by on the street below, but otherwise the world around me was quiet. It was late – nearly midnight – and it had been a long day.

Lizzy had been surprised to hear from me. She hadn't expected my call until Sunday, the day of our usual weekly phone call. And here it was only Saturday. But she had forgotten, or more likely she had never even known, that it was actually Yom Kippur that day. That I knew it was Yom Kippur would have been enough of a reason to call, if only to give her a shock and a good laugh. Neither of us had celebrated the holiday in years. But add to it the fact that I had spent the entire day in synagogue, had fasted and had actually, in some indecipherable way, been moved by it ... well, that was more than worth a surprise phone call from across the planet.

I kept the call short and light on purpose. Just letting Lizzy know I had gone to synagogue at all seemed enough. But now that the conversation was over, I couldn't stop thinking about the day. This Yom Kippur in Moscow, sitting next to Yuri, Natalia, Elena and her daughter, Anna, was like … I couldn't even say what it was like. It certainly was nothing like the last time I had gone to High Holiday services. That was back in Westchester, three or four years earlier, when my mother was still alive. There, I had sat next to Lizzy, Peter and Amanda and as far away from my mother as I could. All I could remember of that day was that it felt like a charade and I had felt full of resentment. Every time someone new, someone totally unknown to me, greeted my mother with a warmly grasped hand or a lingering hug, I became more annoyed. Each new person in my mother's life (and there seemed to be an endless parade of them), felt like just one more empty vessel sucking up her love and care, siphoning off that attention that should have gone, all those years, to me. I remembered sitting there, listening to the Rabbi remind the congregation that Yom Kippur was about repentance and forgiveness. To be written in the *Book of Life*, Jews need to ask for forgiveness, not from God but from their fellow man. It was a nice idea, I had thought and something I would have been willing to do. But my mother never asked for my forgiveness, so I never had the chance to give it.

But this Yom Kippur today, years later and miles away, was a completely different story. When Yuri began to discuss plans for the holiday earlier in the week, I was dumbfounded. "Saturday is what?" I asked.

"Yom Kippur." Yuri then looked at me as if I had suddenly sprouted wings. "John. Really. Yom Kippur. The holiest day of the year. And this year it is a Saturday, so no excuse not to go. We will all go together. We pick you up about nine o'clock."

I couldn't believe it. For the rest of the week I kept asking Yuri things like, "Why so early? "Are you sure it will be that crowded?", "Where are all those people coming from?", "Weren't all the Jews killed or something?" It was getting embarrassing. But I couldn't seem to control myself. The whole idea of a thriving, active Jewish community within Moscow went against everything I had ever heard. And what about Yuri's assumption that I wanted to be a part of it? I was feeling completely bewildered by it all, until he eventually took pity on me. The day before the holiday, over a paper bag lunch in our office, he tried to explain.

"Look. Natalia wants me to talk to you," he started. "And to give you this." He handed me a sandwich of sliced chicken and peppers on brown bread. "She worries you don't eat. But also that you are confused."

"Natalia's right," I said.

"Yes. I know. So look. This is the way it is for us in Russia. Being a Jew is not the best thing. That is true. It never has been. But you must understand. Moscow is different. In the countryside, in Minsk, that was another matter. But that was about poverty, too and there is no one in the world more hated than a poor Jew, you know." I watched him take a bite of his sandwich and a sip of tea. I wondered how he could talk about this so calmly, so fearlessly. My whole life, I had only heard people talk about 'Soviet Jewry' with fury and disgust. They used the same tone of voice speaking about Russia as they did about Hitler's Germany. But here was Yuri, a Russian Jew who had grown up in the Soviet era, talking about it as if he was talking about the latest issue of *Physical Review*.

"In Moscow, Jews always had education," he continued to explain. "They had work. My father was a dentist, you know. Natalia's an architect. It was possible to live. And if you were quiet, to pray, too." Yuri stopped for a moment and seemed to look off into space. "You know, when you think of it, it is not so different from your family. Your father was an architect, like Natalia's, yes?"

"Yes, but..."

"... and he moved to London..."

"But that was different. My mother forced it. You know the story."

"The affair. Yes, I know."

"Right, so I don't see how it's at all the same."

"No? It is the same because, like us, they did what they had to do to live, *da*? Somehow, even in troubles, they continued. That is what we all did. And now, like you are here, there are many of us here. Some have always been. Some have returned. And sure, maybe many still hate us because, sometimes, now we are too rich. But still we continue. We live, we pray, we work. You'll see."

I was completely skeptical, but when the time came, I did see. There was no way I could explain it all to Lizzy, though. There was no way to tell her about it without sounding, well, frightening. After all those years of ignoring my religion, if not actually revolting against it, how could I tell my sister that after one short month in Russia I was a Jew again? Hell, the worst argument I had ever had with Lizzy was over religion. The first Yom Kippur after our mother died, I refused to go to synagogue to pray for her. I never said *Kaddish*. The holiday fell on a Tuesday that year and I used work as an excuse not to go. "How could you be this way?" Lizzy yelled over the phone. "How dare you?" she cried and then hung up on me. So what would she possibly say about me now, now that I had spent the entire day in synagogue with some other family and had actually fasted as well? No, I just couldn't tell her. Not yet.

But the truth of the matter was, this Yom Kippur wasn't like any other Yom Kippur I had ever known. It was different from any Jewish experience I had ever had at all. It began at nine o'clock in the morning when the doorbell rang and there stood Yuri. We were both wearing blue suits and white shirts. Yuri looked serious. As we headed out to the street, he stopped. "Before we go, Natalia said…"

"…to remind me about Elena's husband? Yes, I know. Believe it or not, I thought about that on my own." Nine months earlier, Alexei had drowned in an ice fishing accident. I couldn't understand it when Yuri first told me. Such a weird, freak thing to happen, I thought, until I learned it wasn't so rare, after all. It happened every year, they said, to many people. The ice isn't always as hard as you think. Although Elena never spoke about the accident itself, she did often say things like, "Alexei used to love..." and, "Alexei always told me to..." She always seemed to talk about him easily, even laughing when she remembered funnier times. But any conversation about the subject was always kept superficial. The pain was still too raw. I could see it in the sallowness of Elena's cheeks, the shadowy bags under her eyes. And the first Yom Kippur, the first *Kaddish* after his death was definitely going to be difficult. Even I knew that.

When we reached the synagogue fifteen minutes before services began, it was already packed. Yuri had been right. The foyer was full of people and the fact that the building was being renovated only made the crowd move more slowly. Everyone had to step over drop cloths and around ladders as they made their way to their seats. Natalia slipped her arm through mine, not for support I could tell, but to guide me along. "See, big works here," she whispered. "Paid for by the government. The Mayor said this is an important building. Is wonderful, yes?" Wonderful? I thought it was unbelievable. I still couldn't get over the fact that there was a living Jewish community in Moscow, no less a beautiful old synagogue, not just standing but being rebuilt. The crowd of congregants passed single file through one of those metal detectors that now stood sentry outside nearly every public building in the city. But, after that nod to the modern world, I walked through a set of inner doors and into the world of my grandfathers.

Quietly, one by one, Yuri, Elena, Anna, Natalia and then I climbed up to the balcony, where we found an empty bench right behind the railing. We all sat. Obviously, these were Yuri's family's seats. I looked down at the sanctuary beneath us, which looked just as it must have looked a hundred years before. The benches on the floor were already filled with men in prayer shawls and yarmulkes, mumbling their prayers to themselves and swaying side to side. The morning sun poured in through the clear glass windows and ricocheted off the ornate gold of the ark. I knew the Torah scrolls in that ark must have been ancient and for the first time in my life I looked forward to the moment when the tabernacle would be opened and those Torah scrolls, holding 'the word of God', would be revealed. It was dramatic, if nothing else.

Natalia handed me a prayer book, already opened to the right page. But when I looked down at the pages I saw that not only was one side in Hebrew, as I expected, but the other side was not in English – of course not, why would it be? – but in Russian. I laughed to myself. There'd be no place to hide in that book today. My eyes wouldn't be used for reading. Instead, I'd have to use them for seeing, for really seeing, for looking at the images around me, taking in their full spectrum of light and dark, color and depth and processing them. There would be more than enough to occupy my time, I thought, as I began to look around. Natalia, who had been staring straight ahead at the scene below, must have noticed the way I was studying everything. She turned to me and whispered, "You know, this, here, where we sit, is where Yuri's family always sat, except for when the synagogue was closed. Then we all made believe it was a school. All the seats were different. But now again, this is our place. Generations of Tsypkins pray from just here."

"Generations of Tsypkins." Natalia had said it with such pride. But what about the generations of Rosens? Where had they sat? For a moment I bowed my head and stared at my feet. I was wearing my good black lace-up shoes. I had meant to polish them, but I had forgotten. It didn't matter, though; I rarely wore them anyway. But, I had to admit they did look at home, resting there on the wooden floor of the balcony. I began to wonder if Yuri's grandfather's shoes ever stood on that same piece of wood as my shoes stood now. And what about my own grandfather's shoes? Where had those stood? Just like Yuri, I came from educated, professional Russians. Yuri's father may have been a dentist, but my grandfather had been a doctor and as Lizzy reminded me before I left Boston, the Rosens had all come from Moscow, back when their name was something else. The same was actually true of my mother's side. They were all Russians, as well. Amazingly, all Muscovites. At first, it just seemed like an interesting coincidence. But now, who could say? To be honest, I knew almost nothing about my own family. I had never really been interested in listening to all those old stories. Although my mother had told them constantly to everyone who ever wanted to hear them, I had never paid much attention. But sitting there among those generations of Tsypkins, I started to wonder about my own grandparents and great-grandparents and about my aunts and uncles and cousins all long since gone. I realized, really for the first time, that I was the only one left. There was Lizzy, of course, but she had become as much a part of Peter's family as she was of our own. But there were no aunts, no uncles, no cousins, no grandparents, no parents. Just me.

I began to feel light-headed and remained sitting for a moment, even though the rest of the congregation was now on their feet. Ridiculous as it may sound, I didn't know what would happen to me if I tried to stand. It's not that I was afraid my legs wouldn't hold me. It was just the opposite. Maybe, instead of standing there rooted firmly to the floor, I would float up towards the ceiling like a balloon without air, without a string to tether it to the ground, like something that was full of nothing.

I cleared my throat and coughed. Natalia was standing above me and she looked down at me with concern. She bent over to whisper in my ear.

"Don't worry. Sit. Maybe you are hungry. Fasting is new for you."

"Yes, maybe that's it," I whispered back, although I knew it wasn't. I looked around the congregation. Most everyone was standing now, but here and there others were sitting as well. I could have just sat there for a second if I had wanted. Nobody would have minded. But in the next moment, Natalia's eyes seemed to draw me up to her like a magnet. I felt my legs unbend, my weight flow down to the floorboards beneath me. I realized I began to sway with the rhythm of her movements, just as she swayed with the rhythm of her family around her. At first I thought it was like they were all attached, all one, but then I joked with myself. No, the number wasn't 1. Actually, it was more like they were all 1.0011596 – that number of numbers which had been calculated so carefully over the years. Yes, I thought. It was much more like that number, the numeric expression of the *magnetic moment*, when one single, lonely electron responds to the power of the field around it.

Chapter 29

John:
Facing a Duality (or Who's the Babe?)

So, did I now believe in God? I wouldn't go that far. But I have to admit that after a day of fasting and praying, a remarkable event, crucial to my life, did occur. The Boston Red Sox became unbeatable. Unbelievably and against all odds, they began to win game after game against the New York Yankees, inching their way towards the American League's slot in the World Series. I was nearly out of my mind with excitement and tension. I started to call Marty first thing in the morning after every game.

"Marty, I'm afraid to breathe. I'm afraid to move. Can this be true?"

"I don't know if it can be, but it is," he assured me.

And then, when the Red Sox actually found themselves in the World Series, the tension became unbearable. I didn't know if I should watch the games or not. The team seemed to be doing fine without me. Maybe I should have moved out of the city years ago and just let them get on with it. I tried to explain it to Yuri, who tried to understand and although he did understand a bit, he also couldn't help laughing. I couldn't blame him. I was laughing at myself, too, especially when I heard coming out of my mouth things like, "Maybe they just needed me to get out of the country," or "Maybe Babe Ruth has finally forgiven us for selling him to the Yankees."

But the day before the fourth game, when the Sox had won seven games in a row (wasn't seven a lucky number?) and were possibly, improbably, on the verge of winning the World Series itself, I gave in and bought the most expensive, high-tech radio available in all of Moscow. It still looked like something out of the early 1990's, but nonetheless, it worked. I suppose I could have watched the game later in the day, at the Embassy, with the other wandering, lost fans, but I decided that if I couldn't actually be in Boston on that incredible, historic, clearly once-in-a-lifetime day when the Boston Red Sox might actually, for the first time in eighty-six years, win the World Series, I would at least be awake while it was happening. I made sure Marty called me at 3:30 in the morning Moscow time, to wake me up.

The night before the transmission of the biggest game of my life, I spent an hour setting up the radio. The biggest game of *my* life? This would have been the biggest game of my father's life, my grandfather's life – all our lives. I could just imagine my father doing the same thing in 1967 and even my grandfather in 1946, both Series, like now, played against the St. Louis Cardinals. For a man who professed to believe in nothing but Science (with a capital S), I always had known deep in my heart that for the Red Sox, the road to redemption must lead through New York and St. Louis. Both cities had been the scenes of ignominious defeats. A victory in the Series wouldn't truly be complete unless it included vanquishing those old foes as well. And now it finally was happening. New York was beaten in a clean sweep and St. Louis seemed to be falling fast. But where was I? I was sitting halfway around the world, listening to, of all things, the *American Forces Network* that so-called home away from home for me and all of America's young warriors spread across the far-flung deserts and mountains of the world's trouble spots. That radio was better than a time machine. I could almost hear Bob Hope and Betty Grable chuckling in the ether. But Marty couldn't believe it.

"You're going to listen to it on the radio?"

"Yes."

"You're not going to watch it on television?"

"No. How can I? It will be four in the morning."

"You don't have satellite? Cable?"

"Marty, I don't even have a TV. I just bought a radio, for Christ's sake.""

Everything had to be perfect. I found just the right place in my bedroom where the reception was best, I put my baseball glove and cap on the nightstand and then I tried to sleep. When the phone rang at 3:45, I was already awake.

"You up?" came Marty's voice.

"I'm up. I'm up. How is it over there?"

"Wild. The whole town's going crazy. I don't want to jinx it or anything but, believe it or not, there's going to be a full lunar eclipse out there in St. Louis."

"A lunar eclipse? You mean, a red moon?"

"A red moon."

"Holy shit."

Omens upon omens. Signs upon signs. My heart raced with it all. When I hung up the phone, I just sat there. I didn't put on a light. I didn't brush my teeth or get dressed or anything. I just reached for my Red Sox cap, sat up in bed, in the dark and switched on the radio. The sound was clear and distinct. I could hear the roar of the crowd in the background, the echo of the loudspeaker announcing the teams. I had never been to Busch Stadium. I had never been to St. Louis, but when I closed my eyes I felt as if I was actually there. I could see it all, the green of the field, the white against black of the scoreboard, the giant foam fingers clenched into 'Number 1' signs shooting up into the sky. Then I heard:

" ...and up first for the Red Sox, the lead-off batter Johnny Damon. What a year he's had." And then, the unique sound of hickory hitting leather, and a hysterical broadcaster screaming into his microphone, "It's a home run! Johnny Damon has hit a lead-off home run to give the Sox a one-nothing lead in the first." Within seconds the phone rang. But it wasn't Marty.

"Did you hear it? Did you?" screamed Aaron into the phone, as if his eight-year-old lungs alone had to send his voice across the ocean.

"I heard. I did," I screamed back, jumping out of bed.

"Only seventeen times in the history of the World Series has there been a lead-off home run," Aaron explained. "Did you know that? Do you think we'll break the curse of the Babe now?" But luckily for me, before I had to answer that question of questions, Aaron was yelling again, "Okay. Dad says I gotta go. He'll call you back."

I was now out of bed, pacing the room, holding a base-ball in my hand so tightly my knuckles turned white. Could they break the curse? Was there really a curse that had been hanging over their collective heads for all those years? If you believe that and let's face it – at four o'clock in the morning, in the dark, in a near state of hysteria, I believed almost anything – then the question remained, if curses exist, can they be broken?

Seven forty-five that morning and I felt numb all over. The game had just ended. Victory was ours. I was standing alone in my bedroom in my Red Sox cap and underwear. I couldn't move; I couldn't think. I just stood there, standing and smiling. I didn't know what to do with myself, where to go, what to say, who to say it to. Eventually, I decided I needed to go out into the world, to see what it looked like now that everything was different. I threw on a pair of jeans and a sweatshirt and headed off towards the river. Late October mornings in Moscow are cold, but especially when you forget to wear socks. My ankles started to go red, but I barely noticed. It just made me walk faster, which was, I realized, what I needed to do. This was not the time for a stroll. This was the time for a power walk if ever there was one, when I could breath the cold in deeply and, somehow, inhale all those entangled particles around me as they reacted to the strong forces occurring back in Boston. I looked around as I walked. The trees were still dropping their leaves. The traffic was as loud as ever. Everything looked the same, but I knew nothing was the same. The Red Sox had won the World Series. How unbelievable was that? But this was more than 'just a game'. It was, somehow, everything.

I decided I needed to celebrate. I called Yuri and invited him and Natalia to a blowout dinner at a fancy restaurant in town. I then called Elena and demanded her presence as well. "Anna's a grown up. She can look after the restaurant this once," I insisted. "I'll call her myself – she won't dare say no to me." And she didn't. I then spent the rest of the day puttering around aimlessly. I briefly went into the office, but I couldn't get any work done. I didn't even try. It was a day for amazing events, so after lunch I decided to do another amazing thing. Go shopping. I'd buy myself a commemorative tie, that's what I'd do, I decided. So I took the Metro towards Red Square and headed into GUM. GUM was the most beautiful, awe-inspiring mall I had ever seen. The roof was made entirely of glass; balconies were lined with ornate wrought-iron railings. Imagine if the Tsar had been a commercial real estate developer – that's what it was like. Of course, few locals could afford to shop there, but I was feeling like a larger-than-life rich American so for the first time in my life I headed for the Hermès store and bought myself the most beautiful, expensive silk tie I had ever seen. I wore it to the restaurant that night.

"My friends. *Moy droozya.*" I raised my glass of champagne and looked around the table. Yuri, Natalia and Elena all looked back at me, glasses in hand, smiling, but each with a

259

slightly perplexed look. "Thank you for coming to this celebration on such short notice. But events like this cannot be planned in advance." I remember trying to be serious, despite the suppressed giggles around me. "Today is a historic day. Actually, yesterday was, but for me it was today..."

"Yes, of course," Yuri interrupted.

And then Natalia, laughing out loud, "It is relative. Yes?"

"Yes. Relative. Well, anyway, today is indeed historic, because today, for the first time in eighty-six years, the Red Sox – those few, those noble few (if I may paraphrase Shakespeare)..." This made it impossible for Elena to keep back her laughter, but I stalwartly persevered. "...the noble Boston Red Sox have finally won the World Series. Maybe they just needed a couple of months of me living on the other side of the planet..."

"Of course. It is all about you," Yuri joked.

"Yes, well, look at it this way. It just goes to show that nothing is impossible. If the Red Sox can win the World Series in our lifetime, then anything is possible. All our dreams, our hopes, our unspoken longings in the night..." Okay. So I was starting to go overboard, but I knew Yuri wouldn't let me get out of hand. He jumped up, forcing his way into my toast.

"Yes. Yes. The Red Sox win. You become a poet. Who knows what else? So, to the Red Sox!"

"To the Red Sox!" was heard around the table, then the clicking of champagne flutes and the 'ahhing' at the taste of the most expensive champagne any of us had ever had.

"Well, my friend, we may not fully understand what is so important..." Yuri said.

Natalia interrupted, "Yes. Eighty-six years. Not so long,"

"But nevertheless," Yuri continued, "we are honored to celebrate this with you and benefit from this display of American extravagance." He gestured around the table and the restaurant with a grand sweep of his arms. "Now, let us eat."

That meal was everything I had wanted and needed from that evening. I had hardly been homesick at all since arriving in Moscow. My weekly phone calls to Lizzy and almost daily emails from Marty, had generally been enough. Every day it seemed my Moscow life consumed me more and more. Boston, with its amorphous anxieties and free-floating angst felt more distant all the time. But, even so, World Series day was hard. As happy as I was, I couldn't stop being aware that the biggest day in the history of modern Boston was happening without me. The whole town was celebrating. Everyone had taken to the streets, overcome with a joy that could be born only from an unexpected success after a lifetime of failure. But I wasn't there to share in it. How could I not feel suddenly alone?

But, once again, Yuri and his family came to my rescue. Somehow, without ever asking, they understood what I needed. Their conversation ricocheted between them without time for a breath. Their laughter was loud and their appetites all-encompassing. We had the waiters bring out tray after tray of their best dishes – caviar with blinis, the most tender lamb, roasted with tomatoes and some sort of Georgian spices, smoked sturgeon, pirozhki filled with God-knows-what. It all went on for hours. But after a while, I began to notice that Elena had grown quiet. She was still smiling, nodding her head and laughing, but some distant thought had taken her away.

"Everything okay?" I leaned over to ask.

"Yes, of course," she said.

"You're not worried about the restaurant? You know, your food is just as good as this." That made her really laugh and pat my hand as if I was a small boy trying to compliment his mother.

"You are sweet. Of course, it is not that, not at all. Anna is very capable and my chef knows what he is doing. It is just... " Then she shook her head.

"What?" I asked.

"No. You hate this sort of thing. I don't want to ruin your celebration."

"Ruin my celebration? What can you possibly say that would do that?"

"It is silly. Walk with me after. I will tell you then. But promise now you won't laugh."

After that, she was her usual self. She went back to overwhelming her sister-in-law with compliments and her brother with scolding. Their banter back and forth was piercing and sarcastic, but always followed by a kiss or an embrace. I loved watching them 'in action', even when they forgot to translate their barbs into English. It made me feel at home. But in the back of my mind now was my curiosity about what Elena would later say to me and why she felt she couldn't say it in front of her brother.

The dinner lasted all night. We were the last ones to leave, which was fine with the restaurant, especially considering how much money I had spent. But I was happy, even eager to spend it. It gave me a celebration to remember – after all, I'd be paying for it for months. And it also gave me a chance to thank Yuri for creating this new home-away-from-home for me. And Moscow was slowly beginning to feel like home. Despite the loneliness I might have felt earlier that day, by the end of the evening, I was actually happy to be where I was.

"So, what is this secret of yours?" I asked, after we watched Yuri and Natalia drive away in the family Skoda, leaving Elena and me to our walk and our Metro rides home. I could almost see her blush in the dark.

"Oh, it is silly. I think the champagne made me ... dramatic. Really, it is nothing."

"Oh, no you don't. You've got me walking out here, in the cold. Tell me."

Elena slipped her arm through mine. It was impossible for me not to feel the warmth and comfort of having her close. But I also found it impossible not to remember the last time I had walked like that in the night, so close to a woman. Believe me, it felt very strange to be thinking of Chloe just then, after so much time. That summer night walking across Boston, I had been filled with an uneasy mixture of anxiety and desire. Chloe's first touch was like an electric shock that paralyzed me and held me captive. But feeling Elena's arm through mine was nothing like that. It was, in some ways, even better.

"Okay then. I will tell you. Actually, I suppose it is two things. One, an observation. The other, a favor."

"A favor? Let's have that first. Your observations make me nervous."

"Okay then, the favor first." Elena looked down at the ground and then off across the Square as if the City itself would help her find the right words. "You know, when our parents died, the apartment went to Yuri. That was fine. I was married already. Alexei had his own family home. What they left me was the *dacha*."

"*Dacha*? The country house?" I asked, but actually, I already knew all about it. It was where Yuri and Elena had spent their childhood summers. It was where Alexei had died.

"Yes. But, you know, it is small. A simple wood building with five rooms. Not like in the movies. But it is ours. After Alexei died, Yuri took me back to clean out his things. It was horrible…" Elena's voice trailed off, losing itself in the Moscow night sounds of car horns, laughter, sirens. I had to listen very carefully. "Since then, I have not been back. Yuri and Natalia, yes. Even Anna with friends last summer. But me, no."

"That's understandable. Of course it would be hard for you."

"Yes, it is hard. But, you know, I must. I must make a new life. New memories. Can you understand? I don't want my childhood place to become a … I don't know what … a ghost house." For a while we walked silently. I understood what she didn't want. Of course, I did. But it took me a while to figure out what she did want. And when I did, I knew it was something I could easily help her with, just as Yuri had helped me.

"Elena. What if I went with you? I mean, I'd love to see it anyway and if it would help…"

Elena stopped walking and stood looking at me beneath the light of a street lamp. Now, she was smiling. "Yes, John. Would you? I know it is not proper."

"Not proper?" That, I didn't get.

"Yes, you know – a woman, a man alone in the country…"

So *that* was the problem. Slowly, I began to see why, maybe, she didn't want to ask this in front of Yuri. I tried not to laugh. I certainly would never want to insult her. But really, it was preposterous to be worried about something like that, I thought, especially in this day and age. I chose my words carefully. "Look, Elena, I would never presume to think that you meant anything by this. We're friends, right?"

"Yes. Right. Good friends, so I can ask without embarrassment."

"Embarrassment?"

Elena laughed to herself, again as if she understood so much more than I ever could. "Look. We are at The Bolshoi," she said. "You know it?" She led me across the street to a huge courtyard in front of the enormous yellow-brick building. We both stood, staring up at the statue of Apollo on his chariot which hovers over the columned entrance to the theater, looking as if it is about to take flight.

"Look at him," she said, but it was unclear whom she was now speaking to. "That Apollo. He never ages. Everything changes all around him, but he is always the same." She clicked her tongue like my grandmother used to. "With us, with women, it is different." And then, suddenly, she was back to her old self again, laughing and teasing me just the way she teased Yuri. "But anyway, I know you like young women."

264

"What?" I said, shocked at this new statement of hers. I remember my cheeks even becoming flushed. "What's that supposed to mean? What has Yuri told you?"

"Oh, nothing. He told me nothing," Elena laughed. "But maybe there is something to tell? Yes? Don't look so serious. I'm not stupid. I know you are not married. Young students around you all the time. I know you have many girlfriends."

I said nothing but began to walk around the courtyard in silence. Elena kept laughing, chuckling to herself. I knew she meant it good-naturedly, joking with me the way old friends do. But at the time, it didn't seem so funny. For some reason, I felt the need to explain myself, to make her understand that my love life wasn't what she was imagining. Sure, there had been Chloe, once and never to be repeated. But she made it sound like I had a different teenager every night. What did she think I was? One of those graying old types, ogling each year's batch of new girls? It was disgusting.

"So that's your observation?" I asked. "That I'm some kind of dirty old man?"

"Oh, no," Elena now rushed to say. "I am sorry. I tease too much. I must remember you are not Yuri. You are not so tough – which is a good thing. Come. Let's sit." There was an empty bench beneath the theater's awning. The evening's performance of *Sleeping Beauty* had already let out. The night was quiet. "Forgive me. No, that is not my observation, that you are dirty old man. It is something else." She spoke softly now, drawing me closer. "Just this. When you came to Moscow, you were unhappy. *Pravda*? I could see it. You know, I even asked Yuri if something was wrong; your work, your family, even more than this business about that race with your research. But he said no, nothing. So, I don't know. I start to think maybe it is even worse. Am I right?"

What could I say? I really didn't want to talk about all that now. This was a day to celebrate, not hash over old grievances.

This was a day when curses were being broken, not remembered. But it was useless. I had to say something.

"Yes," I admitted. "You're right." Again, Elena looked around, as if searching the air for words.

"Well, maybe your soul was sad. Don't laugh. We Russians use that word all the time. Yuri calls me 'little soul', *dushinka*. You've heard?"

"Yes, I've heard." Now, I was laughing. "So what are you saying?"

"All I am saying is that, maybe, now, here, things are better. You are better. And, of course, the Red Sox help."

"They certainly do." I thought that was the end of it, but she had more to say. She always had more to say, it's true. But sitting there in the shadow of The Bolshoi, with my stomach still aching from all the food and my face still warm from the champagne, I was happy to listen.

"Do you know, I was a scientist, too," she said. "A chemist at the University. Yes. The *trater* came later for us, with capitalism and Yeltsin. So I may use the word soul, *dusha*, but I know other good words, too. Like 'duality'. That is a good word. Where several things are different but bring the same end? Yes?"

"Yes, it's a good word."

"Okay, then. So that is my observation. Being here in Russia, for many different reasons, makes you feel better."

She looked so earnest, so compassionate sitting there on that bench, that I didn't have the heart to argue. Of course it was ridiculous, all this stuff about soul, duality. But I did have to admit I had been feeling better since I had come to Moscow. I had been having fun. And, truthfully, I hadn't needed one of my pills in days. The reason for it? Why? How? Who knows? In the end, I decided it didn't really matter. We might as well just blame it on The Red Sox.

Chapter 30

John:
Scientific Method

I have to say it – baseball's been very good to me. As a kid, it gave me a place to hide. As an adult, it helped me believe I could stop hiding. There is a force in the universe that makes things happen. Some call it luck. Others talk about dualities and the unavoidable, rapid collision of particles. All I know is that after we won the World Series, I started to feel a sense of release, of movement, as if along with the rest of the universe, I was also expanding.

Since arriving in Moscow I had been diligently working on our holography research. Every day I sat at my little desk in Yuri's office and pecked away, seeing tiny steps of progress here, minor setbacks there. It was a tried and true method for me – peck, peck, scratch, scratch – until eventually 'eureka', only with a lower case 'e'. But now the South Americans were breathing down our necks again and Yuri was pushing harder. It's strange how we would hear nothing about our rivals' research for weeks and then, suddenly, someone somewhere would say, "I saw an early draft," or "I overheard something at a conference..." There was never anything tangible that I could see with my own eyes or feel with my own hands, so my impulse was to ignore the rumors and just get on with the work. But Yuri couldn't do that. He believed in rumors, whether they were true or not. If they were happening, then that was enough to signal trouble and he always tried to confront trouble before it happened. So more and more frequently now and at haphazard moments, he would walk into the office, look over my shoulder and say something like, "Hmmm." Or, he would actually close the door, stride over to the blackboard and scribble while complaining, "But what of this?" All this backroom muttering was frustrating for me, but for him it was worse. He was beginning to show signs of that dangerous indigenous characteristic: brooding Russian despair.

One day, after staring forever at my latest scribblings, I stood up to stretch my legs. I mindlessly began to thumb through some old papers I had brought with me from Boston. There was a stack of them on the radiator, still waiting to be filed. Hidden in the middle was an article written by my hero, Richard Feynman. When I was a graduate student, I swore I would be exactly the type of physicist that Nobel Laureate was – cocky, wild, 'the cowboy of cosmology'. But I realized, as I glanced over Feynman's paper on quantum electrodynamics, that it had been a long time since I had lived up to that promise. Even I had to admit there were sparks of great genius in some of my earlier papers, but over the past few years I had stopped 'rocking the boat'. My ideas had become measured, my calculations over-wrought and the natural scientific curiosity I seemed to have be born with, now looked more and more like distrust. It was generally agreed by scientists that theoretical physics was a young man's game. Well, I was no longer a young man and without even realizing it I had stopped pushing at the boundaries. Yes, my new research was potentially groundbreaking, but I had started to hold myself back, disbelieving that my wildest ideas could really work. I had stopped acting like Feynman.

But now I was in Russia. Why I had come to Moscow in the first place was anyone's guess, but surely one reason had to be to break through the impasse Yuri and I had reached. We had been staring at a wall of wrong numbers for too long. Every time we erased it, it popped back up in some other form. Finally, I'd had enough. Some way or another I had to break through that wall if it took all day and all night for the next two months. I would listen to the Feynman hiding inside me and I would stop playing it safe. If the Red Sox could do it, so could I.

I tossed the article back on the radiator and sat down. Grabbing a new blank notepad, I cleared out a space for it in the center of the table, set it down before me and stared at it. In a matter of minutes, my eyes lost their focus and the blue lines began to blur across the yellow sheet. I twirled a newly sharpened pencil in my hand and then held it over the page and waited. A number seemed to make its way out of my head, through my arm, along the pencil and onto the page. Then came another one. Slowly, characters of my favorite language – mathematic notation – started to appear on the paper. One sign after another. Bit by bit. Not hurried in a flash of inspiration, but quietly, as if they were sneaking up on me, developing on their own. Some unrecognizable amount of time passed and I stopped. I looked at what I had written, scanned the empty air around me and said, "What the..." Something new was on that sheet of paper. It looked wrong. It had to be wrong. But, for the first time in a long time I didn't let that stop me. Maybe wrong was right. Maybe wrong was exactly what we needed. More scribbles. More furrowed brows of disbelief. But something was becoming clearer. Something appeared different than it had before, more plausible but in a previously unimagined way. At this point, I didn't dare stop to think. I made a few more notes on the side of the paper, nothing terribly specific, just hints at what I had begun to see. Then I stood up and headed down the hallway, moving faster and faster with each step. When I reached Yuri's classroom, I did the unthinkable. I knocked on the closed door. A few seconds passed and I knocked again. A student opened the door and just stared at me. I forced my way past him and went up to Yuri, who was now looking worried.

"Tsypkin. Come with me," I whispered.

"What? Natalia?"

"No. She's fine. I just had a thought."

"A thought? Okay. One minute." Yuri mumbled some Russian to his class. They all got up to leave, looking nervous and suspicious. I didn't care. I needed Yuri and I needed him now.

"What is it?" he asked, rushing down the hall after me. "You look like a crazy man."

When we got to the office, I closed the door and went straight to the blackboard. I realized I didn't know where to begin. For a moment, I barely even knew what I had discovered or how. It was all a blur. But out of nowhere came the hint of an idea. I began to write wildly, hurling symbols all over the place. I started with the equation I had just seen develop seemingly without me on that empty sheet of paper. Then I wrote a calculation that Yuri and I had fooled around with over a month before. At that time, it hadn't really worked. The idea had seemed preposterous. Now, though, I was seeing it all with a new brain, as if I was viewing the signs themselves from an acute angle. While I wrote, I talked. "Remember this?" "You see what I mean?" "Now, if you add c2 over c..."

Yuri was silent. I could see that, at first, he was mystified. But soon, a change came over his face. He became intrigued, even excited. Soon, he was on his feet as well, batting at the blackboard with his heavy index finger, muttering "*Da, da,*" under his breath. And then I stopped. I looked at him expecting to hear something from him, but when nothing came I said, "And I guess that's all I've got for now."

"But where did this come from? Why not before?"

"I haven't a clue. But I think that I'm on to something. Don't you?"

Yuri hesitated for a moment. "Yes, I do. But what about...?"

I could have hit him. Those 'what abouts' were exactly what I was trying to get away from and I couldn't let him drag me back into that place of sensible thinking. "Forget the 'what abouts' for now," I said. "I think I've got something here. Leave it with me." I then started rushing around, shutting down the computer, collecting my papers.

"What are you doing? Where are you going?" Yuri asked.

"Not sure. Somewhere. Back to my apartment. But I'm going to figure this out once and for all. Those damned South Americans. Tell your 'Deep Throat' to hold them off. I'll call you." And then I pushed out the door like a man possessed. And I was possessed. Something old and long forgotten was heating up inside me – electricity. It coursed through my limbs, sparking muscles to move, to run, to dash out the building into the cold and rain. But I hardly even noticed the rain. I hardly noticed anything at all, except the murmur of a *"Dosvedanya"* coming from the old security guard as I sped by.

When I finally stood up from my desk at home, it was nearly midnight. Ten hours. Was that possible? The floor was strewn with crumbled drawings and equations. Everywhere I looked I saw arrows and question marks, inequality signs and all sorts of mathematical hieroglyphics. I was tired, but more than that, I was hungry. I opened the refrigerator as if there might be something there waiting for me. What was waiting for me, though, was a whole lot of nothing. But there was milk. I poured myself a bowl of cereal and sat on the couch. I could have killed for a pastrami sandwich, maybe a dill pickle on the side. But Russian-styled corn flakes would have to do. "A silly dinner," I thought to myself. That expression – I hadn't thought of it for years. It was what my mother used to say on nights when she was too tired to cook and I was too lazy to care. Actually, I used to love those dinners. For some reason, they only happened when Lizzy was at a friend's house and my father was working late. Then my mother would smile at me and say, "How about a silly dinner tonight?" as if it was our own special secret.

Thinking about that made me feel pleasantly untethered, as if I was traveling in and out of ideas, of time. I sat there for a while, eating my cereal and staring into space. A series of half-formed thoughts floated around me. Random words. Weird associations from the past, the present. Cheerios. Silly dinners. My mother and her favorite game show, *Wheel of Fortune*. Circles and the forces which make them spin. Quantum spin. Richard Feynman. Weightlessness. Russia. Gravity.

"Shit," I said out loud and jumped up. The empty cereal bowl went flying. Suddenly, it all became clear. Gravity was the key. Of course it was; it always was. But all along, that concept of gravity had given us trouble, screwing up our calculations like some nasty gremlin lurking behind each new set of numbers. But now, I finally realized, or remembered something I had known for years. Yes, gravity was the key, but it was the key precisely because it actually didn't matter. You could add it into the calculation of one theory and not add it into another, but either way those two calculations could still be equivalent. Of course, they could. It's just like speaking two different languages. One merely translates the other. Like 'friend, *droog*' or 'house, *dom*'. Two languages, one meaning. If this had been an old movie, I might even had said my, "Eureka!" with a capital 'E'. I rushed over to the computer and started typing furiously. The next time I stood up, it was morning.

I waited a full twenty-four hours before contacting Yuri. I didn't want to worry him, but I wanted to make sure everything made as much sense in the cool light of day, after a few hours sleep, as it did in the first rush of discovery. Actually, it wasn't really *sense* that I was looking for. Feynman's own work had taught me that. Physics, after all, isn't about what made sense.

Especially quantum physics. Rather, it is about whether a theory, no matter how absurd, agreed with experiment. The theory may not be 'philosophically delightful', to use Feynman's words. It may even seem ridiculous. But, if the numbers worked, they worked. And my numbers worked.

When I finally called Yuri, I immediately heard the concern in his voice. "There you are. At last. You okay?"

"Yes, I'm okay."

"Did you do it?"

"I did it."

"Come here. Fast."

When I arrived at the office, I found a handwritten note, in Russian, tacked to the door. I had no idea what it said, but I was sure it wasn't meant for me. I walked in to find Yuri fidgeting beside the window. "Finally. I am going crazy," he said. "You look like shit. A good sign." I then realized I hadn't even changed my clothes. I had worked in them for two days. I had even slept in them. By now they felt like a suit of armor.

"At least I brushed my teeth. Be thankful for that," I said. "What's with the sign?"

"Oh. It says 'Private Session. Do Not Disturb.' Good?"

"Good."

Yuri placed two chairs facing the frighteningly clean blackboard and sat down. I turned on my computer and unpacked my papers. Suddenly, I was nervous. I knew this was a big moment. I wasn't afraid that Yuri might not agree with me. Actually, I assumed he would find some small problems here or there and that was fine. But I was afraid of something else. It wasn't the science. The science I was sure of. Rather, I was afraid of the way I was feeling. I was feeling too good, maybe too good to be true.

I grabbed a piece of chalk and wrote down my first set of numbers. I started slowly, but soon I was racing to get each new symbol down, hardly ever glancing at my notes. I never said a word. I didn't have to. Behind my back I could hear Yuri making noises of agreement, even occasionally a correct prediction of what came next. By the time I was finished, he was standing beside me, grinning. He threw his arms around me and kissed me on both cheeks, one after another after another.

"Genius," he said. "I do have questions. Minor."

"Of course."

"But, that is later. Even now, I can see this works. I am sure."

"I couldn't have done it without this idea of yours from before. This one, here." I was pointing to a series of numbers somewhere in the middle of the morass.

"I knew at the time it had to be correct," Yuri agreed. "I just couldn't see where to next."

"I know. I couldn't either, until. . "

"Wait." He rushed over to the door and locked it. He even peered out the window and drew the blinds. I laughed, but he scolded me. "No, John. Do not be foolish. We must be careful. I am not saying anyone here would steal this, but..."

I sat in silence as I watched him open the bottom drawer of his desk and take out a small digital camera. Carefully, section by section, he photographed the contents of the entire board.

"Yuri, this is crazy. I have it all in my computer and notes anyway."

"Yes. That is why. This is more secure."

"Okay, Mr Bond," I teased. "Do what you must." Suddenly I felt exhausted. The adrenaline which had sustained me for days had finally run out. "Whoa. I could use a cup of coffee."

When he finished photographing, Yuri erased the blackboard. All of it. Then he said, "When did you eat?" He lifted up a bag, which had been sitting unnoticed in the corner. Out of it he pulled a thermos, a loaf of dark raisin bread, two plastic cups and a knife. "Natalia..." he shrugged and smiled. "But, sorry, there is only tea. No coffee."

"Yuri, you found yourself a Jewish saint." We sat silently eating for a while, but really we were digesting everything we had just discovered. I stared at the floor. He stared at the now empty blackboard.

After a while, he said, "Your notes. Let me see them." Then he started to mumble. The mumbling was in English so it must have been meant for me, but he looked like he was talking to himself. "Yes. Here and here," he pointed carefully. "A slight adjustment? Maybe." He then stood up and shook his head. "I just can't understand…"

"What? Did I miss something?"

"No, nothing," he said as if now changing his mind, but he looked like the words were trying to force themselves out of his lips, whether he wanted them to or not. "Only, you see, I knew, I mean I hoped, if you came to Russia, if we actually were together, over time, we could do it. And we did." He then started to laugh. "I feel like Elena."

"Don't you start talking about my soul, now."

"No, not that. But you have to admit…"

I did have to admit. Something was up. I knew it. But I also knew that it didn't matter why. The *why* was something no one could ever really explain. All physicists understood and accepted that fact. Only the *how* was important and what I had been able to demonstrate, both in my work and, unbelievably, in myself, was this *how*. "All I know," I said, tentatively at first but then with growing confidence, "is that it's something about how you deal with gravity. This idea, me, everything. Do you know what I mean? Gravity is the weakest force of all, but it's the thing that keeps us down."

"Yes, that is true." Once again, Yuri knew exactly what I meant. But he was the one who could in any language find the right words. "But of course you know you only feel gravity when you resist it. When you give in, then you are free."

I raised my plastic cup to him. "I'll drink to that."

Chapter 31

Grace:
Pish Posh

"Time flies like an arrow. Fruit flies like a banana." Groucho Marx, *A Day at the Races.*

Or was it *A Night at the Opera*? It doesn't matter. I watched those movies over and over when I was a kid. In my family, Groucho Marx was God.

It seemed one minute I was eating bananas off a tray in the Hammersmith Hospital, the next minute it was four years later. I can't tell you what happened during those years, but I do know they flew by. There was a period in my life when I experienced time as if it were pockets of turbulence I had to pass through. But as the years went by, I started to feel like it was my traveling companion. Time and I were in this together.

John finished high school. I did what I could to help him, but it wasn't very much. He had always been the sort of kid who wanted to do everything by himself. During that time when I couldn't even cut my own food, John grew even more self-reliant. He got himself up in the morning, did his schoolwork, made his own plans. When I should have been the most reliable person in his life, I was the least. How could I blame him for not wanting my help, when I was finally ready to give it?

Soon after John went back to the States for college, my father started getting sick. It began with little annoyances – arthritis, hip replacements – then moved on to the debilitators – diabetes, blindness, strokes. It seemed like every few months there was some new distressing phone call from my mother. The 3,500 miles to Brooklyn seemed further away than ever.

When my father had his last stroke, slipping into the coma that would eventually become his death, Jack was terrified. How would I handle the death, the funeral, my grieving mother? he worried. I think he was afraid that what happened to me once, would happen again. He would have denied this, I'm sure of it. But I could see this fear standing there beside him as if it had a body of its own. When I decided I absolutely had to go be with my mother (over a month, as it turned out), Jack couldn't contain himself any longer. I think he was afraid that, literally and metaphorically, I just wouldn't come back. I won't pretend I wasn't frightened, too. There were nights, lying in the dark, listening to my mother cry, crying myself, when I didn't know if I could stand it. Sometimes it's hard to remember the lessons you've learned, even if you've gone through so much to learn them.

As it turned out, my mother's pain gave me something outside of myself to focus on. It was plain to see how much she needed me and how much I needed her to need me. My mother had done nothing on her own, nothing exclusively for herself for over sixty years. For all the complaining and bickering, I knew she liked it that way. It's not that my parents were so much in love. Or maybe they were. Who am I to say? But after all that time, they had become a collective noun– *momanddad*. The boundaries dividing them had blurred a long time ago.

It's wrong to say I survived the death of my father. I lived through it. The pain in my heart was physical – it left me breathless. But in the end I remained whole, as I eventually realized I would. The image of my father sitting in his chair, a conspiratorial wink in his eye, came to rest safely at home inside me. People you love become a part of you. They do. And when that happens, you feel better. Jack could see that I felt better and so he began to feel better, too. My mother, on the other hand, never really recovered. When she died herself, less than a year later, I have to say I wasn't surprised. Human beings have this extraordinary capacity to choose. They can choose to remember their joys rather than remember their sorrows. They can will themselves to live and they can will themselves to die. For me, that fact stands as a proof, like a geometric theorem, of everything I have come to believe in my life.

So there we were again; another Brooklyn funeral. Jack and the kids came, of course, but that was basically it. My brother-in-law offered to fly in from Hong Kong, but I told him not to. His firm had moved him there not long after Gina's death and he'd just been back for my father's funeral. Enough was enough. There were a few others with us, neighbors, synagogue members. But all in all, it was a small group.

At the funeral home, the Rabbi said the usual prayers and gave a nice enough sermon, considering he didn't really know my mother. Our old Rabbi had died himself in the months between my parents' deaths. I had never felt very close to him, anyway. I never really felt anything about him at all, except when I was a teenager. Then, his bushy eyebrows looking down at us during services made me feel guilty, even when there was nothing to feel guilty about. But, like it or not, our old Rabbi was a fixture in our lives. He presided over Gina and my Bat-Mitzvahs. He married us and ate big slices of cake at our weddings. He was always there in the background, ready when we needed him, like a card table you pull out of the closet. Except this time. Now, he was gone, too, and it left me feeling like a lone survivor. As the new, stranger-of-a-Rabbi led us in the prayer of *Kaddish*, I was the only one left standing.

When it came time to go to the grave site, it was just me and Jack and the kids sitting in one limousine. There was no motorcade leading to the cemetery. We simply drove behind the hearse, across Brooklyn, to that huge expanse of tombstones you can see from the highway. Those journeys to the cemetery are always terrible, but the drive we took to bury Gina was the worst. I can't think of one without thinking of the other. At Gina's funeral, I sat with my parents, Jack and my brother-in-law in the first car at the head of a long line of cars, all moving slowly, all with headlights on. I remember thinking I would throw up whenever we hit a pothole or stopped short. My parents were devastated. I know what it's like to lose a baby. But to lose a grown child is the worst possible tragedy. How does one move on from there? At the time, I was just beginning to realize how it could be done. But it didn't make it any easier. My brother-in-law was like a zombie. It was unbearable.

The drive to my mother's funeral was much different, though. It actually felt easy. There was no hysteria. No terrible unburdening. The four of us just sat there, chatting quietly, resigned to our latest loss. John talked about his friends at college. We finally got to hear some details about Lizzy's new job. Then came stories about their grandparents, stories from their childhood. Those stories made us all feel better, more normal. I remember looking out the window and watching the old green road signs pass overhead. Grand Central – 1st Left. Long Island Expressway – Keep Right. I heard the voices of my children and thought to myself, *"My mother's dead."* I mean, I knew she wanted to be. She had lived her life and was ready to move on. I guess she was lucky, or maybe, as I like to think of it, her quiet, timely, painless death was her reward for living her life as best she could, with kindness and spirit.

The journey to the grave site was easy. It was arriving that was difficult. There, laid out before our eyes, was my entire family. There weren't many of them and even though I had seen them all there before, lined up side by side, the sight of it still startled me. There were my grandparents, who I knew more from stories than from anything else. They had been dead for so long already, it might as well have been another lifetime. Then came Gina and my father, almost like stepping stones leading to my mother's newly dug grave. "They're all there," John said. "Just waiting," I thought to myself. That's when I really started to cry. My longing for them, the sounds of their voices, the sounds of my childhood, was like a tender bruise deep inside that would never go away. And I didn't want it to. Somehow, it gave me comfort to know that I could touch that bruise, think of them and feel that longing. Standing there, the four of us together, I knew for certain that I wasn't really alone, no matter how long I lasted or who I out-lived. I wanted to say, "Look, Ma. Here we all are." This would make us both rest easier.

After the funeral, we went back to the old house and sat *shiva*. I knew what to do all too well. I covered the mirrors. I found a hard stool to sit on. I pinned a small piece of torn black ribbon to the front of my dress. Lizzy ordered a platter of cold cuts and pastries from the local deli, but barely anyone came and those who did I hardly knew.

Then it was over. The Rabbi said one last prayer. We threw out the leftovers. I urged the kids to go home. John needed to get back to school and Lizzy back to work. I think as the older child and the daughter, Lizzy felt she had a responsibility to stay and help me. She was just living in New York, after all, and could easily come and go back and forth from work. I thought about having her stay, but I realized I didn't really need her. Actually, I didn't need Jack either. It was as if all the hard work was already done. I was content to tie up the last remaining loose ends myself.

Of course, it worried Jack to leave me on my own, but I wasn't eager to have him stay. To be honest, he was never his best around death. He saw death as a time to become his most reasonable and pragmatic. He took on the role of 'The Great Organizer' and that was fine. It prepared him for his own parents' deaths and left him feeling alive and functioning. But I didn't need that sort of help. If Gina had been there, it would have been different. Two sisters going through the final effects of their parents – I could have imagined wanting that. But Gina was gone and if it couldn't be her, then I didn't want anyone.

So, I was alone when I went back to the house for the last time. I put my key into the front door and pushed expecting resistance. It opened with such a force it sent me flying into the hall. That door was always stuck. It swelled with the cold damp of each winter and the summer's humidity made it swell even more. "Jesus, this house will be the death of me," I found myself saying, just like my mother.

There were a dozen pieces of junk mail on the floor and the house had only been empty a short time. I picked it all up and put it on the little, round table under the mirror. I went straight to the kitchen as if it was any day in any year. I took a plastic tumbler from the cupboard and poured myself a glass of water from the tap. "New York City water's the best water in the world," I could hear my father say.

"So, Grace, what first?" I said out loud to nobody, just to hear my own voice. I walked into the living room and there they were, stacks of empty boxes left for me by the movers. What first? Although I had made arrangements to have a moving company come, I still had to go through everything and see if there was anything I wanted. After my father's death, my mother did nothing. Neatnik that she had been, she even stopped cleaning. She didn't change anything. She didn't move anything. My father's things were exactly where he had left them. There was even his Yankees cap, tossed on top of the old television. The house was in suspended animation, as if she knew she would be gone soon, too, so why bother?

I grabbed a box and went upstairs to their bedroom. It was full of old people things, like a crocheted tissue box cover, doilies protecting the surfaces of furniture, an embroidered footstool beneath a small chair. They looked like old people's things, but actually they had been there for years, as long as I could remember. They weren't all just old people's things. They were my parents' things.

I opened the closet. I wanted to make sure there weren't any boxes of photographs or papers hidden away and seeing that there weren't, I closed the door again. I didn't need to look at every skirt, every blouse. I looked in the dresser. Nothing there but old stockings, handkerchiefs, enormous bras and Playtex Living Girdles. Then, my father's. There were his gold-toed support socks and his boxer shorts, sleeveless T-shirts in ribbed white cotton, a cru-neck sweater or two. After he died, my mother refused to let me go through his things. They were all still there as if he was due back from work any minute.

Of everything I found in that house, all I really wanted were the photographs. There were hundreds of them, all scattered around, adorning every flat surface and tabletop. There was the one of the kids at the Cape while they were still little. Lizzy graduating from high school. John graduating from high school. Me holding John as an infant with Lizzy looking over my shoulder. My wedding photo. Gina's wedding photo. My parents' wedding photo. All slightly faded. All neatly arranged. I took them frames and all, sweeping them one-handed into a box resting on my hip.

Thinking about it now, I realize it was all quite methodical. It wasn't automatic, as if I was some soulless robot. I was systematic, organized. Each room got its attention, its last double-check. It was clear what I wanted and clear what I didn't. But I remember being stumped by their bedside tables. "Maybe there's something important in there," I thought to myself. But when I reached out towards one of the drawers, I stopped. I couldn't do it. Those tables were too personal, too private. I remembered how we were never allowed to go into those drawers when we were growing up. Once, when I tried (nine, I think I was), my mother caught me just as the drawer was sliding open. "What are you doing?" she asked. "What are you looking for?"

"Nothing."

"I don't sneak a look into your drawers, do I?"

"No."

"All right then."

Something about those drawers felt sacred. I never looked
in them again after that one time and I couldn't bring myself to
do it now. Whatever private items were hidden in there would
have to stay. Old prescription medicines, often-read letters,
even old, dried-up condoms – I didn't need to see them. They
were the last remnants of intimacy. I let them go.

After that, I roamed around from room to room, touching
old pieces of furniture, smoothing out bits of upholstery. I
stopped one last time in my bedroom. There was nothing there
I needed, but my bed was still a comforting place to be. I
slipped off my shoes and swung my feet up, settling in for a quiet
rest. I didn't close my eyes, though. I just stared into space, un-
focussed, listening to the noises in the street and the quiet in the
house.

I think that's when I truly realized my parents were gone.
That whole generation was over. It was now, somehow, up to
me. I was sad, but I wasn't afraid. My parents had done the best
for me they could. I knew I could take it from there.

After a while, I picked up my one box of keepsakes and
went back downstairs. I was getting hungry. I sat down at the
kitchen table (yellow Formica – what else?) and reached for a
leftover box of cookies. I took one out and bit into it. There it
was, that soft almond paste in the middle, those thin shards of
almond on the top. It was such a familiar, but distant taste. It
brought me right back to those afternoons in the kitchen, doing
my homework or playing dolls while my mother cooked. I used
to sit there, waiting until I could lick her fingers. I saw my own
fingers covered in sticky cinnamon and powdered sugar and
licked them, too.

I opened the small drawer that was hidden in the side of
the table. I was looking for the deck of cards. It was still there, as
I knew it would be. We were a card-playing family, after all.
Come to think of it, I bet in the back of my mind I had been sav-

ing that little discovery for last. I felt the weight of the pack in my hands. The cards were almost still warm, they were so worn. I remember looking at the three empty chairs around the table and suddenly seeing they were full. There sat my family – my mother, my father and Gina. The four of us were sitting there like any weeknight in any year. My father was shuffling the cards, a bridge forming between his fingers that made a clicking sound as it collapsed into a perfectly reordered stack. We were going to play Pish Posh. My parents were poker players. They never really played with anyone else, at least not that I know of. But every night, growing up, I could hear them in the kitchen, smoking cigarettes, drinking coffee and playing poker, just the two of them, their games getting more and more complicated (seven-card draw, deuces wild, aces high), their bets getting more and more exotic (I'll see your two Cadillac Sevilles and raise you a trip to Florida). Eventually, Gina and I would storm in, demanding to play.

"You're too young for poker," my father would tell us.

"No, we're not. I'm nearly ten and Gina's smart for her age."

"What would the neighbors say?"

"We won't tell them."

He raises an eyebrow, winks at my mother and nods. Gina and I sit down quietly, hoping they don't realize how near bedtime it is.

"Ok, girls," Mom says. "We'll play 'Pish Posh'."

"Can Jacks be wild?"

"Yes, Jacks can be wild."

"And sevens!"

"And sevens."

Actually, we could have wanted the entire deck to be wild and they would have said yes. Because 'Pish Posh' I learned much, much later, was a made-up game between the four of us. No one else had ever heard of it or knew how to play, because it was the invention of my parents. The rules changed every time, often in the middle of a hand and although someone was always winning, there never was actually a winner. Everyone put a card down and if you saw a card you wanted to pick up, you could have it, as long as you could come up with a plausible reason for it. If you ran out of cards, you picked five more from the deck. If the deck was empty, you used the discard pile, if it wasn't too late, or you'd 'continue tomorrow' if it was past your bedtime. It was a wonderful game. Anyone could play, as long as they were loved by one of us and it never ended, because as we knew, actually, there always was a tomorrow.

Chapter 32

John:
The Stubbornly Persistent Illusion

Winter finally came to Moscow. Although it had been 'winter coat' cold since the end of October, it took nearly another month for the sky to turn steely gray and for frost particles to start forming around your nose. Now when I looked out my apartment window, I saw a dusting of snow on the trees and below, a parade of fur hats and fur boots. "Pack warm clothes," Elena had said. But I wasn't concerned. After years and years of Boston winters, I assumed I knew cold.

I waited for the Skoda to appear outside my building. It was Saturday morning, but I felt as if I had done nothing but wait since Thursday. On Thursday, I spent the entire day working on the narrative section of our holography paper. All day long I sat there on my own, typing away, pacing around the small room, waiting for Yuri to appear. But on that day, Yuri never did appear. When I finally called his apartment, I waited and waited for someone to pick up the phone, but again, no one. At last, just around dinnertime, my phone rang. It was Elena. "John," she said. "We didn't want you to worry. Everything is okay, but Yuri asked that I call you. Natalia has had another miscarriage."

"Another? Is she alright?"

"Yes. She is fine. It was very early in her pregnancy. Maybe eight weeks. Yuri was with her at the clinic all day. That is why he wasn't at work."

"My God. Okay – what can I do?"

"Nothing. Thank you. They are home now. Physically, she is fine… "

"Should I call? Should I stay away?"

"For now, let them be. They will rest. But I thought Saturday maybe we should all go to the *dacha*. Some country-side. Some quiet. It will be good for her. A distraction. Will you come?"

"Of course, I'll come. I'll distract them. I'll distract all of you."

Elena laughed. "Yes, I know you will. And then, we will do our trip another time – soon."

I was nervous, standing there that Saturday morning, watching for the car to come around the corner and pull up beside my building. I didn't know what to expect. How upset were they? How somber a weekend would this be? And anyway, it was all a bit confusing. Natalia pregnant again? I hadn't heard that a new trial had started. Surely, Yuri would have said something. Could she have gotten pregnant on her own? When the car finally appeared, I leaned over the backseat and gave Natalia a hug to say how sorry I was. She smiled and said, "Don't worry. I am fine. It was not meant to be. This time."

We sped out of Moscow. The roads were nearly empty that early on a Saturday. "This way we miss the traffic and have the whole day," Elena explained. "I brought lots of food from the *trater*. Andrei made his dumplings." I remember groaning. "What?" Elena said. "You don't like Andrei's dumplings?"

"I don't like them, I love them," I explained. "That's the problem. Once I get started eating those things, I can't stop. Do you have any idea how much weight I've gained since I've been here?"

"Ah, you sound like a girl," Yuri teased. "Don't worry, you still look the same, like a twenty year old. And anyway, why do you still have so much hair on your head? What kind of Jew are you?"

"Not that again. You have a Samson complex, you know that?"

"First James Bond. Now Samson. What next?"

"Okay, boys, enough," Elena interrupted. "You are both beautiful. But also both forgetful. Yuri, did you bring the new heaters?"

"Yes. One for each bedroom. Expensive, though."

"Anna said she would help."

"Oh, did she?" Yuri laughed. "Now that she works in a bank she is such a big deal, my niece?"

"Oh, but it is wonderful," Natalia said. "Imagine, twenty-three and making such money!"

"It is a new world," agreed Elena.

"And now, with our heaters, a warm one," said Yuri.

I listened to the family chatter, but really I remember I was concentrating on the sights speeding past us. Within no time at all, we were on a deserted highway in the middle of nowhere.

"You are quiet," Yuri said.

"I'm just looking. It's incredible. There's nothing here but trees."

"What did you expect? This is the forest."

"But we're not even a half hour outside of town. I don't think I've ever seen so much empty space in all my life."

"Yes, just small farms and now and then a village."

"It's beautiful, barren, like the 1800's or something. I'll make you a bet, though," I said. "Now that you have all embraced capitalism, by the time I'm back here in ten years or so, this whole area will be filled with Starbucks and MacDonald's."

"Well, if people get jobs…" Natalia said.

"What ten years?" Elena snapped at me, taking her eyes off the road just long enough to give me a playful grimace. "You will be back long before that, you know."

Within an hour, a small road veered off into the forest. In the distance I could just about make out some fenced-off plots of farmland and a scattering of small buildings.

"Here we are," said Elena. The road's frozen mud crackled beneath the tires. We were driving through a village. Actually, it was more like a settlement. There wasn't a store. There wasn't even a church. But carved among the trees were small gardens, now covered with the winter's first snowfall and behind each one, a wooden building, painted in blue or yellow, each with scalloped wood around the windows and a large brick chimney in the center of a sloping roof. "And this one is ours," Elena announced. I got out of the car and stood there in silence while the others unpacked the bags. I wanted to help – I had meant to – but instead I stood there, rooted, staring, as if I was lost in time.

Eventually, I felt Yuri slapping me on the back. "You like?"

"It's beautiful. Like a fairytale." I had to shake my head to bring myself back to reality. "But, here, let me help."

Elena and Natalia were already in the kitchen making lunch. I helped Yuri with the new heaters. Together we lifted the first one out of the box, gently as if it was some instrument of rare intricacy. Of course, it was no different from the hundred others I had seen before over the years, just a simple, rectangular space heater with a long cord coming off the back, a dial on the side which, in Russian, must have read 'on-low-high', and a wire grill on the front to keep prying fingers off glowing orange coils. I laughed. "Okay. Plug it in and turn it on. Pretty basic, eh? And this was expensive?"

"Yes," said Yuri, more seriously than I had expected. "But I bought three and paid in dollars, so I got a good price."

I said nothing more about it, but went into the other two bedrooms to plug in their new heaters. Each bedroom was the same; a small, square room with a sloping ceiling, an old metal-framed bed covered with quilts, a straight-backed wooden chair in the corner, a painted wooden wardrobe against a wall. Everything was wood, as if the entire existence within those walls had been carved out of the forest itself a century before. As I roamed from room to room plugging in those simple, though longed-for space heaters, I found myself getting embarrassed, once again, at how much I had always taken for granted. In America, I had everything – central heating, satellite TV. But here in Russia, nothing could be taken for granted. At first I thought Russia made me feel as if I was trapped in a time warp, hovering between the new-fangled and the old-fashioned. We all might have forged our way into a new millennium, but you would never know it by looking around this *dacha*, with its simple wooden construction and surrounding acres of dense, undeveloped forest. But then I came to realize that I didn't feel as if I was trapped *in* time. Rather, standing there, cold from the still unheated air, staring into the quiet narrow spaces between the trees outside the windows, I felt *beyond* time. To me it felt as if Russia herself was beyond time.

The smell of simmering chicken stock and dumplings reached me. It lured us to the kitchen table, which was already set with a platter of smoked fish and bread on a carving board. Yuri poured vodka into four small glasses. "For the cold," he said, passing them around."*Na zdarovya.*"

All during lunch, I watched Natalia. I couldn't help myself. She looked fine. She sounded fine. But immediately after finishing eating, Yuri stood up from the table and went over to her chair. "I think now Natalia must rest," he said.

"I can help clean first. Really, I am fine. "

"Don't be silly," Elena scolded. "John and I will do it. There is very little anyway."

"Absolutely. Go rest. We'll see you later," I agreed and watched as Yuri led Natalia to their bedroom. Considering he was such a huge bear of a man, Yuri could be surprisingly quiet and gentle with Natalia. It was a side of him only his wife seemed able to bring out and I loved seeing him like that.

When I turned back to help Elena in the kitchen, she was nearly finished. Cleaning up had taken no time at all. "How about a walk?" I asked.

"Yes, I was going to say the same. Come. We will walk and look for mushrooms." Elena and I tiptoed around, trying to be as quiet as possible while we put on our boots, hats and coats and walked out the door. Elena led the way on a path past one other house and into the woods. The air was very cold, but the sun was even stronger. It shone through the empty branches of the trees and made the icicles shimmer like mirrors. There was so much silence around us, I felt like I should whisper.

"So, tell me. How is it now, for you being here?" I asked.

"What? For me? Oh, that. No, it is fine. Funny, how when you worry about someone else you forget yourself."

"Good. I'm glad," I said and then found myself wondering what to say next. I said nothing for a while. Neither of us did. But then I simply asked, "Mushrooms?"

"Yes. With so little snow, you can still find some. Maybe then a soup."

"I haven't looked for mushrooms since - I don't know. I used to go with my grandmother when I was really little. Funny."

"And did she make soup?" Elena asked.

"I guess. Who can remember?"

I watched Elena stoop down, brush aside some snow and pick up a mushroom. She smelled it and then put it under my nose. "You see? This one's good. We'll find some more." As we walked further into the woods, Elena became busier, sweeping away snow, unearthing more mushrooms. She had put a bag into her coat pocket and by now it was half full. I just watched, following behind, now and then kicking some dirt with the toe of my boot. I remember feeling suddenly subdued, for some reason. I wasn't tired, but there was something about being there in that forest, watching Elena go about her chore, which made me feel strange. An absurd kind of melancholy came over me. Suddenly, all I wanted to do was sit down and rest. I found an old tree stump and brushed it off. "Let's stop for a second, okay?" Elena found one last mushroom and then sat down next to me. Our shoulders touched. We didn't say anything at all for a few minutes. I suppose it was clear I was thinking about something, trying to figure something out. "Elena, can I ask you something?"

"Of course."

"Did you know Natalia was pregnant again?"

"Yes. She had just told me. Last week."

"You know, I wonder if this is safe."

"Safe? Maybe safe isn't so important to her. After all those years of trying, this pregnancy was a surprise. A happy surprise. A bolt from the blue, I think you say."

"But doesn't that make it even worse?"

"Maybe yes. Maybe no. Either way, it is always a sorrow. The loss is still the same. And the hope."

We sat for a few minutes in silence. Now I was trying *not* to think. I would have liked to just sit there, mindlessly, listening to the sounds around me. But I was having trouble. I felt troubled inside, and I was struggling between trying to figure it out and not wanting to think about it at all. I hated feeling that way and I began to regret the fact that I had decided, really to please Yuri more than anything else, to leave my vial of pills back in Moscow. I hadn't actually expected to need them on this weekend. I'd only taken one over the past few weeks anyway and that was – I don't even remember why that was. But now I began to wonder if my pill-popping days weren't really over after all. I started to talk, just as a way to get those thoughts out of my head. But what I said surprised me. "You know, my mother lost a baby once."

"Really? A miscarriage?" Elena asked.

"No, a baby. He was born a few years before me. I think Lizzy was three." I continued to look down at the ground, randomly kicking aside dirt and stray twigs. I could feel Elena staring at me, but I couldn't think of anything else to say. Sure, even I could see why I was thinking about that baby I never knew, but talk about him? I had never talked about him with anyone for years. But Elena seemed to have that affect on me, as if she was forever giving me permission to tell her things I never even told myself.

"So, you had a brother?" she eventually said. "What happened? How did he die?"

"Nobody really knows. They call it 'crib death'. The baby goes to sleep and never wakes up."

"My God. How terrible that must have been."

"Yea, but my parents didn't talk about it much. My father never did. Neither did my mother – well, at least not until she got much older. Then she talked about it a lot, actually. Like she talked about everything, I guess."

"How old was he?"

"The baby? Three or four months. I'm not sure. His name was Sam."

We sat on that stump in silence for a while longer. It was getting colder all the time and although it didn't seem to bother Elena, the cold made me shiver. But even so, I didn't move or speak.

"Didn't your sister almost die, too?" asked Elena in a voice that seemed to come out of nowhere.

"Lizzy? Yea. That's how she lost her eye. And I was sick a lot as a little kid. In and out of the hospital all the time. Crazy, huh?"

"Your poor mother. No wonder."

No wonder? Elena said that as if she now understood it all. But I still couldn't understand anything. I sat silently for a very long time. At one point, I felt some motion beside me and I thought I heard Elena's voice, but it sounded far away. I just

294

kept sitting there, though. There were times when I thought my eyes were closed, but at other times they were open again. Sometimes I felt the air get cold. Other times I felt nothing at all. For a long time my thoughts were whirling, ricocheting from one extreme to another. I tried to think about my mother. I actually wanted to for once, but I couldn't really picture her. I couldn't picture her trapped in a single moment the way I could my father, say, sitting on the couch at Thanksgiving, watching football on television. Or my grandparents, playing cards at the kitchen table, smoking cigarettes. Each image of my mother that came to mind melded into another one, so that I could never really see her at all. Whatever stubborn illusion of her I had been carrying around inside my head seemed to be vanishing. I couldn't see her, but I could feel her just the same. Everywhere. Inescapable. And the more I felt her, the sadder I became for her. My eyes filled with tears and I knew this time it wasn't from the wind. All those losses. Those fears I never knew. No wonder, Elena had said. No wonder was right.

Suddenly it was much colder. I stood up, my legs felt stiff. I realized I had been sitting there for a very long time. I looked around for Elena, but she was nowhere to be seen. The sun was beginning to set. My watch said four o'clock. The days were short at that time of year, I knew, and sunset came suddenly. I could barely see the path underfoot, but the lights from the *dacha* were bright in the distance. I began to hurry; the others shouldn't worry about me. And anyway, I was getting hungry. I could almost taste the mushroom soup I knew was waiting for me, back home.

Chapter 33

Grace:

The Rock, the Fox and the Woman

There is a lovely hotel in Wiltshire with a thatched roof and a vegetable garden. It is surrounded by acres of farmers' fields. I don't know how I found out about it, whether I saw it listed in some magazine or whether I dreamed it, but a few months after my mother died, I woke up one morning knowing I needed to go there.

Being home after the funeral was hard. Although I felt emotionally strong, physically, I was weak. My parents' deaths, coming so soon one after another had drained me. Just like when I first came out of the hospital, Jack was terrified to leave me alone and terrified to be with me. The questions "What should I say?" and "What shouldn't I say?" hung threateningly in the air.

But I was patient. I had learned patience years ago in the hospital, during months of waiting for some unimagined something to happen. I knew there was nothing I needed to do now but be home and love us.

I found myself thinking a lot after my mother's death about the months I spent convalescing. I remembered a conversation John and I had soon after I came home from the hospital. It was a Saturday afternoon. I was finishing my lunch and John was just coming out of his room for breakfast. His eyes were puffy and his short hair spiked up in different directions. I just smiled and offered him a bowl of cereal. I stood against the sink, watching him eat and turn the sports pages of the newspaper. It was quiet and peaceful. In time, John looked up at me, somewhat suspiciously. He shook his head as if he was a parent contemplating some child's silly antics. "Mom, is this really you, now?" he asked. "Yes," I answered. "This is really me."

Now, years later, it was still really me. But Jack and I felt fragile. We had to be reassured.

I decided to start taking long walks again, often following the same routes I had taken with Lizzy years before. This time, it was Katherine who walked with me. She was still in London, her twins now in high school and every few days, we set out together to cover as many miles as our aging legs allowed. We called it exercise. Really, it was friendship. We walked slowly. We stopped to read monument inscriptions. I took notes in a little spiral-bound notebook I carried everywhere. "Who was Charles Napier?" "Where is the Sind?" We wore layer upon layer so we could sit outside with a cup of tea whenever the sun was shining.

It was during these walks through manicured gardens and systematically spaced trees that I began to hunger for a different view. I began to crave scenery without concrete, with wide expanses of green and varying levels of earth. My need for the countryside became almost a physical need, a longing I could feel in the muscles of my arms, like a mother longing to hold her child. Over and over I fell asleep to images of open fields and dirt paths and woke from dreams of empty skies. I decided to take a trip.

Jack's initial reaction was delighted surprise. "Sure, we'll make a weekend of it," he said. But that wasn't really what I wanted. I realized that what I wanted was time out of the city and alone. I wanted to walk through the fields on my own, to hike through woods in the falling light, to sit on a boulder staring blankly at the sky. This was something I would crave more and more as the years went by, but this first request to go off on my own was met with fear.

Jack suggested we call the psychiatrist. Maybe I was having a relapse. Maybe my parents' deaths had been too much for me. That's when I realized that Jack would always be afraid I was teetering on the brink of breakdown. Any behavior out of the ordinary, any prolonged silence or unusual request was met with held breath. I knew this was his problem, not mine. I knew I was fine within myself, the debilitating lump in my throat long since gone. But Jack's fears for me choked him still and all I could do to alleviate those fears, was to live my life and give him time.

I had to take that trip. I didn't want to give Jack any more reasons to worry, but I felt more and more strongly that I needed to go. It could be just for a few days and it needn't be very far away. I became convinced there was some reason why I needed to go there, wherever 'there' was.

Once again, Katherine came to my rescue. I explained it to her one afternoon while we sat in the café in Hyde Park, overlooking the Serpentine, drinking coffee and eating Eccles cakes. It was still late winter. The paddleboats were tied together like a floating island in the middle of the pond. The geese were squawking around our feet, looking for an off-season handout. The clouds were sailing quickly from one side of the sky to the other.

"Listen, Grace," she said. "There is no way Jack is going to let you go off into the countryside on your own. You may not like it, but you have to understand how he feels."

Of course, I understood. But there had to be a solution. There always was a solution. In an instant, it became obvious to me. "Come with me, Katherine. You can be my chaperone. You can make sure I don't hurt myself." I laughed, knowing those days were over. "You can follow behind me, stealing in and out of bushes like Sherlock Holmes."

She was easily persuaded, but persuading Jack was harder. Although I could convince him I would be safe, I couldn't convince him not to be hurt. "Why Katherine? Why can't I come and follow you on your walks?" he asked. It was hard to explain why because it was, undoubtedly, selfish. He couldn't come because I didn't want to have to think about him. I didn't want to have to watch him watching me, wondering what I was thinking, wondering why I was there. "Some things are not about reason," I eventually said, "but about trust." I tried to explain it to him. "I need to be by myself in an open space, not surrounded by walls or rooms or city streets. I'm asking you to trust me. As silly as it may seem, it is something I must do."

A trip to the country. Two days in a lovely hotel, less than a hundred miles away. Not a very big thing at all, you would think. But it's a simple freedom that is hard to win back after you've threatened to give it all away. I knew I had already gone off to be with my mother after my father had died. I had already buried both my parents and survived. But for Jack, this was different. To him, my going someplace familiar, like Brooklyn, was hard enough. My going someplace strange and my going alone, was harder still. Jack had his own fears and guilt, his own 'brush cutting' to do. The best I could do to regain his trust, was to go out into the world and come back home again, safely. And to call him three times a day while I was gone.

I knew the hotel the minute I saw it, as if I had been there before. Two stone pillars marked the curving drive that led us through an ancient stand of trees. A few hundred yards away, the road ended in a circle around a concrete fountain, water erupting out of a stone flower stem, in a cement pool. Behind the drive was a building out of a fairytale. Three rambling stone and brick wings covered in thatch, windows with wooden shutters, a flagstone path leading up to heavy oak doors. We could hear logs crackling in a distant fireplace and before we could set down our bags, Mrs. Crenshaw, as she introduced herself, was checking us in and offering tea.

Katherine took charge of the small talk, explaining that, yes, we were American but no, we lived in London actually and had for some time. Yes, we did get back every now and again to see family, but no, we really did love living in England. I walked around, peering into adjacent rooms, studying the names under two-hundred-year-old portraits. Soon, Mrs. Crenshaw showed us up to our bedrooms that faced each other across a narrow hall at the top of the staircase. That had been another hard-fought battle. Jack had wanted us to share a room so, I suppose, Katherine could stay up all night watching me sleep. But when I reminded him that even in the hospital they trusted me to sur-vive the night in my own bed and bath, he had to give in. When I walked into my room, I gasped. The room itself was nice enough, small with a canopied double bed and chintz wallpaper. But out the window was the view I had seen in my dreams. In the distance were rolling hills, green despite the winter frost. Stonewalls meandered around groups of trees, cows lingering here and there. But even more importantly, in the foreground was a garden with rows set to hold vegetables and wildflowers, long-handled tools leaning against wooden fencing and a small stone bench for the weary worker. I couldn't wait to be out there.

I was already finished with breakfast and sipping my second cup of coffee when Katherine walked into the dining room. "Do you always get up this early?" she asked. "It's barely eight and you're all ready to go."

"I can't help it. I'm excited. But you take your time. I'm just going to have a peek at the garden." I assured Katherine I wouldn't go wandering off. "Look – I won't even put on my wellies. I'll wear my own shoes," I promised.

The air had a cold edge to it, but the sun was shining and the sky was surprisingly clear. I took a deep breath, filling my lungs as if I had been underwater too long. Then, I slowly began to walk along the planting beds, row by row. The dirt was still hard from months of frost, but you could see where some bulbs were getting ready for spring. A few wooden markers lay here and there, left over from the previous year's plantings. I bent down to read the names. The first few were vegetables – cos lettuce, radish and some kind of parsley with curly leaves. But the second bed had clearly been set aside for flowers. I took the marker labeled 'gladiola' which had been lying flat on the soil and stuck it into the ground. My hands were covered with dirt. I brought my fingers to my nose. The scent of loam and manure was almost lost, like a distant memory, but it was clear enough to make me close my eyes with satisfaction. I walked some more until I came to the stone bench I had seen from the window. I couldn't sit there for long. It was too cold. But I did rest long enough to look back towards the hotel, to the fields beyond, to a distant outcrop of rocks near a standing of oak trees. They stood there on the edge of a hill, huddled together like old men waiting for a bus. I went back to the hotel to get some wellies and tell Katherine I had found my walk.

Katherine asked Mrs. Crenshaw to take a picture of us before we headed off. She laughed, saying our old friends in America needed to see this. We both wore over-sized, green, waxed jackets with matching square, waterproof hats. Our jeans were tucked into heavy walking socks, which were in turn nestled into our green rubber boots. "We look like an advertisement for *Country Life Magazine*," Katherine joked.

"Ready?" I asked and strode off. I needed to lead the way. Katherine understood that this was not a time to chat. She saw we weren't taking this walk together, exactly. This was, somehow, my pilgrimage and she walked behind me, uncharacteristically quiet, obedient.

The air felt cold in my lungs at first and although the wind was gentle, it made my eyes tear. But I remember being grateful for the sensations. Everything I felt reminded me that I was alive and when I looked at the greens and browns and blues all around me, I knew a joy I had never really experienced before. The simple joy of mere existence. We walked for almost an hour before we neared the rocks, but as we did I instinctively moved faster and faster as if being pulled forward by the rocks themselves. I could hear Katherine huffing behind me, trying to keep up without being too close. Yet, with every step my own breathing became smoother, deeper and less labored and I remember feeling lighter, as if some hidden weight had suddenly been lifted off my shoulders.

When we came within a few yards of the rocks, I stopped. Katherine, now trotting behind me, head down, arms pumping, nearly ran right into me.

"Oh, you stopped. Jeez, I didn't realize this was going to be a sprint."

"I didn't realize I was walking that fast," I apologized. "But maybe this is a good place for you to rest. I'd like to go up to that stone pile by myself, if that's ok." I tried to be gentle about it. I realized that I was leaving Katherine to rest in an open field with nowhere to sit but against a tree on the hard ground. But there are times when it's important to be selfish and this was one of them. And I knew that this was exactly why I wanted to be there with Katherine rather than Jack, if I had to have anyone with me at all.

I approached the rocks slowly, examining them as if I was a geologist. I knew nothing about rocks — why they were formed the way they were, how they came to be deposited where they had been, how they were connected to the hills and fields I saw all around me. All of this was a mystery to me, but not a nagging one. It was enough for me to notice the striations of lighter and darker browns, the smoothness of one face leaning into the sharp crack of another. Slowly, I walked around the periphery. There must have been seven or eight large boulders, toppled together, with dozens of little stones wedged into the spaces between them. They didn't cover a huge area, but it was large enough to have each side offer a different view of the surrounding landscape. I chose the one facing into the nearby trees, knowing that, although my back was to Katherine, my face was towards the sun. I found a flattened ledge on one of the boulders and sat down. I took a deep breath, placed my hands on my knees and shut my eyes. The image of the trees stayed before me as the sun shone through my closed lids. I sat there content, no, happy, for some time. I have no idea how long. It seemed I heard the movements of every bird, the swaying of every branch. In the open-spaced hush I could nearly hear the rays of light rushing towards me. "This is peace," I said to myself and if that was all that had happened, it would have been enough.

But, when I opened my eyes I saw something else and I blinked a few times to make sure it wasn't some trick of the light. What I saw wasn't really anything all that unusual, although it felt deeply important to me. It wasn't an UFO or some mythological creature. I didn't see an elf or an angel or even God. What I saw, slowly walking out from between the trees, was a fox. Its bushy red tail was unmistakable, as was its long snout and pointy ears. I knew it was a fox immediately, Wiltshire was fox-hunting country, so why not? But there was something about his olive-shaped eyes that held my gaze. I can see them even now. They were clear, piercing. They were aware and seemed to realize that not only was there some other animal sitting there on those rocks in front of him, but that the other animal was me. I know it sounds absurd, but a definite communion took place between us, and as the fox approached, closer and closer, I became more and more aware that I was not, in fact, frightened. Although I had been afraid of strange animals all my life, mistrusting them as if I blamed them for not being human, there I was, sitting calmly, watching this wild fox come right up to me. I think I even whispered, "Hi there," as he came and stood at the base of the rock on which I sat. He looked straight at me. I didn't reach out to him. I kept my hands resting softly on my knees. But we looked at each other, deeply, for a long time. And in that time we had together, he taught me something. As if he was somehow placing the words in my head, I thought as I looked at him, "I am a part of you and you are a part of me." Then, the fox shook as if releasing something from within himself and slowly walked back among the trees.

When I finally stood up and turned back towards Katherine, I found her standing near me with a look of terror on her face.

"Oh, my God, are you all right?" She rushed up to me and put her hands on my shoulders. "You must have been terrified. What was that? A wolf? It almost looked like a tiger, it was so big."

After Katherine saw that I really was all right, she asked if I wanted her to take a picture of the rocks. I told her yes to be polite, but I knew even then that it would be a photo I would never need to look at. I carry an image of that moment inside me, whether I'm looking at that picture or not. It's there, deep inside me, guiding me, comforting me and reminding me that I am not some solitary being, separate and alone. I had become, or actually I always had been without knowing it, one small, though important part of everything around me – all of it the same – the rock, the fox and the woman.

Chapter 34

John:
Many Worlds

After all the thinking, calculating, erasing, recalculating and haranguing, our holography paper basically wrote itself. The whole thing took just a few days. It didn't look like much – three pages of equations plus two pages of text – but I knew that anyone who understood what he was looking at, would immediately realize its value. Yuri was less sure. Once the paper was finished and we were ready to send it off to *Physical Review*, he got cold feet. I was ready to go with it. The stamp was already on the envelope. But he was holding back. It seemed to me like we were now in some weird role reversal. He had always been the supremely confident one. I was usually the indecisive mess. But something was going on with him and I didn't really understand what it was. I tried to stand firm, but he pleaded. "John, we can not be rash. We must show it to others first. Trust me." And although I was eager to get going on the publication process – a process that could take anything from a few weeks to a few years – I did eventually give in.

"Okay. We're in this together," I told him. "I don't know what's gotten into you, but we'll bounce it around first, if it's that important. But, no feet-dragging."

Yuri didn't drag his feet. On the contrary. Within no time at all, barely a few days, I found myself driving over to the Lebdev Institute with him for an *informal* sharing of our findings. Once there, Yuri's confidence miraculously returned. But the Institute had the opposite effect on me. First of all, it was huge, like a palace, set far back from the street and behind large locked gates. And then, when you drove up, you had to state your business to a uniformed guard in a cement booth. He looked at you, looked at his clipboard, and then looked at you again. The whole process made me feel like I was caught in some Cold War spy movie. I felt nervous to be an American. It wasn't by accident I had managed to avoid the place all this time. "When we pull up, you do the talking," I told Yuri. "I'll just sit here in my fur hat and try to blend in." But what I was really thinking to myself was, "Shit – An American and a Jew. We're done for."

Yuri, on the other hand, was totally at ease. Once inside, he stomped the snow off his boots and handed his coat to the old woman in the cloakroom. He nodded to people passing in the hall. He even made a huge walrus noise blowing his nose. Then, he strode off towards the conference room as if he owned the place. I followed behind, carrying the computer and box of slides as if I was the nervous assistant. And that was fine with me. I had already convinced Yuri that the talk should be in Russian and that I would be there simply to help field questions at the end. That obviously had not been his plan, though. I think he wanted me to lead the whole thing, as if he was showing me off to the 'big guys' like some pet gorilla. He must have seen the anxiety in my eyes, because he looked at me, shook his head and asked, "If I make you talk, you will take one of your pills, yes?"

"Maybe. Probably," I said. "If anything would make me take one again after all these weeks of not, it's those dour old Russians in that fortress-of-a-place."

"Okay, then. I talk. But promise, no pills."

To be honest, I had never thought about taking one of my pills before he brought it up. Even I was beginning to think I could start handling stress on my own again without them. But why tell Yuri that now? Let him worry about me. And let me fade into the background this once.

The fact of the matter was that the whole session was remarkably pleasant. Just like me to make a big deal out of nothing. Six of us (four from the Institute plus Yuri and I), sat around a highly polished, cherry table, in comfortable leather chairs, sipping sweet tea and eating pastries. Yuri talked everyone through the equations which I beamed onto a freestanding screen on the side. Sometimes the Russians nodded. Sometimes they interrupted, though politely, to ask for clarification. After about thirty minutes, Yuri was done. For a brief time there was silence. I looked at the faces around the table. Yuri was smiling. Two of the four Institute physicists were checking over some notes they had made. One stared off as if he was about to fall asleep. And the last one, clearly the oldest, sat far back in his chair, stretching his legs. He then began to chuckle. Ordinarily, a chuckling old physicist meant trouble and when this one started to talk in Russian, I turned towards Yuri in alarm. But he started to chuckle, too. "If I may translate," he said, gesturing respectfully to his elder. "Professor Zeldikov here said that as long as you do not think about *philosophical* implications, it works very nicely."

I then had to laugh, too. Zeldikov was right. The philosophical implications of our theory were crazy and very much the sort of thing no self-respecting cosmologist would ever talk about. That was the problem with working on holography. You could see how it worked. But applying it to a model of the universe was another story. It was incredibly bold of us to even try. That's why the South American team's work was so surprising. It had been almost impossible for Yuri and me to believe that anyone else in the scientific world would be willing to risk their careers on such an idea. But clearly, they were. Maybe that's what had spooked Yuri in the first place and given him such cold feet. But now I was more undaunted than ever. If anything, this race of ours showed me how much new and daring work was actually going on out there in the cosmology community. It also made me realize how much I still wanted to be a part of it. Now, cosmologists were talking not only about string theory, but about *m-branes* as well. Suddenly, some were saying that we all might exist on one or more outstretched membranes, and that these *branes* might float around in an expanse filled with even more invisible dimensions. Holography was more pertinent than ever. It was a natural next step, because if the *m-brane* theory worked, then how do we know for sure that what we see is what really exists? Maybe there's more, maybe there's less. And so, maybe it is worth studying holography, even if it does mean that a 'logical' consequence of the work leads to an inconceivable assertion; namely, that our universe, as we experience it, is actually just a three-dimensional perception of a less complicated reality. Maybe there is less to our reality than meets the eye. But, luckily, we were physicists, not philosophers. We didn't need to answer these questions. As Feynman had said, we just needed to make the numbers work.

And the numbers did work. Seeing Yuri lay it all out in front of those somber Russian physicists convinced me of it all over again. The calculations were beautiful, if I did say so myself. Suddenly I was feeling brave and oddly at home. Zeldikov's statement was still hanging in the air and so I spoke up. "But, of course, Dr. Zeldikov, we are lucky," I said. "Our job is not to explain the whys and wherefores of the universe. Our job is only to demonstrate what *is*." And that was, basically, that. No great disagreements or threatening discussions. If anything, the general response to all our hard work was one of bemused comprehension, the Russian equivalent of, "Oh, yea – now I get it." It was too easy. Maybe it meant the peer review would be a nightmare. Maybe it would take years and endless revisions before the paper actually got published. But for now, I was happy,

Yuri was reassured and the Lebdev Institute was looking much less scary.

After a few more pleasantries and a few more pastries, everyone began to leave. Yuri and I stayed behind to collect our papers and any odd scribblings the others had left behind. There was no need to be suspicious, I believed, but as Yuri had taught me, there also was no need to be foolish. Soon, though, we realized that Zeldikov was still there in the room, waiting.

"Professor Rosen. May I have one minute more?" Now I became worried again. What was this about? I glanced at Yuri who simply continued to pick up his papers. But there was something about the way those two Russians looked at each other... I started to realize that, actually, much of Yuri's talk was aimed at Zeldikov himself. Although his eyes occasionally fell on one of the other men's faces, I now saw it was, in reality, Zeldikov we had come to see.

I put down the slides I was holding and gestured to the old man. "Yes, of course," I said. "Please."

"You know, it is very good to finally meet you and see this work for myself," Zeldikov began. "Yuri has told me much about you and your research. He mentioned it, perhaps?" Three pairs of eyes met each other, but nothing was said until Zeldikov continued. "I wanted to ask, though. Your time here in Moscow is over when?"

What was this? An invitation to dinner? I became less worried but all the more curious. "To be honest, I hate to even think about it," I answered. "But, I leave just before the New Year."

"I see. I have been authorized, actually, to ask if you might extend your stay, perhaps through this academic year, as a Visiting Scholar here at the Institute? Of course, you can continue your research, but we are also considering a symposium and would be grateful for your help. Of course, there is some money..."

Flabbergasted. A silly word, but that's what I was. And speechless. It had never, ever dawned on me that such a thing was possible. Had Yuri known about this? I looked over to see him sitting and shrugging. "If I may say so, Professor, it is a wonderful idea," he agreed.

"I am extremely honored," I said.

"And perhaps the University will extend as well," Yuri continued. Or, I now wondered, had they already agreed? How much of a setup was this? Not that I was complaining, but I couldn't help but feel like a marionette who had gotten an unsanctioned glimpse at his own strings.

"Yes. The University's agreement would help, of course. Professor Rosen, I am sure you will need to discuss this with your own University, your family ... you are not married?"

"No."

"Then, perhaps a few weeks to think will be enough? If you could let us know as soon as possible." Professor Zeldikov then reached out to me with both hands. "It has been a pleasure."

I most certainly did need to think. I sent Yuri back to the office and began to wander the streets on my own. As I walked it started to snow, not heavily, but just enough to dampen the sounds of the city and make the pavements slick. To stay all year? I kept asking myself that question over and over, but it didn't lead anywhere. I never expected this. Slowly and rather unhappily, I had been growing aware of the fact that my time in Russia was nearly over. Just one semester was all I, or anyone else, had agreed to. I had been continually pushing the thought out of my mind like a kid does at the end of summer. But what if summer didn't have to end? What if I didn't have to go back to school, to reality? What if this was to become my reality? I walked around, oblivious to everything around me. For the first time in a very long time, I was actually trying to figure out not only *what* I was thinking, but *why*. But, hadn't I just told Zeldikov that this question of 'why' was exactly the one I, as a physicist, didn't have to answer? And yet, there I was, trying to do it, to answer that wretched 'why' not about the universe, but about myself. Of course, "Thanks, but no thanks," was the obvious answer to Zeldikov's offer. My own University would be furious with me if I didn't go straight back. I had obligations, responsibilities. But something was stopping me from saying it.

I came to a Metro stop and automatically went down the stairs. I had no idea where I was going, but it didn't matter. Sometimes I rode the Metro just to look at the stations. They were extravagant, ornate glorifications of the Soviet myth of Everything for the People. Each one had a different set of amazing mosaics, statues and crystal light fixtures. Even before I had a chance to figure out where I was, a train came. Just like clockwork, every few minutes without fail, the trains always came. I took this one to wherever it led. I was happy just to sit there, watching the stations streak by. The sounds of the wheels and the rattle of the carriage anesthetized me. I stared at a poster above the seats opposite me. After living in Russia for a few months, I could now read the Cyrillic letters. Although I couldn't understand what the letters meant, being able to sound them out was almost enough. I grew comfortable sitting there among the locals. I felt like a local myself. But then, eventually, for no reason at all, I got out.

I was in *Ploschad Revolyutsii*, Revolution Square, a station I hadn't been in for a while. I took my time and walked the length of the main hall. I wasn't alone. An old woman with a scarf around her head was also there, pulling a cart filled with groceries. There was a young soldier, too, who stood off to the side, secretly eyeing a pair of teenage girls. But there were many others as well, frozen for decades, life-size bronze statues of normal, everyday Russian people. A farmer. A mother holding a child by the hand. A factory worker. I stopped in front of each one. They all looked surprisingly familiar – the broad face, the deep-set eyes. Undoubtedly, that was the desired effect back when the station was first designed. Of course, the rational part of me understood that this array of statues meant nothing more than some Soviet fantasy of happy citizens working together for the betterment of the State. And, of course, I understood what that had really meant. I had heard more than enough frightening stories from my friends. I knew how difficult their lives were, even now. But at that moment, it wasn't my 'rational part' that was really at work. Standing there in the enormity of Revolution Square Station, none of the *truth* really mattered. The history. The economy. The fear. That all, somehow, seemed beside the point. Because the point was that, nonetheless, there was still life there in Moscow and that life was being handed over to me. Already strangers had started mistaking me for 'one of them'. Just the other day, a guard inside a hotel stopped me and asked, in Russian, where I was going. Clearly, my Russian life already existed and it belonged to me as much as any life of mine did anywhere. All I had to do was decide to live it.

I sat down on a bench and waited. If anyone had asked me what I was waiting for, I wouldn't have been able to answer. It wasn't a train. It wasn't even for time to pass. That old nemesis, time, definitely wasn't going to help me now. Time had never felt so irrelevant. It didn't matter how long I had been wandering around, thinking. It didn't matter when I got back to the office or my apartment. Everything had stopped, even while it was continuing. The world was spinning, as always. Strings were vibrating, branes were floating. Boston was having breakfast, while Moscow was getting ready for dinner. But still I sat there, caught in the middle. I thought how, for a long time now, I had just allowed things to happen to me. Events, other people, had been picking me up and carrying me forward for months, maybe even years. First London. Then Moscow. But now, I actually had to make a decision and it was a bigger one than it seemed. I understood enough to realize that. I wasn't just deciding whether to stay in Moscow for a few months more. If I stayed this year, why not stay the next? And then the year after that? Hadn't I been happier and more comfortable in Moscow than I had been for as long as I could remember? Why should I ever go back?

All these questions buzzed in my ears. I forced myself to think about Boston and all that was waiting for me back there. Lizzy and Peter. Marty, Beth and the kids. My friends. My students. The Red Sox. My 'real' life. But there was that old 'what is realty' joke again. I knew there were people, even respected cosmologists, who theorized that there were many realities, many worlds, where everything that can happen, actually does happen. Some say that given x-number of probabilities, there are x-number of universes to give them reality. So, just as I had one 'real' life in Boston, so could I have another in Moscow, in London, in Alpha Centuri for that matter. Some might even argue that all those lives already existed. All I had to do was choose. It was as simple and as complicated, as that.

Chapter 35

John:
Music of the Spheres

"Now I'm the one who needs to get away," I told Elena on the phone. "Can we go this weekend?"

Throughout all my wandering and Metro-riding, the only decision I had been able to make after my conversation with Zeldikov was to take another trip to the *dacha*. Getting out of the city might help, I thought. There might be something there in that desolate, beautiful countryside that would untangle my jumbled thoughts. Elena was more than happy to go, but she needed to stay at the restaurant through lunch. "It may be late when we get there. After dark. I hope that is okay," she told me. But I didn't mind at all. It gave me a chance to sleep in. Actually, I slept later that morning than I had in ages, finally forcing myself out of bed at eleven o'clock. I couldn't believe what time it was. "I've really lost it now," I thought. But then I remembered Einstein and his habit of sleeping ten to twelve hours a night. Einstein's famous stroke of genius, the Theory of Relativity, came to him at just such a time in his life when he was sleeping more than he was awake. That fact had been one of my greatest comforts and greatest excuses throughout graduate school. Brains do their best work when they're asleep, I used to say. Hopefully, it was still true.

By the time we got to the *dacha*, it was late afternoon and the sun had nearly set over the lake beyond the trees. Quickly, Elena unloaded the car while I got to work heating up the house. I carried a few armloads of wood in from outside and stacked them near the fireplace. "I think the wood pile is getting low out there," I said.

"We have enough for tonight, you think?"

"Oh, yea. That's no problem."

"Good. Then you can chop some more in the morning." Elena saw the look on my face and began to laugh. "Yes, we chop our own wood here. There is no store we can go to, to buy it all neatly wrapped in plastic. Do not worry. I will show you how."

Sure, it was humiliating, but I knew better than to try to lie about the fact that I had never chopped a piece of wood in my life.

"You know, when I was in college, a friend and I started to write a book called *Jews Don't*, I reminisced. "I think the very first page was, *Jews don't chop wood*."

"Very funny. But not Russian Jews, and guess what?" Elena teased.

"Yes, I know. I'm a Russian Jew."

While Elena worked in the kitchen, I put on my boots and coat and headed outside one more time before the sun had completely set. "Do you mind if I take a quick walk before it gets too dark? Do you want to come"?

"No, you go. I am content here."

But as I closed the door behind me, I heard Elena calling out, laughing, "But watch out for the wolves!"

"Now who's being funny?" I called back. But actually, it was funny. The whole scene was funny. The little wooden cabin in the forest. Smoke rising out of the chimney. Snow all around. There was even an ax leaning against the side of the house. "What is this, *Peter and the Wolf?*" I laughed to myself. I had grown up with that Prokofiev music. My parents took Lizzy and me to hear it every year at the Boston Pops Children's Concert. But I never thought I'd be living it for real. Okay. Elena was no old grandfather. But I could almost imagine my own long-gone grandfather out there, somewhere in those woods, hiding behind a snow pile, making sure the wolf never got too close.

I didn't need to walk far. All I really wanted was to stand among the trees and listen to nothing. It was the quiet more than anything else that I craved. But not just the quiet itself. It was the way the quiet seemed to inhabit me, ooze in through my pores or something and silence all the noise in my head. Usually, I walked around, trapped in an endless rush of imagined conversations. Mostly, I had them with myself. I cajoled, argued, scolded. Sometimes I was insulting, sometimes infuriated. But all of this went on like an eternal drone. Yet, there, in those woods, all that noise disappeared. There was nothing to hear outside and nothing inside. All I did hear was a breath or a breeze. The silence was, in fact, liberating.

This is what I needed, I knew without even thinking the words. I stood there with that feeling for a while, looking back at the lights of the *dacha* and letting the cold air fill my lungs. In time, I became aware of one more sensation: hunger and that led me back to the kitchen and Elena.

"No wolf?" she asked as I walked inside. She was sitting on the couch by the fireplace, her legs tucked up beneath her, a book on her lap.   Something wonderful was in the oven and an unopened bottle of vodka was on the table.

"No wolf, but Prokofiev music filled the air."

"At least it was Russian. God forbid, Debussy should haunt these woods . . ."

I poured two glasses of vodka and sat down in a chair beside her. Now that I was inside, I realized how cold it had been, wandering around outside in the snow. But everything in the room seemed designed to warm me up – the stove, the fur throw across the arm of my chair, the smells coming from the kitchen, the shot of vodka sliding down my throat, the sight of Elena curled up on the couch. Everything was peaceful, except for random cracks of air escaping from the burning logs. Suddenly, for no particular reason, I thought about Lizzy. If she could see me now, she wouldn't believe it. Never would she have believed that I could be sitting there, so calm and content, without rushing off to think some thought or do some task.

"John, listen to this." Elena looked up from her book. "Do you know this author, Tynanov?" I shook my head. "Have you heard the story of Lieutenant Kije?"

"Lieutenant Kije? Wait. Didn't Prokofiev write some suite named that?"

"Very good. I am impressed. Yes, Prokofiev again. His music was a sort of response, I suppose, to Tynanov's story. Anyway, this is his autobiography. And he says here, 'If I had not had my childhood, I would not understand history'. What do you think about that?"

Leave it to Elena to come up with something like that to talk about. I was quiet for a while and then I joked, "Remember, we physicists don't do philosophy," knowing she would never let me get away with just that as my answer. "But I don't know," I continued. "Everyone's had a childhood, but not everyone understands history."

"Yes, everyone has a childhood. But you see, perhaps it is not in the having. Perhaps it is in the remembering. Perhaps history is nothing more than everyone's childhoods all linked together? An interesting question, yes?"

I nodded. Actually, it was an interesting question.

Elena was smiling. "Good, *da*? I like this quote. History is something you can believe in, I think, even if you cannot believe in anything else." She began to stare off into space. I could almost feel her moving away into some other place and time, but then she seemed to physically bring herself back. "But,

I promised. No big talks. Right? Just food, drink, resting and relaxing. It is a deal?"

"It is a deal." I raised my near-empty glass in a toast. "*L'chaiyim.*"

"*Na zdarovya.*"

Elena had also promised not to fuss too much over dinner. "I should be cooking for you," I had said when we were making arrangements.

"And what would you cook?" Elena asked, an obvious dare. "Cornflakes? No, I like eating too much. I won't fuss, but it will be more than that." I have to admit, her assumption that I could cook nothing but cornflakes did annoy me, even though I knew it was true. But really, the thought of me cooking was ridiculous. Especially now, as I watched Elena effortlessly bring a lamb stew out of the oven.

"I'm so glad I didn't insist on cooking," I said as I sat down to eat.

"Yes, we all have our strengths and weaknesses. But what if I came to visit you in Boston? What would you do then?" Elena in Boston. Now, that was a strange thought. I couldn't imagine her anywhere outside of Russia. Who would she be if she wasn't here? I took a while to answer and Elena must have misunderstood my hesitation. Quickly, she said, "I didn't mean to say…"

"Oh, don't be silly. Of course you'll come to Boston. You must. I was just trying to imagine what it would be like to have you there. What would I show you? Where would we go?"

"And what you would cook?"

"Well, we probably would eat out mostly."

"Every meal? You never cook?"

"Sad, but true."

"Ah, the American bachelor."

To be honest, I couldn't even imagine myself back in Boston just then. Where did I use to eat? Of course, there was 'The

Chinese Dragon' across the street from the physics building. And 'The Italian Kitchen' on the way to my house. But really, dinner was only something to remember to do, more than anything else. And sometimes, when I didn't remember, it *was* cornflakes in front of the television at midnight.

I opened a bottle of wine. The exercise of turning the screw, easing out the cork and pouring, gave me a chance to refocus on the meal in front of us. Simple, delicious and best of all, easy and unhurried. I would miss these meals, maybe more than anything else, when I went back to Boston. Did I think, *when*, or was it *if?* Suddenly, I wondered if Elena knew about the Lebdev offer.

"If I'm in Boston, you will definitely come to visit. Often." I spoke the words even before I realized I was thinking them.

"*If* you are in Boston?"

Yes, Elena knew. I could tell by the tone of her voice and the arch of her eyebrow. "So, you know about the Lebdev, then?"

"Yes, I know. Do not be angry with Yuri for telling me. He was so excited."

"No, of course I'm not angry. I was going to tell you myself. Are you surprised?"

"No, I am not surprised that they made you the offer. But, to be honest, I am surprised you are seriously considering it. And you are considering it, yes?"

That was a shock to hear. I had assumed that if anyone understood my desire to stay in Russia, it would be Elena. "Sure, I'm considering it. And why not?" he asked. "I've been so happy here. You don't think I should stay?"

"Truthfully, I am not so sure. Yes, you are happy here now. But in the long term? Do you want to live a life where you may not be able to afford a car? Go on holiday? Money is a difficult issue here."

"Yes, but I'm lucky. I have some money of my own. And anyway, I don't own a car now."

Now Elena was the one who was hesitating. I watched her drink her wine and dunk a piece of bread into her stew, but I knew, really, she was thinking. I realized it worried me, not knowing what she thought and I began to understand just how important her opinion had become to me. Eventually, she spoke. "Please understand. It makes me very happy to know that you have found a home here. That you are happy here. I cannot say enough what that means to me. To all of us," she quickly added. "But if you would like my opinion, I will give you my opinion."

"Yes. Of every opinion out there, yours is the one I really want."

"Ah, you spoil me. Then here … I tell you. It is this. You know it will pain me to say goodbye. It will. But still, I think you should go." Immediately, I moved to interrupt. This wasn't what I wanted to hear. I knew it now. But Elena continued. "Yes, you should go. Make things right with your job in Boston. Show yourself that now you can be happy there, too. And then, come back. Maybe for another sabbatical. Next time, in the spring, when the trees are in bloom. It is beautiful. And then another time after that. Why not? You can have two homes at once. Two 'realities' as you say. Can't you?"

"And you will come to visit me when I'm not here," I said, as if it was a statement of fact.

"Yes." Elena laughed. "You send the tickets and we will all come."

So maybe it wasn't so complicated, after all. Why couldn't I have two homes? What about those people you read about in magazines, like: Joe Schmo of Paris and Rio de Janeiro. Why couldn't I be: John Rosen of Boston and Moscow? Admittedly, it doesn't have quite the same ring. But it could be done. Elena was right about that and about something else, too. I did have to show myself that I could be happy again back in Boston.

It wasn't just Moscow and Yuri and Elena that were making me happy. Something had changed in me since coming to Russia. If nothing else convinced me of it, then that half-full bottle of pills left back in my apartment should. But it was true – I did need to believe that whatever change had occurred would stay with me and I could carry it around inside me no matter where I lived.

I went back to my meal, eating and drinking with the appetite of a pardoned man. Then I started to laugh. "Two realities? Are you sure you're not a physicist?"

Dinner lasted for hours. We ate slowly. We talked, listened to the sounds outside the house, then ate some more. It was nearly midnight by the time we were sitting back by the fireplace with our glasses of tea and the remains of the bottle of wine. It was pitch black outside the windows and it looked like the cabin was floating in the depths of space. Some frost particles were forming on the panes of glass, but everything inside was warm and quiet. We had fallen into what could be called a 'companionable silence'. Neither of us spoke, nor read. I didn't even doze off, although I'm sure I could have if I had wanted to. But I didn't want to. I was too happy just sitting there doing nothing. At one point, the fire looked to be lessening and I got up to throw in another log. When I turned back, Elena was motioning to me to sit next to her. As we leaned lightly against each other, I felt a sense of easy intimacy between us, as if we had happily sat like that, together, quietly in front of the fire for years. I couldn't remember when I had last felt that way with a woman. Even with Susannah, my longest-lasting relationship of all, I had never felt quite so comfortable.

I stared at the fire, watching the colors of the flames change with the intensity of the heat. The warmth of those flames reached us despite the density of the air it needed to travel through. That heat would have reached us even if we had been surrounded by a vacuum and in some ways it felt like we were in a vacuum. Sitting there, I felt as if nothing existed anywhere else except the heat from the fireplace, the subtle movement of my chest rising and falling with each breath and the gentle stirrings of Elena who, I now noticed, had fallen asleep. At some point, I must have fallen asleep, too, because I remember suddenly realizing I was cold and my neck felt stiff. Elena had shifted away from me and was leaning on the arm of the couch, still sound asleep. The fire had died out. I needed to be in bed. We both did. So I gently tried to help Elena onto her feet and walk into her room. She let me guide her to her bed as if she was a little girl again, allowed to stay up later than her body could handle. Still dressed, she climbed under the quilts and smiled. "Come," she whispered, her eyes still closed, her hand sleepily patting the pillow. "It's warm." I got in beside her, felt the heat of her back against mine and fell deeply asleep.

I awoke to the smell of coffee and occasional sounds coming from the kitchen. I was still fully dressed from the night before and my shirt felt damp against the back of my neck. But I was happy; and very hungry. I stumbled out of the bedroom. "Good morning," Elena said. "I did not want to wake you." She looked as if she had been up for hours – new clothes, combed hair. "Breakfast is almost ready. Do you like eggs?" What a question. Of course, I liked eggs. But I would have liked anything coming out of that kitchen that morning, eggs or otherwise, because on that morning everything was perfect. The cream swirling like a vortex in my coffee. The crackle of the eggs turning crisp in the pan. The rays of the sun breaking through the icy glass of the windows. Elena's smile. Me. Everything. Perfect.

Too soon, we were turning off the heaters and packing up the car again. I took one more look around the *dacha*. I didn't know when I would be back. As Elena started to drive away I asked her, "When will you be back here again?"

"I am not sure," she answered. "But soon. It feels like mine again."

"Good," I said. "It kind of feels like mine, too."

325

Chapter 36

John:
Perturbation Theory

I spent my last days in Moscow opening doors, so to speak. I realized, somewhere during the ride back from the *dacha*, somewhere in the middle of a dark highway, that the only way I could get myself to leave Russia, was to pave the way for my return. The first door to push on was the Lebdev Institute. I went over to see Dr. Zeldikov and brought Yuri with me to translate. Not that it was necessary. I knew that in Moscow, nearly everyone I needed to speak English, did speak English. Even Zeldikov, somewhere in his eighties, had picked it up along the way. But it was still embarrassing to be forced to have every single conversation in English. "I swear this is the last time I come to Russia without being able to speak the language," I told Yuri for the umpteenth time in three months. "And this is not the last time I come to Russia."

On this visit to the Lebdev Institute, I was the one to march into the building with purpose and confidence. Yuri, not quite sure why he was there, lagged behind. I quickly led the way over to Zeldikov's office and found him waiting for us at the door. "Come in, please," the old man greeted us. "Some tea?" Now this was an office to aspire to, I thought. The difference between the room I shared with Yuri at the University and Zeldikov's 'salon' (for lack of a better word), was like the difference between Stalin and the Tsar. Zeldikov's furniture was lavish. Off to one side, near the window overlooking a courtyard, was an enormous desk with a huge leather chair. On the other side was an ornate table surrounded by two smaller antique chairs and an upholstered sofa. One wall was covered with leather-bound books, the other filled with photographs. I examined each picture. It was like looking at the entire history of Russia's recent past, with an aging Zeldikov presiding. Every famous face was there. Yeltsin, Gorbachev, even Khrushchev. Looking at them all, it was impossible not to wonder what that old physicist's relationship had been with his government throughout the Soviet era and the Cold War. What compromises had he made? What blind eyes had he turned? And if Zeldikov had so successfully steered his way through decades of turbulent Russian history, then the politics of academic science must have been a breeze. And so it dawned on me exactly who Zeldikov was. He was the great facilitator, wasn't he? He was the man who knew what was going on behind every door, within every laboratory and he quietly made things happen. Suddenly, my decision to be standing there in that office, at that time, no longer seemed quite so much my own. I looked from the photograph of Zeldikov shaking hands with Brezhnev to the reality of Zeldikov whispering to Yuri in the corner. Those two now looked as if they were mentor and protégé, father and son. There was definitely something in their relationship which I had never realized before and which Yuri had never shared with me. Despite the fact that he was as close to me now as if he had been my own brother, I began to feel uncomfortable.

"All I need now is one with Putin, yes?" Zeldikov said, moving over to where I was standing. "But there is still time, I believe." I looked at Zeldikov who was nodding and smiling. Could he detect my sudden uneasiness? When he made the friendly gesture of placing his hand on my shoulder, did he feel the tension in my back? Or was it an instinctive sense of comradery that made him lean in close and quietly say, "You know, you do what you need to survive, *da*?" Where had I heard that before? It was from Yuri, wasn't it? Talking to me, before Yom Kippur. "We do what we need to survive." It sounded like a revealed confidence then and it sounded like one now, like a secret handshake, like a deciphered code. That one sentence alone, now worked to soothe me, made me feel accepted and trusted, like one of the team. Maybe I was naïve. But it didn't matter. I knew I both wanted and needed to believe that we were all on the same team, that Zeldikov was completely trustworthy and that he only had *my* interests at heart.

Zeldikov gestured for us to sit – not one behind the desk and the other two in front, like a teacher with his students, but rather all three on overstuffed chairs, around a table set with tea and cakes. That, too, was masterfully maneuvered. By the time he asked the inevitable question, "So, tell me, you have a decision?" I was ready to say even more than I had intended. Actually, I said even more than I had as yet told Yuri. There was something about that old man that drew me out. Even though he sat there surrounded by all the largesse the Russian government could ever bestow, even though he had probably been the living embodiment of all the Cold War's scientific hopes and dreams, I really did trust him. I wanted to like him, but more than anything else, I knew I respected him.

"Doctor Zeldikov," I began. "I would love to take up your offer. Nothing would give me greater pleasure than to stay here in Russia. I suppose not many Americans would choose to live here rather than the U.S."

"More than you would imagine," Zeldikov said.

"Maybe you're right. But I have to be practical, too. My university wouldn't let me stay without a fight. They need me. This is just too short notice. To tell you the truth, I was lucky they let me come over here in the first place. But I do have a proposition for you." I turned towards Yuri, to show that I was talking to him as well. "Let me help you with your symposium from back in Boston. What if I tried to make it a joint sponsorship? The beginning of a real relationship between us and the Lebdev. I'll return to Boston and set that up, then I'll come back to you. Not now, but this time next year."

That was the plan that had been developing during my waking and sleeping hours over the past week. A joint professorship. Part-time in Boston. Part-time in Moscow. I knew it could work. And by the look on Zeldikov's face, he did, too. Yuri assured us, that an on-going position at the University could also be easily arranged, especially if there wasn't much money involved. And then, that was that. Three men sitting around a table, setting my future in motion. When Yuri and I walked back to the car after the meeting, I wanted to ask him how all of this had really come to pass. From that day sitting in the Bird House in London Zoo, to today's meeting at the Lebdev, everything had happened too easily. How could that be? And who was Zeldikov, really? But I stopped myself. Somehow, I found it didn't really matter to me after all and Yuri probably wouldn't have told me, anyway. But there was one question I did really need to ask. "Yuri, the South Americans?"

He just smiled and said, "Our paper is better. For now. And trust me. The right people know."

Driving back to our office, I stared out the window. The trees along the boulevards were all dark, empty branches, their roots were covered with snow. But I had to shield my eyes from the brightness of the sun, as it bounced off the snow, through the cold air and into the car's windscreen. For some reason I thought back to the original money discussion I'd had with my brother-in-law, years ago. It now all started to make sense. There must have been a reason why I had hardly spent a nickel my whole life, hoarding all my money in a couple of measly savings accounts. Now I knew what that reason was. My money was the wedge that would keep all these doors open to this newly imagined life of mine. If all else failed, I could afford to make it happen on my own and in my own way.

I assumed I would need to spend my last full day in Moscow doing chores. First, I cleared out my little desk in Yuri's office, then packed up my apartment. But none of that took very long. I hadn't brought much with me in the first place. Most of the afternoon was left for me to wander around, revisiting my favorite places. I crisscrossed the city by Metro, stopping now and again to look at the stations. I took one last stroll through *GUM* and found a large set of enamel dolls, each one nesting inside the next. A bit touristy, I thought, but still nice and I decided to send it off to Amanda. What she would do with it in the wilderness of East Timor, I didn't know. But it made me feel good to send it. From there, I made my way to Red Square and St. Basil's and then out through the gate and on toward the Bolshoi. Each sight brought a different memory, as if an entire lifetime had been created for me during my few brief months there. If Moscow had changed me at all, I thought, it was to make me appreciate my memories. All of them. They were what made me Me. And if spacetime really was just an interconnecting grid of 'nows', as I had always told my students it was, then it must be memory itself that showed you your own unique position on that grid.

By the time I had made it back to my apartment, it was getting late. I had to rush. Elena had, of course, insisted on hosting a farewell dinner for me at the *trater* and I knew I needed to be on time. Hurrying over, I burst through the doors, tossing my coat into the cloakroom, greeting the regulars with a slap on the back. What a difference from the first time I had stepped into that restaurant. Then, I had hid awkwardly behind Yuri, nervous and tired, completely bewildered. But now? Now it felt like I had simply come to sit in my own living room. I easily took part in the teasing hellos and shots of vodka. The conversation around the table was as animated as ever. But after a while,

I found myself quietly sitting back in my chair, content just to look around. Each person there meant something special to me and, in time, each one raised his glass. Natalia was first.

"To John," she started. "And to what you teached – no, *taught* – us. The Red Sox and the curse of the ... baby?"

"Babe," I said, shaking my head and feigning exasperation.

"Yes, Babe. Sorry. But also, sorry to say, the difference between regular champagne and very expensive champagne." At that, everyone around the table moaned. "Yes, it is a curse you are leaving us with. The taste for expensive things. So you will have to come back to buy us more! But now, really, to John, my new *brat*, my brother."

Then, somewhere between the borscht and the cucumber salad, Yuri was moved to make his own toast. I was already feeling pretty emotional and I hoped he would keep it light. It was hard to tell with him. Although usually matter-of-fact and cool, Yuri could be very intense, as well. I would never forget the look on his face, when he first urged me to come to Moscow. Intense was the only word for it. His eyes got dark and piercing. His eyebrows pointed down as if leading my gaze directly into the deepest part of his brain. It had been hypnotizing, as if he was willing me to think as he thought, feel as he felt. At the time that was easy, since I actually had no sense at all then of what my own thoughts and feelings really were. But now...

"I have not prepared any comments," Yuri began.

"Thank God for that," was the general consensus.

"Because, you know, this is not such a big deal. So, John is going away. So what? He will be back. Just as I knew you would come in the first place, eh?" he said, pointing directly at me. "Now I know you will be back again and again. We will see you here before we know it. And even sooner than that, we will see you in Boston and maybe even in England, if things work out right. Ah, surprised? I can make clever plans, too. Just wait and see." I was suspicious. England? Now what? I moved to interrupt, but Yuri wouldn't let me. "But, please, if I can be emotional for one minute..."

At that, Elena started to laugh and shake her head. "Oh, yes, do," she teased. "We all love that."

"Yes, well..." Yuri continued. "I want to say that what is truly important is that we, all of us here, are connected now, even more than before. And that will not change."

Of all the words spoken that evening, those were the ones that stuck with me the most. Those words took up residence in my heart and have stayed there ever since. Instinctively, I rose to my feet and went over to Yuri. My mother had always told me, "If you go to someone's house, bring a gift." I had been thinking about that all day, but really, what could I give him? A television? A new car? I could have just spent money on him, but that wouldn't have meant anything to him. Not coming from me. But, during the course of that afternoon, I did finally have an idea of something I could give him that he would actually want. And so, when I threw my arms around him after that toast of his, I dropped my vial of little white pills into his pocket. Maybe he would find them when he got home. Maybe the next time he wore that jacket to the office. But either way, I knew it was the one gift that he would really want from me. Sure, it was just a symbol. I could always get the prescription refilled. We both knew that. But, at least, this would be a sign that I didn't think I needed those pills anymore, not now and maybe not ever. And that would make us both happy.

It took a lot of vodka, a lot of wine and a lot of Chef Andrei's dumplings to subdue the lump forming in my throat. Each goodbye was difficult in its own way, but the one with Elena was the worst. Throughout the day I kept thinking that I wanted to make her understand this really wasn't goodbye. She could always rely on me and I would continue to depend on her. As the meal was ending, I still hadn't found a way to tell her, but then she seemed to do it for me. She pulled me aside, took me into the kitchen and made me sit on a stool in the corner of the room. She sat beside me and handed me a small box.

"What's this? Not a gift, Elena. No."

"Oh, don't be silly. Just open it. You will see." I untied the ribbon and opened the box carefully, as if it might crumble to pieces in my hands. Inside, was a folded piece of paper. One side was in Russian, the other in English. "It is a recipe for mushroom soup," Elena explained. "I expect you to make it for me when I come to visit. And this way I will also know, that every once in a while you will have a home-cooked meal."

It was, of course, the best gift, the only gift, she could have given me. After reading it slowly, both sides, I folded the paper neatly and placed it back in the box. "I promise," I said.

"Now, John, I do not want to keep you. I know Yuri is waiting."

"But won't you come with me now?"

"No."

"Then tomorrow?"

"I will see you next time. And then, the time after that. I know goodbyes, John, and this one, between you and me, is not really goodbye. Now, please go."

And so I did.

My plan had been to sleep during most of the flight back to Boston. I felt like I hadn't slept in days, so how hard could it be to sit back, plug in my earphones and close my eyes? But the minute I buckled myself into my seat and looked out the window, I knew it was hopeless. Every second brought a new thought to be acknowledged, a new feeling to sort out. I watched the huge letters – MOSKVA – recede into the horizon as the plane taxied away from the terminal. I remembered seeing those letters for the first time. They had seemed so enormous then, so cold and forbidding, standing against the Russian sky.

The plane lifted off and my stomach dipped. An equal and opposite reaction. I flipped through the music channels. The classical station was playing Tchaikovsky. No way. No, what I needed now, I thought, was some good old American Copeland, some Wild West music, or even better yet, some Sixties rock 'n roll to carry me back to my old home. But that brought another question. How much like my 'old home' would Boston be? It had to be different, didn't it? Boston hadn't stood still while I had been away. Hell, the Red Sox had even won the World Series. Everything was changing all the time. I had changed, too. But, how would those changes fit into the old equation? Hundreds of such questions passed through my brain just as hundreds of clouds passed through the sky beyond my window. Thoughts and clouds were floating in and out of sight, without any great storms of energy, just gently appearing here and there, stopping for a moment to be noticed, then often changing and moving on. Strange, I first thought. But no, it wasn't strange. That wasn't it. It was …I remember searching for the right word. Was it perplexing? No. Perturbing? Yes. And no.

Now that brought a thought that made me smile. There was such a thing as a perturbation theory and that old bear of a concept had been for me, like for all physicists, something I had intensely hated at one time in my studies. The calculation was notoriously exasperating, so much so, that I grew to love forcing my own graduate students to do it, to spend hours filling reams of paper with tiny squiggles, just so I could see that crazy, glazed look in their eyes when they were done. Sure, the calculation may have been torture, but I now also knew that the theory itself wasn't the enemy. That theory was actually a friend. It was the perturbation theory, after all, that forced us to acknowledge the fact that at any one time, we can only know so much. As that theory taught us, all we can ever do is take a complex idea, simplify it by approximating as best we can and then add more details as they arise. No one can ever really know it all. But you can, over time, increase your understanding. You can refine your solution, systematically, step by step, by acknowledging more details as they come to light – even those you may have known before but had for some reason chosen to ignore. You can still recognize them when the time is right and add them into the equation. If there was ever a statement of hope for the future, I suddenly thought, it had to be that blessed perturbation theory. And it gave me real comfort, sitting there on that airplane. Everything outside me might be perturbed, but inside I was growing calmer as I flew from what I thought I knew, to what I thought I didn't know. Know, not know – it didn't matter. Either way, the solution was bound to become clearer over time. And that was worth a drink.

I heard the wheels of the cart come rolling down the aisle towards me. "Something for you, sir?" the stewardess asked. I looked at my watch. It was about seven p.m. Moscow time. But in Boston it was only eleven in the morning. What would it be? Vodka or coffee?

"Vodka, please," I said. For the moment, the decision was easy. I unscrewed the cap of the little bottle and poured it all into a plastic cup. "*Na zdarovya*," I said, toasting the clouds, the sky, the universe and time itself, which was leading me backwards and forwards with, yes, occasional bursts of turbulence, but nonetheless with a reliable sense of symmetry and a not-so-small touch of elegance.

Chapter 37

Grace:
After All

Not surprising, I got old. Really old. After Florence and I moved out of New York and into Westchester, the years just seemed to melt away, turning to mush like biscuits dunked in tea. I got so old that it became hard to talk. I began to have this breathlessness. Shortened, shallow gasps. They're not terrible or painful. I still get the air I need. But what used to happen so mindlessly has now become part of my daily work. Breathe in. Breathe out. Breathe in. Breathe out. It's a struggle, but it doesn't disturb me. It's a struggle I've accepted.

It is true, my body doesn't work the way it used to. Of course it doesn't. Even I have lost track of how old I am. I can see; it's just that it's all gray, like a thin-meshed gauze has been thrown over the world. I woke up one morning and there it was – this watery grayness. I kept rubbing my eyes expecting them to clear, but they never did. I just had to accept that this color-less blur was now my world and once I did, a funny thing happened. I recognized it. I remembered being in the hospital, somewhere between living and dying, and the whole world being gray. The walls were gray. The light coming in through the dirty windows was gray. Even the people were gray. The gray that surrounds me now looks like that, but it feels different. Before, that colorless void grew out of a deadness in my spirit. It was as if the little shimmer of light that was Grace was so faint it could only be seen against a backdrop of nothingness. Now, it's just that my eyes are old and tired. My new gray world isn't anything to be afraid of. It's more like a cool bath after a hot day. It's soothing.

One day, Florence sat down beside me, looked me straight in the face and said, "That's all. We're not entertaining your friends anymore. We're all out of tea. We're all out of cake and you are all out of stories."

I tried to argue, but it was no good. She wouldn't listen. But it didn't matter. My friends still come. I may not see them, but I can hear this buzz, this indistinct whirr of sound. Sometimes, Florence describes them.

"Mrs. Rosenberg's daughter is here. You know, the middle one with the curly hair? She brought you some of her mother's brisket." Or,

"Mr. Arnofsky came by to tell you his wife is back in the hospital. He doesn't look so good."

It's funny how people still come, even though I don't really see them anymore. I think they just come, to come. To be here. To connect. To be somewhere. And that's fine, because let's face it, what does an old lady have to say, anyway? Just stories from her life. That's all. I suppose I used to think that my stories might help someone else, might teach them something. But now I wonder, what can anybody teach anyone else, really? Can you pass on wisdom? I don't think so. Plenty of people tried to teach me plenty of things during my life, but I never listened. The only person I ever listened to was myself.

I used to worry about everyone, even people I didn't know. Like those baseball players who got traded – I used to worry about their families. And what about that ice skater who came in fourth in the Olympics after struggling every day of her whole life? What became of her? I especially worried about myself, though. Who had I become? There was so much promise and energy inside the young Grace. Was it still there, somewhere, packed beneath the troubles and fears? Being a mother brought nothing but worry. Were the kids all right? Did they hate me? But even more, was I the Grace I wanted to be? It took a very long time for me to learn that worrying doesn't help. For me, it just made things worse. So I stopped and now I can't even remember what it feels like to worry. Was it a bad feeling? Maybe I liked it, since I had done it so much.

But sitting here now, there's no worry on the inside and no great discomfort on the outside. I can't complain. Every once in a while, Florence wheels me from one room to another. It doesn't make much difference to me where I am. I'm content just to exist with my thoughts. I don't see anything distinctly. The gray persists. I hear things, but I can't always be sure what they are. Sometimes I think a siren is just some high-pitched squeal. And who's that talking to me? I don't know. It could be Florence or Lizzy. Or myself? No, I know it's not me. I don't think I've said much of anything for a long time. I mean, I still have plenty to say. Don't get me wrong. I just don't say it.

It's like I'm floating in a grayish cloud. No, more like I *am* the cloud. Sometimes I think, maybe I'm already dead. How would I know? What does dead feel like? Would it feel like this? Sometimes I close my eyes and see people. I can see Jack whenever I want. But he's dead. He's been dead a long time, Jack. After all these years, even his name makes me smile. Maybe I'm dreaming when I see him. But if it is a dream, dreaming doesn't feel any different from when my eyes are open. I don't think there's much difference between dreaming and being awake anymore. No matter. Either way – dreaming, awake, dead, alive – it all feels fine to me.

Thousands of people have graced my life. They gave me spirit, love, energy, hope. All the good stuff. I gave them what I could. But I always saved a little something extra for my family, my children. Lizzy. John. Even Sam. Sometimes I thought the love I felt for them would kill me, would make my heart explode right out of my chest and turn me into nothing. Sometimes, I'm afraid, I smothered them with my love. Other times, I'm afraid I didn't love them enough. But, you know, the heart is a magic box. The more you empty it, the more it fills up. And once I knew that, I knew there was nothing more to worry about. I want my children not to worry about me, also now, at the end. I want everyone to know that it's not just about life, about living it and then having it be over. There's so much more to it than that.

A fox coming out of the trees … the English country-side. Sometimes I can see it clearly as if I am there now, sitting alone on that rock. It's the same moment, isn't it? The same thoughts? "I'm a part of you and you're a part of me." There's nothing to worry about. It's wonderful, really, sitting here, alone, in this colorless quiet. This gray silence. This reverberating, darkening, resonant hum.

Chapter 38

John:
Escape from the Black Hole

My re-entry into Boston was hard, at first. I knew I had only been gone a few months, but it felt so much longer than that. Things looked different, smaller even, let's say the way the huge fence you hid behind as a kid looks surprisingly little when you revisit it as an adult. The thing itself hasn't changed, but your perception of it has. Boston felt something like that. The city itself was probably no different. I was just, somehow, bigger. But bigger, different, whatever the change in me, Marty noticed it immediately. He seemed to think it was a good thing, though. The first time we saw each other again after my return, he took one look at me and said, "Thank God."

"What? Thank God I'm back?" I asked.

"No. Thank God you went."

I could tell Lizzy was thinking the same thing, only she didn't have to say it. I went down to Westchester for a visit soon after I got back. I brought Elena's recipe with me so Lizzy could show me how to do it. Within no time at all, she was standing back and staring at me with this sense of satisfaction on her face. It was annoying, but I just laughed it off. It was harder to laugh off her questions, though, once she got hold of Elena's perfect little box and started examining it like it was some rare archaeological find. "I can see she took a lot of trouble doing this for you," she said, turning the paper over and over. "You two get close, did you?"

"I suppose," I said, not knowing what else to say. "But you'll meet her. You'll meet all of them, hopefully this August. On the Vineyard. And did I tell you we might all be back in England in July?"

Things were moving fast in the world of theoretical physics and already there were plans to hold another symposium in England, but this time at Oxford. Inquiries into the Latest Findings, or something like that; our holography paper was being pegged as one of the topics. As soon as I got back to Boston and settled in, Yuri and I started to work on that lecture, revising the theory, generally making sure. That work with him turned out to be the best thing for me in my early weeks back home. I may have been living in Boston, but I was still working in Moscow, as if the two cities were being drawn together by the pull of some enormous electromagnet lodged deep inside me. And there was plenty of work to be done, because Yuri and I both realized that, actually, we were preparing for what could be the greatest and most difficult challenge of our careers so far. Everyone would be at that conference. The entire South American team would be there for sure and they would undoubtedly be looking for a fight. They may have conceded defeat in the early battle towards the development of the holography theory, but they weren't likely to stay down for long. Yuri had already received word from 'his sources' that the South Americans were busily developing their rebuttal. But if anything could be more important than that, it was the fact that Stephen Hawking himself would be there. Where he went, everyone went. To be honest, it was really his work, not ours, that everyone wanted to talk about. He was the big show.

The summer before the Red Sox won the Series, just a couple of months before I found myself in Moscow, Stephen

Hawking had said he was wrong. For thirty years he had convinced the world that black holes not only existed, but that they were so black they swallowed up everything that fell into them forever. Once in, never out. But now, it seems, he had changed his mind. Black holes aren't so black after all, he said and in time, the information that had fallen in would be released. At first, the media went crazy. It was big news everywhere. And now, a year later, everyone wanted to have another look. At the time that it all first came out, I was too distracted to really give the idea much thought. Over the months that followed Hawking's announcement, the rest of the scientific community was arguing about who knew it all along, who didn't and what were the implications. But, at that time, I was too busy obsessing about my own troubles to worry about black holes, Stephen Hawking or anything else. Now, though, as I got ready for that July conference, I found myself thinking about Hawking's reversal a lot. And I discovered I loved it. I loved everything about it. Walking along the river with Marty one April afternoon, I was nearly poetic on the subject.

"It's got to be right," I said. "At least, I hope it is."

"So what, if you want it to be right? That doesn't matter," Marty warned.

"I know. I know. But you've seen the math."

"Yea and ... don't get me wrong, I think it works, too. Shit, it's annoying he's so smart."

"No, it's not. It's great. It's great that he figured it out. Otherwise, if what we all originally thought was true, there'd be no hope. We'd never be able to know anything for certain about the past and the future would be impossible to predict. But now, we have the math to prove the reverse is true."

"Be careful how you play with that word 'prove'. You could lose an eye."

I laughed and walked for a while, chuckling to myself. The more we walked, the more I chuckled.

"What?" Marty finally asked.

"Well, it's just that – think about it. In no time at all, all this stuff has changed. The Black Hole Theory is reversed. The Curse of the Bambino is reversed. You got to wonder."

Just a few short weeks after that conversation with Marty, it was already May. Boston had its fifteen minutes of spring and was quickly changing into summer. I decided to fly down to New York for the long Memorial Day weekend. It seemed the obvious time to carry out a promise I had made to Elena months earlier. "Make the soup," she said. "But also, make amends. Go see your mother. It is not right." So I flew to New York, rented a car and drove out to the cemetery. Lizzy had to tell me how to get there. She offered to go along, too, but I didn't want any company; not this time. And anyway, it wasn't hard to find. The place was enormous. You could see it for miles from the Expressway. Every Jew who ever lived anywhere near New York in the second half of the twentieth century must be buried there and my family was, too. Both sides. I followed the slow moving line of Memorial Day traffic into the cemetery gates and inched my way along until I found the right section. I walked up and down the paths, in and out of other families gathering around their dead, until I found my own. I stopped for a minute beside each grave. First there were my father's parents, who I didn't remember much. We didn't see them that often when I was a kid and then they both died when I was still too young to pay much attention. Next came the graves of my mother's parents, who I did remember. I was stunned to see that their headstones were in both English and Russian. I had forgotten that from the last time I was there, which was for my mother's funeral. I suppose I wasn't noticing much of anything that day. But now, those Russian letters stood out in high relief on those headstones, as if they had been patiently waiting there all this time, like small gifts meant just for me. I could read the Cyrillic letters. I even said the sounds out loud and although I didn't understand them, they still somehow had meaning.

Then, lying next to my grandparents, was my mother's sister, Gina. My only aunt. I stopped there for a while. I had known her very well. She used to tell us stories, make-believe ones, when we were little. And I know she came and sat with me often when I was barely three years old, in and out of the hospital with croup, struggling to breathe, a plastic oxygen tent around my head. But she died young, in her forties. We had been living in London at the time. Cancer? Yes, I thought, that was it. And what a horrible funeral that was, I remembered. So many people and my grandmother nearly collapsing on the grave. My mother, I now recalled, was like stone.

The next grave I found was surprisingly less painful to look at. I knelt down and brushed some stray leaves off my father's headstone. There were twigs lying on the ground nearby. I picked one up and gently dug out the dirt that had become lodged within the carved letters. I laid a few stones on top of the grave and then stepped back. "That's better," I thought.

Soon, though, I realized I was no longer alone. A middle-aged black woman was standing there, just a few feet away. At first I thought maybe I had stumbled over onto some other family's grave site. But why would they have dug a grave right there, so close to my father's, my mother's? I soon understood, though, that it was actually my mother's grave that stranger had come to see. I tried to ignore her, at first, and just stood there staring at the headstone, silently. It was identical to my father's, but tidier, as if someone had already been there, clearing away dirt, planting flowers. My first, instinctive reaction was anger. "What the hell? Who's been here instead of me?" But then I glanced again at the woman who was still quietly standing there, arms crossed over her chest, head gently nodding. I'd never seen her before in my life, but soon she looked at me and smiled.

"This woman saved my life," she said. I was stunned. What could she possibly mean? "She came into my life just when I needed her, you know," she continued. "She'd sit and tell me the craziest stories. We'd drink tea. My aunt was her nurse."

"Florence? Your aunt was Florence?"

"Yes. Did you know her? Then you must have known Grace, too."

And that's when I finally realized that I didn't really know either of them, at all. I had never understood what my mother had been doing in her old age, what she had been saying to all those friends of hers. If anything, I thought it was just ego, conceit and probably even a way to avoid having to deal with us, her own kids. But I had been wrong. My mother had been doing something important sitting there in her living room, serving tea and cake and telling stories about her life. She had been making amends, in a way, maybe even asking forgiveness. And she would have done the same with me, I now was sure, if only I had given her the chance.

A few minutes later, the woman was still looking at me, still waiting for an answer to her question. I turned to smile at her, but it wasn't easy. It took a long time for me to know what to say. Maybe I didn't have to say anything, really. I suppose I could have just continued to smile weakly and nod or something. But this woman was looking at me so sincerely, so sweetly, that I couldn't just let it go. There was a connection there, somehow, and if I had learned anything at all, it was that these connections must be acknowledged.

"Yes, I did know your aunt," I finally said. "And Grace? I knew her, too. But honestly, not nearly well enough." And that, if anything, was the truth.

Glossary

Arrow of Time: The direction in which time, as we experience it, seems to point - namely, past to future.

Babuschka: The Russian word for grandmother, it also means a scarf worn on the head by old women.

Black Hole: Originally thought to be an area in **spacetime** that has such a strong gravitational pull that nothing, not even light, can escape from it. New research by **Stephen Hawking** shows that these holes both give off the aptly-named *Hawking Radiation*, but also eventually open up to reveal the information trapped inside.

Brane: In string theory, an extended object of varying dimensions. For example, a one-brane could be a string, a two-brane could be a membrane (see **p-brane**).

Constant: In physics, a theoretical property or quantity that does not change throughout a series of calculations.

Cosmology: The study of the universe as a whole, its origins and evolution. Some have said that if astronomy is about the trees, then cosmology is about the forest.

Dark Matter: Matter in the universe which can't be seen but can be detected due its gravitational field. Some think that up to ninety percent of the universe is made of dark matter.

Dispersion: The phenomenon or the measurement of a wave's ability to separate into different lengths or frequencies.

Duality: When seemingly different theories actually bring about the same physical results or properties.

Einstein, Albert: (1879-1955) German-born physicist who moved to the US. Everyone knows, or should know, his *Theories of Relativity*, both *Special* (1905) and *General* (1916). Awarded the Nobel Prize for Physics in 1921. He remains, quite simply, the benchmark.

Electron: A negatively charged particle that orbits the nucleus of an atom.

Entangled Particles: A phenomenon of quantum physics where particles, though completely distant from each other, share correlative properties and influence each other's reactions. It becomes impossible to mathematically describe each particle's condition separate from the other. Einstein called it, "Spooky action at a distance."

Entropy: The measurement of the amount of disorder in a physical system.

Event Horizon: The boundary of a **black hole** from which it is impossible to escape. "The point of no return."

Feynman, Richard: (1918-1988) A brilliant maverick of a physicist, born in the US, and best known for his outrageous behavior and his work on quantum electrodynamics. He was awarded the Nobel Prize in 1965. Actually, he shared it.

Gravity: One of the four fundamental forces of nature, it is the force which draws us down towards the center of the earth. Although it is the weakest of the four, it is the one we are most aware of.

Hawking, Stephen: (1942-) British physicist who is probably the most famous scientist of our time. He is the Lucasian Professor of Mathematics at Cambridge (just like Sir Isaac Newton), and is best known for his work on **black holes** and the big bang.

Holography: The theory that the quantum states of a region of **spacetime** can be found entirely on the boundary of that region, just as a two-dimensional piece of etched plastic can, when illuminated by a laser, reveal a three-dimensional image.

Inflation: Theory showing that the universe, in its earliest stages, experienced an enormously accelerated period of expansion.

Interference Pattern: The wave pattern that arises when waves, emitted from different locations or at different times, merge and overlap.

Kaluza-Klein Theory: A theory of quantum mechanics that describes the universe in terms of multiple (i.e. more than three), curled-up dimensions.

M-Theory: A not yet completely understood theory which seeks to unite all five **string theories** plus supergravity into a single framework. The theory involves eleven **spacetime** dimensions. By the way, no one seems to know what the **M** stands for.

Magnetic Moment: The response of an electron to an external magnetic field. Actually, for those who like this sort of thing, the most accurate calculation of this response so far is 1.00115965221.

Maldecena, Juan: (1968 -) Argentinean-born physicist now living in the US. A string-theorist who, in 1997, showed the beginnings of how holographic theory could be applied to cosmology.

Many Worlds Interpretation: A theory of quantum mechanics which says that all potentialities of a probability wave actually exist in separate universes. In other words, a different universe exists for each different possibility.

Morrison, Jim: (1943-1971) American rock 'n roll singer and poet. Lead singer of "The Doors". Also know as "The Lizard King."

Music of the Spheres: As Pythagoras supposed, the celestial music produced by the movement of the planets and stars.

Neutrino: A particle without a charge, and subject to the weak force.

P-branes: Quite simply, a **brane** with **p** dimensions (where **p** is any whole number less than ten).

Perturbation Theory: A way of simplifying a complex problem by first finding an approximate solution that is then improved as more details become known and included.

Pesky, John: (1919 -) A fielder for the Red Sox, Tigers and Senators. The right field foul pole in Boston's Fenway Park became known as **Pesky's Pole** because it sits only 302 feet away from home plate and so is close enough to allow even a hitter of modest strength, like Pesky, to send the ball past it for a home run.

Photon: The smallest bundle of light and the "messenger" particle of the electromagnetic force.

Planck Length: In **string theory**, the size of a typical string, about 10^{-35} centimeters. Named after one of the founding fathers of quantum mechanics, Max Planck.

Proton Accelerator: A device by which two beams of photons are forced to collide head on.

Quantum Jitters: Also known as "quantum fluctuations," these are the unavoidable and rapid changes in a field's value as it occurs in very small scales.

Quark: A charged elementary particle that reacts to the **"strong"** force. There are six different types, surprisingly named up, down, strange, charm, top and bottom.

Relativity: Einstein's theory that states that there can be no independent existence for either time or space, but that their existences are both relative to each other.

Residual Strong Force: Also called the "nuclear" force, the **strong force** binds quarks together to form protons and neutrons. The **residual strong force** then holds these protons and neutrons together to create the nucleus.

Scientific Method: The method by which scientists solve problems via observation, the statement of a hypothesis, prediction of results and then experimentation. The aim is to minimize personal bias.

Second Law of Thermodynamics: The law that states that total **entropy** in any given system always increases.

Singularity: A location in **spacetime** in which curvature becomes infinite, general relativity breaks down and matter becomes infinitely compressed. It is now assumed that the universe must have begun with a **singularity**.

Spacetime: The union of space and time within which events occur. Has been called the "fabric" of the universe. The concept arose first from Einstein's Theory of Special Relativity.

Speed of Sound: An approximate calculation of the speed through air is

$$C_{air} = (331.5 + (0.6 \times O)) \text{ m/s}$$

where O (theta) is the temperature in degrees Celsius. Actually, the speed is greatly affected by the medium and altitude through which the waves travel.

Spin: A basic property of quantum particles which shows that they rotate quickly, much like tops.

String Theory: The unified theory which brings together both quantum mechanics and general relativity. It describes the universe as consisting of particles comprised not of points, but of one-dimensional filaments or strings.

Strong Force (see **Residual Strong Force**)

Theory of Everything: A much sought after theory of quantum mechanics that encompasses all forces and all matter. Cleverly abbreviated as T.O.E.

Third Law of Motion: Newton's famous law that says for every action there is an equal and opposite reaction.

Uncertainty Principle: Heisenberg's principle stating that you can never know both the speed and the position of a particle, and that the more you know of one, the less you know of the other.

Variable: A symbol that can have a wide range of possible values.

Wormhole: A tube-like segment of **spacetime** that connects distant areas of the universe. Some believe it allows for the possibility of time travel.

Book Club Questions

for *Tangled Roots*

1. What is the reason for making the Professor's subject Physics? And why, specifically, Theoretical Physics and Cosmology?

2. John and Grace are both, predominantly, city dwellers, yet the countryside plays an important role in each of their developments. How is this similar and different for each character?

3. In what way are the characters of Florence and Elena similar?

4. Friends and siblings play major roles throughout the novel. In which way are they similar? In which way different?

5. It has been said that the concept of time itself is a major character in the novel. How is this true?

6. What role does language and the idea of "finding the right words" play in the mindset of the major characters?

7. The novel is set in three major political forces – the US, the UK and Russia. How does this underlay the political landscape of the book?

8. Colour and the absence of colour strongly affect each character in various ways. How is colour used throughout the novel?

9. What role does Kendall play in Grace's life? Does someone play a similar role in John's?

10. Parts I and II both begin with an epigram. Why?